INDIAN

COUNTRY

A Kelly Turnbull Novel

By

Kurt Schlichter

Kindle Edition ISBN: 978-0-9884029-5-9

Paperback Edition ISBN: 978-0-9884029-6-6

Version: Final - Full 052117 v32b2

ACKNOWLEDGEMENTS

Many people helped make this novel possible, but most of all my hot wife Irina Moises, who was there from the beginning. This time I actually let her read it while it was in progress, and she was again my primary advisor on whether it made sense. She was also the main editor. She spent a lot of time fine tuning it. Without her help and support, this book would have never materialized. I would have spent all my time tweeting at idiots on Twitter instead of getting this prequel written.

There is a prequel because of the wonderful readers who took a chance on *People's Republic* and made it a success. A lot of people bought it, and that still sort of makes me scratch my head. The notion that some story I cooked up in my head as a warning about the perilous path our country is on could entertain so many people is still a bit baffling to me.

I want to thank everyone who read it, and especially those who gave me their feedback. Except the ones who pointed out typos in early versions. Yeah, I know it's necessary but I still hate it. Anyway, to my readers – thank you!

I got a lot of support from my friends in the conservative media who have tirelessly helped me get the word out about *People's Republic* and, hopefully, about this one. These include Cam Edwards, Larry O'Connor, Tony Katz, Dana Loesch, Hugh Hewitt, Derek Hunter, Ben Shapiro, Ezra Levant, John Cardillo, Howie Carr, and Cameron Gray. There are more who I will kick myself for forgetting to include.

Jim Geraghty took *People's Republic* seriously enough to interrogate me on it and demand more – he was there at its inception as well in that bar that night we started discussing where this nightmare that our country is in might conceivably lead!

Let's not forget my former battalion commander, Colonel (Retired) Bill Wenger. His example taught me what it is to be a real commander.

Once again, I pillaged the minds of people like Michael Walsh, Robert O'Brien, Owen Brennan, Stephen Kruiser, Drew Matich, Adam Baldwin, Daniel Knauf, and John Gabriel for material without them ever knowing it. There are others as well.

And, of course my pal known to most as @WarrenPeas64 did some early reading and told me to keep writing. I also got great support from Christian Collins. There were many others whom I have overlooked. Thank you too!

I also want to remember Bob Owens, who gave me some invaluable firearms 411. He is gone too soon.

I also want to thank all of my Twitter followers (currently 100,000+) for being so very, very #caring.

Let's not forget the amazing J.R. Hawthorne. He turns my silly ideas into awesome covers. I don't understand how. Thanks!

As always, I want to thank the late, great Andrew Breitbart, for sucking me back into this whole conservative thing against my will and better judgment. Our country owes him a huge debt of gratitude, and I owe him a personal one.

And to those who might not dig this book, I want to quote Andrew:

Apologize for what?

Kurt Schlichter

PREFACE

This novel, like *People's Republic* before it, is no volume of giddy wishcasting for violent civil unrest. Anyone who says so is an idiot or a liar, and probably some combination of the two. This book is, like its predecessor, a warning.

When Donald Trump was elected on November 8, 2016, I had two thoughts. The main one was that I was relieved for my country. Hillary Clinton, with her unique blend of malice, stupidity, and middle class college girl radicalism, had a very real chance of ripping this country apart and making my last book come true. Her hate for lesser Americans – and pretty much everyone living more than 50 miles from a coast is "lesser" in her clique's book – plus her utter conviction in her own divine right to wield power was such that she could never, ever stop poking, prodding, and aggressing against red America.

And I feared she would provoke red America to aggress right back.

So I was delighted that evening when I realized that we had dodged the Hillary bullet, and I hoped that we could get back to the urgent mission of making America, if not *great* again, at least *normal* again.

But I was wrong. The Left did not engage in the soul-searching or self-examination necessary to understand why half of America – incidentally, the half with most of the senators, congressmen, and Electoral College votes – rejected it. Or, if it did, the result of that soul-searching and self-examination was a renewed sense of its own absolute moral purity and its manifest destiny to rule over us.

Instead, the Left launched an unprincipled and unlimited attack not just upon the legitimacy of this president but upon the legitimacy of the people who put him into office. Yes, the Left hates Trump, but its hatred is really for *us*. In its hive mind, we have no right to rule ourselves, no moral standing to defy the pagan god of Progressivism. And, as with other religious fanatics, anything leftists choose to do is therefore justified if it serves their perverted vision of the greater good by bringing us heathens to heel.

That's why we have seen blue state governments allow conservatives to be silenced, to be intimidated, and to be beaten, in the full view of blue state law enforcement. My worst fears are slowly coming true, much to my regret. The Left is using all its governmental, political, and cultural power to marginalize and repress its opponents. If you want to see the true frothing hatred of the Left, jump on social media. Don't worry – the leftists will tell you exactly what they think.

Nothing I write in *People's Republic* or in this book is beyond their aspirations; in fact, my dystopian vision may well be *too* optimistic. The bottom line is that the 2016 election did not render *People's Republic* moot. There is still more story to tell and still a warning to be issued. That's what I hope to do here.

Now, the second (and substantially smaller) of my election night thoughts turned to the Kelly Turnbull canon. In *People's Republic*, Hillary wins the presidency in 2016, leading to the Split between the red and the blue states in the early 2020s. Well, that's a storytelling problem for me in writing the prequel – and I have decided to solve it by simply changing the future history in *Indian Country*.

Let the *Star Wars* and *Star Trek* franchises tie themselves in narrative knots to ensure they aren't bombarded with furious tweets by angry nerds infuriated because in Episode 4 Luke's favorite color was green while in Episode 8 it was blue. I'm just going to tell my stories and you're going to like 'em, damn it.

Being a prequel, *Indian Country* takes place a number of years before the events in *People's Republic*. As you will see, *Indian Country* begins in 2022, after Hillary Clinton's disastrous 2020 election and as the country is moving inexorably toward disintegration. It then skips ahead and picks up later a few years, after the country splits in two. I hope this resolves any confusion and provides a powerful lesson to you – always read the Preface.

But the fact that I can still write about our country tearing itself apart without seeming utterly nuts is itself nothing to be happy about. I would gladly write a more traditional action thriller set in a world where people didn't wonder if the sun was setting on America as we know it. Maybe someday I will. But for now, it's me and Kelly Turnbull. And if you and others enjoy *Indian Country*, he'll be back soon.

Maybe someday we will realize that the path we are currently on ends in a place that looks a lot like Kosovo, where I served from 2004-2006 with the United States Army's 40th Infantry Division. The people there chose expedience and violence over the hard work of sustaining the rule of law. To paraphrase that knight in that Indiana Jones movie, they chose poorly.

But we don't have to. We can still choose wisely. As I wrote in my Preface to *People's Republic*, we still can choose not to throw away the greatest, freest nation in the history of mankind.

And I still pray we do.

We are hard pressed on every side, but not crushed; perplexed, but not in despair; persecuted, but not abandoned; struck down, but not destroyed.

2 Corinthians 4:8-9

Baghdad

August 2022

1.

Whenever Kelly Turnbull met someone, he always made a tentative plan to kill him.

Or her. Or xe, if that was xis pronoun of choice. It was August 2022. With Hillary Clinton finally president – the third time was the charm – the US Army, in the years leading up to the Split, might not have been too concerned with winning wars, but it was definitely big on diversity, including diversity of gender identity. And Captain Turnbull didn't discriminate.

Everyone was a potential target, so everyone got a termination plan. Man. Woman. Unspecified.

This was a real timesaver in his line of work.

Some people earned more detailed plans than others; for most, the plan was his default move – shoot them in the face with the tricked-out Kimber Model 1911A1 .45 automatic he kept locked and loaded 24/7 with eight hollow point Federal Premium HST rounds in his extended mag. Plus, of course, one in the pipe. Totally illegal ammo – some of the REMFs called it a "war crime," but never to his face.

Others' killing plans got more in-depth attention. But after years of fighting, his planning process was now just a reflex.

Hi.

How are you?

I think I will use this pen to take you out by going for your left eyeball.

But in preparation for tonight, Kelly Turnbull had made a very detailed plan.

It was still hot in Baghdad at oh-dark thirty – no one ever called it "zero dark thirty." His body armor and battle gear, worn over tan civilian tactical clothing designed to obscure the fact he was a soldier, only made it worse. The young captain paused to wipe the accumulated layer of sweat off of his forehead. Had Turnbull opted to wear the helmet he was supposed to have on, he'd have been even hotter. He wore a ball cap instead.

The whir of a gas-powered generator had covered their movement over the low wall and into the compound. Turnbull and his team paused behind a storage shed, checking out the two-story house, weapons up, covering the windows. Behind them lay a zip-tied and duct-taped sentry who one of his Iraqi commandos had silently taken down in textbook fashion. He probably didn't know it, face down in the dust with a broken nose, but he was lucky.

Turnbull's boys didn't play, and the American advisor trusted his five man team of local fighters with his life. He'd worked with them, trained them, and the hell if he was going to let them go on a mission without him regardless of the standing orders sent down from the desk drivers back in Washington.

The last thing the politicians presiding over the accelerating collapse of the Union wanted the public to hear about was more dead Americans fighting in some distant, endless counterinsurgency. No, the politicians had much bigger problems at home. And so Kelly Turnbull's faraway war was just an unwelcome footnote to a much bigger story.

But that didn't mean he was going to fight his own personal war on the *jihadists* any less aggressively.

There were lights on upstairs. Khalid al-Afridi, known as the Accountant, would be up there. Khalid was all his now. Homeboy had a lot of dead commandos to account for. And dead commando families. Because in the bitter calculus of insurgency, an effective way to hurt a guy inside a well-defended forward operating base was to go butcher his family at their home and have one of your minions drop off a bag of heads and hands at the front gate.

That was the kind of thing Khalid the Accountant was responsible for funding. And tonight Kelly Turnbull was intent on him paying for his actions in a different kind of currency. One that was denominated in calibers.

There was a lot of noise and movement on the first floor. It was 3:00 a.m., Baghdad time, but these assholes were all wide awake, probably sampling some of the meth they were supposed to be arranging to truck out to the desert and into the wild lands of Syria for their Islamic State pals' kid soldiers. After all, if the promise of an afterlife of eternal booty calling wasn't enough motivation, some crank would seal the deal. They sure loved their drugs – being whacked out probably made it easier for them to do what they did.

But Turnbull didn't need drugs to do hard things to bad people. That's what made him so very good at his job.

Too good, according to some.

The bad guys were all exactly where they were supposed to be. It looked like the informer had actually been straight with Turnbull. The Shia militia Turnbull's team uneasily worked with had fingered the informer, meaning the Iranians who pulled the strings were in on it too, so Turnbull's trust meter was pegging zero when they talked. The informer was initially reluctant to assist. It helped when Turnbull had explained that if he wasn't straight, Turnbull would shoot him in the face. One look in Turnbull's eyes and he knew this American was not like other ones he had dealt with.

So he chatted freely and without restraint.

The Iraqi police commando lieutenant to Turnbull's right fingered his M4, breathing shallowly. He spoke English, the only one of the Iraqis who did. But after working together so long, the team's tactical conversations were conducted with hand and arm signals. They were a machine. Still, it didn't hurt to make sure the plan was clear one more time.

"Remember, I'm going in first and clearing the upstairs," Turnbull whispered. "You guys just deal with the shitheads on the bottom floor and everything will be fine." Turnbull made the appropriate gestures to illustrate the plan as he talked.

"Okay," the lieutenant replied, and then he repeated the instructions to his men in Arabic. Turnbull could understand bits and pieces of the speech, but had no trouble feeling his counterpart's underlying fear – the lieutenant cared for the family he was always talking about, and that emotion made him vulnerable. But he was still braver than most. He would not let his American advisor down.

"Are you going to take this guy alive, Kelly?" the lieutenant asked. "I mean, for once." The other guys who made up the team just watched, looking as if they understood the question even though none spoke a word of English beyond "dollar," "whiskey" and "fuck." They'd seen this happen before dozens of raids all through Baghdad over the last year.

Turnbull smiled, then peeked around the corner of the shed at the main house. It was a pretty nice-sized two-story job that some local Baathist flunky had owned and that had been turned over to the gentlemen they would be visiting this evening. The owner had kindly chosen to donate it when the Islamic State goons showed up at the front door and gave the owner four hours to clear out or be disemboweled in the street along with his whole family. Even though the government of Iraq, such as it was, was at war with the Sunni insurgents, through bribes and fear, these guys operated out of this house with impunity.

Until tonight.

Seeing an unobstructed path up to the main door and no goons stumbling around out front, Turnbull motioned for his guys to move forward. As they ran, the rest of the team was breathing heavily, but not Turnbull.

They backed-up against the front stucco wall of the house, in line next to the door, and paused. A woman cried out from somewhere inside, probably upstairs. The police commandos always got meaner when they felt they were protecting women, and there were always fewer explanations required afterwards. Turnbull understood that, as a practical matter, he was going to have a free hand.

The dudes downstairs were in for a shitty evening, though no doubt orders of magnitude less shitty than the ones who were about to encounter Turnbull.

The other guys carried M4 variants, but Turnbull had left his back at the FOB. Instead, he carried his black Remington 870 short-barreled pump action shotgun with special shells – he used Federal Flite Control Law Enforcement Number One, a buckshot round with 15 pellets and a tight pattern. It cost him a lot out of pocket to score them on the economy, but in this kind of fight, he preferred to vaporize whatever he hit the first time he shot it. As for his pistol, the JAGs always said that any US soldier carrying hollow points was officially a war criminal. Turnbull figured these Islamic State bastards could file charges, if they lived.

He did not anticipate that being a problem.

The American didn't need to rack in a shell – there was always one in his chamber. He nodded, and the team set for entry. Turnbull swung out about four feet back from the door, took aim at the top hinge and blasted it out. The guys inside went nuts as Turnbull pumped in a second shell and blew out the lower hinge. It should have been another team member who took down the door, but contrary to protocol, Turnbull hit the loose door running with his shoulder, knocking it into the foyer.

The stairway was right in front of him, just like the source had drawn it. The source had hesitated for a moment when asked to draw it. Turnbull stuck the Kimber to his temple and told him in broken Arabic that in 60 seconds the piece of paper that was just slid in front of him was either going to have a diagram of the house on it or his frontal lobe all over it. Turnbull made it clear that it didn't matter to him which one it was.

All sorts of chaos was going down on the ground floor to Turnbull's left – dudes running around, shouting, kicking over tables, kicking up piles of powder into toxic clouds. He didn't see any of them with a weapon in hand yet, so they were the police commandos' problem. Turnbull's job was to clear the upstairs, and he bounded over the fallen door and onto the steps, taking two at a time upwards into the dank second floor, slipping two replacement shells into the Remington's feed along the way.

The stairway rose up to the end of a long hallway going left; a couple of dirty, bare 60 watt incandescent bulbs hanging from cords dropping out of the ceiling threw off the only light. Not very climate change conscious, he noted.

Turnbull hit the landing and pivoted, 12 gauge up and ready. Just as he expected, there were two doorways leading into rooms off of the hall to the left, and then another room straight down at the far end.

Movement left – a big guy popped out of the first door, his face registering utter, fatal confusion.

The terrorist had a battered AK in one paw, but it was pointed down at the grimy carpet. Amateur, Turnbull assessed. Turnbull was already charging down the hall so he could not have stopped even if he had wanted to, and he didn't want to. The terrorist froze seeing the American coming at him, shotgun barrel pointed directly at his face. Turnbull went straight on and speared him with it – the barrel caught one of his cheek bones and ripped through the skin with Turnbull's 200 solid pounds behind it. The terrorist staggered back, a bloody flap under his left eye where the barrel had hit him.

Given a couple more seconds, the terrorist might have remembered that he was carrying an assault rifle, but he didn't live that long. Turnbull half-stepped back, then shot him in the face. The buckshot went in through where his nose had been and out the back, painting the grimy walls with a sheet of crimson terrorist brains. He dropped to the floor like a sack of wet shit.

The American racked another shell into the chamber and scanned for targets. None, no movement. Ignoring the yelling from downstairs, he peeked around the doorframe into the first room. It seemed empty and he didn't bother clearing it properly. No time. If some other shithead came out behind him, he'd deal with him. Right now, Kelly Turnbull had bigger fish to fry.

A few more steps and he was looking into the second room, his 870 searching for targets. None.

Instead, a girl, probably late teens, was tied down and bent forward over a wooden table. She was naked, of course, and bloody. She tilted her head around and back toward the American, eyes blackened and swollen, lips puffed up and red between her teeth. She looked right into his eyes, with no emotion or anger. She didn't seem to want from Turnbull any outrage or concern. She saw in his eyes what Turnbull was going to do to her tormenter and that was enough.

Turnbull left the girl tied there and threw himself against the door of the last room at the end of the hall.

The flimsy door almost broke apart, but it held together enough to swing open and out of Turnbull's way. It was the bedroom of Khalid al-Afridi.

Until Turnbull had wandered into his life, he had been happily handling millions of dollars for the rebel groups and, of course, kidnapping and sodomizing the occasional girl or boy who caught his eye.

The Accountant had been educated in Los Angeles before 2001; his dad was a secular government bigwig. After the liberation, the whole family had gone into the Sunni *jihadist* business. Sycophants of a secular dictator to enablers of fundamentalist savages – the al-Afridi family was nothing if not adaptable.

Now, the Accountant himself was standing there utterly naked, hands up, shaking. The girl's blood was smeared across his stomach through his pubic hair and across the front of his thighs. There was a Makarov pistol about two meters away on the bedside table. There was no way he could reach it, no way he could effectively resist.

"Stop! Put down the gun!" Turnbull shouted perfunctorily, loud enough for the commandos to hear downstairs.

"Wait, I'm…" he stuttered, just as Turnbull fired a swarm of buckshot into his groin, making sure to obliterate his bladder and as much of the pelvis itself, and the nerves running through it, as possible. Khalid collapsed onto the floor at a terrible angle, bending at a place people just aren't supposed to bend. Stunned, the Accountant, simply moaned. Blood was pouring out of him and onto the floor.

The American racked another shell into the chamber and quickly assured himself there was no one else in the room. Then he took the Makarov off the nightstand, walked over to the wounded man, and squatted. Turnbull could hear the ruckus downstairs dying down, so he needed to work fast. He bathed the Makarov in the blood spurting out of the Accountant's ruined gut.

"You have a ledger, right? Look at me, pal." Turnbull grabbed his chin because his eyes were starting to roll back. "Point to where they are for me and I'll get you patched up and you'll be out paymastering and fucking teenagers again before you know it. You hear me?"

Hope is a powerful ally. Khalid pointed to under a dresser. Turnbull got up, scanned it for wires, and then reached underneath into the hiding place. Bingo, the ledger.

Satisfied, Turnbull turned back to the Accountant.

"Drop it!" he shouted, again loud enough for his team to hear it downstairs.

The Accountant seemed surprised. He started shaking his head "No," then began sobbing.

Turnbull nodded.

"Yeah, I totally lied to you," Turnbull whispered, and shot him in the sternum. Then he tossed the Makarov to the dead man's side. It came to rest in an expanding pool of red.

The lieutenant and another police commando were racing up the hall to rescue him when he stepped out of the Accountant's room. One of them split off to take care of the girl; from the fury in his eyes, it was pretty clear the lieutenant had seen her.

"Sorry. He pulled a weapon. I had to defend myself," Turnbull said, shrugging.

They could hear the freed girl's sobbing now.

"Good," said the Iraqi lieutenant.

The heart of the U.S. military's police commando advisory presence in Iraq was at a non-descript compound of buildings at an old Iraqi-turned-American-turned-Iraqi-turned American again army base on the outskirts of Baghdad. It held the hundred or so Green Berets and their support personnel, none of whom were supposed to be there. To the north, on another base, was the official U.S. presence, dedicated to America's half-hearted efforts against the reconstituting Islamic State, which had been largely annihilated in Iraq under President Trump's administration.

Turnbull preferred to stay with the police commandos he was working within their quarters – rough conditions didn't bother him. The benefits of good food and many big screen televisions at the US compound were outweighed by the costs – too many people trying to talk to him and interfere in what he was doing. Plus, the only way to really develop local forces was to embed with them – you had to be there, right beside them, eating with them, fighting with them, even dying with them.

But occasionally he had to come in and, not surprisingly, the colonel wanted to see him. Turnbull walked through the compound toward the command building, listening to the gunfire in the distance. There were a lot of bad guys out there; Baghdad was slowly going to hell again, the bloody gains of the last few years squandered by the feckless hacks in the Clinton White House. He could stay busy here for a while.

Turnbull sighed. It was a pain being at the task force HQ. On earlier deployments, when he was leading a Special Forces "A" team instead of working alone with the indigenous forces, his unit operated almost completely on its own, tens or even hundreds of miles from its higher headquarters. On one Afghanistan rotation, his unit had helicoptered in on October 16th, and Turnbull didn't see his commander again until December 23rd. Both of them were pleased with that arrangement. But now, there were always plenty of the battalion's staff weenies and civilian "advisors" around to watch and "help," and to narc the teams out. If the commander wasn't so squared away, it would be unbearable.

Things were tightening up on the teams. Less freelancing than before – much less. Instead of running a specified area, cultivating their own contacts, the teams were acting largely on intel other folks gathered. Usually, it was bad. That's why Turnbull tried to work his own sources, though it was not always possible. Sometimes he had no choice but to take tips from people he'd otherwise be inclined to shoot. The Shia militia, backed and run by the Iranians, had terrific sources. But, of course, they also had their own agenda.

If he was forced to rely on someone else's source, he always insisted on having a personal chat with the source before going on a mission. What a military intelligence guy or some Iranian spook thinks is important is often a lot different than what the guy kicking in the door thinks is important. And a source provided by an Iranian Revolutionary Guard officer might send you into a trap that ends with your head getting sawed off on YouTube.

Turnbull could be a little more persuasive than some E4 with 16 weeks of HUMINT training at Fort Huachuca. Those guys would talk to the source, and as they were trained, try to create a rapport based on shared values and cultural cues. In contrast, Turnbull would take his .45, shove it into the subject's face, and count to three. And if the source didn't interrupt him with some interesting tidbit before he got there, it would be a short conversation.

This was a startlingly effective technique, but it was just one more source of friction between Turnbull and the REMFs, the rear echelon motherfuckers who seemed to live to ensure victory always remained just out of reach. Turnbull found the staff pukes' short-sightedness tiresome.

They found Turnbull dangerous.

So now, Turnbull worked alone with the natives – everyone preferred it that way.

Turnbull went into the tactical operation center after flashing his ID to the unsmiling guards. Inside, the staff majors and captains glared at him. His clothes were ratty and his unshaven face made him look less like an Army O3 than a roadie for Motörhead.

Turnbull ignored them and went to the back where Lieutenant Colonel Jeff Deloitte was sitting. Deloitte had a cup of coffee and a bad Army haircut. If he had wanted, his uniform could have been covered with so many scare badges –Special Forces and Ranger tabs, Combat Infantryman Badge, airborne, HALO, SCUBA – that they would have made him look like a walking PX.

But that wasn't Jeff Deloitte. And that was why if some asswipe had tossed a hand grenade into that tent right then, Kelly Turnbull would have made sure he beat his commander to jump onto it.

"I told you I wanted prisoners, Kelly," Deloitte began. "I mean, not just flunky prisoners."

"Just didn't work out that way," Turnbull replied, pausing before adding a "Sir."

"It *never* seems to work out that way with you," the colonel replied. "You know Kelly, when a commander – and I'm yours – expresses a wish for something to happen, or not to happen, that's still an order even if he doesn't announce 'This is an order?' You know how command works, right?"

Turnbull just stood there and shrugged.

Deloitte went on. "The MI guys went over the Accountant's room. The S2 thinks you just dropped the gun."

"Well, if he didn't have one, then maybe I mistook his bloody hard-on from raping that teenage girl for a gun. Or maybe I was worried he'd pull a pistol out of the crack of his ass," Turnbull suggested helpfully.

"You have a lot of anger, Kelly," he said.

"I have a lot of police commandos whose families that bastard paid to have butchered. Anyway, the rules of engagement allow me to defend myself – at least, they do for now – and I did. I was in fear of my safety and stuff." Turnbull suppressed a smile at the thought of being court martialed for blasting the Accountant in the nutsack, with him on the stand explaining to the jury of my fellow officers about how the Accountant had been sodomizing a young lady right before the 12 gauge interrupted his party. They'd probably give him a medal.

"Kelly, you're great at direct action. Great. Too good, because our real mission isn't doing the trigger pulling. We're supposed to be training the locals to do for themselves."

"I can't lead from the FOB, sir."

"You also can't win their war for them all by yourself."

Turnbull would have ignored it coming from anyone else. And if he hadn't known Deloitte so well, he might have mistaken his commander's reticence for weakness. But Deloitte had walked the walk as far as developing indigenous forces. In fact, after turning a primitive tribe of rural Afghans into a top flight fighting force, he and his team had cleared an entire district of Taliban. Deloitte put down his lessons learned in a field manual, and then he taught them in the Q-course at Ft. Bragg. Among his students: Kelly Turnbull.

"One more thing. You have a meeting at 0900 at the embassy annex," the colonel said. "Clean up."

"What's it about, sir?"

"I'm not quite sure. But you're supposed to have all your stuff ready to go."

All of Turnbull's stuff consisted of his guns, a backpack and a duffel bag with some clothes and a single paperback book – some early Vince Flynn novel he had read on the C-17 coming over. No photos, no diary, no iPad. He piled it all into a Blackhawk that had dropped out of the night sky into the base's landing zone, obviously summoned long before the encounter with the colonel. Turnbull figured it was a temporary assignment or debriefing or something and expected to be back with his commandos soon.

Still, it wasn't like the old days when there were helicopters all over the place. Someone with some heat had dialed up this ride. Since no one was trying to put handcuffs on him – a contingency he was mentally prepared to respond to with massive violence – Turnbull figured he'd wait and see how this all played out.

The flight was uneventful and short. Looking out, Turnbull could imagine the Saigon 1975 scene that would ensue there if (when) the Islamic State got its wish and took Baghdad. The few special ops guys were certainly helpful, but that wouldn't be enough to keep the animals at bay forever. Then he thought about how he was going to get himself out into the field again. After all, there were a lot of *jihadis* out there, and he meant to kill every one of them that crossed his path.

In Afghanistan, during his second tour, Turnbull stopped counting after he shot his thirty-fifth al-Qaeda guy. Of course, his definition of an "al-Qaeda guy" was never that strict – he was perfectly happy to do any kind of terrorist, or terrorist-enablers, or even terrorist friends and well-wishers, but the real points came from a genuine al-Qaeda guy. Still, Taliban, Islamic State, Baathist, *Wahhabi* nutjob, generic *jihadi* enabler, random child-abusing pervert; it was all good. Turnbull shot them all equally.

The Blackhawk landed inside another compound while it was still dark. There was a pair of big, beefy guys with large weapons and civilian clothes waiting. Turnbull was ushered into a dimly lit building inside its own ring of concertina wire. Spook Central.

Turnbull hated spooks.

The guards didn't come inside the building. Instead, they shut the door behind him, leaving Turnbull alone with an obviously American guy in his mid-forties dressed in casual slacks and a collared shirt – no tie, since it was still 80 even though the sun was just coming up. His hair was grey and styled like a Roman senator's, almost like a bowl. And there was a second man, in civilian clothes and Middle Eastern, who Turnbull recognized.

"What's he doing here in a secure area?" Turnbull asked, pointing at the Persian.

The American gestured for Turnbull to sit, and his eyes followed the captain to the sofa running along the far side of the room. It looked like it folded out into a bed. Turnbull adjusted the holster on his thigh so he could sit comfortably, and left his M4 leaning against the wall.

The man had a manila file sitting beside him under a water bottle. That would be Turnbull's file, of course.

"You can call me Clay," he said. "Clay Deeds."

"Is that your real name?" Turnbull asked.

"No," he said. It was a stupid question.

"Who do you work for?"

"Think OGA," Clay replied evenly. "Other Government Agency" – that could be CIA, or something else Turnbull had never heard of.

Turnbull had worked with these kinds of guys before. They always had their own agenda, but theirs and his had never been mutually exclusive, so it worked. Still, this guy was clearly not a field guy anymore, not like the rough ex-special ops contractors they'd dumped into Afghanistan. He was a suit, or at least *now* he was a suit. Turnbull couldn't get a feel for what he had been before that. No bulge, but that didn't mean there wasn't a gun somewhere within reach. Of course, with those two slabs of beef outside, he didn't need his own piece.

"What is an Iranian Revolutionary Guard field grade doing in a secure American compound, Clay?"

The Iranian smiled. So did Clay.

"You've already met Colonel Javadi. I take it you've worked together."

"Yeah, enemy of my enemy and all that shit."

"Hello, Captain Turnbull," Javadi said.

"Fuck you," Turnbull replied. Javadi grinned.

"Kelly H. Turnbull, born Los Angeles, California...."

"I know my bio ..."

"What does the 'H' stand for?"

"Hugs."

"Basic training, OCS, Infantry branch, Airborne, Ranger school. Brought into SF on the accelerated SF expansion program as a new first lieutenant."

"Is there a point incoming? I'm getting super bored."

Clay looked up, considered Turnbull's expression, and lowered the file.

"Do you want to shoot me for asking you questions?" he inquired.

"Well," Turnbull replied evenly, "I do want to shoot *someone*, but I'd prefer to go with Javadi here, you know, given the choice."

Clay smiled. "You ever thought of channeling that anger in a positive direction?"

"I thought I have been."

"You've killed a lot of people, Captain."

"I like to make a difference. Are you ever going to tell me why we're talking?"

"I want you to work for me," Clay said. "Here, in Iraq, for the time being. Then … elsewhere."

"Doing?"

Clay took a drink from his Desani water bottle and said, "You are uniquely qualified for a special project. *My* project."

"What's your project?"

"Protecting our country and our Constitution, assuming they continue to exist in some form we recognize. And doing it your way."

Clay seemed happy to wait for a response, pausing for almost thirty seconds before he spoke. Turnbull just watched him. Clay seemed mildly disappointed.

"The report said you'd be more enthusiastic," he said, lifting the folder and smiling.

"That's a psych report?"

"Uh huh. They thought you would be intrigued by the challenge."

"I'm happy where I am. Thanks for the chat." Turnbull got up to leave.

"Sit down, Captain," he said. Sometimes you can tell when not to make a stand. There was something in his voice that told Turnbull this was one of the times to sit down and shut up.

Clay leaned forward. "Do you know why Delta rejected you?"

The man certainly knew how to push buttons.

No, Turnbull didn't know why, at least not *exactly* why. After he got back from a tour in Afghanistan, a colonel and a sergeant major in sanitized uniforms with no nametapes pigeonholed him at Bragg and invited him to try out for Delta Force, though they never used that name. At 0330 the next Saturday, Turnbull showed up in a parking lot with a stripped uniform, a rucksack and a canteen. There were a few dozen other guys there – Turnbull knew some of them, all squared away SF guys. They had told them not to talk among themselves, and they didn't. It started to rain, and when a couple of 5-ton trucks showed up an hour later, they got in silently and rode silently for an hour into the North Carolina hills.

In the middle of nowhere, the trucks stopped and the candidates piled out. The cadre – scary NCOs likewise without nametapes – handed them maps and compasses and told them each to go to a different point on the ground as fast as they could. Turnbull's point was 13 kilometers away over three ridges and two large streams. Off he went. When Turnbull got there, three hours later, exhausted, a bored looking master sergeant who probably could have broken him in two with his little finger gave Turnbull another point to find. It was 18 klicks south.

This sort of thing went on for three weeks, with intermittent breaks for food and sleep. At the end, just three of them had neither dropped out or been kicked out. The cadre trucked them into camp, fed them their first hot meal in nearly a month, then sent them one after another into a series of long interviews in front of a half-dozen cadre members who pelted them with questions, some difficult, some incomprehensible. The candidates filled out pages of forms asking even more bizarre questions – probably some kind of personality profile. When that was all over, Turnbull collapsed. He hadn't slept in 32 hours.

The next morning, the colonel thanked him and told Turnbull he would be sending a letter commending his efforts to his commander. But they did not need Turnbull's services at that time. Turnbull had never been rejected for anything in his Army career.

"I suppose you'll tell me," Turnbull said, doing his best not to take the bait and get angry.

Clay's face brightened. "They did predict that you would say something like *that*. They certainly predicted that the issue of your rejection by Delta would agitate you, which it has."

"The reason?" Turnbull asked.

"Oh yes. Well, your physical skills were top notch. All of your scores were exceptional, in fact. You were off the charts in pure aggression and your stubborn refusal to quit. There was only one problem, Captain Turnbull. Delta rejected you because you habitually violate known norms, rules, and laws. You find them…frustrating, so you just ignore them. Now, the good news is, you're not a sadist. You do not seem to get unusual pleasure from the suffering of others."

"Just the normal amount?"

Clay smiled. "So you're not a sociopath, which is good."

"That's a relief."

"You're just not reliable, in the sense that they *could* rely on you to complete your mission but they *could not* rely on you not to go and take it to the next level," Said Clay. "Delta wanted a xacto knife. Subtle, precise. And you're a battle axe with a mind of its own."

"Not subtle, not precise."

"No. Kelly, a man like you isn't given an assignment. You're unleashed. And that's exactly what I need."

"Thanks, I guess. So, are you ever going to tell me why he's here?" Turnbull asked. Javadi grinned again.

"You are going to be working with me and him directly."

Turnbull looked over the Iranian, and not in a nice way. "You know, Javadi, someday we're probably going to be shooting each other. I mean, overtly, not just covertly."

"But not today," Javadi said. "Not for the time being. By the way, thank you for last night. For the Accountant."

"Sorry I couldn't take him alive," Turnbull lied.

"I am not. He knew things that were…what is the term? 'Inconvenient.' So thank you for solving our problem, as we expected you would."

"If you think telling me you played me makes me want to cap you any less, you are terminally mistaken."

The Iranian smiled. "I think we will work together very, very well, Captain."

Turnbull drummed his fingers on the table. Clay motioned to Javadi, who got up and left the room without another word.

"Sometimes we have to work with bad guys to get other worse guys," Clay said after the Iranian closed the door behind him.

"Yeah, I get the whole ambiguity thing you people have to deal with. I prefer being straightforward. There's the bad guy. I go shoot him."

"And I need a guy who's direct, but also who can take it to the next level when necessary, if you get my meaning," Clay said. "This is only a short term op, Captain. A couple months. Then you come home. This war here – at least our part of it – is ending. Everyone's going home. They're bringing us back from almost everywhere. You've read about what's happening at home, haven't you?

"I don't follow the news much. Got other things on my mind."

"Well," said Clay. "Did you know we're leaving Europe? Three brigades pulling out. Have to appease the Bear and all. NATO Article 5 isn't worth the paper it's printed on – President Clinton always talked a big game about Russians when she was slagging

President Trump, but she isn't going to war for Poland. I guess she's just not that into our allies. You could ask the Baltic States about that, if there were any that Putin hadn't grabbed as soon as she was sworn in. And back home it's getting ugly. You heard what Texas said about her fracking ban yesterday?"

Turnbull shook his head.

"Texas said 'No,' and pretty much dared the President to do something about it."

"I make it a point not to pay attention to politics anymore."

"Yes, but soon politics will be paying attention to you," Clay replied. "You work with me here for a couple months, then we go back home. And you work for me there."

"Doing what back home?"

"Whatever needs done."

"Which side?" said Turnbull.

"The one with the Constitution."

"Sounds like a great deal. Now, am I volunteering or being voluntold?"

Clay shrugged, and Turnbull nodded resignedly.

"Understood. So, there are always details. What are the details?"

"None of this exists. This interview, this discussion, none of it," Clay said. "Agreed?"

"I kind of assumed that."

"And if I need to take you out to protect our country, you are history. I hope it won't come to that, but if it does, *adios*. Mission first. Know that going in. I'll always be straight with you, Kelly. Relatively."

Turnbull had the feeling then that if he left that room without signing on the dotted line, it was going to be *adios* anyway. "Guess I'm in."

Clay smiled and nodded.

"And they predicted I'd accept."

"Oh yes," Clay said.

"So what now?"

"The paperwork is done; you're seconded to the Department of State as an agricultural liaison. The Army is probably happy to have you become our problem. You settle in here and tonight the three of us will meet and start planning."

"Okay," said Turnbull, unconvinced. "But I don't trust that Javadi guy."

"Nor do I, but it's in his interest that we succeed so I expect we will. I'm not particularly concerned about what happens here in Baghdad."

"You're not? Seems pretty significant to me."

"It's what's happening back home that concerns me. We'll finish up here, and then we'll go home," Clay said. "It's getting ugly, Kelly."

"Ugly enough that you need a guy like me?"

"I truly hope not," said Clay.

America

June 2027

2.

Dale Chalmers kept his shower short for two reasons. First, in 2027 in the People's Republic, hot water was expensive; his power bills had tripled since the Split. Second, a long shower was a waste. It was an odd day of the month and the license plate on his Dodge ended in "8," so like all the other evens without a special pass, he was walking to work today in the June heat. That meant putting his suit and black shoes into a bag and changing in the bathroom at the office after wiping off his sweat with the towel he kept there for that purpose – paper towels had been banned as an "environmental outrage."

On the upside, his sacrifice was going to help save the polar bears or something. Yet the new climate change laws didn't seem to be helping to temper the heat wave that was turning Southern Indiana into a sauna.

He toweled off and put on shorts and sneakers and came downstairs. Liz and the kids were already around the table eating breakfast.

"Why won't you buy Count Chocula?" Jimmy complained.

"I told you," Liz said. "There's no more Count Chocula."

It was true. All the sugary cereals that kids actually liked were long gone from the supermarket shelves. They announced the new regulation from the Food Justice Commission on the news one evening and the next day shelves were bare. The broadcast had featured interviews with several moms excited about the opportunities presented by their narrowed options, but none of Liz's friends were happy about having to hear their kids complain.

Dale ate his corn flakes dry – the store was out of milk and the kids got what they had left in the carton. The empty went into the cardboard recycling bin – Liz was careful about that, not wanting another $100 fine if one of the snoops who went up and down the street pawing through people's bins on trash day caught them misdividing their recyclables again.

Beth, the high schooler, was at the table reading her American history textbook, *Legacy of Hate*.

"Test today?" Dale asked.

"It's all such bullshit," she replied.

"Beth!" Liz snapped. "Watch your mouth. You can get in trouble talking like that."

"Honey, you need to not be difficult. You want to get into college, right?" asked Dale reasonably.

"You think I'll ever get into college? From here?"

"Your grades –"

"Grades don't mean anything. You're an insurance salesman. Mom's a housewife. Our name is freaking 'Chalmers.' You don't know anyone with connections. I'm fucked!"

"Beth! Don't say things like that," Liz said. "And don't say the f-word either," she added.

Beth took her book and left without another word. Jimmy shrugged and followed. The bus might or might not be coming and they needed to be at the stop in case it was their lucky day.

"Should we leave?" Liz asked, again. Dale crunched down the dry flakes in his mouth and put down his spoon.

"Now you want to go? I thought we agreed to stick it out. And what about your brother? Your mom?

"We could take Mom with us," Liz replied.

"She would never leave. She's been here all her life. Hell, *we've* been here all our lives. What would we do in wherever – Texas?"

"We don't have to go to Texas. Maybe we head over the border to Kentucky. That's still close to home."

"They're talking about sealing the border. And leave the business? I built that office for 20 years. I'm 45. I can't just start over in a different country."

"A lot of people are. Todd and Katie Terrell left with their kids. Just picked up and left their house last week. Supposedly, they went to Florida."

"So we go and we have no money because you know we can't take anything with us. So I have to find a new career. You have to get a new job. We can't vote because we're not vets. Our kids have to join the Army if they want to."

"I can't see Beth in the Army...," said Liz.

"Right? Is that what we want?"

"No, but it's just – everyday it's something new. We can't drive our car on odd days, the reparations taxes, all the politically correct stuff. The fighting –"

"There's no fighting around here. Look, all this politics – it's got to get better soon. People's Republic, USA, none of it matters to us – everything's going to calm down and get back to normal. It has too. We just have to wait it out. Anyway, I need to get to work."

"Is your new employee going to show up for once?" his wife asked.

Dale frowned. Three weeks ago, a sour-faced bureaucrat from the Fair Employment Commissioner had walked into the offices of Chalmers Insurance Brokers and informed him that one Leon Williams was to be hired immediately as part of the new full employment program. It was not a request.

Williams looked fidgety and disinterested; Dale suspected he was one of the drug convicts granted blanket pardons as part of the criminal justice reforms designed to make amends to those who had been caught violating racist, classist, and similarly terrible laws. But Dale tried to show him the ropes and Williams paid attention for a few minutes then announced he needed a break. He showed up for three days, then on the fourth day he called in sick. On the fifth he didn't call at all. But when Dale stopped paying him, assuming Williams had lost interest and quit by default, he got a prompt call from the Fair Employment Commission informing him that he had failed to meet the new good cause standard for terminating an employee and that Mr. Williams would be by to pick up his check. And Mr. Williams did come by for his check, then smiled and walked right back out the front door.

Dale muttered something, and left for work.

It was two miles to the office in downtown Jasper, but it was a beautiful day in Indiana. The road had no sidewalk along that stretch, just a ditch off the shoulder to catch the run-off. A gentle uphill slope of green grassland on one side of the road led up to a line of trees. On the other, corn grew out to the blue horizon. Dale wiped his brow, then turned around upon hearing the crunch of gravel under tires behind him.

Cop car.

Ted Cannon, his brother-in-law, was at the wheel, in his tan uniform. The door read "Dubois County Sheriff" Dale relaxed, then thought it odd that he had tensed up seeing the light bar. He had always considered the police his friends. Until now.

"Odd license plate, huh?" Ted said when Dale walked back to his driver's window. "Hop in."

Dale came around and got in the passenger side. An old 12 gauge Mossberg was in the rack between them.

"Thanks."

"I'm really not supposed to," Ted said, maneuvering the cruiser off the shoulder and back on the street. "But whatever. I'll deal."

"You busy today?

"Not really. I'm not allowed to do real police work anymore, so that makes it easy. It's oppressive to hassle scumbags these days."

"You don't want to be oppressive."

"Yeah, well, the people worried about the scumbags being oppressed aren't the ones getting their houses broken into. Since they collected up the guns, the scumbags think it's open season."

"I have a feeling that not all of them got turned in," Dale said.

"Hell no," scoffed the deputy. "There are guys I know – guys I hunted deer with – who I know for a fact had dozens of guns who shrugged when the collections officers came to their houses and swore they didn't have a one. Searched their places and nothing. Man, I bet if you go into those woods and turn over a shovel full of dirt you'll probably find an arsenal."

"That seems risky, you know, just for a gun."

"Five years minimum. Remember Joe Jordan from school?"

"Of course. He puked in my house at a party when my parents were away."

"They brought him in yesterday. Deer rifle. Five years, man. He had it broken down, but if it had been assembled when they came I bet he'd have capped a couple deputies. Bad shit. This is getting ugly. You know, the day after they announced that we will be absorbed into the People's Security Force, four deputies disappeared. Went South, I hear."

"You ever thought about going south?"

"Your wife would kill me if I even suggested leaving. Our mom would too."

Dale didn't mention his talk with Liz that morning. He trusted Ted, but it just didn't seem...wise.

They were passing the skeletons of the old furniture factories, now closed due to environmental regulations. Apparently the chemicals Americans used to make beds and desks and tables were so damaging to the environment that the Americans had to be laid off; apparently these same chemicals had no effect when used by the Third World laborers the work was outsourced to.

"We have to start wearing those black PSF uniforms too," continued Cannon. "Tan uniforms are soothing, you know. People see you as one of them, a local. Black ones are scary."

"Maybe that's the idea."

"Yeah, maybe. I know we're getting a lot of pressure to start enforcing all these new rules. I thought the new constitution had free speech in it too, but I'm not sure they meant it when they put that in. You know – don't tell anyone – we're supposed to be looking for people who are illegally organizing political groups. Supposedly from the US. Infiltrators."

"*Illegally* organizing political groups? I thought this was supposed to still be a free country after the Split." said Dale. "Maybe freerer."

"Yeah, I'm not so sure. Just watch who you talk to about politics. They seem a lot more interested in pointing us at people saying the wrong things instead of real criminals. This is your stop."

The cruiser idled in front of the Chalmers Insurance storefront office as Dale thanked the deputy for the ride and got out onto the sidewalk. Cannon pulled back into traffic and headed down the street. Many of the businesses were closed – the town had never been particularly prosperous even when he was a kid in the 1990s, but now it was worse than ever.

Clumps of sullen young men hung out on the corners, probably either transferees moved in from the cities to take over the houses of people who had picked up to go south to the United States, or refugees from the former red states who had moved north. The post-Split welfare reforms in the US – essentially, a policy of not giving money to people who did not work – had finally motivated the hardcore dependent population to take action. And that action was to move to the People's Republic, where the new government had massively increased social programs once free of the constraints imposed by their former co-nationals.

Cannon ignored the loiterers – it was clear they were up to no good, but proactively interacting with them was not worth the hassle of the inevitable complaints that would follow.

A blue pick-up truck pulled ahead of him and the stars and stripes sticker on the lower right quadrant of the back window caught his eye. He knew that truck, and he knew the driver was often his own worst enemy. Cannon flicked on his cruiser's light bar.

After a few tense moments, the truck pulled over – Cannon was grateful for that – and the deputy got out, approaching slowly and at an angle, just in case.

Larry Langer lived outside of town and his whole family had a reputation as troublemakers – not dishonest, but just rowdy. The Langer brothers, first to fight, first to get drunk, first to tell anyone who tried to tell them what to do to go straight to hell.

Cannon peered into the bed of the pick-up and the back of the cab as he walked – not really expecting anything, but he always said you aren't really a cop if you aren't a little paranoid.

"Hi Ted, how's it hanging?" Larry asked. He had a short beard and a ZZ Top cap. It took Cannon a moment to remember what a ZZ Top was.

"I'm fine. Why are you causing trouble, Larry?"

"Now how am I causing trouble, Deputy?"

"The sticker."

"You mean the US flag?"

"Yeah, the US flag."

"What about it?"

"Well, it's going to offend a lot of people."

"Is it illegal?"

"Not officially, but like I said, it's going to offend a lot of people."

"Well, then fuck 'em."

"Come on, Larry."

"Come on what? I fought for that flag and I'll damn well put it or any other flag I want on my truck if I damn well please."

"Okay, things have changed, Larry. This isn't the United States anymore. This is the People's Republic of North America and you need to get that sticker off your truck before someone who isn't as patient as me pulls you over. I'm telling you for your own good."

"How about I choose what's for my own good like a damn American?"

"Because you aren't an American anymore," Cannon said, then immediately felt strange.

"Ted, they've been pushing and pushing and pushing and they better understand that some of us are ready to push back."

Cannon did not like the sound of that.

"You got something in your glove box, Larry?"

"You sure you want to look in there, Ted?"

"Nope, because if someone has, say, a .38 in his glove box, that's five years, and I wouldn't want to be the guy to bring someone in for that."

"You want to look, Ted? You want to bring me in?"

"No," the deputy replied. "No, I don't. I just want you to…get along. Just take it easy and everything will work out. You know?"

"I'm a Langer, Ted. Hell, I'm an *American*. You ever know us to just get along?"

"Look…Larry, I'm trying hard to keep this town calm and peaceful. That's all. In all this, I just want to keep my little town and my people safe."

Larry Langer smiled. "Someday, you're going to have to pick a side, Ted."

And he drove off.

The coffee tasted tired and thinned out, which it was. "Responsible coffee" they called it – running the water through the wet grounds a second time to minimize the devastating impact upon the earth of a decent cup of Joe. Deputy Cannon drank it anyway, creamless even though he liked cream. There was none to be had in the stores this week for some reason. Part of the new normal.

The station was crowded with unfamiliar faces, strangers from elsewhere in black People's Security Force uniforms mingling with the local deputies still wearing tan. On examination of the locals' uniforms, one could see the faint outline on their right shoulders of where something rectangular had once been sewn on and later removed. That was the US flag they had all worn up until the Split. The new People's Republic flag kept changing, so they never bothered sewing it on to replace the Stars and Stripes.

Sergeant Dennis Dietrich was standing outside his office, a banker's box filled with the mementos from his 20 year career in hand.

"Denny, what's up?" Cannon asked.

"I've been kicked out of my office." The Sergeant nodded his head at the new occupant, a short, angry woman in PSF black busy hanging a rainbow flag on the wall behind her new desk.

"I'm sorry."

"Yeah, well, they're coming in in force and I don't know why. We got twenty new officers assigned in today."

"Twenty? The whole department has never had twenty deputies total ever. What the hell for?"

"I don't know, Ted. Most of them don't look or act much like cops. I think they have some sort of shake-and-bake school to turn out PSF officers. Look at them. Half these guys we'd stop if we saw them in civvies walking down the street. That one has a skull tatt on his neck."

"Can't the Sheriff tell her to step off?"

"I don't think he has any juice anymore. The Sheriff's still the Sheriff, at least in theory, but this Lieutenant Kessler has got him spooked. She told him she needed my office and bam! I was packing my shit."

"I don't know what to say, Denny."

"Shit's changing, and I don't like it. Not sure what I'll do."

Cannon said nothing; it was obvious that to "do" something meant going south – and this pumping up law enforcement on the border was not a hopeful sign that going south would be an option for much longer.

The sergeant put his box down on an adjacent desk.

"She's calling a meeting in the assembly room at four," the sergeant said.

"Probably to tell us how the new real sheriff in town is going to run things."

"I don't like any of this, Ted. None of it."

Cannon finished the last of his responsible coffee, lost in thought.

"For too long, this department has tolerated sexism, racism, classism, homophobia, and…" Lieutenant Kessler paused, trying to remember what sin she had forgotten.

Greely, the PSF officer who Cannon had noted following the lieutenant around like an eager beagle puppy, piped up.

"Sexism?"

"I said 'sexism' already," the Lieutenant snapped back.

Greely looked wounded.

"Transphobia!" she said, triumphant. "For too long, this department has refused to challenge the paradigm of hate left over from the former United States. That changes now. We will no longer tolerate the systemic hate criminality that remains dug into this county and this whole region."

Cannon was standing in the back with the other local deputies; the new PSF officers had taken the chairs. There was some low mumbling of disapproval around him, but not so loud as to draw attention. That there was tension between the locals and the newcomers was no surprise. When the Crisis had come and the reds and the blues were negotiating the mechanics of the Split, the Hoosiers of Southern Indiana had simply assumed they would go along with the red states. After all, in temperament and voting patterns, that's where they belonged. But the negotiators had agreed that the existing state borders would be honored – it would be all or nothing. Perhaps that was necessary to avoid even more violence – the number of dead in the growing series of clashes was rising – but the people of Southern Indiana were ceded to the People's Republic along with the rest of the state, and the Split consummated and the Treaty of St. Louis was signed and sealed before they could react. Since then, they had always suspected that the faraway powers that be looked upon them with distrust.

Their suspicions were correct.

"As the PSF integrates existing law enforcement agencies, it is important that we break with your oppressive traditions and demonstrate the new path the People's Security Force will take from this point on," the Lieutenant said. "We need to show that intolerance will no longer be tolerated. We need to stamp out resistance to the people's will."

Denny Dietrich leaned in toward Deputy Cannon.

"This is not going to be good," he said.

"We have identified known subversives and we intend to sweep through and collect the illegal firearms that you failed to collect after they were banned. Also, these criminals have been burning wood for heat in violation of the Carbon Crime and Denial Act. I have here warrants for five members of the Langer family. We are going to raid their compound tonight. Officer Greely will brief you on the tactical details..."

"Lieutenant," Deputy Cannon began. "A raid is a really bad idea. A dangerous idea. We can talk to them. We know them."

"Yes, you know them. That's apparently the problem. You know these social criminals and you therefore refuse to act."

"Lieutenant, they are probably armed. A couple of them have military training..."

"We will be armed too, Deputy. And we will outnumber them and have the element of surprise when we hit their compound."

"Look, it's not a 'compound.' It's a farm. And there are young kids there. If you come in heavy, they'll fight. If you want to take them, grab them when they come into town on errands..."

"You miss the point, Deputy. They are defying the People's Republic. That's intolerable, and I intend to show it will not be tolerated. Sergeant Greely, brief the plan."

Cannon and Dietrich rode in the last cruiser in the 12-vehicle convoy. Greely's plan called for a direct, frontal assault on the compound. No recon, no perimeter. Drive in, jump out and grab everyone.

"We'll hit them so fast they'll give right up," Greely had said, proud of his plan. Greely had clearly never met a Langer.

Cannon and Dietrich immediately volunteered to be in the last vehicle. They figured that would be the one least likely to be shot to pieces.

About a mile out, Sergeant Dietrich racked his Mossberg. Cannon looked at him quizzically.

"Just in case," the Sergeant said. Cannon, driving, looked down at his own.

The eager PSF officers had been excited to break out the Army surplus M16s and the new AKs they had brought with them. None appeared to have any advanced tactical training. But they did have enthusiasm.

"I'm gonna shoot me some redneck, ride their asses back here tied to my hood," one officer had crowed as they prepped to deploy. His PSF pals had giggled. Cannon double checked the plates in his body armor.

Up ahead, Cannon could see the head of the convoy pull off on a dirt road to the right. Down at the end was the Langer family farm, maybe a quarter mile in. The radio crackled with static.

"We see the house, over," someone reported.

Cannon turned right onto the dirt road, the last of the cars.

BAM! BAM! BAM!

"We're taking fire!" shrieked the radio.

More fire up ahead, some automatic. The cars in front of Cannon were still going fast, headed right into the meat grinder.

"Screw this," Cannon said, hitting the brakes. His car stopped. The others ahead kept going.

There was a hurricane of gunfire ahead by the house. Cannon and Dietrich looked at each other.

"Aw, shit," Cannon said, and they both bailed out onto the dirt road. "I'll flank left, Sarge."

Dietrich nodded, and Cannon moved into the woods, maneuvering toward the western side of the farm buildings he could faintly make out through the trees.

More gunshots – many of them, and shouts from men and women. There were cries for help. And always more shooting.

Remembering his Army training, Cannon moved forward with his shotgun ready in three-to-five second rushes, taking cover as best he could after each movement to ensure it was safe to make the next one. As he got closer, he could see the situation better. It was a nightmare. The police vehicles were bunched up in a large open space in front of the main house. Off to the side, he made out Larry's truck – flag sticker still there, of course. The PSF that weren't down – and a number were down – were firing as fast as they could into the house. There were civilian bodies on the stairs and in the grass. A couple men, at least one woman. What looked like two kids.

It occurred to Cannon that a figure walking through the woods off to the flank was as likely to be shot by the PSF idiots as by the surviving Langers, and he redoubled his efforts at stealth. He kept moving, unsure exactly what he would do when he got to wherever he was going.

A shirtless boy, maybe fifteen – that would be Jimmy Langer, who Cannon had made pour a 40 of Miller into the gutter last year – ran out of the back of the house. If he had gone straight, he would have been able to reach the cornfield and freedom, but instead he turned and came back around to the front, pistol in hand.

Cannon opened his mouth to shout, but the kid came into the view of a pair of PSF on the left of the cluster first. They pivoted and opened fire on full auto. Most rounds missed, but at least a couple slammed into the boy's gut and tossed his skinny body backwards onto the grass, where he writhed and cried out.

Cannon, heedless of the danger, began to run forward toward the wounded boy, even as the two PSF shooters charged their victim.

"Wait!" he shouted, but the pair reached the young man and shot him to pieces as he lay on the grass. Cannon stopped, stunned.

One shooter was the officer who had promised to bag himself a redneck; he was beaming and sounding off about his achievement to his buddy until his forehead exploded out and all over his partner in a fountain of red.

Larry Langer was behind the falling PSF thug, a smoking Colt Python in hand. The second PSF officer started to raise his AK but Langer was too quick and too accurate. Shooter Two died from a .357 round through the bridge of his nose. Langer surveyed the corpses of the men who had slaughtered his little brother dispassionately, and then darted into the woods.

Cannon's shotgun was up when Larry Langer ran up on him. The fugitive stopped.

"You gonna kill me, Ted?"

Cannon said nothing. The shooting at the house continued; there did not seem to be any more return fire. Smoke was coming out of the windows.

"Well, go on. You bastards killed everyone else. You can kill me too. At least it won't be a stranger who does me."

Cannon stood there, pointing the 12 gauge.

"Run. Don't stop," the deputy said.

Larry Langer took off past him into the deep woods. And Ted Cannon just stood and watched the house burn.

3.

Captain Kelly Turnbull, clad in camo with none of his scare badges or tabs, surveyed his basic training company as its recruits navigated the obstacle course. They were men and women, some too fat, some too skinny. One was in a wheelchair. All were stumbling between, or trying to scramble over, the wood and rope structures, exhausted, hungry, and sweaty. Worse for them, every moment they were under the exacting observation of Turnbull's cadre of drill sergeants, who made it abundantly clear that this pathetic corps of half-stepping dumbasses was undoubtedly the biggest bunch of fuck-ups to ever be dumped off buses into a US Army recruit depot.

Watching them was comedy gold, a festival of tripping and fumbling, falling and groaning. A young woman on the rope swing let go too soon, and plopped into a muddy puddle with a brown splash. It could have been worse; when Turnbull had done his basic training at Benning, it was January through March. Here at Fort Sill, Oklahoma, if it had been winter instead of summer, she would have wrecked herself on the ice. The mud was probably a welcome relief from the heat.

"Are those my men, First Sergeant?" Turnbull said, puffing out his chest. Top, who was also a fan of *Stripes*, smiled.

"*Those* are *your* men, sir."

Turnbull laughed a little, and for the first time in months it didn't hurt. That was good. He was healing nicely. No one could say the same about the guys who had hurt him. There was no coming back from what Turnbull did to them.

He and Top walked toward the struggling recruits – they did not get the rank or title of "Private" until they graduated – carefully observing the circus. The new soldiers were in only week six of their fourteen week Basic Combat Training course. Turnbull's own Basic was as part of the old US Army, and it had been only ten weeks long. A lot of that time had been devoted to diversity and sexual harassment training. Those subjects had gotten less than a minute here: On Day One, Top told the assembled cluster of newly-shorn recent civilians, "You screw up and you're out." Once the first knucklehead grabbed a female's breast and got dragged through the company area after one of the drill instructors knocked him out with a right cross, the entire unit became crystal clear on the Army's harassment policy.

In the post-Split US Army, Basic was also harder than before. It was more serious, and where the old Basic had been designed to pass recruits, this one was designed to force them to choose whether or not to succeed. The old Basic meant to prepare warriors. The new Basic meant to do that too, but also to ensure that each recruit had to *want* it.

You didn't just get full citizenship by virtue of being born in the US anymore. The right to vote and hold public office had to be earned. These recruits were at the very beginning of their two-year citizenship service. If they volunteered, they could try no matter what their physical condition. If they performed to the standard – modified where need be for recruits like the one in the wheelchair – they graduated. But if the suck got the better of them, well, there was always The Bell.

Turnbull looked it over, a brass bell with a little rope hanging down from the clapper. The drill sergeants ensured that the recruits carried it with them everywhere. It was always there as they trained, beckoning the weak-hearted. A drill sergeant would jump your shit for anything – a look, a pause, a bootlace out of place – but if a recruit was headed toward The Bell, no drill sergeant would do anything more than watch.

Ring it, and you were gone – after you talked to the company commander.

"Anyone ring out today, Top?" asked Turnbull, his right hand dropping to his holster to ensure his service SIG 320 was still there. Constantly check your stuff – that habit was ingrained in him. Like all non-recruits, he carried his weapon at all times, on duty and off.

"Nope, none yet," replied the first sergeant with a hint of pride. When a recruit failed, he felt the failure even if he didn't show it. Top was a big, mean-looking NCO with a 101st Airborne patch on his right shoulder and a Combat Infantryman Badge on his chest from the pre-Split Army – though he saw action long before enlisting while growing up on the mean streets of Detroit. The recruits were scared of him, but they were scared of everyone. But what distinguished Top was the respect bordering on fear of the drill sergeant cadre.

When Turnbull had arrived a few months before to take command of the company while recuperating from his latest Middle Eastern escapade, it took him about three seconds to know two things. First, he might have orders into the CO slot, but the sergeants owned Alpha Company, 2-80th Field Artillery. Second, if he let Top do his job, this company command tour was going to be the easiest assignment he had ever had.

"Think we'll make the average pass rate?" asked Turnbull, still getting into the swing of this training unit gig.

"I'd say about seventy-five percent," Top replied. "The Army's a shock to a lot of them, especially the ones coming from the blue states. They are all gung ho to vote, but then they see what they have to do to earn it and they think again."

Over at the eight foot wall obstacle, a fat kid fell on one of his buddies, sending them both sprawling on the ground. They picked themselves up, and this time they got over by working together.

"Jessup's down 12 pounds," Top said. "He might just make it. Now sir, watch Marshall there."

Marshall was a strong, good-looking college grad whose attitude always called in fire on his own position. Turnbull had read his record – his family had money and came from the blue after the Split. Marshall was either going to be a leader or a pain in the ass.

Marshall and a couple others ran to the base of the wall just as Autry, the recruit in the wheelchair, rolled up. Marshall ignored him and pulled himself up and over.

Top was off like a shot.

"Marshall! Get your ass over here!"

The recruit trotted over after seeming to ponder whether to bother responding, then assumed something remotely like the position of attention.

"Yes, First Sergeant?"

"Why'd you leave your buddy behind?"

"Huh?"

"Don't you 'huh' me, recruit! Autry. You left him."

"So?"

Turnbull put his hand on Top's shoulder to keep him from committing manslaughter. The First Sergeant continued.

"Recruit, you talk to me like that again and I will put my boot so far up your ass that you'll taste shoe leather."

"I don't think so," Marshall said, turning and walking to The Bell. He grabbed the rope and clanged it.

"My office," Turnbull said.

The company commander's office was on the ground floor of the main building in the Alpha company area. A large counter and admin area blocked access to Turnbull's front door; several NCOs were there working. Inside his office, which was completely bare except for the desk and chairs, was a second door in the back leading into Top's identical office next door.

Turnbull closed the front door, walked over and sat at his desk. He put the DA Form 444 his clerk had prepared down in front of him, along with a blue pen. He had expressed that he needed a DA 444 and it had appeared – the power of command. He wondered whatever happened to Colonel Deloitte, who had taught him about how being a commander worked.

Sitting down, he realized that nothing hurt – that was a change. He had been healing from his injuries here in the rear with the gear, and it was certainly nice not having all sorts of people trying to put holes in him for once, but lately he had been starting to feel ready to get back into the game. Dealing with assholes like Marshall was already getting old.

There was a rap on his door that brought his attention back to his present problem.

"Enter!" Turnbull shouted.

First Sergeant came in and formally reported; Turnbull returned his salute. Marshall walked in next with a smirk on his face, slouching as he stood before the desk.

"I'm technically a civilian now, so I don't have to 'sir' you, right? Or salute?"

"True," Turnbull said. "You don't have to do anything. Except listen."

"To what?" Marshall said insolently. Turnbull wondered if this punk understood the risk he was taking disrespecting Top's commander – the only thing keeping him out of a full body cast was First Sergeant's professionalism.

"To me try and talk you out of quitting."

"Go ahead and try."

"Yeah, don't expect me to put my heart into it because I think you're a little shit and exactly the reason why now we make people earn the right to vote in the United States. But the Army still has regs, and since this is a big decision for you – because you won't get a second chance to serve if you bail – the regs say I have to make sure you understand the implications of your decision."

"I understand."

"You understand that you will not be able to vote in any election?"

"Yeah."

"Or hold any elected office or any appointed office of significant responsibility?"

"Yeah."

"You understand there may be social consequences to your decision?"

"Social consequences?"

"Yeah, like people – especially women – may think you're a pussy."

Marshal snorted. "Women are not going to be a problem. I make a little more than you Army guys."

"Well, technically, your dad makes more than us Army guys and gives some of it to you, which, of course, is the kind of character-wrecking parental malpractice that led you to be standing here quitting."

"I want out. Where do I sign?"

"I have your DA Form 444 right here, awaiting your signature. But I really hate to see someone who probably could succeed choose not to. I'm just kind of curious. Why?"

"Why what?"

"Why are you quitting?"

Marshall laughed sourly. "I'm quitting because I don't need this shit or want this shit. I wish my father had never left Chicago when this redneck country broke away. I'm going back where they appreciate education, and I don't have to pretend I don't think you Jesus freaks are clowns, and I won't have to crawl around in the mud with idiots just to vote."

"Those sound like awfully good reasons. Sign here," Turnbull said, sliding over the pen and paper. Marshall wrote out his name and tossed the pen down, smiling. Turnbull took it and signed that he had advised the recruit of the consequences of his decision on the "Commander" line.

"Am I done?" Marshall asked.

"Oh yeah, you're done. And thank you," Turnbull said pleasantly.

"For what?"

"For not pissing in America's gene pool. First Sergeant?"

"Yes, sir?"

"Please get Mr. Marshall the fuck out of my company area."

Top smiled and placed a huge hand on the new civilian's right shoulder.

"Time to go, *Mr.* Marshall," he said, none-too-gently pulling the young man outside.

Paperwork. Readiness reports. Assessments. Turnbull threw down his pen and looked around his office. Were the walls closing in on him? He could swear the room looked smaller than it did when he sat down a couple hours ago.

Then again, he could always go back to his spartan bachelor officer quarters and be smothered by *its* walls.

Turnbull rubbed his face and looked out his window into the company parade ground. Across the way the lights were on in the troop barracks.

"Someone got caught with a Milky Way bar and now they're paying the price," said Top from the inside doorway. "The whole company is having a GI party. By the time the recruits get to sleep, my barracks will be *gleaming*."

"And a Milky Way is the *worst* kind of candy bar," Turnbull said. "Like a Butterfinger, maybe that would be worth it. I never got caught with any pogey bait when *I* was in Basic, but you know I had it."

"Yeah, sir, you strike me as that guy in the platoon who always had something going on the side. You know, I knew when I met you that you had been a NCO, that you went Officer Candidate School."

"My worst career decision ever. Landed me behind this desk."

"Well, sir," said the NCO, coming in and sitting down. "I don't think that's exactly what got you here. You're not a cannon cocker, but you have a company command in a Field Artillery unit. Tells me they needed to find a shelf to keep you on until they needed you again."

"Just trying to get my command time, Top."

"Uh huh, sir. Yeah, I figure you can't talk about what got you so beat up you had to recuperate here, but you can't fool this old NCO. I ran your record as soon as you signed in. You know what comes up?"

"I'm guessing not a lot."

"Nothing. Everything is sealed. You're something … unusual. I don't quite know what you are, and I know you can't tell me, but you're something unusual."

"Well, I'll try to do my best while I'm here."

"You seem better, so I'm guessing that won't be too long. They always have something for guys like you to do. Of course, my problem is your replacement. What if I end up with a slug?"

"Hell Top, if anyone can square away a dicked up O3, it's you."

"I've had to square away a *lot* of young captains in my time."

"I bet. That's what a first sergeant does. Captain-squaring away is core NCO business."

Top laughed. "Well sir, I gotta go walk through the billets and sow some righteous terror in the hearts of our young recruits. You have a good night."

"You want me to come along?"

"Nah, sir. Sowing righteous terror is core NCO business too. Plus, you probably don't want to see what happens if they're as dicked-up as I bet they are."

"Roger, First Sergeant. Then I'll see you at PT tomorrow at…?"

"Oh-five thirty." Top smiled. "Unless they piss me off. Then it'll be oh-four thirty."

The bachelor officer quarters on main post were still as depressing as he remembered from when he left them 18 hours ago, also in the dark. The building was five stories high, full of a lot of lieutenants in training and some permanent party officers like Turnbull, mostly company grades but with a smattering of a few divorced majors and the occasional light colonel. A pair of first lieutenants slipped into the elevator with him, a male and a female. They chatted about some bar in Lawton they would be hitting with their pals later. Turnbull ignored them. He had long ago left their world for a darker, more brutal one; he was an alien who outwardly looked like his peers, but in reality they were not his peers at all.

The pair got off on the fourth floor and Turnbull was glad to be alone again. It occurred to him that the female had been pretty, that at one time he might even have talked to her, chatted her up. But now, what was he going to say to her? How would he break the ice?

"Kill anyone interesting lately? I have."

The door opened on the fifth floor and he walked into the corridor. A low-bidder fluorescent bulb flashed and flickered, casting its unnatural light on the ancient, industrial carpet that had seen a million pairs of combat boots trudging over it.

BOQ Room 555 was at the end of the hall, and without a conscious thought he scanned the frame and the seal and…saw a space.

Had he forgotten to shut the door at 0440 this morning?

No. He always checked to make sure it was snug. Always.

Housekeeping? The local ladies who vacuumed and dusted and who also did his laundry for $100 a month had been doing their thing for generations of officers. They would never forget to close a door.

Turnbull drew his SIG and stepped off center of the doorframe. He listened.

Nothing.

He slammed his tan boot hard into the door, sending it flying hard into the doorstopper on the wall. But by the time it hit he was inside, weapon up and seeking targets.

He could see most of the living room from the entry hall – clear. The kitchen was through a doorway to the right. He sliced it and advanced as a shape filled the doorway.

It was wearing camo – *he* was wearing camo, a big, middle aged soldier with a shocked look.

Turnbull, still charging, dropped his left hand from the pistol and grabbed the front collar of the intruder, pushing him back hard against the fridge and thrusting the pistol into his stunned face.

"Do *not* fucking move," Turnbull hissed. Judging from his expression, this guy was not going to move.

Turnbull looked him over, and noted the eagle.

"Okay Colonel, why are you in my quarters?"

"Kelly," said a familiar voice behind him in the entry hall. "Could you not shoot the nice O6?"

"He's with you, Clay?" The gun did not waver.

"Oh yeah. He's okay."

Turnbull waited a moment, then lowered the weapon and released the colonel, who took in a deep breath and regained his composure.

"Well, come on in," Turnbull said, turning to face Clay Deeds, who was also dressed in a colonel's uniform but with a nametape reading "JOHNSON." "You know, there is probably a better way to set up a sit down than sneaking into my quarters. This could have ended really badly. For both of you."

"I thought Colonel French here could use a little demonstration of your unique Kelly Turnbull style."

"Colonel French," Turnbull said, nodding.

"Captain Turnbull," the officer replied. "Colonel Johnson told me you could be aggressive. *Highly* aggressive. But, you do seem to be able to control it."

"I think maybe you got lucky this time," Deeds said. Turnbull holstered the pistol as he tried to get a sense of the odd dynamic.

"No," said French. "I think he can do what we need him to do."

"And what's that, sir?" Turnbull said. Who was this guy?

"Let's talk in your living room. I'd suggest we open some beers but your fridge is empty. Well, you do have some mustard and what used to be a half of a Domino's pizza a month ago," Deeds said.

"If I knew you were coming, I'd have stopped at the Class Six, Colonel *Johnson*."

Deeds nodded and the three went into the sparely furnished living room. The intruders took seats on the nondescript couch. Turnbull sat in an old chair facing them. It had a dark stain on the cushion that looked like a horse head. The fabric felt like sandpaper.

"So, what's going on?"

"How's your health, Captain?" French asked.

"Good?" Turnbull said suspiciously, his eyes flicking over to meet Deeds's own.

"Excellent," said French.

"And my health matters why, Colonel?"

"We need to send you in," French replied.

"In *where*?"

"This is all classified, of course," French said. Of course it was – Turnbull shot Deeds a "*Who is this idiot?*" look, and Deeds looked up at the ceiling.

"Okay," Turnbull said. "So where do you want me to go?"

"Indiana."

"What?"

"The state."

"Sir, I know *what* Indiana is. What I don't know is why you would want me to go there. I mean, what's in Indiana?"

"What is there are a bunch of red Americans trapped on the other side. Look, when the Split happened, it happened fast. Clinton took over in 2021 and immediately started retaliating against the red states. The executive orders, the regulations – and when the red states finally said 'No more' we were on the brink of all out civil war."

"I remember. I was there."

"I know. Well, I don't know exactly what you did during the Crisis, but I expect it was pretty intense."

"Intense is one way of putting it."

"Our mutual friend Colonel Johnson here, whoever he really is, did not fill me in on all your past activities when we asked for you. But it's clear you've operated in the People's Republic before. And in even less permissive environments."

"What exactly do you want me to do in Indiana?"

"Southern Indiana, to be exact. It should have come with us in the Split. There are a lot of places like that, red splotches on the map that got left on the other side because the negotiators chose to stick with state lines when splitting up the country. It was probably a good idea at the time. It had to happen fast or a lot more people were going to die than already did. You remember the hatred, don't you?"

Turnbull did. He had been in the middle of it, the palpable contempt and fury of Americans against one another. He'd seen the blood on the ground – hell, he shed some of it. Colonel French continued.

"There are these little enclaves across the continent, red in the blue, some blue in the red. People who belong on the other side, *with* the other side. And the situation is getting worse. The People's Republic – I can't believe they chose that name just to spite us – is getting more and more oppressive every day. And they are concentrating on the red enclaves."

"What do you want me to do? Do you want me to go in and smoke somebody? Because as Colonel – what's his fake name? Johnson? – will tell you, that's kind of my wheelhouse."

Deeds broke into a smile. "It really is, which is why I'm not sure you're right for this mission."

French continued: "There are talks coming up, secret talks. Negotiations to resolve the border once and for all. Our position will be stronger as to the red parts we want with … appropriate facts on the ground."

"Appropriate facts on the ground?"

"If these places are hard to govern, the blues might be more willing to let them go."

Turnbull leaned in. "How hard to govern are we talking about?"

"Not violence. Oh no, we don't want a violent insurgency."

"You want a peaceful one?"

"There's resistance already. It's informal. Mostly peaceful, though earlier this week a bunch of People's Security Force officers were killed raiding a family outside Jasper."

"What's Jasper?"

"The town where you will center your ops. It's strategically significant, near three main arteries – the old I-69, I-64, and US-231. Look, you're Special Forces. You're not just trained to kill people and break things. You're trained to organize indigenous forces as well as do recon and feed us intel. You go in, evaluate the situation, work with the locals to demonstrate to the blues that Southern Indiana is not worth the trouble. You – and the others we're sending in elsewhere – set the conditions for a successful negotiation."

"But you don't want me to kill anybody?"

"No. Absolutely not. This is not a combat mission. It's hearts and minds. You're not even taking weapons."

"Well, this sounds super appealing and a nice change of pace from getting shot at in weird foreign countries, but I think I'll have to pass."

"Captain, you're still in the Army," Colonel French said.

"Well, kind of. I usually work for him."

Deeds leaned in. "Well Kelly, that's the thing. You still belong to the Army. That's why you're here, doing a command tour.

They realized you were on their books and when they got you back for a little while they decided they wanted to keep you for a while."

"You'll certainly work with Colonel Johnson here. He's representing whatever agency he represents on this mission. But you're a soldier first. Remember that."

"So, you're ordering me to volunteer?"

"No," Deeds piped up. "He's just ordering you."

French nodded.

"Since it's decided, I guess I should get some specifics."

"Colonel Johnson will fill you in on those. He'll also liaison with you when I don't."

"And what's your role, Colonel French?"

"I'm military intelligence. You're under my overall command."

"Sir, I still think I'm missing something here. You could send me any place. Why Jasper and Indiana? I've never even been there."

"There is one other thing. The Military District of Southern Indiana – they call it the MDSI and it's pretty much everything south of Indianapolis. It's commanded by Colonel Jeff Deloitte."

"He went blue?"

"Yes. He chose to go with the blue states when they split off. His family is all in New England. Now he's the military commander for that region. There's an infantry and an armor battalion there as part of the 172nd Brigade, which he commands too. But understand, he's not the commander of the PSF or the secret police. They are independent, and our intel is that the military does not always play well with the civilian law enforcement."

"Deloitte knows counter-insurgency," Turnbull said.

"And you know him," French replied, and stood up. "I'll leave you two to talk details. Glad to have you aboard, Captain."

"Glad to be shanghaied, Colonel."

French disappeared out the front door. Deeds sat back as Turnbull looked him over.

"How did I get sucked into this clusterfuck, Clay?"

"Numbers, Kelly. They're sending in a bunch of people to embed in these disputed areas. And they had you – I couldn't hide you off the books, since you're currently turning civilians into Army guys."

"No gun? That's not going to work for me."

"Of course you get a gun. What, do you think I'm listening to him? But they don't want a war. They just want to know what's going on and for you to facilitate some nonviolent dissent."

"The blues will object. Dissent stopped being patriotic in the People's Republic a long time ago. I hear they are getting more serious about their oppression. I guess all those rights in their new constitution have an asterisk."

"Well Kelly, they came for the guns and took whatever people admitted having. They were at kind of a disadvantage finding them without records. Thanks to you, of course, the federal firearms data all went poof during the Crisis."

"Yeah," Turnbull said, smiling. "That was a real tragedy."

"They're doing more. New laws, new rules. People are getting angry. Especially about the pressure on churches, at least the ones who won't play ball. You just need to help guide the anger in a constructive direction until the negotiations finish. Hopefully, they'll decide Southern Indiana is too much trouble to keep."

"What if they don't?"

"Don't start a war, Kelly. Nobody wants that. We want a nice, peaceful resolution. We give up some ground, and so do they, and then we live in peace."

"You've been in there, right?"

Deeds shrugged.

"I don't know if they want peace, Clay. They seem to hate us pretty good."

"Just try not to kill anyone. It would make Colonel French upset."

"I'll make pleasing him my main goal. How long am I in?"

"A few weeks, tops. They're trying to get the negotiations done fast. Your main contact's a minister. Knows everyone in town. I've had him as a source for a while."

"Is your network compromised? Do they know I'm coming?"

"No. That's the advantage of not having much of a network – they can't infiltrate what doesn't exist."

"Enemy forces?"

"Local sheriffs, but they are getting taken over by the People's Security Force. Those are the guys that shot up the family farm last week. A real bloodbath, but they lost some too. No People's Bureau of Investigation in town – it's too small. They haven't sent in any People's Volunteers yet; those guys are real winners. And your boy's military units are 40 miles away. So keep out of the way of the local yokels and you're good."

"Seems super easy. Like every mission I get from you," Turnbull said. "And yet, they never are."

"If it was easy, Kelly, I'd send someone else," Clay said. He tossed Turnbull a Cincinnati Blues baseball cap. "Enjoy."

4.

"You sure you want a .45?" Clay Deeds asked Turnbull.

They were inside a customs interview room with the door locked. Outside, a 787 thundered down the runway. Dallas/Fort Worth International Airport was now the busiest airport in the new United States, serving the capital city and the huge metroplex that expanded relentlessly in all directions out across the plains.

"Yeah. I like killing what I shoot the first time," Turnbull said, his meaty hand out.

Deeds passed him a black 1911A1 in a small, inside the waistband Uncle Mike's holster. There were thick serrations on the sides of the carbon steel slide to facilitate cocking, and nicely grooved black grips with a pewter eagle emblem. It was maybe seven and a half inches long, about three pounds, with the sharp edges rounded for concealed carry.

"It's a Wilson Combat XTAC Elite Compact, fake serial number. It predates the Split, so it's not going to give you away as a red stater. It's pretty much stock, not much use on it. Our people didn't have a lot to do to it to recondition it, except change the number."

Turnbull slid the weapon out of the holster and looked it over, then pulled back the slide. Clear chamber. Good tolerances, solid. He approved.

"Kelly, how about a Glock 19? Fifteen plus one rounds. Lighter, faster rate of fire. And nine mil ammo is easy to get."

"Pass." Turnbull took one of the three eight round extended mags of .45 Federal Premium HST rounds and slipped it into the well. The mag stuck out a little below the grip, but he'd deal with it for the extra shot.

"The ammo is all pre-Split too. So are the mags. It's all sterile. They can't trace it to us, but they're locking people up for five years for having a gun so don't get caught with it."

"I don't plan to get arrested." He released the slide, then carefully dropped the hammer and slid the weapon into the holster and slipped the holster inside his pants in the small of his back under his sport coat.

"You're carrying the gun on the plane on you?"

"Uh huh. They might search my luggage and maybe my carry-on, but I've yet to be patted down going through customs. After all I'm what? An accountant?"

"Michael David Nesmith. Twenty-eight. CPA from Indianapolis."

"At least you named me after the smart Monkee."

Deeds looked at him, a bit pleasantly surprised.

"I grew up around classic rock," Turnbull said.

"Nesmith's mother actually got rich inventing Liquid Paper."

"I have no idea what that is," Turnbull said. "Anyway, I've got the back story memorized." He took the other two mags and slipped them into the pockets of his tan slacks. "Wife is Darlene, kids Cindy and Kaden. The dog is Tiger."

"Here's your iPhone 14," Deeds said. "There are photos of the family and the mutt. The home number goes to a controller inside the PR – 'Cindy' will answer if someone calls. The other numbers are cut-outs except for one special one and Pastor Bellman's. He's real. He's your point of contact. You meet him tonight, six p.m., at his church."

"The safeword is 'Utah.'"

"'Password.' Please don't get those terms mixed up, Kelly."

There were a few dozen apps loaded into the phone. The Justice Air app was right there on the front. Turnbull hit it.

"Your Justice Air app doesn't work."

"It's buggy. I printed you a paper boarding pass. You got the wallet and passport?"

"Yeah. Car keys?" Deeds handed him a ring with a remote and what looked like house keys. All fakes.

"Blue 2015 Chrysler parked in the long term lot, fifth floor. Photos on the phone."

Turnbull flipped through the pictures. "You could have picked me a hotter wife."

"That's my sister, Kelly." It was unclear if this was a joke.

"No wonder she's not my type." He flipped through a few more snaps until he came to a couple photos of a blue sedan in a parking structure next to a pillar with "5-B" painted on it. In the background was a poster: "Report Racism! No Tolerance for Intolerance!"

"The phone has about 100,000 alternating electronic signatures. It won't sign in to a cell tower the same way twice, so it's hard to trace. Your password is one-two-three-four."

"You're kidding."

"You're Army so I kept it simple. Punch in one-two-three-four-five and you wipe the memory, so be careful. Now, the special contact is Peter Dolenz."

"Really? Or am I just a daydream believer?"

"Come on, your plane boards in ten. Now, under Dolenz's contact is a phone number. That's your 'no shit emergency' number. It comes to or from us and it means something significant is happening. The email address is to a Canadian account. We'll get it. The phone will auto encrypt, but remember – those bastards got most of Silicon Valley in the divorce and don't think they can't intercept and trace you."

"Don't worry. I'm a believer."

"Just stop. The carry-on has a laptop we've loaded with accounting stuff. No password; they can dig through it all day and all they'll get is bored. We gave you a paperback suitable for your cover's background as an accountant so you can read on the plane. Your suitcase is already in the baggage system. It's full of business clothes in your size, all from the PR. There are no work clothes, just some jeans, so on your way stop at the surplus store on the outskirts of Bloomington and get yourself some boots and other gear. The address is in your phone. You were here in Dallas on business for a week, so the clothes are all dirty. That should discourage the customs folks from poking around. Which is good, since there's $25,000 in real dollars in the liner."

Turnbull said nothing.

"What?" asked Deeds.

"I was just trying to think of another Monkees song and I can't."

"Come on, before you miss the last plane to Clarksville."

Deeds walked him out of the customs office, the US customs officers all wise enough to ignore the pair. Turnbull carried a doofy vinyl computer bag as his carry-on. His tan sport coat was too big, but it hid the .45 nicely. At the door into the passenger terminal, well beyond the security gates, Turnbull paused.

"Any last guidance?"

"Try not to start a war."

"Okay. I promise not to *start* one," Turnbull said, then opened the door and slipped into the stream of passengers.

Turnbull entered the terminal alone – Deeds did not do public appearances. It was crowded, with travelers pulling their carry-ons and kids crying and running rampant. The Justice Air gates were at the end of the terminal; the People's Republic's new "public option" airline was one of the government competitors it had established in many industries to balance out the capitalists. The PR had little choice but to create a government airline – soon after the Split, all the major carriers moved their headquarters to the red. Though many flew into the PR, for now at least, the new government aggressively regulated them. Slowly but surely, they were pulling out – and the political tension that was ratcheting up did not help.

The flights out were crowded – this one was full, and the passengers looking to fly into Indianapolis were backed up out of the gate area and spilling into the terminal hallway. A 737 in Justice Air livery was unloading passengers from Chicago, but they were diverted downstairs into customs. You could travel freely between the two countries, at least for now, but this was a vivid reminder that they were now, in fact, two separate countries.

A bitter looking woman at the counter picked up the hand mic. "This flight is delayed an hour," she said over the loudspeaker, adding, "It's not Justice Air's fault."

Turnbull frowned. It was almost certainly Justice Air's fault.

He kept to himself as he waited, looking over his fellow passengers for any PR security types who he should avoid. There were not any. The PR would never admit it, but it could rely on the US's strict security measures and aggressive border controls – the same ones it regularly labeled racist, sexist, and Islamophobic.

Fox News was playing on the video monitors. There were a couple jabbering talking heads, one a perky blonde and one a salty looking dude, and the chyron read "Travel Ban Threatened As Tensions With PR Increase."

A man nearby mumbled to his wife, "We might be getting out just in time."

"I hate this place and these racists," hissed the wife. She seemed angry; her face might be moderately attractive if it wasn't twisted with bitterness. Turnbull assessed that this guy's marriage was a never-ending delight.

The flight finally boarded 90 minutes late. The first to load were a pack of well-dressed people. There was no announcement or fanfare – they just went first. As the last one disappeared down the jetway, the woman at the counter picked up the mic again. "Justice Air does not believe in privilege and there are no boarding groups. Please demonstrate your commitment to cooperation and consensus as you board."

It was, of course, chaos. The crowd swelled and bunched around the entrance to the jetway, shoving and pushing. Turnbull hung back, not wanting someone in the scrum to rub up against his piece. When the throbbing mass thinned a bit, he darted in. Stepping onto the plane, he passed the first class area, except it wasn't called "First Class" anymore. It was simply not acknowledged, and the travelers passing in the aisle instinctively avoided making eye contact with their pampered betters.

The loading took 30 minutes, plus another ten inside as the crew argued with irate travelers about their luggage, demanding random pieces be checked because of "luggage privilege."

Turnbull was on an aisle seat next to some pale college age kid who was on his cell talking way too loud with a buddy.

"D-Yazzy? For realz? His rhymes are lazy and derivative."

This was not Turnbull's wheelhouse. He was vaguely aware that there was a rapper named Kanye West who was married to some Kardashian and whose 2020 third party presidential bid had evolved from a bizarre joke into a serious threat to Hillary Clinton's electoral coalition. Kanye had dropped out of the race after the first three-way debate had turned into a profanity-laced, incoherent screaming match, a decision he claimed he made because, "God told me I should heal the world with my music instead." Turnbull later read that West had immigrated to the red states as a post-Split tax refugee, telling reporters, "I gotta keep my money. Plus, Hillary is gonna kill me with polonium."

Turnbull assessed the nearby passengers – all probably harmless. He relaxed a little. The pistol in the small of his back was remarkably comfortable. He picked up a copy of the in-flight magazine, Sky Justice. The cover story was a hagiography about a differently abled Justice Air pilot. She was blind.

"Oh swell," thought Turnbull. He wondered where her dog sat in the cockpit.

The other passengers finally settled into their places, though there was a short shouting match between two travelers who each felt entitled to a window seat and proceeded to call each other "Racist!" at the top of their lungs until the crew sorted it out. Then a very beefy-looking white female in a light blue polyester uniform got on the loudspeaker.

"I am your lead flight attendant Pat. I am a person of girth, but privileged by birth." She did not smile as she said it – apparently it was not meant to be humorous. "My preferred pronouns are 'she' and 'her.' Our flight to Indianapolis will be about three hours. Our delays were the fault of the local government's racist policies." She hung up the mic and proceeded to work her way down the aisle, which was much too narrow for her extensive carriage.

A row ahead were the man and the unhappy wife from the lounge. The attendant's hefty flank brushed him hard, and he was flustered and sputtering.

"Don't be fatist," snapped his appalled wife. He shut his mouth and ceased his fussing.

The plane finally took off, and Turnbull settled back. He could feel the gun in the small of his back, but it was fine there. Next to him, the collegiate hip-hop critic was bopping away to some rap song via his earbuds. Satisfied no one was paying inordinate attention to him – or anyone, since people seemed reluctant to make any eye contact at all – Turnbull pulled his carry-on up from under the seat and felt inside the front pocket for something to read. He pulled out a paperback that bore a cover depicting a green woman with pointy ears wearing a jewel-encrusted bikini writhing around some sort of magic scimitar that was wreathed in golden flames. The title was *The Runewench of Zorgon: Part XII in the Elf-Blade of Norxim Saga.*

Yeah, that fit his identity as an accountant all right. Turnbull turned slightly and saw the hip-hop college kid looking at his book and smirking.

"You'll pay, Clay," Turnbull muttered.

The rest of the flight was relatively uneventful. When they went to provide the in-flight snack, the attendant preceded the service by reading a lengthy disclaimer about how the airline regretted any possible implication of cultural appropriation entailed by offering salsa and tortilla chips. Turnbull dipped a chip and took a bite, then spit the hateful mouthful into his napkin. It tasted like cedar with ketchup. Yeah, to associate that mess with the Mexican treat would have been a grievous insult to those south of the border.

Turnbull pulled down the bill of his Cincinnati Blues cap and tried to sleep. It was an old infantry habit – if you aren't moving, prepping, eating, or fighting, you should be sleeping.

The customs line in Indianapolis was pure chaos, at least for the people in back of the plane like Turnbull. The people who were in first class, though no one called it that in the new egalitarian People's Republic, were quickly guided through. The rest of the passengers were left to fend for themselves. Once they finally got their luggage off of the conveyors, they next proceeded to fight to escape the dank, stifling hall.

First come, first served was a relic of the pre-Split racist paradigm, so the order through the three bored customs officers' station was determined by some sort of pyramid of relative victimhood that no sign or official offered to explain. The queue degenerated into a series of conflicts and people shouted and shoved. One frustrated customs officer had to referee between two shrieking women, one of them a Hindu, the other with a severe limp, arguing over who fell where in the oppression spectrum.

Turnbull hung back, avoiding drawing attention and hoping that by the time he got to the counter the customs officers would be exhausted. One official walked by him as he waited, pointed at him, and asked "Do you identify as gay?" Apparently, this would propel him up a few rungs in the great ladder of wrongs.

"Sorry, I like girls," Turnbull said, shrugging. The officer scrunched up her face with distaste.

"I totally like men," interjected a guy Turnbull had watched check out every female derriere that had crossed his path starting back in Dallas. The officer waved him ahead.

But his plan ultimately worked. Turnbull was near the end, one of maybe a dozen forlorn cis-het guys bringing up the rear. The customs officer at the gate waved him forward, and Turnbull quickly assessed his targets should this go bad and he were forced to shoot his way out of the terminal. But it didn't go bad. The officer asked him to open his suitcase, which he did. The worn undies were on top. The customs officer waved him through.

The parking garage was well past the ground transport area. There were cabs, along with a large sign that spent four lengthy paragraphs affirming that the cabbie-passenger relationship was now one of mutual respect and shared power here in the People's Republic, despite the sordid racist origins of the industry.

He pushed on to the parking structure. It was hot and humid and he was sweating in the sport coat he dared not remove. People were passing him without making eye contact – not just the non-contact you often see in large, anonymous hubs like airports, but what seemed to him to be a more determined refusal to interact.

He walked by two People's Security Force officers handcuffing someone. It was not clear what the perp had done, but they had been shouting "Sexist" at him.

The elevator in the garage was out. A sign taped to it read "Brokin" and it had been there for a while. Turnbull dragged the suitcase and his carry-on up five flights, sweltering in the sport coat.

The blue Chrysler was right where it was supposed to be. He put the bags in the trunk and sat down in the driver's seat. The tank was full. Deeds's agents had done this right. He got out his phone and opened the nav app, setting course for the surplus store.

The roads were bad, but there was less traffic than before since gas was now about $10 a gallon, or $17 in People's Dollars, the new currency that was being phased in here. But everyone seemed to prefer the old-fashioned dollars the red states still printed – the red states had gotten the printing plates during the great divorce.

Turnbull headed south, out of the Indianapolis metro area. He saw no military, and he was looking, but observed a fair number of People's Security Force cruisers. Turnbull carefully kept within the speed limit, and drove as timidly and cautiously as he could manage.

By about three, he was through Bloomington – a sign at the outskirts warned "Intolerance Is NOT Tolerated" – and he exited when the phone told him to exit so that he could stop at the surplus store. It was a beat-up old place without much activity – actually, there was not much activity in the town at all. Turnbull parked out front, looked around and went to the door. A bell jingled when he pushed it open.

It looked like every other surplus store in the world, though of course there were no guns for sale – nor bows or fishing poles, since fishing was now an environmental crime just like hunting. The outlawing of hunting was clearly going to do this place in eventually – the camouflage clothes market needed good old boys chasing whitetails. There was no way the bearded proprietor was going to feed himself selling to the occasional hipster college student looking to spiff up his, her or xis wardrobe.

There was a wide array of stuff in stock – old US military uniforms, boots, camping gear and the like. Turnbull knew exactly what he wanted. He gathered sturdy, but plain utility clothing that would hold up to use outside and keep him from freezing if he got caught overnight, along with a civilian jacket, and brought them to the counter.

"You got an old Army sleep system?" he asked, plopping the goods down. The proprietor, in his mid-fifties and with considerable mileage, smiled – this was already his best sale all week.

"Yeah, Gortex outer layer, two inside layers. You know your gear."

"Guess I'm just an outdoorsman."

"You ex-US military?" the proprietor asked. "I'm a Marine. Well, I was. There used to be no such thing as an ex-Marine, but that was before the politicians shut down the Corps. Well, at least shut it down *here*."

"I just want to go camping."

"Camping, huh? Okay." The proprietor smiled. A small radio on the counter had been playing music, but the music had stopped for an "Oppression Resistance Bulletin." The announcer began encouraging people to turn in "denialists, racists, and red state agents to your local PBI office." The proprietor clicked it off.

"I used to listen to Tony Katz on WIBC out of Indy," he said sadly. "Before they took him away. They can't even let me have my music in peace. Luke!" he yelled.

A young skinny kid of about twenty with bad skin came out of the back.

"Get that sleep system we got in stock," said the proprietor. He looked back at Turnbull. "You need anything else?"

"I could use a good knife and a Leatherman."

"We're not really supposed to sell knives," the proprietor said. "It's not illegal, but it's *frowned* on. I think I can square you away though. You aren't a cop?"

"Do I look like a cop?"

"Ten years ago I'd say yes. Now the damn cops look like criminals. This country is going to hell." The proprietor paused, wondering if he had said too much.

Turnbull nodded. "The knife?"

The proprietor rooted around under the counter for a moment and came up with a used Ka-Bar with a tan leather scabbard and a Leatherman multi-tool.

"I'll take them both. And that battle rig." Turnbull pointed to a tan plate carrier with six mag holders across the front and what looked like an aid pouch. It had cobwebs.

"Ain't sold one of those in a while."

"Guess I'm a weekend warrior at heart."

"I think I'll close early," the owner said as Luke put the sleep system on the counter next to the pile of stuff. The proprietor tallied it up, and Turnbull handed over the cash. Then he saw a tan ball cap and took it. He tried it on, was satisfied, and tossed it onto the counter.

"Also, those sunglasses. Are they ballistic protective?"

"You need ballistic protection?"

"Can't be too careful."

"Yeah, they'll keep frags out of your eyeballs."

"Them too then," said Turnbull. The proprietor eyed him warily. "It's a fashion thing."

The old rotary phone on the counter rang as the owner was shoving everything into a duffel bag he had thrown in gratis. "Grab that, Luke."

"Ringler Surplus," the young man said, then his face turned serious. "Okay," he said, and then he hung up.

"What?" asked the owner, concerned.

"The PVs are in town again. They're at the market."

"We need to hurry," said the owner. He reached under the counter and pulled up a sack, then opened the register and began unloading his cash.

"What's going on?" asked Turnbull.

"Nothing. You should go, quick."

"*Something's* happening."

"The damn People's Volunteers are back again. We aren't cooperative enough, I guess, so they come through to teach us who's boss. And they never pass this store by. They come in here, take whatever they want, and I can't do shit." He finished loading the sack, leaving just a few bucks in the till. Luke took the bag and left without a word. "They aren't getting my money this time."

Turnbull pulled the duffel bag over his shoulder. "Sorry," he said.

"Nothing we can do. They took all our guns. Well, all they could find. But how do you fight the damn government?"

"Good luck," Turnbull said.

"You too. Now get going before they get here. You don't want to meet these PV sons of bitches."

Turnbull turned and walked out with his gear, not explaining that it was really the People's Volunteers who did not want to meet *him*.

5.

Deputy Ted Cannon shifted uncomfortably in his seat. The ceremony was being held in the gym at Jasper High School, with dozens of People's Security Force officers and the half-dozen remaining tan-uniformed deputies sitting in folding metal chairs on the same basketball court where he had played center almost two decades ago. There were few locals in the bleachers – the three PSF officers shot dead in the raid on the Langers' farm were from out of town and no one really cared.

Pastor Bellman of the Jasper First Baptist Church had been told not to have a service for the dead Langers under the authority of the Anti-Hate Act. He held one anyway.

This ceremony for the dead PSF officers was not actually a "memorial" or a "funeral" – it was hard for Cannon to figure out what exactly it was. A severe, square-looking woman in a yellow robe and cropped hair was at the front of the crowd under the basketball net waving a candle. She was flanked by several versions of the ever-changing People's Republic flag.

"Our Earth Mother/Father Spirit surrounds and nourishes us!" she howled. Then she paused. Cannon wondered if he was supposed to do something in response. After an awkward few seconds, the woman did an odd little jig.

"We dance with joy and with sorrow! We dance in the light of our mother the *sky!*" Her voice went high and cracked on the final syllable.

The crowd sat watching silently as she capered about, her robe twirling. After about a minute of this, she suddenly stopped and went away.

Lieutenant Kessler arose while the Sheriff himself, still wearing his tan county sheriff's uniform with three silver stars on the collar, remained seated uncomfortably in the front row. Kessler was the highest ranking PSF officer present, and that was bizarre. Three dead cops pre-Split would have drawn the Governor, if not the vice-President, and thousands of cops from other agencies. Now three dead and a half-dozen wounded could barely fill a basketball court.

It occurred to Cannon that if he was shot dead in the line of duty, this was what they would do for him. Not exactly a morale builder.

"We will redouble our efforts to battle the legacy of hate that led to the murder of these fine People's Security Force officers by racist hooligans!" Lieutenant Kessler said, her voice remarkably free of emotion. She was reading off of a 3x5 card.

Cannon turned to his side, expecting to whisper an incredulous "Hooligans?" to his friend Sergeant Dietrich, but Dietrich wasn't there. He was gone, disappeared the night of the shootings. His family too – Cannon had driven by his locked-up, empty house at the edge of town. Probably over the border and away from all this.

It was tempting, but Cannon had grown up here. He knew these people. They were *his* people. And leaving them now just seemed wrong.

"There will be no mercy for those who disrupt the new order! We will never allow the hate we drove out when we expelled the racist states to return to our community!"

Our community. Cannon stopped himself from rolling his eyes. Kessler had never set foot in town until a few weeks ago. She went on.

"We will bring the criminals and those who sympathize with them to justice! And we are fortunate to have help in our mission by the People's Volunteers."

The PVs – a bunch of shitheads the government handed guns and let loose on uppity citizens. The night before, there had been a net call ordering all the deputies back to the headquarters. Once Cannon rolled in, he was ordered to stay. Then the phones started going crazy with calls. A bunch of People's Volunteers had shown up on Main Street with AKs and started shooting into the air. Then they decided to shoot out a couple windows and beat the hell out of a couple citizens. When they got tired of that, they walked through some stores and took whatever they wanted.

And the deputies couldn't do a damn thing about it.

Lieutenant Kessler had smiled as the remaining local deputies fielded the desperate phone calls. "This town needs to learn," she said. The PSF officers, all out-of-towners, thought the whole situation hilarious.

Luckily, the PVs didn't murder anyone, not this time at least. But that was hardly reassuring. Sooner or later.

Cannon quashed the urge to speak up, to tell the outsiders that these people could only be pushed so far. But that would be the end of his job, and then there would be one less local to protect the natives. Plus, they wouldn't listen anyway.

Kessler went on with her eulogy for a couple minutes – it was entirely unmemorable – and then sat down. The priestess came back up front and led the crowd in an awkward acapella attempt at a Katy Perry song about girl power, even though the three dead officers – whose names were never mentioned – all identified as "male."

"Are these song books approved?" asked Darcy Puig, the regional Inclusiveness Inspector. About 24 and a recent graduate of Notre Dame, where she had majored in Oppression Studies, she had come to Jasper's First Baptist Church as part of her regular inspections of licensed religious organizations. She was squat and had dyed black hair cut in a bowl shape. A stainless steel spike protruded from her lower lip.

"We call that a 'hymnal,'" answered Pastor Tim Bellman. "And I don't understand the question. Do we have to get our hymnals approved now? I thought the People's Republic's constitution protected freedom of religion."

"Well, it does," she answered. "And you don't *have* to get your church books approved, not yet." She sounded disappointed.

"Well, that's good to hear."

Puig jotted some notes down on her computer pad, then looked up. "You know, a lot of churches are moving toward a more inclusive framework that puts aside the patriarchal and racist elements of a lot of old religious practices. You should think about it. I can email you some recommended Christian principles."

"Thank you, but I think I know the tenets of my own religion, Ms. Puig."

"And you are free to practice whatever things you choose to believe *inside here* in whatever way you want. But you need to understand that *outside of here* we believe in science and inclusiveness and diversity. And there's no room for Jesus-based intolerance."

"That sounds kind of like the opposite of diversity."

"Mr. Bellman –"

"*Pastor* Bellman."

She ignored his correction. "We are simply not going to allow any group to undercut the progress and evolution we are putting in place after breaking away from the racist states. If you refuse to cooperate, you need to understand that there will be a price."

"So my congregation is free to practice its faith however it likes except when you disagree with it?"

"In a democracy, the people choose what's allowed and what isn't. And they have chosen not to allow hate, *Pastor* Bellman."

"Are you done here?"

"I'm making a note about this," she said firmly, typing into her pad. "But I'm done here for now."

"Then go."

"I will be back."

"There's the door. Don't let it hit you on your ass on the way out."

Puig frowned, then turned and walked through it without a word. Out the doorway, Bellman could see the sun was setting. And he wondered if those PV punks would be coming back again.

Turnbull saw a young, dumpy woman with a weird piercing stomp out of the sanctuary and down the stairs as he approached from the parking lot. She carried a computer pad and seemed to have the officious attitude of an aspiring bureaucrat. There was no weapon visible so Turnbull went to his default.

If he had to take her out, it would be one to the face with the Wilson .45 he carried in the small of his back. He smiled, all friendly-like.

The woman marched past him as if he wasn't there. Turnbull continued up the steps and through the doors into the sanctuary.

A man in his early fifties was standing near the altar. He turned and faced Turnbull. Good bearing, relatively in shape, probably ex-military.

"Pastor Bellman?" asked Kelly.

"Yes?" replied the man.

"I'm in need of guidance. You can call me Kelly. I'm visiting from Utah."

"Come with me."

"Tenth Mountain Division, Afghanistan, 2004," Pastor Bellman said, handing his guest a Coke. Turnbull took it and thanked him – he knew how expensive soda was here now. The pastor continued.

"I was the battalion chaplain. Good unit, good guys. Worst place in the world to be wearing a US Army uniform and not have a gun. Some of the local nationals fought with us for 20 years and Clinton just abandoned them. Fucking disgrace."

Turnbull lifted an eyelid at the profanity.

"Son, I was an *infantry* chaplain."

"All the pieces fit."

"And you? I was with the grunts long enough that I can tell what you *were* just by looking at you," said the minister. "The big question is what are you *now*?"

"Just a guy here to keep an eye on things, maybe help you folks keep from getting ground down."

"You here to start a war, son?"

Turnbull shook his head. "No. No war. I just watch, report, maybe give you some helpful hints to keep the assholes from stomping you. That's it."

"I'm a shepherd who wants to see his flock grow and be happy, not see them be slaughtered."

"Like I said, it's not my job to pick a fight. Observe, report, provide some suggestions. And they were pretty clear on the no killing part."

"They were clear, but I'm wondering if *you* were clear."

Turnbull shrugged. "Well, I haven't killed anyone since I've been here, so that's something."

"Well, let's try and continue your streak. You hungry? Food's getting scarcer, but I think I have some chili."

"Whatever you got. I appreciate it."

"I live about —"

In the distance: *Bam. Bam bam bam.*

Turnbull was on his feet, listening.

Bellman too. "They're back."

The People's Volunteer butt-stroked Dale Chalmers in the face with his AK-47 because he felt like it. Then he laughed.

Chalmers was with his wife Liz and Jimmy, his youngest kid, at what had been a Union 76 until the oil companies were nationalized, pumping his ration of gas into his Dodge when three cars tore into town. Two cars headed toward the center of town; the other one pulled up on the other side of the pumps from Chalmers, who was kind of stuck there. He tried to mind his business. That was not in the cards.

Four punks poured out, and two headed inside to see what they wanted to take from the quickie mart. One of the others, wearing the black coveralls of the PVs and a do-rag, crossed the island, pointed at the nozzle in Chalmers's car, and said, "Gimme that, bitch."

"What?" Chalmers said, not understanding that the punk wanted to fuel up on his prey's dime – and his ration card.

The punk could have just grabbed the nozzle and taken it, but hitting the guy was definitely more fun. He slammed the wooden butt into the man's face, blood and teeth spattering and scattering as his victim fell. Inside the car, the wife and the kid were shrieking, and on the ground the man was stunned and the red was flowing. The fourth punk, watching over the roof of their car, just laughed.

"Damn, you fucked him up!" he shouted, gleeful.

"Bitch," the People's Volunteer laughed, taking the nozzle. He thought briefly of squeezing a little gas onto him and lighting it, but he decided against it. The toothless punk had learned his lesson.

He slid the nozzle into his Chevy and squeezed, ignoring the ruckus around his victim.

From the center of town: *Bam. Bam bam bam.*

The nozzle popped, the tank full. He pulled it out and dropped it to the ground.

"Come on!" he shouted to the pair coming out of the store loaded up with beer and chips.

They were missing all the fun.

When Kessler finally released the deputies from the station, Cannon rushed to his cruiser and headed the four blocks to the town center. A Ford truck was sitting in the middle of the street, its windshield shot out. He was gratified not to see any bodies. People were out and about – he could feel the tension. Some were sweeping up glass. Others stared at him as he parked and stepped from the cruiser.

"Where the hell were you?" asked Roy Coleman bitterly, an older man who often worked as a greeter at the Walmart on the north side of town.

Cannon ignored him, but he was drawing a lot of angry looks. It occurred to him that the townspeople saw him as an outsider, and that stung.

Pastor Bellman was ahead, his arm supporting someone – shit, Liz was with them. It was Dale, his face bloody, his front teeth a cracked and shattered wreck.

"The PVs," Bellman said as Cannon approached. No judgment, just the fact.

"What happened?" Cannon said, because he could not think of anything else.

"What do you think?" Liz shouted, half angry, half frightened.

"We called Dr. Klein. He's coming to open up his office," Bellman said. Dr. Klein was the dentist, but his milieu was fillings and braces. Dale would need much more to restore his wrecked jaw.

"They ordered us to stay inside the station," Cannon said, not to anyone in particular, and no one was particularly interested in his explanation for why he had been unable to stop thugs from rampaging through his town and beating his people to a pulp.

Cannon's eyes settled on a tall, large man with a serious face following a few feet behind the others. The first thing he felt was a twinge of fear. The man looked him over, as if he was assessing the deputy. The man's eyes went off him and somehow, Cannon felt relieved he had not been assessed as a threat.

"They attacked Becky Collins," Bellman said. "They didn't rape her, but they groped her. She's upset. And they hit Bill Simms in the leg with a round. Flesh wound. Maybe you should go see them."

Cannon nodded, and moved off toward the Sunrise Diner where Becky worked.

Dr. Klein arrived quickly, pulled from dinner and wearing a polo shirt. He unlocked the office and brought the group inside. Liz stayed with them in the exam room. Jimmy was quiet and sat reading in the waiting room. He's barely spoken since watching his father being assaulted. Turnbull took the minister aside.

"They're going to kill someone next time."

"I know."

"Tonight was a message. Maybe I'm screwing up your metaphor, but the wolves want your flock to be sheep. Nice, quiet sheep. And they'll do what it takes to make that happen."

"I know," Bellman replied, thinking.

"So what are you going to do?" Turnbull asked.

"You're the expert. What are my courses of action?"

"I guess we've taken killing the bastards off the table for now, so maybe we let the People's Republic know there's a cost to this kind of bullshit."

"How?"

"Strike."

"Strike?"

"Sure. Strike. Non-cooperation. No one cooperates with the government. You ignore it. And you create your own shadow government. Cut the PR out of the loop. If you can convince your people to do it."

"A shadow government…. sounds like you're an insurgent, Kelly. Sounds like you're trying to make me into one too."

Turnbull shrugged. "I guess you can all get your teeth bashed in. Your women can get groped. Or worse. You can live that way, if you want."

Bellman assessed the outsider. What was this man's agenda? Bellman was certainly happy to help the new United States – he'd move there if he wasn't needed in Jasper – but clearly the newcomer was pushing him towards…what?'

"Remember, we have to live here," Bellman said.

"If you call it living," Turnbull replied. "I call it serfdom. Now, I'm going to tell you something. Something I probably shouldn't, but I'm going to anyway." Turnbull looked over at Jimmy; he was still ensconced in his book.

"Yes?"

"There are negotiations going on to redraw the boundaries from the Split. Southern Indiana is one of the places looking to be traded. In a month, this could be red – if the blues let it go."

"That's why you're here."

"Our interests correspond, Pastor. I have an interest in making sure this area is a pain in the PR's collective ass. And you have an interest in not seeing your congregation get its teeth smashed down their throats."

"We need to organize. Which is why your people recruited me."

"Churches are about the only extra-governmental organizations left," Turnbull said.

"Yes," the pastor said. "The VFW was outlawed as warmongering and the Rotary Club spends its meetings talking about systemic racism. Even the Boy and Girl Scouts are gone. They're now the 'Genderchoice Sharers' and all the kids have to wear green skirts."

"I'm guessing there's a merit badge for denouncing thought criminals."

"Merit badges are patriarchal. Everyone just does macramé."

Turnbull leaned in. "It's time we met up with some locals you can trust. And that cop – who was he?"

"Tom Cannon. Local guy. I think he's okay. They are taking all the local agencies and folding them into the PSF."

"Will he help us? We can use someone on the inside of the security forces."

"You want to get him arrested?" Bellman looked him over. "This is a dangerous game, Kelly. Assuming that's even your name."

"Freedom's a dangerous business. If you people want to go on like this, you can."

"We don't."

"Then find some people you can trust and let's get together. Stay off the phones."

"I may be a country preacher, but I'm not that dumb," replied Bellman, irritated.

"I'm used to operating in enemy territory. You aren't. And this is now enemy territory for you. If you do this, if you defy the

PR, they *will* come down on you. You saw what happened to those people at that farm."

"The Langers were nuts with guns."

"They killed the Langers because the Langers *defied* them, not because they were nuts with guns. The whole PSF is nuts with guns. If you choose to defy them too, there's no limit to what they'll do to you. You have to understand that."

"We can't keep living like this."

"No, you can't. I just want to make sure you are going in to this with your eyes open."

"They're open," Bellman said firmly, but Turnbull wasn't sure he believed him.

Turnbull slept in a small caretaker's room in the back of the church. Bellman went off to contact the key folks he needed for the face-to-face meeting; he would stay the night at his parsonage a few blocks away. There was a small television set and Turnbull tried to watch the news. There was a summer shower coming, which the determinedly ugly weathercaster of unspecified gender attributed to the United States' "racist climate crimes."

Turnbull flipped the set off. His .45 sat on the bedside table. He read for a while, though all he had was his paperback copy of *The Runewench of Zorgon*, and the fact he had not read the prior eleven books meant that Part XII was utterly incoherent. He still had no idea what the "Elf-Blade of Norxim" was, but apparently it was a sword that talked because it gave a seven page libertarian-themed speech that sounded like something Ayn Rand would have written if she had dated J.R.R. Tolkien.

He tossed the book at the wastebasket and missed. It was quiet; he settled back on his pillow listened for a while. Satisfied that it was safe, he allowed himself to fall asleep. He dreamed that he was short of ammo, and he tossed and turned.

The center of town was already largely cleaned up. The damaged Ford truck was gone, and the broken glass from its windshield and several of the plate glass windows the PVs had shattered the previous night had been swept from the street and the sidewalks. But the people were on edge, walking faster than usual, and fear hung like sullen fog. It reminded Turnbull of some of the dictatorships he had operated in, and then it came to him that this should be no surprise. It saddened him that he felt the same oppressive gloom in his own homeland.

Or, at least, what had been his homeland until four years ago.

Turnbull had spent the day in the church thinking about the meeting and cleaning his .45. When Bellman came to get him at about five, he had put the weapon in its holster in the small of his back. Bellman saw it, but said nothing.

The meeting would be at the Sunrise Diner.

"It's a nice little place right there on Main Street," Bellman said.

Turnbull smiled. "Main Street." That was almost too on the nose. But then the town had been founded and its roads laid out long before the discovery of irony.

Turnbull had originally been leery of meeting in a public place, but Bellman assured him that unless he wanted word of a secret rendezvous to get out they had best do everything above board. Everyone already knew there was a stranger in town; if he started having secret meetings that would certainly get around, and there were informers. So better to do it in plain sight.

They took Bellman's Ford Taurus and kept to side streets most of the way. The pastor pulled into a small parking lot behind the row of storefronts. Turnbull surveyed the area without thinking about it – clear. He stepped out and onto the pavement.

Something growled at him.

A small brown puppy, some mix of terrier and spaniel and who knows what else, was blocking his path, snarling, with something in its mouth. It looked like a flattened frog.

"You don't have a lot of rabies around here, do you?" Turnbull asked.

"A lot of dogs went feral when the government decided you needed a license for an 'animal companion.' Of course, the animal control people rarely do anything since they know they can't be fired. It's sad."

The dog growled again, his dead toy quivering in his jaw.

"I think he wants to play fetch," Turnbull said. "Go away, dog." He stepped around the puppy, and they began walking. The puppy trotted behind them, proudly carrying his squashed amphibian prize.

They walked around to the front, Bellman greeting various townspeople on the way, but never introducing the large stranger with him. And in the current environment, no one asked.

The small, cozy Sunrise Diner was only partially full with the early dinner rush – "rush" being a relative term. Turnbull assessed the space quickly – plate glass frontage, one door in the front, a corridor heading rearward, probably to the restrooms and the kitchen. There would be an exit back there somewhere.

A pretty girl in her twenties dropped off a couple of plates of thin sandwiches; their French fry servings were pretty skimpy. The waitress was red-eyed, and Bellman stopped beside her on the way to the back.

"Are you all right, Becky?" he asked. She nodded. Bellman hugged her. Turnbull stood uncomfortably, unsure exactly what to do. She looked the stranger over, but said nothing. The pair moved on.

Bellman had arranged for a table in the rear. The table was already populated with three women and four men – including the unlucky man who had gotten his teeth bashed in. He looked only marginally better than he did last night.

Turnbull slid into a chair facing the front door, but with easy access to the corridor leading to the rear. From there, he could dominate the entire room.

Bellman sat at the head of the table.

"Hello. Thanks for coming out. This is my friend Kelly. He's…not from around here."

"What are we going to do?" Dale Chalmers said, his voice muffled by his ruined teeth and swollen lips.

"That's what we're here to figure out."

"I went to the Sheriff's Department to report what happened this morning and they laughed at me," said an older woman with her grey hair in a bun. She seemed genuinely surprised, as if she had been asleep for the last decade.

"Martha, we need to realize that the situation has changed. We can't rely on the government to protect us," Bellman said.

"We should just leave, all of us," said a middle aged man. "Go south. Get out of here."

"We can run," Bellman said. "That's one option. But this is our home."

"Maybe I can work with them, come to some reasonable arrangement," said a middle aged man in a sport coat.

"This is Larry Silvers, our mayor," said Pastor Bellman. "His real job is real estate – or was, before it became almost impossible to sell property."

"You think that might work?" Kelly asked.

"It might. Better to try and make a deal then go on like this. At least that's how I see it."

"Be my guest," Turnbull replied, his optimism meter far into the red.

"We should dig up our guns and kill those sons of bitches," Chalmers said, sputtering. Turnbull looked him over; he was no soldier, but he was certainly pissed.

"I know you're angry, Dale, but don't talk like that," Bellman said. "We're not here to talk about killing."

"What else will they understand? Should we have a demonstration? March? Carry signs? Vagina hats maybe?" Chalmers was getting hot.

"You fight when you are out of options," Turnbull said. "Not while you have other ones. Because if you fight, then you don't know where it will end up."

"I'll take my chances."

"You'll probably get yourself dead. Lot of other people too."

"They came into my town and smashed my face in in front of my wife and kid," Chalmers said. "You think I won't fight?"

"No, I think you'll fight. I'm not sure how well. But we're not there yet. We can do other things. We need to consider...nonviolent solutions," Turnbull said, hardly believing those words were coming out of his mouth.

"The Founders didn't look for nonviolent solutions to the damn redcoats," Chalmers said.

Turnbull said nothing – the guy had a point. And he wondered if his advice might be different if his orders were not so specific.

There was a disturbance at the front of the restaurant; people were getting up out of their seats staring out the window. Becky the waitress rushed back to Bellman, her eyes wide, frightened.

"They're back," she cried.

Turnbull was past her and at the front door, staring down the street, assessing. Bellman joined him.

"What do we do, Kelly?" the minister asked. People were already rushing off the sidewalks, terrified.

"*We* don't do anything."

Turnbull stepped out of the diner into the street, his Wilson .45 nestled in the Uncle Mike holster in the small of his back.

Bellman watched from the diner doorway, holding the puppy. It had wanted to come along.

The People's Volunteers numbered eight, four per sedan. They were in a couple of Chevys, late '00s, obviously "liberated," with "PV" spray painted on the front doors. The thugs were smiling, happy, in fact, very happy. One fired five rounds into the air from an AK, and he giggled as the already scattering townspeople ran even faster. The sound echoed across the town, just as it was meant to.

This was going to be fun. And easy.

Except for the man walking down the middle of Main Street from the direction of the courthouse, his left hand held up in the air. A big man. A man with a wan little smile.

A man who did not seem afraid.

The PV leader, who wore his black coverall uniform unbuttoned down the front, displaying a concert t-shirt from some rapper with silvery lettering, saw him first.

A man, walking down the middle of the street.

Why was his left hand up in the air?

The leader laughed.

"What the hell?" he said, holding his AK up toward the sky with one hand. He was smiling. His friends went silent and their eyes went to the approaching gentleman with the odd left hand.

The man stopped about ten feet away, a half dozen of the AKs trained on him.

"Hi," Turnbull said.

"Hey bitch," said, the leader, now walking forward, AK still pointed upwards, laughing a little. "Don't you know how to give up?"

His cohort found this highly amusing.

The man just smiled.

"Give up?" Turnbull asked.

"Yeah, you put *both* your hands in the air."

"Oh, I see the problem," Turnbull said. "We have a misunderstanding."

"Yeah, you're right. We have a *big* misunderstanding."

"See, I'm not giving up."

The leader blinked, computing.

"You're not giving up?"

"No," Turnbull laughed. "Why would I do that?"

"Cuz I'll cap your country ass."

"Nah, you won't shoot me."

"Oh yeah, I will."

"No. Curiosity. You *really* want to know why I have my left hand up in the air."

"I don't give a shit ..."

"No, trust me on this. You really, *really* do give a shit why I walked out here with my left hand up in the air."

The leader said nothing. From behind him, one of the gang, his head wrapped in a do-rag, shouted.

"Hey, just shoot that motherfucker!"

Turnbull stared in the leader's eyes, and the leader paused, uncertain.

Why *did* he have his left hand up in the air?

"You could do what the particle physicist in the do-rag says, but I think I've piqued your interest," Turnbull said.

"Why are you holding it up?" the leader asked.

"Do you deer hunt?"

"*What?*

"Deer. Like Bambi, except all grown up."

"I know what a deer is."

"But have you ever *hunted* for deer? Perhaps this is outside of your experience since the new government recruits you People's Volunteers out of cities and there's not a lot of large game animals wandering around there, unless you count the women and children you guys always seem to hit when you're shooting at each other. So, let me share with you," Turnbull said evenly. "Okay, hunting is banned now, but just about everyone around here *used* to do it, so we have some experience with it. To hunt deer, you can walk around the woods looking for a deer, and that's good. It's a challenge."

"Shoot that bitch!" shouted Do-Rag, impatient to get back to pillaging, and maybe worse. The leader ignored him, his attention fixed, trying to figure out exactly what was happening here. And it began to occur to him that it could not be anything good.

"But some guys hunt deer another way," Turnbull continued. "They set up a blind and hide in it and then they wait. Let the deer come to them. Sometimes – and this is usually against the law, but people do it anyway – they even bait the deer to come on in right in front of their deer blind, all unsuspecting, thinking everything's fine. Then the hunter – who's using a hunting rifle with a scope and big old bullets – just...*pow*. Drops 'em."

The gears in the leader's mind were turning; Do-Rag's not so much.

"You know all these country boys around here? *All* of them were deer hunters," said Turnbull. "And *not a one of them* turned in his deer rifles."

The leader looked around, his eyes darting to roofs, windows, cars, doorways.

"So," asked Turnbull. "Since I don't have a radio or anything fancy to communicate with, what do you think happens if, for *any* reason, this hand drops?"

The leader swallowed, then puffed out his chest.

"And you know you'll be the first to get shot," the leader said.

"No, I'd be *second*. But I'm betting you're smart, at least smarter than Do-Rag over there, which can't be hard. Still, I'm rolling the dice, but I'm feeling good about my chances. And now you're thinking about whether *you* ought to roll the dice, and all I can say by way of advice is '*Fürstenfeldbruck.*'"

"What? *Fürstenfuckfeld?*"

"*Fürstenfeldbruck*. Ah, don't bother trying to pronounce it. It's a German airfield – damn, my arm's getting tired so I better hurry. *Fürstenfeldbruck* is the airfield the West Germans had the Palestinian terrorists who kidnapped the Israeli athletes at the 1972 Munich Olympics go to to meet their getaway plane."

The leader blinked, baffled. Turnbull continued, patiently.

"See, except it was an ambush. The Germans were waiting there for them. But the operation went really wrong. They teach you all about it in sniper school. See, the Germans only had one sniper per bad guy – actually, *less* than one shooter per bad guy. So you can probably guess what happened. When they opened fire, they missed taking out all of the bad guys out on the first volley. Tragically, the dirtbag Palestinian terrorists survived long enough to murder the hostages."

All the PVs were watching now, but the only one who seemed to be seeing where this was headed was the leader.

My point is, gentlemen, that you always have *two*. Two snipers per target. That gives you say, in a place like, well, this street, with this light, and high competence with quality high-powered rifles and, well, targets totally out in the open, about a 98% certainty of a first shot kill."

The PVs looked around, nervous – at least, most of them. Do-Rag still seemed puzzled.

"Let me break it down for you," Turnbull said, seeing Do-Rag's bafflement. "If for some reason, *any* reason, this left hand comes down – because you shoot me, because I trip, because I feel like fucking with your dumb asses – these pissed off townspeople kill you all. My left hand is a lot more efficient than a radio. Hand up, check fire. Hand down, smoke you all."

"If you got sixteen snipers," the leader says, pausing to multiply, "where are they?"

Turnbull smiled, hand still up, but wavering a tad. "Well, since they undoubtedly had some time to prep because they saw you asswipes coming down Route 231 miles ago, they're probably in really good, concealed positions since it doesn't take a rocket scientist to figure that you geniuses are going to stop in the center of town for your little party."

"I don't believe you have sixteen guns on us," the leader said, his AK starting to drop toward his opponent.

Turnbull smiled, stepped right a foot to position the leader between him and the other thugs, and in a swift, fluid motion drew out his jet black Wilson .45 from the small of his back with his right hand and pointed it at the face of his opponent.

Its hammer was cocked. Turnbull's left hand remained upright.

The leader froze; the rest of the thugs scrambled, their weapons now all pointed at Turnbull.

"I only need *fourteen* shooters," Turnbull said. "And you can't swing a dead cat around here without hitting fourteen ex-deer hunters just aching for the chance to take some PV asshole as a trophy. There's no limit either, and it's the opening day of the season."

The leader said nothing, did nothing.

"Okay, maybe I've taken the metaphor too far. I do that a lot. So let me get to the point. Get back in your tacky ass Chevy shitboxes and get out of my town before we kill you all."

The leader stood there for a moment, thinking.

"The best case scenario is that I'm lying and *only* you die," said Turnbull. "Maybe I get Do-Rag too before the rest of you get me, but that's your *best* day – just you dying. Now, do you really want to die just so your pals can loot some shit from this town?"

"I ain't afraid to die. I'm a warrior."

"No, you're a punk with an AK and a stupid D-Yazzy concert tee. *I'm* a warrior," Turnbull said. "By the way, Yazzy's rhymes are lazy and derivative."

The leader blinked.

"Go," said Turnbull. "Just go."

"Okay, you got me. This time. We'll roll."

"Great, because my left arm is totally cramping. My trigger finger's still good, though."

"We're leaving," the leader shouted over his shoulder.

"Fuck that," shouted Do-Rag.

"You got him, or do I…," Turnbull wiggled his left hand.

"Get your dumb ass back in the car!" the leader shouted over his shoulder.

"Oh, and leave your guns," said Turnbull.

"*What?*"

"The guns. Leave the guns, and any spare mags, if these dipshits thought to bring any."

"Ain't leaving our guns."

"Well, you ain't leaving *with* them. I mean, we're willing to pass on shooting you and burying your asses somewhere in those woods you passed coming into town, so I think you're getting a really *good* deal, and you should take it. Now put the fucking guns on the deck right now because my arm is getting tired *for real*."

The leader considered, the black Wilson's yawning barrel looming a foot or so in front of his face. He squatted, placing the AK on the asphalt. The rest went along, then wordlessly got into their cars.

"We're coming back," said the leader. "And with a lot more of us."

"I know," said Turnbull. "But you seem smart, so let me recommend you get yourself a desk job, because the next time you PVs show up in Jasper, we're going to kill you all."

As they drove away, Turnbull waved good-bye with his still raised left hand.

People shyly poked their heads out of the buildings and businesses, and stepped back outside. Bellman and Chalmers stepped over to Turnbull in the middle of Main Street. The puppy was along too, still clenching the flat frog in its mouth. It growled.

"Collect these AKs and dig up your guns," Turnbull said. "I think we just ruled out a nonviolent solution."

6.

"Who is he?" she demanded.

Deputy Cannon stood there in front of Lieutenant Kessler's empty desk, his mind racing. He finally spoke.

"I don't know."

"*You don't know*? You know everybody in this shitkicker town. You freaking grew up here!" she yelled and slammed the desk with her dainty fist.

"I don't know who the guy who scared off the PVs is. I have no clue."

Of course, that wasn't quite true. He had *something* like a clue; more like a gut feeling. He had seen that big guy the day before when they were helping Dale to the dentist, but he didn't recognize the guy. He just knew the stranger looked like bad news. And this was all bad news.

"They have weapons now, eight AKs plus ammo stolen from the PVs. Where are they? Somewhere in this town. We're going to find them, and the people who did this."

"I can ask around. I'll talk to the mayor."

"The mayor – what's his name? Silver? He's everything wrong with this town. Another smug, privileged cis-het male. When he finds out his kind is going to be disqualified from holding office, it'll break his heart." Lieutenant Kessler smiled.

"Look," said Cannon, ignoring her rant. "I can try to get whoever took them to turn them in. Maybe we give amnesty to whoever turns them in."

"Sure, amnesty. Just allow them to point weapons at the servants of the people because they don't feel like being punished for their arrogance. No, we're going to find and deal with everyone involved in this, Deputy. And these people are going to learn."

Lieutenant Kessler settled back at her desk, her voice returning to normal. "Your townies are on my last nerve, Deputy. You saw what we did to the Langers when they provoked us. This isn't a game."

"Lieutenant, I know it isn't a game. But you can't have these People's Volunteers punks coming into town and beating the shit out of our people."

"*Our* people? That's your problem. You have dual loyalty, Deputy. Your people, your *only* people, should be the people of the People's Republic, not these renegade fascists who won't accept their place in the new order. They never do. We always have to teach them."

"What did they ever do wrong, Lieutenant? These are normal people, good people. Just leave them alone. Let them live their lives."

"They think they can just keep sitting back, privileged and powerful. We've got news for you and your townsfolk, Deputy. Things have changed. They aren't in control anymore. Time for them to shut up and listen. And they're going to conform."

"Look, let's stop this before it gets out of control."

"It's already out of control, but I'm going to get it back under control. I'm going to Indianapolis for a security meeting this afternoon, and when I get back, these people are going to learn what control is. Now you get out there and you talk to your backwoods brothers and sisters and figure out who the hell is behind this. That's the best thing you can do for them – it'll go a lot easier if we find them fast and we don't have to get rough."

"Get rough?"

"Yes Deputy, get rough. It means what it means," the lieutenant said. "And you need to change into the PSF regulation uniform and get out of that Andy Griffin tan costume. It's a new reality, and you need to accept it just like this town does."

He didn't bother correcting her about Andy *Griffith*. "If you want me to talk to the people, you better let me dress like a friend instead of an enemy."

"Once again you've put your finger on the problem, Deputy Cannon. These people see the People's Security Force as an enemy, not as a friend. Which tells me that they are enemies of the people. Now get out of my office."

Cannon stepped into the squad room and shut the door. There were only one or two tan uniforms left; the rest were in black PSF utilities, and all of those were strangers.

Turnbull pulled back the bolt on the AK and locked it open. He checked for a round and seeing the chamber was clear, stuck his little finger inside the action, rubbed it around, and pulled it out again.

His finger came back jet black.

"Why am I not shocked that these asswipes never clean their weapons?" he asked aloud. The three other townspeople in the garage looked up. Davey Wohl owned the gas station, or he did before it was nationalized in the name of providing cheap petroleum to the people. Wohl's "fair compensation" for his business barely covered his People's property tax assessment for 2025. He now did odd jobs and auto repairs out of his home's garage.

Wohl was already breaking down one of the other assault rifles, as was Mayor Silver. Lee Rogers was working on a fourth. She did logistics for the big Walmart at the north side of town. The company was now the town's biggest employer, having made its peace with the Elizabeth Warren administration and received a government-chartered monopoly on big box stores outside urban areas. For the people, so the President said.

"Let's just get these all at least basically functional," Turnbull said, taking a cloth to the filthy innards of the Chinese-made Kalashnikov knock-off. "I'm taking one and five mags. We need to secure the rest somewhere. That's on you, Lee. Keep them out of houses in case the PSF decides to do a sweep looking for them. Mr. Mayor, you need to organize a watch on the town, so we know who's coming and who's going. We need to cover People's Route 231 both ways. We need to know if they're bringing in reinforcements. And we need eyes on the PSF station 24/7."

The Mayor nodded. "I know everybody. I'll get it done."

"Be careful," Turnbull said. "You know everybody under normal conditions. It's about to get stressful. Make sure you don't trust anyone who isn't going to hold up under what's coming."

Pastor Bellman came in through the door to the house, shown to the closed garage by Davey Wohl's wife.

"Hi to you too," he said, staring down the barrel of the .45.

"Sorry, habit." Turnbull put the pistol away and went back to cleaning the rifle. Bellman surveyed the scene.

"Kelly, I hope you haven't brought us a war."

"I think that's out of our control," Turnbull replied, rodding the weapon's sooty barrel.

"Not adding fuel to the fire is firmly within our control," the pastor observed. "So what do you think their next move is?"

"They're going to increase the police presence, maybe by a lot. There will be roadblocks and checkpoints, ID checks on the street, maybe some raids. We need to set up some sort of informal communication system to get the word out within the town."

The pastor smiled. "You've never been in a small town, apparently. Information moves pretty damn fast all on its own around here. There aren't a lot of secrets in a small town."

"Am I still a secret? What do the cops have as far as informants?"

"They have a problem," said the pastor. "There are still a few hometown deputies left, local folks who haven't been fully integrated into the PSF yet. No one will talk to the regular PSF officers. They're all from out of town and they don't mix much with us anyway. We see them around, getting coffee or whatever, but people are afraid of them."

"If they're smart, they'll start being friendly, cultivating the people. But then, I don't see smart as one of their go-to moves. What about the guys on the inside? What about that deputy the other day?"

"Ted Cannon? Dedicated guy. Community oriented. Probably doesn't want to take sides. That's not his style."

"Cannon's not gonna have much choice about taking sides. It's them or us. So is he going to rat me out?"

"I don't think so, and I'd kinda worry about his health if you thought so."

"Yeah, that would be a good thing to worry about if I thought he was going to go supergrass on us."

"Supergrass? I like the IRA terminology."

"You like that, huh? We can learn a lot about insurgencies from those Fenian boys," Turnbull said.

"We're going to blow up bars now?"

"I was talking old school IRA, not those commie provo punks in the Seventies. Still, we do need to establish a few things with in town."

"Such as?" asked the pastor.

"Establishing the standard that you don't rat out the resistance, that you help, that you report to us what you see and hear. That you do what you have to do to help."

"These people just want to be left alone."

Yeah, well history had another idea about them being left alone. Call it the curse of living in interesting times. Anyway, they aren't spectators anymore. That's a luxury they can't afford."

"Kelly, like I keep saying, I'm not gonna let you turn my town into a battlefield."

"Like I keep saying, I don't intend to start a fight, but I'm not running from one either. We both have jobs to do. And we don't have to get in each other's way."

"I've got somebody who wants to meet you."

"Oh yeah?" said Turnbull, as he finished rodding the barrel.

"Yeah, somebody you probably want to meet."

"Sounds covert. I like it. Intriguing. Who is it?"

"Tell you when we're alone. But you need to make the meeting tomorrow morning."

"I thought I was going to come to church tomorrow."

"You don't strike me as a churchy kinda guy, Kelly."

"Let's just say I respect the holy chain of command. Where is this meet?"

"Out in the woods. I'll give you an azimuth and you can relive the Fort Benning compass course."

"Delightful. Nothing like a little land nav on a Sunday morning. You're on. In the meantime, I think it's a little dangerous to stay at the church. I'll come get my stuff."

"Got somewhere else to stay?"

"Yeah. I got a bag, so I can stay wherever it's relatively flat. If people don't know where I am, there won't be a problem."

"You seem to think through all the angles," Bellman observed.

Turnbull smiled as he polished the action of his AK-47.

"Well, I was taught by the best."

Colonel Jeff Deloitte sighed, pulled up his left camo sleeve, and looked at the cheap Seiko on his wrist. 1348 hours – that meant 48 minutes of priceless time wasted waiting for the Southern Indiana Security Region Fusion Cell meeting to actually get underway.

"There are unacceptable levels of transphobic normative bias within our security apparatus," said Xeno, pounding on the table. Xeno was the civilian security advisor to the governor of Indiana. Xeno used only one name, and leaned slightly toward male identity stereotypes in appearance while tending generic for xis pronouns. Deloitte's S2, the brigade intel officer, had provided a bio of each of the participants for his commander; according to the report, before the Split, Xeno had been named Phil and worked for the IRS.

"I agree, eliminating anti-trans bias *must* remain a key priority in everything we do," responded Chief Roberta Clemens, who commanded the People Security Forces for the region. She was in uniform; a female lieutenant sat uncomfortably at the chief's side. Unlike everyone else at the table, the lieutenant did not have a nameplate listing her name, organization and preferred pronouns in front of her.

The one before Deloitte read:

Colonel Jeff Deloitte

Commander, Military District of Southern Indiana and 172nd Brigade.

Pronouns: "He," "His" and "Him."

Deloitte sullenly looked over the cast of characters sitting around the table. Also in attendance was Franco X, the head of the region's People's Volunteers. He was about 25, and he was decked out in the usual PV coverall uniform, which looked hamper-fresh and had a mustard stain on the belly. Franco X, who the S2 reported had been a petty thief before the Split, was drawing what looked like stick figures with exaggerated genitals on his note paper and barely paying attention.

Only one of them impressed Deloitte – Senior Inspector Darin Kunstler from the People's Bureau of Investigation. He sat quietly, watching, listening – which in Deloitte's eyes made him potentially formidable.

At 1355, Deloitte decided that his patience was fully expended. Xeno had moved on to discussing South Pacific Islanders' Day events and had just inquired how many tanks Deloitte would be sending for the parade in Indianapolis when the colonel spoke up.

"You are wasting my time," he said, and the eyes all went to him.

"I work for Governor Bayh!" Xeno snapped.

"And I work for President Warren. If we aren't going to talk about security, I'm going to go train my soldiers."

"Well, if you don't think racism against South Sea Islanders is an important problem…," began Clemens.

"They prefer 'South *Pacific* Islanders,'" corrected Xeno.

"Sorry," said Chief Clemens, chastened.

"Stop," said Deloitte. "I think the only problem that matters is security in this region, and how you are losing control of it. I assumed that was the purpose of this meeting, which is why I took time away from doing my job to come here to Indianapolis to attend this circle jerk."

"Security is only one piece of the puzzle" Xeno said. "We in the People' Republic are about disrupting paradigms of oppression."

"I didn't have the dubious benefits of going to a college where they taught us about paradigms and made fine distinctions between South Pacific Islanders and South Seas Islanders. Sadly, my West Point education focused on soldiering, as has my career, and I'm at this meeting because if you people don't get your shit together, then I'm going to have to deploy my brigade to practice that skill right here in my own country and I don't want that. *You* don't want that."

"Maybe we should move on to the matter at hand," suggested Kunstler of the PBI, though the way he said it did not make it seem like a suggestion at all.

"The problem is," said Franco X, looking up from his etchings, "that some country motherfuckers drew down on one of my boys in Jasper the other night. My boys deescalated though, but they could have had to regulate. And we need some payback."

"I debriefed your men," Kunstler said evenly. "One man pulled a pistol on eight of them and they ran. They dropped their weapons and ran."

Deloitte laughed, disgusted; Franco X glared.

"You got a problem?" challenged Franco X.

"Yes," said Deloitte. "You and your untrained, undisciplined punks are a joke."

"The People's Volunteers are an important expression of the people's anger against racist fascism!" shouted Xeno.

"Uh huh. We'll just have to agree to disagree then, Xeno. In the meantime, we seem to have a more tangible problem – Jasper. Maybe we can talk about that."

"That's a typical linear military response," Xeno sneered.

"Well, that's the problem with being a military leader, *xir*. I'm forced to deal with tangible reality instead of college campus bullshit."

"Colonel, we all appreciate your input," Kunstler said. "And your point of view. Your region is critical. It supplies a significant amount of the Republic's agricultural output and it contains key transport routes. And we know that the red states want it."

"Inspector, I have a brigade to command. It has to be trained and ready. I have a lot of things to do and a lot of restrictions put on me that keep me from attaining the kind of combat readiness I need to do whatever President Warren might have me do. And sitting in here listening to this nonsense is not helping me get the mission done."

"That's a patriarchal –," Clemens began.

"Sorry that five thousand years of military leadership and experience don't fit into the *paradigm* you learned at Wellesley." Deloitte knew the PSF chief's pre-Split law enforcement experience had consisted of getting tear gassed by D.C. cops while protesting Donald Trump's election back in 2016.

Kunstler sat back and watched Deloitte engage. He knew the colonel's record well, and the Command Diversity Officer reported directly to him regarding the commander's loyalty to the Republic. Deloitte was a holdover from the old United States Army. His family was from Vermont, so when the country split in two he stayed with the blue and in its army. Tactically, his ratings were near the top: Special Forces with a focus on counterinsurgency. But his loyalty ratings were iffy at best – no outright treason, no contacts with the red states, just a refusal to go along and understand that considerations of form often outweighed considerations of substance.

Kunstler assessed him as a skilled professional soldier, which meant he probably did not understand that military competence was far less of a consideration to those in power than reliability. Stalin had gutted the Red Army of its most talented officers even as the Nazi menace loomed, prioritizing loyalty over skill. And Kunstler fully understood and appreciated that cruel logic.

But when push came to shove, what would the colonel choose? That was the question, and the fact that it was a question made him a potential liability. For now, though, he was useful.

"Lieutenant Kessler is here from Jasper. Maybe we should hear from her," Kunstler said. The group's attention fell onto the uncomfortable officer.

"Well, we had a problem with a revanchist family," said the lieutenant. "They had retained firearms, they had flouted other laws. We moved to apprehend them and there was a shootout. We lost three and killed several of them. The main perpetrator is still in the wind, but we will find him. There were rumblings in the town after our operation, so I called for support from the People Volunteers, who patrolled twice. On the second time, they were met by armed resistance."

"Who was this resistance?" asked Kunstler.

The lieutenant shifted uncomfortably. "We think it was outsiders."

"*Outside* of where?" asked Deloitte. "Of Jasper, or the country?"

"We are engaging our sources in the town. If there's someone there, someone new, we will find out who and from where."

"Could it be an infiltrator?" pressed Kunstler.

"That's what I'd send, if I was in the red," said Deloitte. "Send outsiders to organize and mobilize and make Southern Indiana a headache for us."

"We're going to find them and arrest them," promised Lieutenant Kessler.

"Maybe," said Deloitte. "If they screw up you might get lucky and get them. But if they did come from the red, then they're trained and they know how to evade you. I know, because I probably trained them."

"Well, then what do we do?" asked Kunstler.

"Do? If you're smart, you do nothing."

"Nothing?"

"Nothing. You stop pushing. You stop provoking. Let things cool off and calm down. You've already spilled blood. Now the locals are angry."

"A bunch of farmers and bourgeois cis-hets!" said Kessler.

"Who do you think drove out the British? Communications majors? Baristas? Diversity coaches?" said Deloitte. "The goal of insurgents is to mobilize the people against the government. One classic way to do that is to draw down a heavy-handed response from the counter-insurgents and drive the uncommitted to take the rebels' side."

"What *specifically* do you suggest, Colonel?" asked Kunstler.

"First, you keep these bums" – he pointed towards the People's Volunteer commander – "the hell out of town."

"Fuck you, man!" shouted Franco X, rising from his chair.

"Tell me 'fuck you' again, punk, and you're going to have the worst day of your life," Deloitte said evenly. Franco X sat back down.

"Enough," said Kunstler. "Elaborate, Colonel."

"You can only push people so far. You're not leaving them an out. Most people just want to get by, live their lives, and avoid conflict. You want them to be able to do that. But if you get in their faces and you keep pushing, eventually they're going to push back."

"With what?" said Clemens. "We took their weapons."

"Yeah, I have your confiscation numbers. When the weapon seizures went down, you gathered up …," Deloitte consulted his S2's report. "It looks like you collected 12,312 weapons in all of the Military District of Southern Indiana. There are probably city blocks in Indianapolis that have more than 12,312 weapons. You take a shovel, walk out to the woods and plunge it into the dirt, and you're going to hit a buried rifle."

Clemens fumed; Kunstler's face was stone.

"People don't want to rebel," Deloitte continued. "Most people just want to live their own lives being left alone. That's why to start an insurrection in a place like Southern Indiana – before you started pushing – you would need to send cadre in, to train and motivate the indigenous population to fight. But you don't need cadre if you provoke them enough. If you push and push and push, they're eventually going to fight back."

"This is ridiculous," Clement said. "I know how to handle these kinds of racists, these religious nuts. We did it on campus when the fascists tried to speak. You punish them. You crush them. You make them understand that things are different now, that they aren't in control anymore, that they no longer have privilege and that they are accountable to all the people they shit on before the Split."

"Who again were the regular folks in Southern Indiana oppressing ten years ago?" asked Deloitte, disgusted. "I know the area, and I have yet to see much privilege."

"They were Trump voters and before that they were for Romney," Xeno said. "They've always resisted progressive change, and they're never going to change. They have to be *broken*."

"What we need to do is increase our forces in the Jasper area," said Lieutenant Kessler. "I've got an extra twenty PSF officers now and give me maybe twenty more and some detectives from the PBI. Plus some PV support. We will root the infection out."

"You're not hearing me," Deloitte warned. "And you're going to force me to come in and clean up *your* mess with *my* soldiers."

"I think for the time being that this is a civilian matter that we can handle on a civilian basis," Kunstler said. "But let's not make any mistake. The region is vital. Tell them why, Xeno."

Xeno licked xis lips, nervous. "There are border negotiations coming up, and we believe that this area is going to be one of the regions that the red is going to seek to recover. We don't want that. We need its agriculture. We need its road network. We have to make it secure so it looks loyal, so they don't want it. We have to remain in control."

"I'm telling you, I've done this before," said Deloitte. "If you want to keep control, give it up. Leave them alone. They don't want to fight. But they will *if* you force them to."

"My people can handle a few hicks with deer rifles," Lieutenant Kessler said confidently. "Maybe with a little PBI and PV support, but we can stomp this out before it gets out of control."

"With this guy's untrained flunkies, and your thugs with badges? Five half-competent hicks with deer rifles could shut down your entire operation. How many bodies do you have, anyway? How many can Chief Clements here give you? Get you up to maybe 200?

Let's assume 100 of them are going to be logistics, admin, and command and control, and that you've achieved a 50% tooth-to-tail support ratio, which is unheard of in modern warfare. And make no mistake, we're talking *warfare*. So, you got maybe 100 actual bodies to patrol and secure thousands of square miles. They have to retrain, refit, eat, sleep, shit, shower, and shave, so maybe you have 25% on duty at once. That's what? Twenty-five bodies at any given moment? For four or five counties? You can't guard every inch of road. You can't guard every piece of vital infrastructure. You can't guard every target for assassination."

Clement spoke up. "We will find the leaders and arrest them! Cut the head off the snake, destroy their network."

"You don't get it. There's no network. There's no organization. They're going to decentralize. They're going to operate on a cell basis. We're not just seeing it around Jasper. We've seen these problems all through Southern Illinois and Ohio too. You need to understand that you don't have a good kinetic solution to what you're facing."

Franco X was baffled by the word "kinetic." It seemed to puzzle Xeno too; xe scratched xis head before speaking.

"Well, if the PSF can't handle it then we'll call you in to save the day," said Xeno.

"Let's say I give up my mission to deter and defeat red invaders and focus on counter-insurgency. I have two battalions, plus support – about 3,000 troops. You think I can control the Military District of Southern Indiana with a two-maneuver battalion brigade? I can defeat any grouping of rebels should they be dumb enough to let me catch them concentrated in one area, but if this thing blows up – if you light a fuse that makes this thing blow up – there's not much I can do to stop it. And if you tell me to do it anyway, you'll need to authorize me to do things that even you don't want me to do."

"If we have to scorch the earth, Colonel, we will scorch the earth," said Xeno. "We are not giving up Southern Indiana. And it doesn't matter how many racist knuckle draggers have to die to keep it that way."

"Those are your own citizens," Deloitte said bitterly.

"I agree with Xeno, Colonel, I respect your views, but the time for firmness is here," Kunstler said. "We cannot allow this to continue. We need to stop it before it gets out of control. I'm authorizing the additional People Security Force officers and the PBI detectives to support Lieutenant Kessler's program. Lieutenant, you are going to have access to the People Volunteers as you need them. Do what you have to do. And Colonel, if we are forced to call you in, I am confident that you will do your duty."

"I know what my duty is. You don't need to tell me. I've been doing it for 30 years."

"But now you are doing it for a new country, a better country," Kunstler said.

"Well, then I should go," Deloitte said, standing. "Looks like I need to do some more training for my brigade. Oh wait, I can't do any training for three days because I have a mandatory shutdown because one of my guys wolf whistled at some E-4 and I now have to do three days of sexual harassment training instead of combat training."

"Colonel, I sometimes wonder about your priorities," Xeno snapped.

"My priority is accomplishing my mission," Deloitte said as he headed toward the door. "I'm still wondering about yours."

7.

Deputy Ted Cannon was rebelling – if he was going to get called into the station at 7:00 AM on a Sunday morning, he was damn well wearing his tan uniform.

He drove down Main Street as he always did, heading out from his house where he used to live with his wife before she took off, and slowed as he saw something up ahead. There were two PSF cruisers, front to front, blocking most of the road at 5th. A checkpoint – four PSF officers stood about, one of them gesturing to a guy in a pick-up truck they had stopped. The officers stepped back and looked into the bed, then peered inside the cab, and finally waved him through after he showed his ID.

In the People's Republic, they were big on ID. Apparently somewhere along the way, identification had stopped being racist because they were always asking for it.

Cannon rolled up in his cruiser slowly, intending to pass, but the lead officer held up his palm. Cannon stopped and rolled down his window. The PSF officer was one of the new ones that Cannon had seen around the station. He stepped forward, looking Cannon over.

"Where's your black uniform," he asked.

"In the hamper."

"You're supposed to wear the new uniform."

"Am I working for you now?" Cannon snapped. The officer frowned.

"Where is your ID?"

"In my ass," Cannon answered. "What the hell is this roadblock for?"

"This is a checkpoint," said the PSF officer.

"No shit," said Cannon. "Why do you have a checkpoint here in the middle of town on a Sunday morning?"

"Because we're tired of your hick friends' bullshit."

"Get out of my way," Cannon said. The PSF officer seemed to think about it for a moment, then thought better of it and stepped aside. Cannon drove through and down the street to the station.

He parked outside in the lot, having managed to snag one of the now-scarce empty spaces. With the station packed with newcomers, he often had to park down the street.

There seemed to be an unusual level of activity for a Sunday – officers were walking about, some in tactical gear. They all stared at him and his old school uniform. Cannon went inside.

Kessler saw him and scowled upon seeing the deputy's uniform. It was the only tan one in the station. Everyone else was now in black. And there were long weapons and other gear lying about – what had been a friendly local sheriff's station now looked paramilitary, and distinctly unwelcoming.

Cannon approached Lieutenant Kessler, who was consulting with several sergeants.

"Is there an operation going on?"

"Why do you want to know?"

"Because this is my town."

"You're not involved. Stay out of the way."

"Where's the Sheriff?"

"Relieved. This is my station now." She turned to one of the sergeants. "You make sure that *Officer* Cannon stays off his cell phone and doesn't leave until the operation's over."

"What are you talking about?" Cannon asked.

"Oh, you'll see soon enough. We are reasserting control," Kessler said, walking away.

"Where'd you sleep?" asked Pastor Bellman, leaning against the railing of the stairs up to the church. The doors behind him were wide open. It was still an hour before the 9:30 service and it was still cool.

Turnbull smiled. "I got myself a room. Okay, it's a garage."

"Did you already get your stuff out of my handyman's room?" the pastor asked. "There was a towel and some paperback book. Looked like porn."

"I wish it was porn. Yeah, I got them. So who am I meeting this morning?"

"Somebody right up your alley, I think. Just don't make any sudden moves."

"Oh yeah? Sounds edgy. Should I have brought my AK?"

"Not sure that would help you a whole lot if you got on his wrong side. He's that way." Bellman pointed to a tree line a few hundred meters north of the church across an overgrown field.

"Go inside the tree line about 100 meters north and there's a creek. Head west. Keep going about a mile. And then you'll find the mystery man." Pastor Bellman smiled. "More likely he'll find you first."

"He knows I'm coming, right?"

"Oh yeah. He's not the kind of guy you want to surprise. Better get going. People are starting to show up." Turnbull noted a Chevrolet pulling into the parking lot with a family.

"How many do you get on your average Sunday, Pastor?"

"A lot more than I used to. Half the churches around here are closed down now. People had either left or they've been foreclosed on since they cancelled the religious property tax exemption. I guess we're just stubborn."

"You know it's only going to get worse for you guys?"

"I know. But a little oppression hones the faith."

"I guess so. Just don't let yourself get too honed. I'll see you after the service, if your mystery man lets me live."

Bellman smiled and went inside the sanctuary, Turnbull turned and began his long walk across the grass towards the woods. The heat, the stickiness, the bugs his feet kicked up in the unruly grass – it was like walking through the savannah.

People just sort of assumed that America was always a civilized continent, that there was nothing wild about it, but they couldn't have been more wrong. There was something primeval, something untamed here, almost jungle-like, when you stepped out of civilization's realm. It was masked by all the tens of thousands of square miles of pavement and buildings. But it was out there, at the fringes. Something wild.

Turnbull got to the tree line. Inside it was dark, and as soon as he stepped inside rays of sunlight streamed down through the canopy of leaves. It smelled rich and earthy, a different world.

His booted feet crunched as he stepped clumsily on the detritus littering the forest floor. That cued him to shift into stealth mode. He slowed up, watching the ground in front of him, carefully calculating where he placed his feet on each step. Now he was back at Fort Benning, at Dahlonega, at Hulbert, walking through the woods on patrol. Fifty meters inside the tree line he stopped and took a knee and waited, getting used to it, hearing the noises of the forest, and just as importantly, hearing the silences.

After about ten minutes he felt comfortable and at home, so he arose and began walking, each step calculated, each step careful. After a couple minutes, he came to the creek. It was slow moving and quiet, maybe a meter or two across, most of it less than a foot deep, but there were some pools where he could not make out the bottom. A dark green frog leapt off the bank and into the water with a *plunk*. Turnbull froze and listened. Nothing.

He kept going, holding to the south bank, backed off a couple meters from the water, moving quietly, looking down at each step, and then around him. Every few minutes he would stop again to listen, usually pausing behind a bush or a tree trunk. He was back on patrol, albeit without his battle gear, without a rifle. He felt the weight of the .45 in the small of his back under his long shirt.

Turnbull counted his steps, as he had been trained to do, knowing his stride was exactly 33 inches in the open, but adjusting for the smaller steps he was taking in that confined space. It was slow going, moving around trees, avoiding roots, and stepping over logs after peering down on the other side to make sure he didn't step on a copperhead.

No copperheads. That was a relief. But he kicked up a garter snake, which slid off of the bank and into the water and swam away like a big green "S" with a yellow stripe running down its back.

Turnbull figured he was a half mile in, then about a mile. Now far out of town, the sounds of the cars rumbling along the roads had faded. He was in the deep woods. He was in his element.

Did he smell smoke?

Turnbull dropped and listened again. Nothing, but there was something more going on. He *felt* it somehow. He was getting close.

"Y'all just hold up now," he heard a male voice say, and Turnbull dropped and rolled, taking cover behind a log, his weapon now ready.

"The pastor says you're an okay guy, and I want to believe him, being a man of God and all, but if you're gonna start pointing guns at me, you and I are going to have a problem, mister," said the voice. It was coming from up ahead, but Turnbull couldn't place it. The guy was well-concealed.

"How do I know you're not pointing a gun at me?" asked Turnbull.

"Well, I am, but then this *is* my house, and I figure I got a right to point a gun at anybody who comes in to my house, if you know what I mean."

"Maybe so," Turnbull said. Damn, where was this guy? "So how about neither of us point any guns at each other and we can take it from there?"

"Okay sir. That sounds fair to me. Why don't ya stand up, let me take a look at you?"

"How about we both stand up and take a look at each other?"

"That seems fair to me too." There was a rustle about seven or eight meters to his front. A shape was rising out of the brush. Turnbull stood up too, slowly, careful not to do anything that could possibly be interpreted as hostile.

The man in front of Turnbull was skinny, wiry and weathered with a scraggly beard. He didn't seem afraid. Instead, he seemed rather confident, totally at home, and he had a big .357 silver Colt Python revolver slipped into the belt at the front of his jeans. He wore a black T-shirt, a little bit tattered, with an eagle rampant over an American flag. Not exactly consistent with the PR's evolving fashion sensibilities.

"My name is Kelly," Turnbull said.

"I'm Larry Langer. Pleased to meet you."

"Langer," said Turnbull. "You're the one that got away."

"Yes, sir. I got away. But I ain't *going* away, if you get my meaning. I'm just biding my time. I got accounts to settle, if you know what I mean."

"I think I do. And I can't say I blame you."

"Pastor said I needed to meet you. Said you and I might share some common interests."

"We might. But I'm not exactly interested in settling any scores."

"Pastor said that too. Well, we still might have some common ground. But I'm not done with the sons of bitches who murdered my family quite yet."

"You've been living out here?"

"Sure have. It's my second home. Been running around these woods since I was four years old. Hunting, fishing. Got a little tent and a cook stove over there. Dug a nice privy too, back from the creek of course."

"Of course."

"I'm pretty comfortable. Like to have a big fire, but if they see smoke then they'd get all excited and send somebody else to give me a citation for climate violations. And if they did that I'd have to shoot the son of a bitch, and that'd attract even more attention. When the shooting starts, I intend to be the one starting it, and when I'm good and ready."

"Seems to me you want to get your own private war going on," Turnbull said.

"Guess I do. Are you here to start your own?"

"Just here to be difficult. I don't intend to do any killing unless I have to. Though these PR bastards seem intent on pushing things that way."

"I gotta say, I liked being part of the United States. This Split's been nothing but trouble. You think you're gonna be able to deal with these people without killing a few of them?"

"I'm not optimistic," Turnbull said. "I have experience with these bastards too."

"All we ever asked for was just to be left alone," said Langer. "We just want to keep doing what we've always been doing. Never hurt anybody. Never stole anybody's stuff, never got sideways with anyone who didn't get sideways with us. But they just couldn't leave it be."

"They can't, because if they see you doing what *you* want to do, then other people are going to want to do what *they* want to do, and then pretty soon our People's Republic friends are not going to have anyone to boss around anymore."

"Yep," Langer said, walking slowly forward. "So where do you come from anyway? Down in the red?"

"I came from where I came from. It's not important."

"Oh yeah, OPSEC. You know, I was a Marine. And a good one. I did one tour and made Lance Corporal three times." Langer smiled. His teeth could have used some work. "Fought in Falluja. Never occurred to me I might have to fight here at home."

"Maybe it won't have to come to that. I just think maybe that, since you know the area and the people and have some training, maybe you can help me make things a little more difficult for these folks."

"Maybe I can. But that's not saying that I'm not going to expect some payback at some point. They killed my family, and that's got to be answered."

"I hear you. And I –"

Shots, in the distance, to the east. A lot of them.

Both men froze,

A burst, then more shots. *Bam Bam Bam Bam Bam Bam Bam Bam Bam.*

"AKs," said Langer. "You don't forget what they sound like."

"PSF or PVs," Turnbull said.

"It's back in town," Langer said.

"Back from where I came," said Turnbull.

"The church," Langer said.

"You coming, Larry?"

"I'm with you."

"Let's go."

They began running through the forest back the way Turnbull had come. There was no deliberation now – they were moving full speed.

Pastor Bellman looked out over his congregation and observed that nearly every space in the pews was filled. Before the Split, he'd have been overjoyed. But the fact was that First Baptist had inherited a lot of families from the other churches in and around town that closed since the Split. Pretty soon he was going to have to add another service at 11 a.m. to handle the attendance – people just wouldn't all fit in the 9:30 service. And it seemed to him that people are paying more close attention to his sermons. In times like these, people looked for the comfort of God.

He called out the next hymn, "Amazing Grace," one of his favorites. Some of the other churches had done a lot of Christian lite rock in their services. They would get a couple guys with a six-string and a bass and a drummer and sing some up-tempo songs no one had heard before and a lot of people liked that. Not Bellman. He was about the basics. "Amazing Grace" was the gold standard that Christian music was going to be measured against, and that was what they would sing in his church.

They finished the hymn and he gestured for the congregation to sit. The congregation did, and people put their hymnals back into the racks and settled in for the sermon. Bellman never wrote his sermons out. He kind of got an idea about what he wanted to say and then simply said it. He figured it was best if your sermon came from the heart. Anyway, his old audience of grizzled infantrymen wasn't going to take some overly prepared performance seriously. You had to look those guys in the eyes and really talk to them, and that's how he tried to do it in his preaching.

Bellman stepped to the pulpit and opened his mouth but then paused and said nothing. There was the screech of tires and the roar of engines outside. A lot of them. Something was happening.

The congregation heard it too, and they looked around confused. One man at the back stood up and went to the closed door and pushed it open a crack. It flew wide open and the People's Volunteers were there, a dozen of them, smiling slyly, strutting as they walked inside, AKs up.

The foot soldiers pointed their rifles at the congregation, which sat staring and silent, as their leader swaggered down the center aisle. He had gotten his mojo back since his encounter with Turnbull. Bellman's face registered nothing but contempt.

"If you're not here to hear my sermon, you need to leave," said the pastor.

The leader laughed. He was back in the role he loved, the only guy in the room with a gun, the one in charge.

"Fuck you, preacher. You make me leave."

"You use that language in the Lord's house again and I will."

"Oh, your old ass is going to do something about it?"

"If you're asking if I will walk down there and throw your ass out of my church, the answer is 'Yes'."

"Well, come on, old man." The others laughed. One of the PVs stepped to an old woman in the aisle and grabbed her purse. She shrieked, and a man in the row behind her stood to defend her. Another People's Volunteer hit him across the gut with the butt of his rifle. The other PVs burst into laughter as the man crumpled.

"Get the hell out of here!" Bellman roared.

"Where's your friend?" asked the leader. "We're here for him. And to collect some donations."

"Go to hell," said Bellmen.

"For a preacher, you got a mouth on you," said the leader. He turned to his men. "Find him."

The PVs commenced looking down the rows, scrutinizing the parishioners and grabbing purses. Three of them broke off to head to the back and they went through the door into the administrative areas, weapons up.

Do-Rag was greatly enjoying the party. "Get your wallets out, bitches! I'm taking a collection!"

The leader turned back to Bellman, who was gripping the sides of his pulpit so hard it seemed he might break them off. "You think you can just have your little church like you used to? You think you can just do whatever you want? You think you can disrespect us? No, you can't do shit. You think this is your town, but it's our town."

A woman with her cell phone caught his eye – she was dialing 911, and the leader just laughed. "Go ahead and call the PSF. Call them! Hell, walk outside and talk to them because they're here with us. Nobody is coming to rescue you. You belong to us. You're ours now. You're going to do what I say you're going to when I say you're going to do it, and you're going to give us what we want, and you're going to shut the fuck up about it."

Do-Rag was a couple feet behind his boss, smiling broadly, when he saw Will Collins move his hand behind his back. Where Do-Rag came from, that's where you kept your gun, and he reacted instinctively. Do-Rag swiveled and leveled the AK, firing a burst that caught Will Collins in the chest and sliced into his wife Sarah, blowing out her eye.

The other PVs reacted instinctively, opening up, panic spraying rounds into the seated crowd. The leader was stunned for a moment, and then he began yelling.

"Stop shooting, stop shooting!"

Bellman was on him grabbing his arm, going for his rifle. The leader kicked Bellman in the gut, pushing him back, and without thinking he raised his rifle and fired. Five bullets ripped through the minister's abdomen, and Bellman sprawled back into the aisle.

"Stop shooting, stop shooting!" the leader yelled. The PSF officers who had been outside securing the area were at the door now, weapons in hand, looking in, horrified.

The shooting stopped.

Smoke wafted across the sanctuary. It was silent for a moment, and then there arose a chorus of moans and screams and yells. The three PVs who had gone off to investigate the administrative rooms burst back in, looking panicked at the chaos.

"Let's go!" shouted the leader. "Let's go!"

He stepped forward and found his Nike submerged in an expanding pool of blood from an elderly woman his men had shot in the face.

The People's Volunteers ran out the door and to their cars, wasting no time clearing out of the area.

Turnbull and Langer burst out of the wood line in a full run heading across the grass towards the church. The stained glass window facing them had been largely shot out – it did not take a genius to know what had happened well before they arrived at the sanctuary door.

Bodies, some alive, some clearly not, were strewn across the floor and the pews. Some people were focused on first aid; others shook and cried, useless. Others carried the wounded out to their own vehicles.

Dale Chalmers was there, dazed. Turnbull came over to him and he looked up, his jaw still bandaged, as he leaned over the corpse of the pastor. None of his family had been hit, but the brains of the school teacher sitting in front of him were splattered across his white shirt. Turnbull knelt beside him as Langer went to help other casualties. He checked for a pulse on Bellman, but knew there would not be one.

"Who?" Turnbull said, knowing the answer.

Chalmers blinked dazed.

"*Who?*"

"The Volunteers again. They're gone now. And the PSF were here too. They didn't do anything to stop it. They just started shooting for no reason."

"Call 911. Do it now."

"We did, a bunch of times. They, they won't come. Not the PSF, not the paramedics. The dispatchers just hang up on us."

Langer was putting pressure on a teenager with a sucking chest wound; his eyes were black with rage. But Turnbull allowed himself to feel nothing. He was in operational mode.

"Who has medical training, military combat lifesaver training, nurse school, anything?" he shouted.

A hand went up, a middle aged man who was helping a boy shot through the right arm. "I was an EMT."

Turnbull pointed to the open area behind the pews. "That's the casualty collection point. You take it over. You're the doc until a real one shows up or we get them all out of here. The rest of you, if you have an SUV or a station wagon, back it up here. You're our ambulances. Everyone else, if you have a wounded family member, you stay with them. Everyone else, our EMT is going to tell you what to do. If you have a sweater or something you can use to apply pressure to a wound, take it off and put it where the EMT says."

People began gently moving the wounded to the casualty collection point as others ran to get their vehicles. Turnbull began his own triage, walking from casualty to casualty, coldly assessing which was likely to live and which was likely to die – or was already dead. He counted 12 dead, including Pastor Bellman. He organized the evacuations, selecting the most seriously wounded who would have the best shot at the hospital to go first.

Ten minutes after the first SUV left with a serious abdominal wound, Dale's cell rang.

"What do you mean the ER won't take the wounded?" Dale shouted into his iPhone. Turnbull turned to the EMT.

"You keep evacuating these wounded. I'm going to the hospital," Turnbull said to the ex-EMT. He motioned to Langer and Dale; they headed out to the parking lot at a sprint toward the insurance salesman's Dodge.

What had been Memorial Hospital and was now Chuck Schumer People's Health Center, was a modern-looking building on West 9th Street. A crowd of SUVs was bunched up by the emergency room entrance. Dale parked and Turnbull and Langer were out the door.

The wounded were still in the backs of their vehicles.

The pair rushed up to the glass doors, which were shut tight. Several parishioners were pounding on them, but a severe-looking nurse was standing inside, just shaking her head.

"Everyone, get back," Turnbull said. The crowd retreated a few feet and Turnbull rotated to face the nurse through the glass. He motioned her forward with his index finger.

She stepped up tentatively, shaking her head and shouting "We're closed."

Turnbull smiled, reached behind him, drew his .45 pistol and shouted "You're now open."

She stood, terrified.

"I'm counting to three, and then I'm shooting out this door. One!"

She shook, but did not move.

"Two!"

Nothing.

"Screw it," Turnbull said. He fired six shots down the pane of glass, then kicked it hard. It shattered and fell inward. The nurse screamed and cowered. Langer slipped in and hit the OPEN button and the doors slid apart.

"Get stretchers and get them inside. Dale, put someone on security. If the blues show up I want to know." Turnbull stepped up to the nurse.

"Where's your boss?" She pointed. "No, *take* me." Turnbull and Langer followed, Turnbull holding his guide by the rear of her uniform collar.

She led him to a tall, thin man in a white coat. His badge said "People's Doctor Dr. Gorman." He was probably doing an involuntary hardship assignment down here in Jasper – after all health care providers had been nationalized post-Split, the government simply ordered them to work wherever it needed them at its pleasure.

"Hi," Turnbull said. "We have multiple gunshot wounds. You better call everyone in, and you better do it right now."

"We are not authorized for this level of treatment. We're officially closed. You need to take them and go to Indianapolis."

"Oh," said Turnbull, releasing the nurse. "Larry?"

Langer drew his .357, grabbed the doctor and pressed him against the wall. Then he stuck the massive pistol under the doctor's chin.

"You open now, doc?"

"Okay, okay."

"And unless you want a firefight in your ER, you should probably not follow through on that idea you had about calling the PSF," said Turnbull. Behind him, people were starting to wheel in the wounded. "Larry, can you hand me the doctor's wallet."

Without removing the pistol, Langer reached into the terrified man's pocket and withdrew a black leather billfold then passed it to Turnbull.

"That's my ID – I need it!"

"You sure do," said Turnbull, selecting his driver's license. "Okay, Dr. Ronald Vernon Gorman of 1324 Heathcliff Street in Indianapolis, let me tell you how it's going to be. Now we know where you live. So, if you don't do a really good job on these wounded people, one of us will come visit you, and you are not going to like how that turns out. If you're lucky it'll be me because all I'll do is shoot you in the head. You do not want it to be *him*."

"No sir, you do not," reiterated Langer, shaking his head.

"Now go do your job," Turnbull said. Langer released the doctor, who fled down the hall toward his patients.

They stood outside the hospital, Larry taking a drag off of a smoke he had bummed from an orderly – in fact, the terrified orderly had generously given over his whole pack. Dale was still shaken. Turnbull causally slid a fresh mag into his pistol and put it back in its holster. He slipped the mag with three rounds into his pocket.

"Well, we got us a war now," Larry said.

"Yeah," Turnbull replied. "We need to get ready. Dale, you're a pretty useful guy."

"I want to fight," Dale said, his words still muffled.

"I don't think fighting is your strong suit. I think you can do more for me on the intel side than on the shooting side. I can get plenty of trigger pullers. You know almost everyone around here. I need you to start gathering information on the enemy. The PSF especially, since they stay here. Where they are, what they are doing, their chain of command."

"I can do that," Dale said. "So what's your plan?"

"Plan?" said Turnbull. "My plan is to kill them all."

8.

Larry Langer walked out of the woods and into town at 10:38 Monday morning, careful to avoid the enhanced patrols that went up to try and keep a lid on the town in the wake of the First Baptist massacre. There was an obvious increase in the number of PSF on the street, but Langer kept to the residential streets and approached downtown from the north. A fair distance away, the checkpoint in the middle of town was still operating, but there just weren't enough officers to completely cover even a small burg like Jasper – much less the other villages and townships within their zone.

Everyone knew what happened the previous morning, even though the licensed news outlets made no mention of it. Moreover, Jasper was small enough that everyone knew at least one or more of the dead or wounded. Only a few people were outside on the sidewalks – those who worked were working and most others simply felt it was better to stay indoors that day. But some of the ones who still had permits for animal companions were walking their dogs, while others felt simply being outside was their own act of moral resistance.

They all recognized Larry Langer. He wore a loose shirt over his familiar tee, and wore a tattered backpack, but it was Larry all right. Some people went to school with him, others knew him as a town fixture – usually the subject of a parent's warning to behave lest "you end up like one of those Langers!"

They knew he was wanted by the PR, so they knew his presence out in the open meant something was up. Most simply looked away. Some nodded at him, with approval, while others stared. If they looked too long, he stared back. They got the message.

No one reached for his phone to call the PSF.

The city's administrative annex had been taken over by various People's Republic agencies, which had largely displaced most of the old city government. The mayor still had his office, but the city council wasn't necessary, they had been told. Now that freedom and social justice had descended upon America, there was no need for local control. The bureaucracy would take good care of them.

Langer hung back across the street and checked his watch. It was 10:43. The annex itself, was a storefront located in a plain, one-story brick building with the latest version of the PR flag flying outside. Next door was a closed Subway sandwich restaurant and a shuttered vacuum cleaner repair shop.

The agencies it housed were listed on a sign out front – the Fairness Commission, the Inclusiveness Bureau, and the Truth Agency. There was no security, no PSF in sight in front or anywhere along the street in either direction.

Langer checked his watch. 10:44:13 a.m. It was all good. It was going to go down in about 45 seconds. He walked gingerly across the street, leaned back against the brick and lit a cigarette. It was a Marlboro, a real one, from a pack his cousin the trucker had brought back from Kentucky and that Langer had been saving. Then he listened.

The clock hit 10:45 a.m. and from the southeast he heard a "pop." Then, cig clenched between his teeth, he drew the .357, pushed open the glass doors and walked inside.

There were several agencies sharing the open space. The Truth Agency was to his immediate right. A sad woman with mousy hair was marking up the *Dubois County Herald* with a red pen for her meeting with the editors later that day. She had been particularly irritated by the paper's total invisibling of trans citizens' experiences in the front page corn harvest story.

A young male in a vintage dress coat and sporting a goatee was in the Fairness Commission section, staring at some approved pornography. He would never admit it, but he liked smuggled-in, unapproved red state porn DVDs much better – too bad you couldn't get that stuff on the blue internet. The approved porn always took ten minutes to get started while the participants obtained express consent and discussed how what they chose to do sexually should not be construed as validating traditional patriarchal sexual power structures. And you could not fast forward through any of that to get to the good stuff.

Darcy Puig, the county Inclusiveness Inspector, was seated nearby. Her name plate gave her name, her job, and alerted all that her pronouns were "her" and "she." A poster on the wall behind her featured a cartoon crew of multi-cultural children dancing on some prostrate Scandinavian-looking guy with a moustache and, for some reason, a top hat. It declared that "All Peoples Reject White Cis-Het Male Privilege."

Puig looked up at the strange man, wondering what he was doing there, since no one ever came inside willingly. Most of the other workers simply ignored him; they were not being paid on the basis of customer satisfaction, and they acted accordingly.

Langer aimed his big revolver and shot out the monitor on Puig's desk, which exploded in a shower of sparks.

That got their attention.

The dozen bureaucrats in the office froze at their desks, staring.

"Don't do nothin'," Langer instructed them. The workers were mostly young, having been hired at their colleges to come and run Jasper since the townspeople were obviously incompetent to do so themselves. Over 40% of blue college grads found jobs in the PR bureaucracy.

The porn boy slowly reached for his Android 29 phone, and the barrel of Langer's .357 found him with his hand hovering in mid-air.

"Y'all think that's a good idea?" asked Langer. Porn Boy withdrew his paw and placed it back on his lap.

"Okay, everyone on your feet. All of you. Stand up." They did. Langer motioned them to the corner to the right of the door around the Truth Agency desk.

"I'm gonna tell you all this once, and one time only," Langer said. "If I see any of you around here again, I'll shoot you. You understand?"

The dozen PR bureaucrats stared in horror, silent.

"We're not playing and negotiating," Langer said. "You ain't welcome here anymore, and I'm giving you fair warning so you can leave and go back wherever the hell you came from. If you come here again and mess with our people, I'm going to put a bullet in you. You all feel me?"

Nothing. So Langer shot Porn Boy in the kneecap.

Porn Boy screamed, falling to the ground, clutching the ruined joint in his hands as blood poured through his fingers. Their ears rang; cordite wafted through the room.

Some shuddered, some cried, some begged.

"Please, don't hurt us!" the Truth Agency woman whimpered, confused and terrified.

Langer stood calmly, his weapon trained on them, cigarette hanging from the corner of his mouth. "Take a good look at him," he said. "Your job ain't worth limping for the rest of your life."

The wounded man rolled, and moaned.

"You all might want to help your friend. Go on! Wrap something around it so he don't bleed out. Now you –" Langer pointed at Puig. "You, come here and take this pack. Come on, I won't hurt you."

Puig stepped forward, shaking, streams of tears running down her face.

"Take it," Langer said, handing her his back pack. She took it, reluctantly. "Open it up."

She unzipped it.

"Quick, take out that jug."

She removed a gallon milk jug full of pale yellow liquid – the reek of gasoline was already escaping from under the twist cap.

"You just open that top up and spread that gas around the office. Don't forget the computers. Get everything nice and wet down," Langer instructed.

She did as Langer instructed while he covered the others. He took a puff on his dying cig.

"Get the file cabinets – open them up and splash a little on there. You don't need a lot. Get those computers. Come on. Hurry up, now!"

He could see what they were thinking – someone had to have heard the gunshots, so where was the PSF?

Langer smiled. The PSF wasn't coming anytime soon.

It took her two minutes to empty the jug, and after she splashed the last out on Porn boy's computer Puig looked up and stared. The place reeked of petrol fumes. The wounded bureaucrat was still crying on the floor.

"Pick up your friend and y'all get out of here. Like I said, this is your one free pass. If I see you again, you're going home hoppin' on one foot. Now get going!"

The ones who could run ran out the door; two others helped their injured co-worker out onto the sidewalk. Langer walked to the door, turned, and took his fading cigarette out of his mouth and tossed it onto the Truth Agency womyn's gasoline-soaked desk. It bounced across the surface, kicking up some sparks, and then the whole desk erupted in a fireball.

Langer jumped out the door and the fire roared through the office. Outside on the sidewalk, he could hear sirens wailing, but he knew they were not coming for him. He slid the pistol into his belt, covered it with the flap of his shirt, and strolled away as if nothing happened.

"You sure you can make a 500 meter shot?" Turnbull asked Davey Wohl. Turnbull was watching the mid-town PSF checkpoint at Main and 5th through a pair of Bushnell binoculars he had borrowed. Wohl was lying next to him with the Winchester 700 rifle the man had dug up from his cache out in the woods the previous evening. The shooter was peering downrange through a Nikon Buckmaster II 4-12x40 scope – deadly to deer, but not so pricey that it was deadly to him when his wife saw it on his credit card statement a dozen years before.

"Oh easy," Wohl said. "I was the designated marksman in my unit back in Desert Storm. Shot an Iraqi major in the temple at 400 meters outside of Kuwait City. He was just sitting there on the edge of his hatch on top of his BTR. Dumbass."

There were four PSF officers around their patrol cars at the roadblock in the middle of the intersection. One was talking to the driver of a silver Toyota Corolla they had stopped. The other three were lounging around, barely engaged, their AKs either leaning on their vehicles or strapped across their backs. They were clearly expecting another fulfilling day of hassling locals.

Turnbull and Rogers had selected their shooting position on a small rise in a wood line that offered a view a straight up the street to the north. They would be hard to see from the roadblock, and far enough away that it would be hard for the officers to effectively engage with their AKs. Naturally, there were good routes for withdrawal.

Turnbull checked his watch. Just fifteen seconds till 10:45.

"You got a round in the chamber?" asked Turnbull.

"Of course I do!"

"Can't hurt to ask. Try not to take this guy in the head. Better to keep him alive. It'll be noisier."

"Okay," said Wohl, taking aim.

Turnbull stared as the second hand ticked off the time. "Four, three, two, one. Take him."

The rifle kicked immediately, and loudly even though Turnbull had his earplugs in.

Through the Bushnells, Turnbull watched one of the PSF guys near his cruiser suddenly slammed against the rear quarter panel as if someone had just pounded his thigh with a sledgehammer. He fell to the ground, rolling, spurts of red visible even from that distance."

"Nice shot." They could hear faint cries from that direction. The other PSF took a moment to figure out what was happening and they were now scurrying like ants hit by a splash of Raid.

"Next shot. Take out a window." No sense in trying to hit one of the scattering PSF officers – anyway, they needed to be alive to call in for help.

"Roger," whispered Rogers, letting out his breath then squeezing the trigger. The big deer rifle kicked up again.

Downrange, the rear window of one of the cruisers exploded. The other three officers had taken cover; one of them had the limited presence of mind to fire a series of bursts from his weapon in the general direction of the noise. The guy in the Corolla opened his door and ran away; he forgot to put it in "Park" and it started rolling forward. One of the other PSF decided to shoot it full of holes for some reason as it drifted toward the curb.

"Not a bad shot for a Walmart guy," Turnbull said.

"It's like riding a bicycle," said Wohl. "Except louder."

Through the binoculars, Turnbull could see a second officer was not shooting while a third one had gotten inside a cruiser and was shouting into his radio.

"He's making the call. Shoot out another window."

Wohl said nothing. Aim, breathe, squeeze.

Another cruiser's window blew out. The return fire, which was aimed nowhere near their position, ceased as they ran dry and reloaded.

"I think we've got a sufficient distraction. Let's move out." Turnbull paused to pick up the three empty .30-06 shells Wohl had ejected. No need to provide the PBI with any evidence.

The pair moved off to the rear, heading quickly back into the woods and away.

Inside the station it was chaos since the call from the checkpoint came in. Since the previous morning, they had been expecting something, but no one was exactly sure what. Now it was here.

"This is Unit 15! We're under fire, we're under fire! Over!"

Ted Cannon watched the squad room freeze, then burst into activity. Everyone was rolling, but not him. He had been restricted to the station, assigned to assist in integrating the 20 new PSF officers and several PBI detectives down from Indianapolis early after the bloodbath at First Baptist the day before.

When the report of the PV shootings came in, he had to be physically restrained from leaving the station. Even Kessler was stunned – she hadn't anticipated that her instruction to intimidate the townies would be interpreted as orders to commit mass murder. They were just supposed to find that big guy, and break a few heads – help the locals get their minds right, as it were. They were supposed to send a message, but not *that* message.

Still, perhaps the inadvertent message would prove useful. Kessler had recovered her composure quickly once her higher PSF headquarters essentially shrugged when she broke the news. Now she was ordering the PVs out of town and doubling patrols on the street, just in case there was a reaction.

"We did not want to have this happen," she told her officers. "But the racists and Christianist extremists brought this on themselves. Understand that we will defend the integrity of the People's Republic, and we will not allow the forces of reaction to delay or derail our journey to true freedom!" Some of the PSF officers clapped.

"Only twelve?" sneered one male-identifying officer a little too loudly. Cannon lunged at him and had to be held back by several others.

Kessler stepped between them. "Deputy Cannon – *Officer* Cannon – you will control yourself. Your connections to this community are useful to us, but remember that your duty is to *all* the people of the People's Republic, not just the ones here. You can help these people most by helping them accept what has changed, and commit to the new reality. Now get back to work."

It was about six that Sunday evening when Cannon was finally able to leave the station. He headed out and drove directly to his sister's house. There were only a few people on the streets – Kessler's curfew began at 7:00 p.m.

The first place he went was the Chalmers' house to see his sister. Liz and the kids were fine. She gave her brother a beer, then started crying. Dale came in a few minutes later while Ted was still hugging her; his church clothes were caked with dried blood.

He ignored them, went to the kitchen, and brought back a Budweiser. It was in a rainbow can, and it tasted like Old Milwaukee backwash. The PR had nationalized all the breweries after the Split; too many brands was "inefficient."

"You okay?" Ted asked, letting Liz go. Upstairs, Jimmy started crying – he'd been crying a lot after what he saw that morning – and she left the living room to go to him.

"Do I *look* okay?"

"It wasn't supposed to happen, Dale."

"Twelve people. Twelve of our friends. Will Collins, Patty Enright. Some of this is Pastor Bellman's blood, Ted. And your people just let it happen."

"They didn't mean to let anything happen," Ted replied, miserable. "That wasn't planned. They just came looking for the guy who drove off the PVs. It wasn't supposed to turn into a massacre."

"You think giving a bunch of gangbangers guns and sending them out to threaten us, to come into our church, is going to end well? You think they care that this happened? They don't. They think it's going to scare us into giving up. A bunch of dead hicks isn't a bug. It's a feature."

The deputy said nothing. What could he say?

"You need to choose a side, Ted."

"What do you mean choose a side?"

"I mean choose a side for what's coming. Because this can't go on."

"I'm not choosing some side, Dale. I'm just choosing to try and keep some order, keep people safe."

"How's that working out?"

"What the hell do you want me to do? It's me, maybe two other locals left and a few support people and that's it from Jasper. Everybody else is from outside. They're sending in another couple dozen people and some detectives too. I can't do anything."

"You can't?" said Dale leaning back on his couch and taking a swig. "You're inside."

"What the hell are you talking about?" Ted said. "Do you want me to quit? Walk away, go south like all the others and leave you with nobody from here in that station?"

"No Ted, I want you to stay. I want you to do your job. I want you to be the very best PSF officer Jasper's ever seen."

"I don't understand," Ted replied, but he really did – he just did not want to go there.

"I want you in there, telling us what's happening. From the inside."

"What do you mean 'us'?"

"I mean *us*. Our people. This is war now. They started it, and we have no choice. None at all."

"You aren't hearing me. We're going to have 60 officers here, plus detectives."

"That won't be enough."

"What, are you and your *us* going to start some guerrilla war?"

"We're going to finish one. My question is whether you're going to help us or not. *That's* the question."

"You want me to spy."

"Yeah. Get us information. You're on the inside. You know what they do, you know who they are, you know where they're watching. You know what's happening."

"They already don't trust me. They won't even let me call out when there's an operation underway. They don't let me leave until the op is over."

"You still have more access than anyone else. You still see the bigger picture. The question is what are you going to do to help us?"

"What, help you kill them?"

"It'll probably come to that."

"Who the hell do you think you are? You're an insurance agent, Dale, not a guerrilla."

"The guys who won World War II weren't soldiers either, until they were."

"You're crazy. You need to never tell anyone else any of this or you'll end up in a cell, or worse. You and all your stupid friends, digging up your deer rifles and playing war."

"We're not playing. Like I said, you need to choose a side."

"Is this your idea? Who's in charge of your little rebel band?"

"It isn't little, Ted. It's big, and it'll get bigger."

"You're really going to do this."

Dale nodded and pointed at his bloody shirt. "That's real, and so is what's coming. You in or out?"

"What, what do you want from me?"

"Tell me about who is in charge."

"Lieutenant Kessler. She's a female – at least she uses female pronouns. She got sent down to take over a few weeks ago with a bunch of outside officers. She moved the Sheriff out. She's converting us from deputies to PSF, and I'll have to wear black too."

"Okay, that's good to know. What does she do, where does she live?"

"What are you going to do? Kill her?"

"Maybe."

"Is that your plan?"

"Our plan is taking back our town."

"I'll tell you what I can. You want to do some vandalism, write some graffiti about how the PR sucks, go for it. But I'm not going to be a participant in murder."

"You think you're not already? Whether you like it or not, you're part of the People's Republic, and it just killed a dozen of our friends. You need to make your choice."

"This is crazy," Ted replied.

"This is happening," Dale said, and finished his beer.

"Get the tactical team assembled!" Kessler shouted from the squad room floor. The lieutenant should have been planning and supervising – she was stepping into sergeant's business, something the old sheriff would have never done when he was still in charge.

The PSF officers were scrambling following the call about the sniper attack on the cruiser. The officers assigned as the quick reaction force ran to the supply room to draw their body armor and AKs. Cannon sat at his desk, watching but not offering assistance, the other administrative staff, a few men and women from around Jasper who acted as clerks and receptionists, simply kept their heads down as the uniformed officers ran about.

"Lieutenant," a sergeant yelled across the chaotic squad room. "There's reports of shots fired at the administrative building, and a fire."

Kessler stared for a moment, then said, "We need to respond to the sniper call first. The firemen can put the fire out."

"But, there were shots –" began the sergeant.

"The sniper is the priority!" Kessler ordered.

Ten minutes later eight of the station's cruisers roared out of the police lot heading towards the checkpoint. Cannon monitored the operation on the radio. The casualties were light – one rifle round in the leg and some damage to one of the vehicles. There was no sign of the snipers. Nobody on the street saw anything – the PSF was canvassing everyone within sight of the checkpoint. They were able to generally pinpoint the direction of fire as from the south, probably in the woods somewhere. A search yielded nothing.

With the station almost empty, Kessler finally assigned Cannon and another PSF officer, a young man with curly hair and a surly mien, to respond to the continuing calls from the administrative building. Cannon parked his cruiser down the street. Firemen were putting out the flames and a young man with a bad leg wound was being lifted into an ambulance.

Cannon's temporary partner just stood there.

"Maybe we ought to interview some witnesses?" suggested the deputy. The PSF officer seemed put out by the imposition.

"You can talk to them," he said, fingering his rifle. Cannon left him and began corralling onlookers.

Interestingly, the descriptions by the bureaucrats was consistent. The citizens were all over the board. It was some tall skinny guy, or a short fat guy, depending on who you talked to, who had walked into the People's Republic administrative building, shot one of the diversity workers in the leg, and set fire to the place. All while the PSF was out responding to the sniper call.

"Langer," thought Cannon. He scribbled down his notes, making sure to include all the different descriptions. The PBI people would not be happy about it, but too bad.

The plainclothes PBI detectives had taken over a suite of offices and began their work. They ignored Cannon except to demand he retrieve or move various things for them; they saw the PSF officers as fodder and a PSF officer who had been a local deputy was even lower in their esteem.

The detectives were bringing in a lot of computers. Cannon heard some of their cell calls – he couldn't quite make out what they were saying, but it looked like they were increasing monitoring of cell phone traffic within the county. And there was talk of software that would help define terrorist networks.

The people of Jasper who would not roll over were, apparently, terrorists now.

Kessler was afraid of the PBI contingent, though she tried not to show it. The lead detective was a man named Kunstler; he had her shaking in her boots every time he spoke to her. Or rather, spoke *at* her.

It took them some time to learn what Cannon already guessed, that the admin building shooter downtown was the same Larry Langer who had capped two PSF while escaping during the raid on his family farm. He obviously had not left town and the PBI "recommended" she increase patrols and random stops for ID on the street and at checkpoints.

"Have you set up surveillance on his known frequented establishments? Is there a bar or something he usually frequents?" asked Kunstler calmly.

"I, I don't know," Kessler stammered. "I just got here a few weeks ago."

Kunstler looked her over, annoyed. "Starting now, I'm assuming command. Get your officers ready to go out on the street. We are going to tear this town apart."

9.

"Look, we're not calling ourselves 'Wolverines,'" Turnbull said, annoyed. "Stop suggesting that."

One or two of the assembled insurgents looked disappointed.

"What we are going to do is turn this map red," Turnbull said, pointing to an AAA roadmap of Southern Indiana that they had tacked up to the wall of the barn.

There were about a dozen men and a couple women there, gathered around, watching the stranger. There were deer rifles, some AR15s and a few AKs leaning against the wall. One of the younger guys, a trucker from a nearby town, looked at the map, then at Turnbull, then back to the map. Turnbull had heard him called "Kyle."

"You mean red, like in 'red state'?"

"No," Turnbull said, now even more annoyed.

"You mean like blood?"

Sometimes, I hate civilians, Turnbull thought. "No, not like blood. Look, when you're doing an insurgency there are three colors on the map. White is where the counterinsurgents hold. That's cleared of the guerrillas and the troublemakers. Right now, this whole map is white."

The groups nodded, listening as Turnbull continued. "Next, pink. That's the at-risk area. That's where there's some trouble, but the government has got it sort of under control. Then there is the red. The red is insurgent territory. Our territory. That's what we are going to make out of all this white territory on this map. First, we make all this white space outside the towns pink, then red. Then we make the towns pink, then red. That's when we take Jasper itself.

"I thought it meant blood," said Kyle, disappointed.

"It doesn't mean blood."

It had been eight days since the attack on the administrative building and the checkpoint, eight days of organizing and training. True to his word, Dale Chalmers the insurance salesman had identified the likely rebellion's early adopters and set up the cells. Reliable contacts turned them on to other reliable contacts. Each night, Dale and Turnbull met to assess the new prospects and to analyze the information that was coming in.

They were organizing by cells, and not just in Jasper. There are other towns around, a few miles down each road, small and tight-knit, none with their own PSF station. Turnbull wanted a cell in each dot on the map, and Dale set to it. The cells were made up of neighbors and relatives; Turnbull knew that was the best way to keep them secure. Kind of like the mafia, but with pick-ups and Protestants, as well as the Catholics who settled the region.

There was tension – everyone could feel it. Some wanted to hide their heads. Others wanted a more active role. Turnbull generally left it to the locals to decide who was allowed how deep in the organization. Dale, the Mayor, Lee Rogers and Davey Wohl would sit around at night tossing names back and forth.

"He's dumb as a box of Illinois rocks," Wohl declared about one candidate.

"No, she never shuts up," the Mayor said about a woman he had greeted on the street as a long lost sister earlier that afternoon. "Worst gossip in town. We can't ever tell her anything, but she'll tell us everything."

"Not Jake Cole," Lee Rogers said. "He's a meth addict and people saw him talking to some blues. People are saying the PSF is trying to use junkies as snitches."

"Oh yeah?" said Larry Langer. That night he went out at about 11 p.m. with Lee, and didn't say where. The next day word spread through town how a moaning Jake Cole had been found with a bullet through his right knee, wearing a tourniquet and tied to the courthouse park's new statue of Ruth Bader Ginsberg. There was a sign around his neck that said "Rat."

Langer also paid a visit to Andy Houk out at his remote farmhouse, approaching from the woods and catching Andy on the porch coming out with a satchel of the meth he sold in town.

"Hi Andy," Langer said, shoving the barrel of his massive .357 into the big, bald man's multiple chins.

"Hey Larry," the dealer said, with more composure than was warranted.

"Things are getting a little *confrontational* with the government, and I wanted to make sure you and your customers weren't going to get sideways on us. Seems Jake Cole was talking to the blues and, well, his dancing days are done."

"I don't have no use for cops either. You know that, Larry."

"Well, it seems they're letting you run pretty free in town. I was wondering if you were kind of doing them any favors in return for being let alone."

"I don't talk about terrorist stuff to them."

"You calling me a terrorist, Andy?"

"I mean freedom fighters! The TV –"

"Okay, okay, calm down. I'm just saying, if you help them and not us, I'm going to have to find you and I'm gonna have to shoot ya."

"I won't help 'em, I promise, Larry. Swear to God!"

"That's good. Now, we're the ones really in charge now, so here are the rules. You can sell your meth to your regular junkie customers, but you tell them if they ever whisper to a blue you're cutting them off. You got that?"

"I got that, Larry."

"Okay. Now, I get if you got that meth demon you gotta feed it, but if I catch ya selling to any kids, I'm shooting you. Starting at the toe and working north. You feel me, Andy?"

"I feel you, Larry."

"Good. Then you have a nice day."

Most locals weren't chosen as fighters, but most tasks did not involve direct fighting. Much of it was observation and intelligence. The PSF noticed that there were always a few locals hanging around outside of the station, watching who went in and went out. They would deny it when confronted – *"We're just hanging out? Why are you hassling me? Is it because I'm part Hispanic?"* – but drop-ins by locals with good info dwindled to nothing.

Others contributed in their own way. The first graffiti soon appeared. It was usually obscene suggestions about what the PSF or the PR itself should kiss or suck. When the lazy public workers finally got around to scraping one tag off a wall, the next night two more would appear.

There were other, smaller acts of rebellion. A PSF officer coming into a restaurant could always expect a little something extra in his sandwich. One or two officers a day were usually out with the stomach flu. At the Starbucks favored by PSF leadership, the word passed among the baristas that their lattes should always be prepared with "extra loogie."

The maids at the former Best Western – that chain and all the others had recently been nationalized and were now simply called "Economy Hotel" – were enlisted to survey the rooms of the out-of-town PBI detectives when they cleaned them. USB sticks often went missing; if confronted and accused of with stealing, the maids were instructed to claim "sexist and classist oppression."

This same strategy was why Davey Wohl was selected to drive weapons and ammo across town in the trunk of his car – no one expected him to be stopped by the no-notice check points popping up around town. But one evening he was, and when the PSF officer demanded that he open his trunk he flew out of his Buick in a fury, screaming, "I'm not going to stand for this racial profiling bullshit! I am a proud black man and I want my Anti-Racism Representative and I'm going to make a complaint about your cracker ass!" The PSF officer quickly apologized and pleaded with Wohl to just go, please go. He did, laughing hysterically as he drove away with a trunk full of sixteen rifles, six shotguns, twelve pistols and about 5000 rounds of various ammunition.

The reinforced PSF stepped up its patrolling, but for the approximately 60 new PSF officers now assigned to the Jasper sector, there were only about half that number of vehicles. And there were detectives, according to Ted Cannon. He was passing on some information, in bits and pieces, but he was adamant that he would not pass on anything that would get any of his fellow PSF officers hurt. They might be assholes, but they were still *his* assholes – sort of. Turnbull told Dale to take whatever was given; at some point, Turnbull knew Cannon would need to choose.

The detectives were gathering, collating and examining data. And they were going out and talking to people. In fact, the orders had come down that the People's Security Force was to go out and mingle too, an idea which the rank and file did not like. They hated the locals, and they feared them. But they did do some walking patrols, trying to show they were not afraid. They were usually not afraid in groups of six or more, all carrying long weapons.

But out in the country, outside the city limits, they still made their presence known one vehicle at a time.

"We're going to own the countryside first," Turnbull said. "We're doing it starting tonight. Understand that this is coordinated. It's happening in other places too. So, nobody goes home until it gets done, and I don't want to see anybody near cell phones. You shouldn't have them on you at all."

The rule, announced immediately to all their recruits, was no personal cells. Never. Cells would give the bad guys a road map of where you'd been and who you talked to if they ever decided to look at you hard. Plus, as he learned in Iraq, they were an easy way for informants to tip off the bad guys to an op. Turnbull didn't expect they were infiltrated with any informants, but he was taking no chances.

The group nodded. They ranged from teens to an older man in his sixties who still operated a farm, though how long that would go on with the never-ending imposition of new regulations was uncertain. They all lived and worked around Bretzville, a small community a few miles southeast of Jasper where State Routes 162 and 64 crossed.

They knew their mission. It was pretty simple, but they did not plan and rehearse it as if it were simple. Turnbull had gone over it with them again and again, first drawing it out and diagraming where all the players would be. Then he took the shooters and made them walk their positions and their routes of ingress and egress, until they knew the choreography perfectly. The spotters trained too, practicing spotting PSF cruisers and calling them in on the Motorola hand-held radios that had previously been used to coordinate deer hunters. They practiced the timing, from where they spotted the cruiser until it crossed into the proposed kill zone. They ran through other scenarios and options for the plan – "branches and sequels," Turnbull called them.

Turnbull would go with them this time, as an observer. Langer was off with another team that would pull off its own mission tonight. But the locals would do the work. They would pull the triggers.

"All this to take some pot shots at a police car?" asked Kyle.

"Yeah, all that to shoot a few bullets," Turnbull said. "Let me ask you something. How many lives do you have? Are you a cat? Do you have nine lives?"

"No," said the confused would-be guerrilla.

"Let me ask you something else? You know everybody in this room, right?"

"Yeah."

"Lived by them, went to school with them, and related to more than a few of them? Maybe all of them?"

"So?"

"So how many of them is it okay for you to lose tonight?"

"None."

"That's right. None. This is real. People can die in this, *your* people. So we plan and rehearse. I'm not promising you won't lose anybody, and if this goes the way I think it will, I can pretty much promise you that you're going to lose people you know. Know that going in. But every time we rehearse, every time we plan, every time I get a map or get a sand table with a little army man and make you mark out exactly what you're going to do and how you're going to do it so everybody knows the plan and there are no screw ups, then that makes it a few percentage points more likely that you all walk away from this. Yeah, we're just shooting at a freaking police car. But what if they shoot back?"

"We'll be at 450 meters. They are going to have a hard time hitting us."

"See, you know that because we planned. We planned it so the edge is ours, that we have the advantage. You know exactly where you are going to hit them and you know exactly when. You know the terrain. You know how to get in, how to get out, and what they have to cross to get to you. You know how long it's gonna take for them to get back up, maybe even air support. Yeah, that's why we plan and rehearse. Because let me tell you guys something. You are outgunned. You cannot win a standup fight. They will always be able to generate more combat power against you. Every single time. Maybe you kill the first ten to get there, but what about the next ten and the next ten and then the next hundred? This is a guerrilla war, guys. We don't have the numbers. We don't have the combat power. So we have to make up for it. We make up for it by stealth. We make up for it by planning. We make up for it by picking our battles so we fight on our ground on our terms where we choose against an outnumbered unit of the enemy. That's how we win. That's how you don't have to go home and explain to your mother how your brother got his brains blown out because you started some bullshit, off-the-cuff firefight that went south. So, are you guys ready for this?"

"We're ready, Kelly," the young man replied. "We're pissed off and ready."

"Well, that might be the problem. Because if you're pissed off you're not thinking. If you're pissed off, you just want revenge.

You need to be cold. You need to be calculating. You need to have arranged all the pieces of the puzzle so in the end it's them dead and not you. I know you can shoot. You're all deer hunters and you all grew up with rifles in your mitts. But let me tell you another thing. Pulling the trigger is your least important skill. I want to say it again, because it's important. Your least important skill is the ability to pull the trigger. The PV assholes can pull triggers, and they are completely screwed up, tactically and strategically. We're going to train. We're going to plan. We're going to rehearse the tactics that keep you alive. We're not going to fight until we are good and ready, on our terms. Now everybody, get your shit. We're rolling in an hour. I'll do the inspections myself."

"Inspections?" the young man asked.

"Yeah, Kyle, inspections," said an older guy. He spent most of his time listening instead of talking, only taking a moment to correct one of the others when he observed something tactically wrong in the rehearsals. His name was Banks. He motioned Kyle to come over and then he started helping the young man arrange his battle gear.

"You were an NCO?" Turnbull asked.

"Marine staff sergeant," Banks replied.

"Now you're one of my NCOs," Turnbull said. "When I'm not here, you're in charge."

"Roger," said Banks. Turnbull didn't need to tell him anything else. Banks knew exactly what to do.

The radio in Banks's hands went off. "Cheeseburger, cheeseburger. Out."

Turnbull watched from his belly a few feet away as Banks stayed low and moved along the line of three shooters with scoped rifles, all looking down from the ridge across the wheat field to the south at State Route 64. It was a two-lane highway, and it often got confused with Interstate 64, which ran parallel a few miles to the south. They had selected a stretch of road west of a wide curve that ran through the little collection of buildings known as St. Anthony. That's where the spotters had seen the PSF cruiser heading west. At the posted speed of 55, it would be in the kill zone in about 60 seconds.

The radio went off again as the other set of spotters, watching the road to the west, confirmed there were no PSF vehicles coming from that way.

"Pizza, pizza. Out."

Now Banks was whispering to his people, reminding them of what he expected. He himself carried his prized M14, which he had secured out in the woods when the People's Republic declared privately owned firearms illegal. He was not going to fire tonight unless he had to – if it went bad, he had a few 20-round magazines of powerful .308 NATO bullets he could use on semi-automatic to suppress anyone moving on their position from a distance while the rest of the unit escaped.

Banks took his place and pulled up his binos. Turnbull raised his own and looked toward St. Anthony where 64 left it behind. There was one set of headlights coming from the east – if there had been a civilian vehicle nearby, they would have scrubbed the mission. He swung the binos south to the kill zone once more to make sure no knucklehead had wandered into it. The illumination was poor – no moon yet and some cloud cover, but he didn't see anything. Off on the periphery, lights from farms, houses and businesses twinkled. There were a lot more occupied shelters out here in the sticks than one might imagine, and with the powerful rounds they were using they had to be very, very careful of their background less someone drop a stray .270 slug through some farmer's dining room wall.

The PSF cruiser was headed into the kill zone, probably at the speed limit.

"Get ready," Banks said.

The riflemen aimed.

The PSF cruiser disappeared for a moment behind a willow tree growing on the banks of the small creek that ran north-south through the field. When it emerged, Banks barked.

"Fire!"

The three rifles erupted – the noise was deafening. The first volley off, all three pulled back the bolts on their rifles, jacked in another round and took aim. The three shots of the second volley were staggered, first one then two more in rapid succession. The shooters immediately began jacking in their third round.

Turnbull, ears ringing, was watching the cruiser through his binos. After the initial volley – nothing. The car kept going. But after the second, it swerved and ran off onto the shoulder before recovering. The third volley roared, and the front passenger's headlight was snuffed out. The cruiser accelerated, crossing the median and back and then tearing off to the west unsteadily.

It vanished out of sight.

"Get your brass and on your feet!" Banks barked. The shooters grabbed up their empty shell casings and arose, and so did Turnbull, carrying one of the liberated Kalashnikovs kindly donated by the People's Volunteers. The first shooter led them off the ridge and back into the woods along the path they had already reconnoitered. Banks was last out of the position, ensuring that there was nothing and no one left behind.

They tramped through the woods silently and in single file for about 15 minutes until they returned to the barn. They slipped inside, and then began to laugh and congratulate each other. A few minutes later, the two pairs of spotters entered and the whole team was assembled. While Turnbull watched, Banks conducted the after-action review – what went right, and more importantly, what went wrong.

Kyle seemed disappointed. "Well, it doesn't look like we killed them," he said.

Turnbull spoke up. "Doesn't matter. That wasn't the purpose."

"I thought in wars you killed the enemy,"

"In wars you *beat* the enemy. Sometimes that means you kill them, sometimes that doesn't matter. Alive or dead, after tonight they'll know that the countryside is ours, and they either have to move in force when they come out here or give it over to us."

"What the nice officer is saying," Banks said, "is that tonight we turned Dubois County pink."

Banks lit his cigar, then Turnbull's. The air was a bit chilly, but neither showed it.

"This is your area now. Unless we're doing something bigger, you deal with them when they come through," Turnbull said.

"The Department of Agriculture inspector is supposed to be coming tomorrow," Banks said. "Every time, it's more land ordered out of production, more new rules, and more 'equality contributions' of a part of the harvests."

"When he gets here, have a little talk with him," said Turnbull.

"Him? I don't even want to go there – last time some government asshole came through I assumed it was a chick because it had tits and that cost me 20 minutes of crying about how I was imposing my idea of gender identity on it."

"If it does that again, shoot it," suggested Turnbull.

"Yeah, that's my plan. We're also going to start setting aside food in case things get uglier. The prices are going down – see, because the government loves us – so naturally, there's less in the stores to buy every week. My wife couldn't get coffee at the supermarket; you gotta go in town to Starbucks to get any anymore. Nice to be pals with the government, huh? You get a monopoly."

"They like big companies fine if the big companies do what they say," said Turnbull.

"And when the government takes over the grocery stores like it says it's going to, the shortages will only get worse. So, down there, in the red, it's not bad like the news always says, is it?"

"Well, you can get coffee in the supermarkets and Starbucks isn't the only coffee shop."

"You can say what you want, right?" Banks asked, exhaling a cloud.

"Yeah, they kept the old First Amendment and didn't do what they did here – add a whole bunch of exceptions."

"I'd go," Banks said. "But on the other hand, fuck that noise. This is my land and no one's driving me off it."

Ted Cannon was still assigned to a desk inside the Jasper PSF station, and he saw firsthand the chaos that followed the four separate sniper attacks on cruisers across the Jasper sector the night before. Walking in for his shift at 0700, he saw the four vehicles that had been shot at. A couple were short side windows; one's rear window had a bullet hole almost dead center. All four had holes punched through the sheet metal. One had a headlamp shot out; another had blood in the passenger's seat where a slug went through the door and shattered the officer's humerus.

The detectives were all over the vehicles; they had retrieved some of the slugs, which were deformed but they were obviously large caliber hunting rounds.

Cannon went inside, where Kessler was fuming in her office, sipping a Starbucks coffee. Her subordinates were not looking to her for solutions. They were exploring their own.

"I ain't going back out there on those backwoods *Deliverance* country-ass roads," one patrol officer told another. "I'll pull my shit off on a side road and hide until my shift's done. Get high!"

His pal half-laughed and half-considered that course of action.

"It's the coordination that should worry you," PBI Inspector Kunstler was telling the lieutenant. He was in plainclothes and calm; she was shaking with rage and fear. "Four incidents, identical incidents, within a few hours? That's not a coincidence. They are getting more sophisticated."

"I don't understand how this is happening," Kessler said. "I thought we took all the guns."

"Well, Lieutenant, apparently they still have quite a lot of them. And I expect ammunition as well. What we need is the people of this region to identify the criminals so we can break up this ring – or rings. But it seems the people here refuse to help. "

"They're all racist reactionaries," Kessler offered. Kunstler's expression did not change.

"Obviously, we can't allow any of this into the media," Kunstler said. "We'll need more checkpoints and ID checks by your people. We can increase media and communications monitoring. We're already mapping relationship networks on our software. And we can use the schools, interview students and encourage denunciations."

"More ID checks and checkpoints. Yes, we'll do those."

"And are you going to take any retaliatory action?"

Kessler looked around, as if she were caged. "Sergeant, what are the nearest towns to these terrorist attacks?"

The sergeant, another out-of-towner stared at the map on her wall. "St. Anthony is close by where Unit 14 was shot at."

"We'll send the Volunteers in there tonight," Kessler said. Kunstler did not reply. He turned and went back to his suite of offices.

Cannon headed to the back door.

"So, we know they come south from Indianapolis. We know they'll come into Jasper and pick up some PSF escorts like last time. The question is, which way will they come?" asked Turnbull. Langer didn't bother looking at the map Turnbull had spread across the work bench in Lee Rogers's garage.

"Gotta come down 231," Langer said. "Now, the question is whether they keep coming down 231 after Jasper to 64, or if they come down on 162 and hit 64."

"We can't know," Turnbull said. "We need to hit them before they get to Jasper, somewhere along 231, before they pick up their PSF escort."

"You got a 20 mile shot straight south from Loogootee," Langer said. "Gotta be somewhere that's good near the middle."

Turnbull pulled the keys to Lee Rogers's Ford truck out of his pocket and jiggled them.

It was an even day, and Lee's truck had an even-numbered license plate to avoid attention and climate crime traffic stops. The pair took side streets until they got to 231 just south of the Walmart and turned north. There was not much traffic in the late morning. About half-way up, they found what they were looking for – a narrow stretch, with a wooded rise on one side and a long field stretching away in the other. Deep ditches paralleled both shoulders.

"We could seal it off there with a big truck or something," Turnbull said. "And then another behind to block them in the kill zone."

"Plenty of big trucks around," Langer replied as a semi whipped past northbound.

"At least 15 minutes until help arrives, assuming they even get a call off. Lots of roads heading west, so afterwards we can get away fast and work our way back south. The meet-up in Jasper is supposed to be at 2030 hours, so this probably goes down around 2000 hours."

Langer nodded. "We hook us up a spotter with a cell phone up in Loogootee, and he gives us a heads-up when they're coming south."

"We can bounce the calls around so it's hard to track to someone around here. Dale can figure out who calls who.

"I got a team I want to use," Langer said. "They did good the other night."

"I want to use Banks's team from Bretzville," Turnbull said. "Though if we miss their area is undefended."

"Reckon we best not miss then."

"Yeah. Let's go. We got nine hours 'til show time."

They kept to the speed limit heading south, and it was as they crossed the low span of the East Fork of the White River that a PSF cruiser pulled off the side of the road and fell in behind him.

Langer said nothing. He pulled out his .357, opened the chamber to confirm he had six magnum rounds loaded. Turnbull carefully and with little fuss pulled the Wilson Combat from behind him and placed it on his lap.

"We got the right plates, evens, right?" asked Langer calmly.

"Not sure that matters," Turnbull said, eyes on the rearview.

The cruiser hit its lights.

"Better make this quick, before they can call it in," Langer said. "Lee'll be mighty pissed if she finds out there's a BOLO on her truck."

Turnbull eased the truck to the shoulder and released his seatbelt. Langer hadn't been wearing one.

Turnbull's right hand took the .45; his left reached over and grasped the door handle.

The cruiser rolled up close. Two officers. Their doors cracked open. No big deal, apparently.

Turnbull and Langer each threw their respective door open and rolled out onto their respective feet, catching the PSF officers as they were in the midst of exiting their sedan.

It wasn't clear who fired first, Langer or Turnbull. Turnbull aimed center mass on the officer through the window of his target's open door.

BAM! BAM! BAM!

The window was down because there was no shatter. Instead, there were three eruptions on the front of the PSF officer's uniform. He staggered backwards and onto the road, trying to draw. He had a vest, and probably some broken ribs. Turnbull fired again and again, then pivoted upwards and fired four more headshots. At least one connected – there was a puff of pink and the officer dropped dead on his back on the road.

The .45's slide was locked back. Turnbull dropped the extended mag and slapped home a full one then released the slide and returned to seeking targets.

Movement left – no, it was Langer by the PSF car, pointing the big magnum at something on the ground and firing.

The last gunshot echoed in the air – fortunately, the nearest house was some distance away.

"You clear?" shouted Turnbull, searching for targets. His own was not moving – even his twitching had ceased.

"Oh yeah, I'm good," said Langer. "This son of a bitch ain't so good, though."

"Help me get them in the truck bed before someone comes along and sees us.

They loaded the bodies in the back of Lee Rogers's pick-up and covered them with a tarp.

"Follow me," Langer said, trotting back to the cruiser. He did something under the dash, then fired it up and turned it around, heading back to the bridge. Turnbull followed him as he made a right onto a dirt road running parallel to the river and about 15 feet above it. They went in about a quarter mile to a quiet bend, where Langer stopped. Turnbull parked.

"Pulled out the GPS," Langer said, holding up a grey metal device with a couple of wires hanging from it.

"Get the radio out too. Maybe we can listen in."

Langer nodded and went to work as Turnbull kept watch. After a few minutes, he produced the radio. He also took the AKs out of the vehicle, along with the extra ammo. They had already liberated the side arms. To Turnbull's disappointment, the dead PSF carried 9 millimeter Berettas. He had only about one and a half magazines of .45 left. But he did retrieve a fairly decent Kevlar plate from the back of each one's vest. The front plates were terminal. Those would go in his own plate carrier rig, front and back. And he liberated a thigh holster from one as well.

Langer put the sedan in neutral and pushed from the driver's door so he could steer; Turnbull pushed from behind. The sedan went forward over the bank and down into the river with a splash. The windows were all open, so it flooded almost immediately. With a final gasp in the form of a huge air bubble, it sunk into the muddy water.

"I'd plant those two here, but I need to go back to Lee's and borrow her shovel too," Langer said. They returned to the truck and headed south toward town.

Turnbull was taking the lead on this one personally. There were two cells involved, one Langer had trained and Banks's from Bretzville. Their vehicles were left guarded about a mile west off a little used farm road. They made the march east to the ambush point with the sun still up, so they kept to the woods. They had all taken off work early to plan and rehearse; most worked for themselves or each other, so no one outside the circle of trust noticed.

The mission was much more impromptu than Turnbull liked, but they would be fighting somewhere tonight, and his vote was for on the ground of his own choosing. He planned it and rehearsed them as best he could in the time he had.

"How did your discussion with the ag inspector go?" Turnbull asked Banks as they walked between the trees.

"Pretty well. A couple of guys in masks pushed his car off the road, dragged him out from behind the wheel and kicked his ass pretty good. Told him things had changed and that his services were no longer needed," Banks replied. "He won't be back."

"He?" asked Turnbull. "You didn't misgender xim, did you?"

"I'm pretty sure he was a he," Banks said. "From the way he cried when I slammed the butt of my fourteen into his nutsack."

"That's the moment genderfluidity becomes much less fluid," Turnbull said. "So is Kyle going to be able to pull off his part of all this?"

"Drive a truck badly? Yeah, I figure he can do that right, especially when he's trying to."

The two cells rendezvoused, but Turnbull and Langer did not let them interact – OPSEC. The pair handled the coordination between the teams. Langer's crew took the north part of the wooded embankment and the north security position that would seal off the kill zone along the 100 meter asphalt strip. Turnbull's team took the south, including the southern security element. There were 18 bodies there, not counting Kyle and the rear truck driver Langer's group supplied.

Turnbull carefully positioned each shooter, and reiterated the plan. Each shooter set up right-left limit stakes to help ensure his fire was into his assigned sector of fire. Maybe five were prior service military in some form – they got it right away. It took some effort to train up the others. To the extent their training was incomplete, now it was time to learn by doing.

The call came in on a burner cell at 8:17 p.m., routed through a half-dozen people who had no idea about the nature of the message they were passing onward. The four People's Volunteer vehicles had passed through Loogootee at 8:05 p.m. Turnbull huddled with Langer for a moment, and then the local took off to his troops.

"Three minutes," Turnbull said to the men to each side. He lay down, his AK ready. He had passed five others out to the shooters. He would initiate the ambush with automatic fire and the others with Kalashnikovs would join him in trying to run up the count fast. The rest, with their deer rifles or AR15 semi-autos would provide pinpoint fire.

Banks had his M14. He would put holes through anything the bad guys tried to hide behind.

Kyle sat in the cab of a moving company semi he had taken at gunpoint outside Jasper an hour ago. The driver was sitting zip tied in a gas station washroom where he'd be discovered the next morning – a small sacrifice for the cause. Kyle held the Motorola in his hand.

"Inbound," barked the radio. The northern spotters had the enemy in sight. Kyle started the engine with a gloved hand and glanced at the AR15 he had selected for tonight that was perched on the passenger seat. He carried six other 30-round mags of 5.56 millimeter ammo in his web gear.

Turnbull had taken him aside and, after explaining his special mission as the blocker, told him, "This time, when it goes off, kill as many as you want." Kyle thought of that and swallowed.

It seemed more thrilling when it was less abstract.

The lights appeared up ahead at the curve. It looked like four sedans heading south fast. Kyle gripped the steering wheel with one hand and the gear shift with his other.

Turnbull watched the convoy and noticed it was followed a hundred meters or so behind by a tractor-trailer rig. That would be the rear blocker.

He turned his eyes south. Kyle's rig was idling by the side of the access road. The convoy was coming fast.

"Any time, Kyle," Turnbull said to himself.

The rig lurched forward as if obeying Turnbull's command. It pulled straight across the four-way intersection, blocking it. To the right, on the northeast corner was a ditch parallel to the highway, and then the embankment where the shooters were positioned. To the left, at the northwest corner, there was another parallel ditch, then a field rolling out a half mile to a far off tree line one could barely make out in the fading daylight.

Thanks to the two ditches, when Kyle sealed off 231, there was no way around the block.

The lead sedan, a familiar Chevy with the black letters "PV" spray-painted on the front doors, waited too long to slow down and ended up screeching to a wobbly stop. The other cars did the same – the fourth car actually rammed the rear bumper of the third. Their doors flew open and 16 men in PV uniforms leapt out, waving their rifles and swearing in incoherent rage at the "cracker motherfucker" driving the truck blocking their way.

The rear truck slowed down too, and turned to position itself to block the way back north. The PVs, eyes fixed south, did not notice.

Turnbull aimed, exhaled, and fired a burst of 7.62 millimeter rounds at the targets 75 meters down and to his front.

The rest of the Kalashnikovs lit up, and then the other weapons too. Glass shattered, steel punctured, tires blew out, and the concrete exploded in a hundred tiny eruptions.

Turnbull's first burst caught a short PV who had been looking up at the tree line while the others were shouting at the trucker. One of Turnbull's guiding principles was to always try to kill the smart ones first. Whether or not the guy had actually figured out that this was a trap was a moot point; three rounds sunk hard into his chest and sluiced out his back, splattering blood and chunks across the concrete.

He didn't fall right away, though; that took a second burst, which caught him in the shoulder, then the throat, then the chin, and then the forehead in rapid succession. That fusillade finally convinced him to sprawl on his back and die, freeing Turnbull to seek his second target, a skinny one sprinting for cover in the far ditch. His next burst of fire tore up the unlucky Volunteer's spine like a series of five little red volcanos.

Skinny's bladder and his legs were freed from their slavery to his faraway brain when Turnbull's rounds severed his spinal column. His legs went in opposite directions as his sphincter relaxed. Skinny collapsed face-first in the dirt of the soft shoulder, his urine turning it to mud, his dignity taken along with his life.

Everyone was firing down the line, though fire from the AKs slackened as they ran their first magazines dry. Turnbull dropped his mag and inserted a fresh one, then sought a new target.

Was that Do-Rag there, near the front of the second car, with crazy, panicked eyes? He had no weapon, having dropped it when the shooting started. It turned out that it's scary when they shoot back at you. Turnbull took aim center mass and pulled the trigger. Nothing. It was jammed. The former PV rifle was apparently trying to help out its former owners.

Do-Rag turned and bolted east, toward the open field. He didn't stop at the ditch – he leaped over it and sprinted.

Do-Rag was getting away. No time to clear the AK.

"Sergeant, can I borrow your rifle for a second?" Turnbull asked.

"It's almost dry," Banks replied, handing it over without any questions.

"Oh, I only need one shot," Turnbull said. Banks shrugged. He turned toward the man on his other side and began directing his teammate's fire at the few targets still standing down on the road.

Turnbull lay flat and took up the heavy rifle. Banks was using iron sights, so Turnbull did it the old-fashioned way. He put the front sight post on Do-Rag's back as the PV ran away and aligned it. Maybe a 200 meter shot on a moving target. Hard, but not that hard.

Turnbull exhaled and pulled. The trigger broke unexpectedly and the gun sounded like a howitzer as the .308 round streaked out of the barrel.

Do-Rag looked like someone had hit him in the lower back with a pile driver. He was down for good.

"Here's your gun," Turnbull said, handing it back and assessing the situation. There was still some shooting, but nothing was moving down there.

"Cease fire!" he yelled. Langer and Banks and then the rest of them picked up the "Cease fire" call, and the firing ceased.

Drawing his .45, he got on his feet. "Assault! Let's go!" he cried, and he and most of the shooters charged down the embankment into the corpse-strewn kill zone.

Turnbull crossed the ditch and hit the asphalt, his pistol up, seeking targets. Nothing. Movement right – Turnbull pivoted. Kyle stepped forward from over near the ditch, AR15 in hand.

"I shot two that were hiding in the ditch," he said. He looked shaken and uncertain.

"You did good," Turnbull said.

"There's one alive in that car, I think," Kyle said.

"Did you shoot –" Turnbull began, but the PV in the car was upright now with an AK and he was firing. Three slugs slammed into Kyle's side; the young man, stunned, dropped his AR15 and fell.

Turnbull was on the shooter and firing fast, two handed, the rounds ejecting out of his action as fast as he could pull the trigger. He was scoring hits. The PV twisted and shuddered under the impacts, and he fell back out of the driver's door onto the pavement.

Turnbull's slide was locked back and he dropped his mag and reloaded the Wilson with the one with three rounds left after he had blasted out the hospital door.

He glanced right and Kyle was there on the concrete, pale and coughing as he bled out. Two of his friends were with him, and Banks was coming fast.

Turnbull came around the vehicle and found the PV leader, his chest riddled with .45 slugs, twitching on his back. The hyphen in "D-Yazzy" on his hamper-fresh concert tee had been obliterated by one of Turnbull's hollow points.

"I told you that if you came back here we'd kill you all," Turnbull said evenly. The dying leader's eye went wide and Turnbull shot him right between them. Then he walked west toward the field.

"Kelly!" shouted Banks. Turnbull raised his empty hand, waved him off and kept walking through the grass. Banks went back to his business in the kill zone. From behind him, Turnbull heard the loud report of a big handgun. Langer was taking care of loose ends too.

Do-Rag had run a good distance and, from the blood trail, managed to crawl another few meters after taking the slug. Not bad for a guy with a .308 crater where his spleen used to live.

Do-Rag was on his face in the dirt. Turnbull put his boot on the man's rib cage and kicked him over onto his back. Do-Rag groaned. It was not clear if he recognized his tormentor.

"Fuck you," Turnbull said and shot him in the face.

Turnbull walked back across the field, now shaking in anger. He noticed the intense ringing in his ears from all the firing. That only made him angrier.

They didn't get it yet. They didn't get what war was, and that misunderstanding of its fundamentally brutal nature would get them killed.

He leapt over the ditch and was back on the road. The guerrillas were gathering up guns and ammo from the dead. Banks was talking to two men holding something heavy wrapped in a blanket – Kyle.

He caught movement to his right as he passed the lead car. One last wounded PV was trying to crawl under the Chevy. Turnbull causally fired his last round into the back of his head, and a pair of the local guerrillas just stared, horrified.

"What?" asked Turnbull. "You wanted war right? That's fucking guerrilla war. If you can't take it, go back to being the PR's bitches!"

He noticed the slide on his .45 was open, his last mag empty.

"Does anyone have any .45?" he bellowed. "I'm fucking out!"

10.

Lieutenant Kessler was in her office with the door closed, one hand holding a Starbucks cup, the other the phone. She was doing substantially more listening than talking.

Cannon watched her through her glass window, as inconspicuously as possible, from the squad room – but then, everyone was trying to watch her without being caught watching.

He had been called back to the station at 9:33 p.m. along with everyone else – Cannon had a suspicion about why, but it was not until he got back to the station that he learned that four carloads of People's Volunteers had been wiped out on Route 231 not ten miles north of town. He wasn't sure how he felt, especially knowing that his information probably led to it, but he had heard whispers about what the PVs intended to do to punish the locals for the sniping, and he knew exactly how he would have felt about *that*.

As a real cop, it was hard for him to accept that he just didn't care.

It was obvious Kessler cared, but only about her own hide. The PVs were expendable – that and the deniability the ostensibly extra-governmental PSF provided the authorities were precisely why they were so useful for getting rough with the recalcitrant citizenry. But sixteen dead? That was clearly raising questions, and Cannon watched through the window as, inside her office, Kessler tried to answer them.

Outside, in the nearly empty squad room, the few remaining PSF officers who were not cleaning up the bloodbath out on 231 were scared – there was no other word for it. A week before, the station's reinforcements had swaggered around town, unchallenged, unconstrained. But now? The locals were fighting back, and they hadn't signed up for that.

First, the Langers had waxed three of them. Then the sniper attacks. Now Unit 71 and two officers had just vanished, gone, poof. They were sitting on the side of the 231 near the river the prior afternoon, then suddenly they weren't there anymore – they weren't *anywhere* anymore. Not a trace. They probably pulled their GPS unit and skipped town, but who knew? And then this massacre, out in the open, right there on the main road into town.

It was not supposed to be like this. The People's Security Force was supposed to be in control.

But if these guerrillas – yeah, that's what they were, and there was no denying it anymore – could wax a whole bunch of PVs, they could do the same to a whole bunch of PSF officers. It was just a matter of time.

"Screw this town. I am done with this shit," one blue told another as Cannon sat nearby. The officer was in his mid-twenties, with a scraggly little beard and the mutton-chop sideburns favored by recent college grads. He had been transferred into town with the other reinforcements and made no secret of the fact that he despised the locals. Cannon had often seen him come back into the station from patrol with cargo pockets full of candy bars that he had liberated from the old 7-11.

"I can quit, go back to Chicago and get on assistance and make almost this much and not get shot at by these backwoods bunnyfuckers," replied Candy Bandit's partner. Candy Bandit nodded.

On the operations wall, two officers were tacking up a large map of Dubois County and the surrounding region. They then began to work on it with colored pens.

From the dispatch area, a radio call came in, and the squad room fell silent. "This is Unit 27 – they're shooting at us! Shit! They're shooting at us!" The GPS monitor display showed Unit 27 was on a rural road southwest of Jasper outside of a little town called Duff and hauling ass, doing maybe seventy.

"We're past them! Over," called Unit 27 in a female voice. Even via the radio, the squad room could hear that she was breathing heavily, which did not surprise Cannon. She was short but weighed in at about 200 pounds – 90 kilograms, since the metric system was now mandatory – and she had been hired under the PSF's "Heft-Positive" quota program that was designed to allow people of girth into the ranks following the elimination of the discriminatory physical fitness standards that had previously excluded so many of the alternatively capable.

"The PSF has no higher priority than crushing fatism!" Kessler had informed the ranks at one of her first briefings. All of the local deputies and even some of the transferees had snickered at her unfortunate formulation.

Now Kessler was coming out of her office, her face fierce, charging to the dispatcher. She grabbed the hand mic.

"Unit 27, investigate and apprehend the shooter, over!"

There was a pause – no one in the squad room said a word.

"Uh, say again, over?"

"Stop your vehicle and arrest them!"

"Uh, I can't because…," the voice began and then there was screeching and static-like sounds.

"Is she *making* those interference noises?" wondered Cannon, and everyone else.

Kessler was shouting now. "Unit 27, come in!"

More fake static.

Kessler threw the hand mic across the room, except it was connected by a wire and bounced back, hitting her in the chest. She stomped back toward her office.

Cannon noticed Kunstler of the People's Bureau of Investigation, apparently just returned from the ambush site, watching from the shadows. He was holding a sheet of paper, and taking in the scene.

Sergeant Greely walked over to Candy Bandit and his pal. "You two, get rolling out there."

"Hell no," Candy Bandit said. "I'm not going outside of town. They'll shoot us!"

"I said get out there!" shouted the sergeant.

"I'm not going! I quit!"

Kunstler approached and stood by Greely.

"What did you say?" he asked.

"I, I –" Candy Bandit began.

"You said you quit. Did I hear that correctly? You *quit*?"

"I just…I can't," the officer stammered.

"Can't what?" asked Kunstler

"They'll kill us!" Candy Bandit cried.

"You're not willing to die for the People's Republic? Is that what you are saying?" The entire squad room was watching now. Kessler came out of her office and watched too. Candy Bandit's eyes darted frantically around the room.

"Look, if you go out into Indian Country, they'll kill you!"

"*Indian Country*? Is that what you and your friends call it? So you're racist too?"

"No, it's just...*other* people call it that. I –"

"So, are you comparing Native Americans to criminal terrorists? Using an illegal stereotype in order to justify your criminal insubordination?"

"That's not true!"

"Are you insulting President Warren as well? Wasn't one of the racists' lies before the Split based on attacking her Indigenous Peoples' heritage?"

Candy Bandit couldn't get any more words out. He just sat back in his chair at the desk, terrified.

"Take his weapon, Sergeant." The sergeant reached down and pulled the Beretta from the quivering officer's holster.

"Please," whimpered Candy Bandit.

"Take him into custody," Kunstler said. The sergeant nodded at Candy Bandit's partner, who helped hustle the pleading prisoner back to the holding cells. Kunstler walked over to Kessler, who said nothing, and handed her the sheet of paper. She started reading it.

"These are the actions we are taking. We are going to put a stop to this, regardless of what it takes." He turned and walked back to his office. Kessler kept reading.

Cannon's eyes moved back to the map as a pair of officers were coloring it in with markers. They had colored everything except the city of Jasper itself in bright red.

Turnbull and Langer sat in the living room of one of Jasper's many zombie houses, the homes abandoned in the dead of night by the owners who had fled south to the USA post-Split. It was comfortable, if a bit dusty. The power was still on, since the PR had decreed that electricity was a human right and no one at the newly nationalized People's Power Cooperative had any incentive to make the effort to turn it off.

Turnbull was cleaning one of the 9 millimeter Berettas he had liberated from the PVs. Without any .45 rounds – why the hell no one had any .45 rounds was beyond him – his tricked out Wilson was just a brick. But there was plenty of nine mil. He had five mags full.

"I don't understand why these people can't clean a weapon to save their lives," Turnbull snorted.

"I guess cuz you don't get a participation trophy for taking care of your gear," Langer suggested. "You okay?"

"I'm fine," Turnbull said, releasing the slide.

"You seemed a little out of sorts."

"Are we sharing our feelings now, Langer?"

"See, I got a reason to kill these sons of bitches after what they did. But you? Why are you even here?"

"To help you people help yourselves."

"Yeah," said Langer. "But you know, whenever the government sends someone to help people like us, they aren't really coming to help people like us."

Turnbull stopped wiping the pistol for a moment and looked over.

"No, when the government sends people to help us," Langer continued. "It's really trying to help itself."

"I don't work for your government," Turnbull said.

"No, maybe not, but you work for *a* government, and in the end they're all more the same than different, if you get my meaning."

"I can't make you people do anything you don't want to do," Turnbull said.

"No, I reckon not. And sometimes you gotta do what you gotta do. But I know where this ends for a not-so-nice guy like me. I'm just not sure where it ends for all these nice people who are fighting your war for you."

"Their war," Turnbull said.

"Yeah, their war. But you're more than happy for them to be having it."

"My personal happiness doesn't matter," Turnbull snarled.

"No, but I'm just wondering how you want it to end, if you even do. I figure I'm going to keep taking payback until one day they surround me and I go down fighting. That's okay with me – it ain't like I'm throwing away any great future. I always figured I was gonna end up in jail or bleeding out on a barroom floor with a knife in my liver anyway. But these folks? Do they think if they cap some PVs and some PSF eventually the PR's just going to let them be? Just gonna walk away and say bygones are bygones? How's this end? And why'd the USA decide to send you up here?"

"I didn't say I came from the red."

"You know, I'm country, not stupid, Kelly. You trying to take Jasper back into the red? Is that the plan?"

"That's above my pay grade, Langer."

"When an officer doesn't want to answer a question, that's what he always says," replied the former Marine.

"You got me there. Hit the TV. Find some news."

The cable box was still working – Article 366 of the People's Republic Constitution guaranteed "free access to cable television and internet service, as appropriately regulated to eliminate hate speech, including but not limited to racist, sexist, and anti-LGBTQN$%EÜ speech and paradigms." The right to be protected from "unprogressive paradigms" was also enumerated in various forms in

Articles 3, 47, 234, 562, and 722 through 771. Those articles set forth the list of banned mindsets in significantly greater detail.

Langer changed channels until he found what he was looking for. There used to be hundreds of channels; now there were dozens, because the People's Republic had decided that people did not "need so many choices," as the elderly Rationalization of Production Minister Bernie Sanders had put it. So many different options was wasteful and irrational in the government's view. His first initiative had been to limit the number of deodorant types to two, "men's" and "women's." That had created an entirely new controversy as genderfluid individuals protested. Now there was simply one deodorant, called "Deodorant," which smelled like wet cardboard and stained your shirt, blouse, or burqa.

The People's Republic was hoping to soon be able to expand the constriction of choices to products throughout the economy as part of its quest for greater freedom.

Langer aimed the remote and clicked past a dance contest show where the best participants wore weights to negate their advantages, as well as a documentary documenting the many hate crimes the red states still allowed, like sex-separate bathrooms. He settled on CNN. Its headquarters moved from Atlanta to Boston after the Split, and CNN was proud to have obtained the first television news reporting license from the new People's Republic. It billed itself as "CNN: Your Trusted Source For Approved Information."

Tonight, CNN had nothing about the attack, but it did have vague rumblings about an increase in "racist hate crimes" across Southern Illinois, Indiana, and Ohio in recent days. These criminals would be swiftly punished, the announcer assured the audience. Apparently, Jasper wasn't the only area getting uppity with the overlords.

And there was another important bit of news. The anchor was one of the lesser Cuomos and about twenty-five years old. Xis gender was difficult to ascertain and xis eye patch gave xe away as differently sighted. Xe announced, "And as of today, the border crossings with the racist states have been closed. President Warren today announced that the citizens of the People's Republic will no longer provide a safety valve for the racist states' victims of economic oppression and social injustice."

There was some footage of the doddering President Warren being helped to the podium. "These restrictions," she said, her eyes wide but unfocused, "will provide a new dawn of freedom and diversity as we eliminate the influence of illegal and unapproved ideas and…."

She stopped, blinked and looked confused, and then the camera cut away.

There was a title card reading "OFFICIAL PEOPLE'S REPUBLIC ANNOUNCEMENT FOR THE SOUTHERN ILLINOIS, INDIANA AND OHIO REGIONS."

Turnbull stopped cleaning the Beretta and watched as a different newsreader, this one pretty clearly identifying as male, appeared on screen.

"Good evening. Terrorists supported by the racist states are at work undermining our progressive progress. These criminals and their accomplices will be held accountable! Because of the epidemic of racist hate crimes throughout the southern portions of Illinois, Indiana and Ohio, the people have demanded strict action. Until further notice, the following activities are banned. All religious services, except Muslim and Wiccan services. Also, witches and crones are authorized to continue their moonlight rituals to the Earth Mother Ge-ga-gia-," the reader stammered, staring hard at his teleprompter.

"Gaia," he finally said, triumphantly. "Also, all sports leagues, and all unapproved large gatherings are banned. Travel will be restricted within these areas. Random identification checks will be in effect. Petroleum and food supplies will be reviewed."

"So they want to starve us," Langer said.

"Starve the people who grow all the food?" asked Turnbull.

"Also," the newsreader continued, "due to the demands of students to protest these hate crimes, tomorrow all students will participate in voluntary and spontaneous protest marches in their towns. These protests will be organized by the school staff and are mandatory. Finally, all citizens are urged to support their People's

Security Forces as they continue their successful operations to suppress these racist criminal terrorists. Citizens are urged to report any terrorist activity to their local People's Bureau of Investigation units. Together, we will hold these terrorists accountable!"

The shot went back to the regular newsreader. "The people of the People's Republic stand united in defense of diversity and social justice," the newsreader assured the viewers. "And thank you for watching. This is Castro Cuomo, for CNN, reporter's license number 474497T."

Langer picked up the remote and clicked it off.

"I haven't watched much TV since they banned ultimate fighting," he said. "Ain't missed it."

"It's on now," Turnbull said. "These are your folks. You think these people can handle it? Think they'll fight through it or roll over?"

"Well," Langer said. "I don't know about *my* folks. We were always kind of white trash, the people everyone else told their kids they'd end up like if they messed up. But they're good people, and you can only push them so far. I think these People's Republic sons of bitches are underestimating them."

"Ah, our *zampolit* is here," Colonel Deloitte observed as Major Kaden Little entered the operations center. It was located inside an old National Guard armory in Bloomington, one that had not been refurbished in decades. The military had been last in line for everything in the blue since the Split. That, however, might be changing if things continued as they were going.

"I know what that means now," snarled the Command Diversity Officer. Technically, as CDO, the major had authority to override anyone in the command other than the commander himself – and if Little needed to do that, he had the phone number of Deloitte's boss on his cell.

"Oh, you do?" Deloitte said. The other staff officers, all either selected by Deloitte or left after he subtly purged the non-hackers and quota fillers from those randomly assigned to him, watched amused.

"It means 'political officer!'" Little said, having finally looked it up on Guugle, the breakaway, licensed and regulated search engine that remained in the blue states. Following the Split, Google departed to the red after the People's Republic demanded real time access to its citizens' web searches.

"So it does," Colonel Deloitte said. "And you're late, not that you contribute anything to this unit anyway except to thicken the fog of war." The staff stifled a collective gasp – no one ever spoke like this anymore and got away with it, except Colonel Deloitte.

"You can't talk –" Little began, turning red-faced.

"Shut up and sit down," Deloitte replied icily. The *zampolit* sheepishly complied. The colonel turned to his staff.

"All right, understand we have no orders yet besides a basic alert. This is my planning guidance. The executive officer will give you a timeline for the process and the decision brief, but I want to tell you what I'm thinking and seeing now. There's unrest across the sector. Minor sabotage, graffiti, and now worse. Evanston, three PSF cars under sniper fire. Other incidents in Salem and Croydon and elsewhere. And of course, 16 dead PVs north of Jasper. They drove straight into an ambush. Whoever set it knew what he was doing. We are not facing just a bunch of farmers with deer rifles, though that would be bad enough. They're being organized. I'm betting US Army SOF, because they are doing exactly what I'd be doing. Colonel, put the overlay on."

The operations officer, a squared away lieutenant colonel with a high and tight haircut, pulled an acetate sheet over the map. It was old school – no computerized maps that might fail when the electricity went out during one of the increasing frequent "Climate Caring" brownouts. The overlay divided the territory into three colors – red, pink and clear.

From Ohio to Iowa, it was almost all red in the southern half of the states. A few of the small towns were pink. Only a few of the areas around the bigger towns showed no red at all.

"Now the fun part. You know the President closed the border tonight. That's an indicator. We also have credible intel of a build-up of red armored and infantry forces south of Evansville, Owensboro and, of course, at Fort Knox. At least three US divisions. They could come north at any time. If they do, our 172nd Brigade defends the western half of Indiana, with the Hoosier People's Forest as our east boundary. The 363rd is moving south to be ready to occupy positions in the eastern half. The 416th is on our other flank in Illinois. Of course, the 416th's troops are on strike right now because their mess hall does not offer a vegan alternative," Deloitte said.

"So, if you look at the map," he continued. "You see we'd be defending alone, at least until we get reinforced, deep inside red territory. That means there is no rear area for us. Everywhere is the front line."

A sergeant appeared with a cup of black coffee. Deloitte had mentioned off-handedly that he was tired and could use some a few minutes before, and even in a little thing like this his soldiers were trying to fulfill his intent. He took a sip. Good. The mess sergeant had somehow come up with real coffee. He resolved not to ask how – best he did not know.

Deloitte looked out at his officers and senior NCOs. Most had never been in action; only a few had held over like him from the old US Army after the Split. The PR military was a low-prestige institution, having to beg for every penny from a government more focused with paying off domestic constituents than providing for a defense from outsiders. The US, on the other hand, was highly militarized – a result of the red states' martial tradition, the pro-military bent of its conservative founders, and because it had to carry the full weight of defending North America after the blues went back on the deal they made to share the burden in the Treaty of St. Louis that formalized the Split.

"There is some good news. We are getting a helicopter package of four Blackhawks," Deloitte said.

"Jimmy Carters!" Major Little piped up. The name of the PR's utility helicopters had been adjudged "problematic" and had been changed to honor one of its most revered former US presidents.

"And four Apaches," continued Deloitte.

"Woodrow Wilsons!" shouted Little.

"The helicopter package will be here in Bloomington centered at Monroe Municipal Airfield. We are also getting two Predator drones, with Hellfire capability. They and the controllers will be collocated there. It's out in the boonies, but we need the runway. S3, slice off a platoon for security. S4, figure out the feeding, fueling and arming." The ops and logistics officers nodded and jotted down their instructions.

"We also need to make sure the operations order addresses issues of intersectionality –," began Major Little.

"Sergeant Major, help the major leave." Little got up and ran to the door ahead of the senior NCO, who seemed disappointed not to have a chance to assist.

"I'm calling HQ!" the Diversity Officer shouted, and then he slipped out the door. It slammed shut behind him.

"We don't have orders to assist the civilian police yet," Deloitte said. "That may come to pass, because they don't know shit about counterinsurgency and it may all fall onto us to fix this mess for them. If they do, the drones give us 24/7 surveillance and recon. We can use the *Jimmy Carters* to drop in scouts to interdict guerrillas. But we may have to defend against a conventional red move north. I don't know what's going to happen, so we need to plan for both. If we have to roll, it's pretty obvious where we need to focus. There's People's Interstate 69 as one enemy axis heading north-south, and 231 in mid-sector is the other. People's I-64 runs east-west. These will be critical main support routes for us too if the red forces come north, and they are key targets for guerrillas. They cut those and that's a lot of food and other supplies that can't move out of, or through, here. So, here's my basic commander's intent for when you're preparing my courses of action. If it goes down and we get the order, we're going to focus our ops at the center of all those key routes."

"We're going right here," Deloitte said, gesturing to a clear island in the middle of the ops map. "To Jasper."

Turnbull was just lying down in the guestroom bed, Beretta on the nightstand, when his cell rang. The name that came up was "Peter Dolenz." He unlocked it, 1-2-3-4, and answered.

"This is Mike."

"We don't have long," Clay Deeds said unnecessarily. "We're aware of your situation."

"Sorry about the whole guerrilla war thing. I tried to behave."

"You're not the only one who's had that problem, but you probably figured that out. It's starting all across the region. We have 50 seconds."

"Do you want me to slow it down now?" asked Turnbull. "I'm not sure it's something you can set on simmer."

"No. I want you to keep it up. The negotiations – they're at an impasse. Warren closed the border tonight. We need the facts on the ground changed, Kelly. Forty."

"So you want me to crank it up?"

"Do what you do. Make it ungovernable. Thirty seconds."

"What about all these nice people who may die because we're cranking up our secret war?"

"What about all the ones who won't die because we're going to get them out from under the PR's boot. Twenty seconds."

"How long do you need?"

"Seven days to see if negotiations are going to work. You hold out that long, then we're coming in one way or the other. Ten seconds."

"We can hold out for a week, unless Deloitte sends in his troops. Then it's something wholly other."

"Jasper's the key to the whole region. You have to hold it. And that's zero. Good luck, Kelly."

The line went dead.

There was a knock at the door.

"Come in," Turnbull said, the pistol aimed at Langer's face as he opened it.

"I'm not lonely," Langer said. "Just heard you get a call and talking. Something I should know?"

"No," Turnbull replied. He lowered the gun and placed it back on the nightstand next to a glass of water and a paperback.

"What's *The Runewench of Zorgon?*" Langer asked.

"Nothing," snapped Turnbull, pulling the book out of sight.

"M'kay," Langer replied, backing out part way, then stopping. "You sure there's nothing going on you aren't telling us?"

"Nope," Turnbull replied. Langer closed the door, and Turnbull switched off the lamp. He lay there for a long time, staring into the darkness.

Two PSF officers, both male, walked into the Sunrise Diner with a third man wearing plainclothes. Turnbull put down his watery coffee and slipped the locked and loaded Beretta onto his lap. He'd kill the big uniformed one first, and the smaller one second – both headshots, just in case they weren't flabby and were wearing vests under their uniforms. He'd do the detective last, then out the back door. If that stupid dog followed him as he ran, he'd consider shooting it too.

His planning process completed, Turnbull returned to his breakfast. Dale Chalmers was sweating and the Mayor swallowed hard even though his food had not arrived.

"Just be cool," Turnbull said, sipping. The three blues were talking to Becky the waitress, all friendly-like. Were they attempting to woo the populace and win their hearts and minds, or were they just trying to score a little small town strange? Becky seemed to be having neither.

"We're hiding in plain sight," Dale said. "That's the best place to hide."

"No, it's actually a terrible place to hide, but we don't have much choice now," Turnbull said. He agreed to meet at the diner because he could watch this morning's proceedings. There were wall-to-wall PSF outside today in anticipation of the "Voluntary Youth March Against Terrorist Hate Criminals and Intolerance." Turnbull had come in the back door from the rear parking area. It was a small miracle that that stupid dog's barking had not alerted anyone; it was beyond him how it could bark so loud being so small and with a dead frog in its mouth.

The big PSF looked over at them and then tapped the detective on the shoulder and pointed. It looked like he was pointing at the Mayor, an assessment by Turnbull that saved their lives. The trio approached. Turnbull did not reach for his gun just then; he smiled harmlessly as he thought through exactly how, if necessary, he would reach for his gun and kill them all.

"Mayor Silver, you need to come with us," said the detective.

"Where?" the Mayor asked.

"Just some questions. We're talking to a lot of leading citizens today. So, you need to come to the station with us. Now."

"And miss the march?"

"Let's go," said the detective.

The Mayor looked over at Turnbull, who met his eyes. The Mayor rose and the PSF took him by the shoulders.

The detective turned to the two remaining men. "And who are you?"

"Dale Chalmers," said the insurance salesman.

"Mike," Turnbull said. "Mike Nesmith."

"ID?"

Chalmers handed his over. Turnbull took his wallet out of his shirt pocket and removed the driver's license. He handed it to the detective, who looked it over. He then ran them both through a portable reader.

"Why are you so far away from home, Mr. Nesmith?"

"I'm a CPA," Turnbull replied.

"And why are you here in Jasper?"

"I'm CPAing," Turnbull replied innocently. He decided that if the detective asked him to stand he would shoot the detective first, then kill the two PSF. After all, you always had to be prepared to change a plan as the situation developed.

"He's doing accounting for my insurance agency," Dale said. "The new reparations taxes, you know."

"He's one sixteenth Chippewa," Turnbull said. "So, we have to factor that in and it's complicated."

"You're telling me you're an Indigenous Person?" the detective said to Dale.

"Well, yes," said Dale, snippy. "You know, I resent you questioning my First Peoples identity. President Warren suffers from that same kind of racist hate doubt too. We might as well be in the United States again!"

"Are you heritage shaming my client?" asked Turnbull, furrowing his brows with all the intensity he could muster. Now the other diners were starting to stare and the two PSF officers began to look uncomfortable.

The detective handed them back their identification. "I didn't mean to say you weren't an Indian," he said.

"Indian?" Becky the waitress exclaimed from across the diner. "Did you just call him an 'Indian'?"

"Are you profiling him?" said Turnbull to the stricken detective. "What next, are you going to call him a wagon burner?"

"No, I never –" stuttered the PBI detective. The PSF officers visibly stepped back from him, as if they thought him contagious. He turned around and walked fast out the door. The PSF officers followed at a distance, bringing along the Mayor.

"Wagon burner?" asked Dale.

Turnbull shrugged. "We had some stupid diversity session back in basic training and they encouraged us to share all the epithets we'd ever heard. That was supposed to build bridges or something. A guy from Oklahoma shared that one. And we had an Apache who called him a 'cousinfucker' right back. Then they started kicking each other's asses. So, it was memorable."

"The protest is almost ready to start," Dale said.

"We don't want to miss that," Turnbull said. "You got it all squared away?"

"I think so."

They walked out front on the sidewalk. Across the street, a pair of workers were desperately trying to scrub something off of the brick face of the old hardware store. Via the medium of white spray paint, someone had rendered the crude image of a large penis next to the words "PSF SUCK THIS."

Main Street was crowded, not only with PSF but with regular citizens too. The local businesses had been ordered to have their workers attend and observe the "Voluntary Youth March Against Terrorist Hate Criminals and Intolerance." To make sure everyone did, the PSF had blocked off not only the streets for the march but also the key roads out of town lest anyone try to sneak away home.

There were a lot of people milling about near the front of the diner, mostly grumbling. A woman with long, straight hair and a purple crystal around her neck was there too, smiling and yapping about how, "This is so wonderful to see youth spontaneously reject hate crimes!" She checked her watch. Only a few more minutes until the spontaneous protest was scheduled to begin.

The children from all the local schools were gathered at the north end of Main Street where it intersected 15th. Their teachers were busy attempting to wrangle them into something like order. The PSF had forced the town's only licensed print shop owner to open up the prior evening after the principal had received a special permit to print up a variety of placards and banners. The eager principal was shouting in her bullhorn, having her subordinates herd the high school kids up front and the elementary school kids to the back.

Carl Hyatt was a senior, and his pockets were full of rocks. Like everyone else, he was wearing jeans and the white school sweatshirt – on the front in red letters it said "Jasper High School" and on the back it read "Our Most Important Subject Is Diversity And Inclusion." The sweatshirts had been distributed at the beginning of the year, and none of the teachers had yet noticed the plural problem.

At seventeen, Carl's prospects were unpromising. He got good grades – very good grades, in fact – but his guidance counselor was very clear. This son of a single mom who worked as a bookkeeper for the grain storage co-op was much too privileged for his dream school, the newly-nationalized Notre Dame, since his great-great-great grandfather had immigrated to Indiana from Dusseldorf and not from some more favored locale.

"Maybe you could start identifying as trans," the counselor helpfully suggested. Carl just walked out.

And maybe he could go spin his wheels in the community college system and then go on assistance and collect a weekly pittance. Without a degree from one of the prestigious colleges – and the connections he could make there – he was never going to gain admittance to the People's Republic's elite. The door was shut to him. It would be a life of taking the scraps the masters chose to toss him from their table. His friends didn't see that, but Carl was smart enough that he did so with crystal clarity.

And it gnawed at him.

Since then, his grades had declined and he had received several warnings from the principal for "lack of commitment to progressive change" and "incorrect thinking." Ms. Marfull took seriously her task of providing the People's Republic with thoroughly committed participants in the struggle for change. Without intervention, privileged youths like Carl Hyatt would embrace and perpetuate the racist and sexist paradigms that unconsciously formed their worldviews. It was up to her to help them in their battle against their original sin; she could at least neutralize the contagion, though the carrier himself was a lost cause.

She paid Carl special attention, especially lately as the local hate criminals turned violent. His kind was potentially dangerous.

"Let the voices of the children demand justice!" Marfull shouted through her bullhorn as her subordinates continued to try to form up the kids for the march. She checked her watch. They needed to start in just eight minutes.

Carl Hyatt had gotten the news of Turnbull's confrontation with the PVs just like everyone else – from fellow townspeople. Some were delighted, others frightened, for they feared the repercussions. They wanted to hunker down and hope the bad times would just pass them by.

And some locals had been horrified – these were mostly the people who dutifully flew whatever the current People's Republic flag was and berated their neighbors for carbon insensitivity for grilling hamburgers. Now those people were called "Tories" – Carl recognized the term from the American Revolution, but not from his school, which taught "people's history," not *history* history. Instead, he got it from books he secretly borrowed from neighbors – well before Turnbull arrived, there had been secret clubs that covertly passed around books that were no longer available to buy.

The Tories were PR loyalists, and they were a threat to people like Carl.

The news of the PVs being run out of town had thrilled him, and a number of his pals who likewise had packed their pockets with rocks before the march. Word spread that something more was happening, that people were organizing, that folks were going out in the woods and digging up their rifles, that they would finally be standing up to the PR.

Carl wanted in.

"You're too young," Dale Chalmers had told him. Carl had shown up at the office after school and demanded to talk to him alone. Dale had no idea how the kid had figured out that he was part of the resistance, but the fact Carl did was impressive. Still, at seventeen, the kid was too young to be running and gunning, as Turnbull had put it. But there were other things teens could do that would hopefully keep them out of the literal line of fire.

Carl selected several friends with similar sympathies – and he avoided the suck-ups and go-along types who the administration allowed to run the student government or who joined the Obama Youth Club and monitored fellow students for improper thoughts and attitudes. With their blue sashes, they wandered the halls and reported their findings to the administration at the end of each day. Carl had been tagged a number of times for "after school reeducation" – luckily, the teacher who got stuck running it, because of his own bad attitude, was an old PE teacher. The guy had been in the Navy before the Split and didn't hide the US flag tattoo on his right bicep. Instead of haranguing the imprisoned students about their thought crimes, he would lock the door, shut the curtains, and burn up the time screening forbidden films like *Dirty Harry* and *Animal House* on an ancient DVD player.

Carl was in the church in a back pew when the PVs opened fire. He and his mother were unharmed, but he was splattered with blood from an elderly woman they had shot in the face.

Carl asked Dale for a weapon. Turnbull, who would not meet with Carl personally due to security concerns, directed Dale to exploit the young people's greatest assets. Teens appeared harmless and with their bikes – driving was forbidden until 23 in the PR because of climate change – they had exceptional mobility within town and could easily avoid check points and roadblocks without drawing attention.

Soon, Carl was organizing his friends to spy on and report PSF and PBI personnel movements and deployments. He would then take the information his cell gathered, compile it, and report back to Dale. Carl was aware there were other cells out there – obviously someone was responsible for the shot-up PSF cruisers his people were reporting being towed back into town – but he did not know who they were. He just knew he'd rather be doing that than spying.

But just gathering information was not enough for him. He and his pals started by using a sharpened screwdriver to poke holes in the tire sidewalls of PSF cruisers left unattended. After disabling three cars the first night, the PSF took to leaving an officer to guard the vehicle when the others got out. They could do so since they had now taken to traveling with four to a vehicle for safety.

Carl remembered some spray cans that had been left in the garage by the family down the street that had picked up and left in the middle of the night. He liberated them, and his cell began tagging walls around town with graffiti of increasingly profane and insulting intensity. They had created a very special one for just this march, but Carl was disappointed to see some government workers actually working and trying to remove it. Too bad – he was pretty proud of his phallocentric masterpiece.

Well, he thought, then they'd have to do something else to liven up the protest.

Ms. Marfull was shouting through her bullhorn, and while the Obama Youth were eager to obey, filling the front ranks of the march in their blue sashes, the rest of the students moved sluggishly and passive aggressively. As they failed to comply with all deliberate speed, the principal's amplified hectoring increased, and the kids – sensing her growing frustration – only moved more slowly as they fell into order.

The march began twelve minutes late, with the high school Obama Youth Club at the head holding a long banner across the front rank that read "JASPER YOUTH IN PROGRESSIVE SOLIDARITY WITH PSF." Behind the beaming blue true believers were the regular students, many half-heartedly holding signs with slogans like "PEOPLE'S JUSTICE AGAINST TERRORISTS NOW!" and "PR AND PALESTINE: THE STRUGGLE CONTINUES."

Another placard read "YOUR GENDER IS YOUR CHOICE!" while a few feet away, a kid used his "SOCIALISM IS SCIENTIFIC" sign, which featured a picture of President Warren for some reason, to poke another boy, who shouted "Stop it, racist!" and started crying. Following them were the junior high and elementary school kids, several of whom ran out of the ranks to pet some stray dogs that had come over to bark at the spectacle.

At the end of the procession came the high school band, which struck up "We Dedicate Ourselves To Inclusiveness," the song that had been the national anthem of the People's Republic until it itself had recently been declared insufficiently inclusive – specifically, because it "ignores and denies the existence of differently-sized, abled and gendered beings." There had been a lot of controversy about trying to write a new national anthem, so they finally settled on an instrumental. Unfortunately, the band did not know the new tune yet, so they stuck with the old tune and hoped no one would notice. Only the blue-sashed Obama Youth Club kids even attempted to sing along, most forgetting the majority of the lyrics except for the chorus. The chorus concluded, "And every village/rejects white privilege!"

The march began its slow progress south on Main Street past perpendicular east-west streets blocked off with sawhorses. The ranks, except for the first ones in which the blue sashes tried to keep in some semblance of order, soon disintegrated into a mass cluster of uniformed students. Carl and his friends, about a half-dozen of them, maneuvered themselves into the middle of the pack, hidden from the view of the teachers marching along the flanks in order to keep the group moving forward.

There were a lot of PSF deployed along the route, including what appeared to be the head of the local station – she was surrounded by a half-dozen officers. And they all carried long weapons.

The people of Jasper were largely indifferent to the march. They sort of stood there, their attendance noted, but offering no more enthusiasm than the minimum they could get away with. There were exceptions – a few Tories applauded a bit too loudly and shouted encouragement.

"Fight hate criminals and denialists!"

"Progressive youth is our future!"

"There's no need to fear expressing your chosen gender identities!"

Jasper was a small town, so Carl recognized most of the collaborators – and made a mental note of them.

The march moved at a leisurely pace toward the center of town and the old courthouse, with teachers shouting and gesturing for their charges to stay in line. The band was playing something no one could hear over the chattering students.

There were a lot more people in Courthouse Square. Except for a few Tories waving and cheering, must townspeople just stared in sullen silence.

Carl slipped the pre-knotted bandana he was carrying around his neck and reached into his pocket.

"Get ready," he told his friends as they did the same.

"What exactly are they going to do?" Turnbull said to Dale as the protest march entered the square.

"Not sure," Dale replied. "He told me not to worry about it, that no one was going to get hurt – he said 'really hurt' but he wouldn't say anything more. Said I didn't need to know."

"I like the OPSEC," Turnbull replied. "But this is the downside of decentralization. Sometimes it's just too damned decentralized."

"I got folks getting video though," Dale said. "So I hope it's at least entertaining."

When Turnbull had seen the news report promising the march, he knew the resistance had to react somehow. The whole purpose of the march – and of forcing the populace to watch – was to rub the power of the State in their faces. The message – we have your children, and we have you – was loud and clear.

It could not go unanswered.

Turnbull had quickly dismissed any thought of an attack on the PSF guarding route. That was an invitation to a bloodbath. A fair chunk of the town was actively supporting the resistance, and there were the Tories supporting the PR, but most of the townspeople – while to some extent supportive of the goals of the resistance – were still uncommitted. The killings at the church were sad, but they were also out of sight – what wasn't on video simply wasn't. And the tragedy could be (and was) blamed on overzealous People's Volunteers, who were supposed to be simply some concerned citizens spontaneously acting outside of the government's control to protect progressive change from haters, denialists, racists, and anyone else the PR declared bad.

But if the resistance recklessly sparked a massacre involving these kids in the middle of town in broad daylight, the guerrillas would alienate the populace and that would mean their demise. The insurgency could continue if the majority of people simply averted their eyes; if the PR won back their hearts and minds, then the guerrillas would die like fish trapped in a dried up pond.

"I could walk out and shoot that principal," Langer had suggested the prior evening. "I don't have to kill her, just put one in her leg. As an example."

Turnbull shook his head. "Same problem. If we start shooting, we buy every kid who gets killed."

"What if they start shooting?" Langer said.

"Then they do."

Now, as the march approached, Turnbull and Dale moved north to get a better view.

"Those kids don't have any guns, right?" asked Turnbull.

"Nope," Dale said.

"How about anything that *sounds* like guns, like firecrackers?"

"No, those are way illegal and hard to get too. Don't worry, Carl's not stupid."

"I'm not worried about Carl being stupid," Turnbull said, pausing to glance at a PSF officer standing guard in the street, AK slung over his back, eating from a bag of the generic potato chips they got as part of their additional food allotment.

The gaggle of students was now nearly all inside of Courthouse Square. Ms. Marfull had led the blue sashes with their long banner around the east side of the courthouse intending to circle back and march the students back up to the northern assembly area again.

In the midst of the mass of white sweatshirts, Carl and his friends each drew a rock from their pockets. They would have used eggs if they could, but eggs were hard to carry and besides, they were very expensive. You didn't just throw away perfectly good food like in the old days.

They weren't big rocks, but they weren't small rocks either. They were just the right size to get the right reaction. Together, the students pulled up their bandanas to cover their faces.

"Now!" shouted Carl, and he threw his rock over the heads of the other students into the packed ranks of blue-sashed Obama Youth Club members. A volley of a half-dozen more stones followed, then another volley, and another.

The Obama Youth kids didn't react as a group to the first volley; several cried out and clutched their scalps. They did react at the second, as rocks found soft heads and they began to scatter as they realized they were under a rocky attack. The front rank, several of its members cradling sore skulls, dropped the "JASPER YOUTH IN PROGRESSIVE SOLIDARITY WITH PSF" banner on the street, where the scattering students trampled it as they fled. Others shrieked and howled, scrambling to get away.

More rocks flew. Now Carl and his friends were shouting and yelling themselves, half profanities and half "RUN! RUN!" to stir the pot even more. Some of the kids around them saw what was happening and joined in. Placards flew into the air. The regular students, smiling and laughing, took advantage of the chaos to scatter, some running toward the courthouse, others toward the sidewalks. The middle school kids broke ranks too; only the little elementary kids stayed put, watching the march break apart with wide, frightened eyes.

The band kept playing, not seeing they were serenading pandemonium.

Carl had a few more rocks and with the Obama Youth dispersed, he searched for targets. Ms. Marfull was up ahead, shouting incoherently into her bullhorn. He took careful aim and let fly. The rock sailed straight toward her and hit inside the speaker cone. The principal dropped the bullhorn like it gave her an electric shock. Feedback roared, and so did Carl – in laughter.

Ms. Marfull saw him.

The children were running wild through the square, teachers trying desperately to corral them, the spectators starting to laugh and point.

Turnbull smiled. The authorities looked ridiculous, and Dale's people were recording it all on video. They would upload it, and before the internet controllers could snuff it out it would hopefully go viral and the PR would be a laughingstock.

Ms. Marfull turned and saw a chunky and perplexed PSF officer watching the remnants of the disintegrated protest running rampant through the square.

"Officer, officer!"

He looked at her, puzzled.

"Huh?" he said, not sure what she expected him to do about her uncontrollable charges.

"That boy! That boy there! He did this! Him!"

Carl saw the principal and the officer talking, and her pointing him out, and he stopped smiling. Students running in all directions darted between them, but now Marfull was pulling the officer along behind her as they came at him, trotting. Then Carl smiled again – he realized that PSF guy could never catch him. He laughed, and Marfull halted, furious, humiliated.

Carl turned to run.

"Stop him!" Marfull shouted.

The PSF officer was almost out of breath already. Carl turned and began to sprint, and the officer raised his AK and put a burst of three bullets through Carl's back at lung level.

The crowd seemed to pause for a moment at the sound of the gunshots, and then true chaos erupted. Joy and laughter became fear and terror as everyone, student, teacher, and spectator, sought to escape.

Carl staggered for a few seconds, and then fell face first into the street. Marfull and the PSF officer stood there, stunned, and then the officer ran away. Marfull just stared until Turnbull pushed her out of the way and Dale followed.

They knelt at Carl's body and Turnbull checked his pulse. Dead.

"Turn him over," Turnbull said.

"What?" Dale said, not quite believing what had happened.

"Turn him over!"

Dale did.

"And pull down the mask."

"Why?"

"Do it!" Turnbull yelled, and Dale did it.

Blood was trickling out of the corner of Carl's mouth.

Turnbull stood and pulled out his phone. He took five photos.

"What are you doing?" Dale said.

"I'm making sure Carl didn't die for nothing," Turnbull said. And then they disappeared along with everyone else.

11.

Just after sundown, Larry Langer and two others knocked on the front door of Donny Moss's modest two-story house on the west side of town.

Moss opened the door, puzzled. He thought he recognized Langer from the television. Wasn't he some kind of criminal?

"Yes?" Moss said, cautiously.

"Get your shoes, Mr. Moss," Langer said. "You need to come with us back into town to open up your print shop."

"What? It's almost nine…"

"I'm not asking you, and I don't really care if you have your shoes on or not. I was just being polite. But you are coming with us."

A few minutes later they were in a Buick navigating the side streets toward the center of town. Moss was in back with Langer; the two up front kept watch for PSF cruisers, but there weren't any roaming the streets tonight. The security forces were hunkered down in the station house on the other side of town, expecting retribution after what happened at the demonstration earlier that day.

They didn't use the headlights, and Langer had opened the trunk and pulled the wires from the brake lights, so they drove through the dark using the ambient light. Near the print shop, they parked and Langer took his passenger up to the front door. After some fumbling with the keys, Moss got the door opened and they went inside.

"I don't understand what you want," he said, frightened. Moss had always done his best to avoid trouble. To his horror, it appeared now that trouble had sought him out.

Langer took a thumb drive out of his pocket and held it up. Moss stared, confused.

"I need some posters, Mr. Moss. About a hundred, if you please."

"I can't print any posters," Moss said, miserable. "You don't have a permit."

"You guessed right there. I most certainly do not have a permit to print the posters of what one of our more artistically-inclined compadres did up on this computer stick. But you're going to print 'em up anyway."

"I can't," Moss whimpered. "They'll arrest me. The printers, they have counters and the government checks to make sure I haven't printed anything more than allowed."

"Well, Mr. Moss," said Langer. "Then when they come and check your machines and see you've printed a hole shitload of extra posters, then you can honestly tell them that some of the local boys came in here and told you that if you didn't do it, they were going to splatter your brains all over your shop."

Moss swallowed, and took the thumb drive.

"I expect you saw the town this morning," Kunstler said coldly to the wide-eyed Lieutenant Kessler. He was standing in the doorway of her office in the station. She put down her Starbucks latte.

"Yes, I saw." What the inspector was describing was hard to miss, and there was no doubt what he was referring to.

But Kunstler still wanted to make his point and he produced a tattered poster, the edges ragged where it had been ripped off a wall. The photo was in full color and showed the dead Carl Hyatt lying on the street. The blood flowing down from the corner of his mouth and collecting on the asphalt was bright red.

In large white letters – Arial Bold – it read "THE PSF MURDERS OUR KIDS."

Kunstler gave Kessler a moment to take it in, then crushed it into a ball in his hands.

"Dozens of them, everywhere. Get your officers on the street, Lieutenant. Right now. All of them. We need to demonstrate that we control this town, not these terrorists."

Kessler's eager nodding was interrupted by a ruckus across the squad room. Two plainclothes PBI detectives were frog-marching Donny Moss into the station.

"The printer," Kunstler said.

The PBI agents brought Moss before their boss. Kunslter looked the miserable little man up and down.

"I didn't do anything! They made me! They said they'd kill me!" Moss whimpered.

"Interrogation," Kunstler said, and Moss's eyes went wide as they dragged him away. Kunstler turned back to the lieutenant. "Get on it. In the meantime, I have an interrogation to finish myself."

The PSF officers went out on the street fully armed and ready, hiking up and down the main streets in a show of force. The people pointedly ignored them; for the most part the citizenry pretended the armed invaders weren't even there.

A few lost it and their curses got them tackled, hooked up, and roughly dragged back to the station. Even as the PSF officers hooked up a protestor, a crowd would gather – not too close, not too aggressive, and respecting the AKs pointed at them, but still there, watching.

The PBI detectives, drawing on their pattern analysis software and input from electronic surveillance, headed out on raids of likely insurgents. A teacher, a plumber, a fireman and more – all were dragged into the station and hauled into interrogation rooms where the PBI read them their rights with fists and batons.

By sundown there had not been too many incidents, and they had made a dozen arrests, but there had been no shootings and no real attacks on the security forces. Kessler breathed a sigh of relief.

"This town is ours," Kessler said proudly to her PBI counterpart.

"We've only just started," Kunstler replied, wiping the blood off his hands. "Tomorrow we continue. We show them we are in control."

"What did he tell you?" the lieutenant asked.

"Nothing interesting yet," said Kunstler. "But we have all night."

The inspector walked back to Interrogation Room #2 and opened the door. A beefy PSF officer, stripped down to his t-shirt, was standing over a slumped and bloodied man handcuffed to the suspect's chair.

"Wake him up," Kunstler said, and the big officer smashed Ted Cannon hard in the jaw. If the chair had not been bolted to the floor, he would have gone flying into the wall.

"So Deputy," Kunstler said, leaning in at Cannon's swollen face. "As we've discussed for lo these many hours, you're the only real candidate for being the spy who told the terrorists about the People's Volunteers. So why not just do your duty and admit it and we can move on to who you told?"

"I told you," Cannon said, his fat lips and shredded mouth muffling his voice. "I didn't tell anyone anything."

"Well, then who did?

"How the hell should I know? Maybe one of these assholes looking to score a bribe," he said, gesturing to the big thug beside him. The officer did not bother to wait for the inspector's signal and drove his fist hard into Cannon's gut. The deputy coughed and retched.

"You know, the problem with you and your terrorist friends is privilege," Kunstler said. "You were privileged before the Split and you think you still are. But you aren't, not anymore. Not in the People's Republic."

"Like I said, I don't know who dimed out your punks," Cannon said. The thug smacked his head hard.

"Those were patriots, Deputy, murdered by your friends for daring to speak truth to power."

"What does that crap even mean?" That drew another hard blow.

"Look, Deputy Cannon, I'm sure Davis here will be happy to pummel you all day and all night if need be, and I'll be happy to watch. But I don't think we're getting anywhere this way, as delightful as our discussion has been so far. So," Kunstler said, picking up a folder off the table and opening it. "Maybe tomorrow we start off again, only this time we bring in your sister and her husband the middle-aged insurance agent and their kids and Davis and I talk to them while you watch? How about that idea? Sound fun?"

Cannon lifted his head and stared, breathing shallowly, his face inscrutable under the swelling and blood.

"Well, you take tonight and think it over and if tomorrow morning you aren't more cooperative then we'll invite your family to participate. Sound good?"

Cannon said nothing. Kunstler shook his head.

"You're right-wing scum," Kunstler said.

"I'm a real cop," said Cannon. "Not a thug."

"A cop. Pathetic. And you're probably proud of it." Kunstler looked over at David. "Throw this hate criminal in a cell."

"I don't know where Cannon is," Dale said. "He was supposed to be here already."

Turnbull considered for a moment. "Then let's hurry this up. Do we all have our targets?"

There were a half-dozen other insurgents, men and women, in the living room of the zombie home – a different one than where Langer and Turnbull had stayed. All of them nodded.

"You sure you want to do this yourself, Larry?" Turnbull asked Langer.

"Oh, this one is most definitely mine," Langer said.

"It's a woman," Turnbull said.

"Well, I try not to be too much of a male chauvinist."

"Okay, we know ours. Everyone else? Are you absolutely clear on what you'll do?" The others nodded. Turnbull stood up.

"Then let's do it. 0715 hours tomorrow. Let's synch our watches."

Becky the waitress woke up at 6:52 a.m., grabbed her clothes off the chair then went straight into the bathroom and turned on the shower. Though the name had changed, the Best Western logo was still on all the old towels.

"Becky?" a man shouted from back in the room.

"I'm taking a shower!" she answered. Something muffled came back.

Becky slipped into the shower and scrubbed herself hard, then turned it off and stepped out and dried herself with the threadbare towels. She pulled on her clothes and combed her hair.

7:07 a.m.

She sat down on the toilet lid and waited.

In the former Best Western's tiny gym room, two PBI detectives got onto the exercise bikes and began pedaling. The television set was on the People's Republic's number one network, MSNBC. Morning anchor and national institution Rachael Maddow was touting the upcoming segment where she would read her dream journal.

Three PBI detectives walked out of the ex-Best Western and into the front parking lot. No one around, they noted. They walked quickly to their 2022 government issue Ford Fusion. The PSF officer guarding the parking lot nodded to them. The driver backed out, and pull onto North Newton Street.

Lieutenant Kessler and three PSF officers in battle gear with AKs walked down Main Street toward the Starbucks. There were a few passers-by, but no more or less than usual. She lifted her head up a little higher as the locals averted their eyes.

"This is my town," she thought.

Becky opened the bathroom door and stepped back into the room. The man in the bed – the same PBI detective who had come and taken the Mayor the other day – lifted his head and smiled.

This shitty assignment got a little less shitty last night, he thought to himself. Guess these hick gals were starved for some city lovin'.

"Big day at work today?" Becky asked as she walked past his suit and the detective's holstered Beretta on the bureau.

"Lots of terrorists to catch," he replied, sitting up.

Becky walked to her purse and glanced at her watch. 7:14.

In the exercise room, Rachael Maddow was reading aloud and intently about her dream of a world where there were no red states anymore, where their oppression had been wiped from the face of the earth. The detective on the left shook his head.

"You think she really dreamed that?"

"Probably. Don't you dream about dead racists?"

"I usually dream about ass –"

His insight was interrupted as the gym room door opened.

The Fusion was headed south on Newton, which was Route 231 inside the town. They passed St. Joseph's church on the right – it was boarded up and the sign out front on the dying lawn said "PEOPLE'S SHELTER COMING SOON."

A hundred meters or so on, they came to 9th Street and stopped at the red. The driver glanced in his rear view mirror. A tan Ford van was idling behind them.

The clock radio read "07:14."

The van pulled to their left, straddling the line of the oncoming lane and started moving forward.

"What's that guy doing?" the driver asked.

Becky picked up her large purse and stood over the bed.

"I've got something for you," she said.

"Good, because it would be sexist for you to expect something from me. I'm glad even here in bumfuck Egypt you're escaping primitive and sexist gender roles."

She glanced at her digital watch, as 7:14:50 turned to 7:14:52.

"So," he said, leering. "What is it? Because I know I deserve something good after how hard I fucked you last night."

Becky reached into her purse and pulled out a Smith & Wesson snub-nosed .38 Chief's Special. The man's creepy face turned frightened.

"I fucked you harder," she said, and shot him in the face.

The cleaning woman – her job title was actually "Room Reconstitution Specialist" – opened the back door and Davey Wohl and his companion walked into the hotel laundry from the rear parking lot. She handed Wohl a key card and walked away back to her work.

Wohl and his partner knew where they were going. They went through the opposite door and into the first floor hallway, walking fast. The gym room was coming up. They drew their pistols from under their coats. Wohl had a Sig Sauer .40 caliber and his partner one of the Berettas liberated from the PVs.

Wohl paused outside the door for twenty long seconds until his watch read "7:15," then swiped the keycard and pushed open the door. There were two men in their thirties on exercise bikes pedaling away while Rachael Maddow spoke into the camera.

Both bikers turned and looked at them, puzzled. Wohl and his companions stepped in and they raised their weapons. There was a thud from somewhere upstairs that Wohl heard over Maddow's droning monologue. They aimed.

"Hey wait –" one rider began.

The insurgents fired again and again, then each finished off one of the PBI men with a headshot. Ears ringing fiercely, they walked out the door, leaving the two detectives dead on the floor. Back in the gym room, to her silent audience, Maddow concluded,

"And that's my dream, a dream of final victory over the forces of hate."

The van whipped around the Fusion on the driver's side looking like it would pass them and roar through the intersection, but it skidded to an immediate stop right beside them.

"What the hell?" sputtered the driver.

The side door of the van slid open. Two men and two women were inside, aiming semi-auto rifles.

They opened fire, shattering all of the windows on the driver's side. The driver himself took the first round through his forehead, splattering brains on his passenger beside him. Then several more rounds slammed into him and into the detective in the back seat as well. They didn't try to flee – they just jerked under the impacts and died where they sat.

The detective in the passenger's seat was hit twice but didn't know it with the adrenaline, and he was big enough and the 5.56 mm rounds were light enough that they didn't stop him from opening his door and tumbling out on the street.

The dead driver's foot came off the brake, and the Fusion began the drift forward even as the firing continued and the roof erupted in bullet holes.

The passenger rolled out onto the asphalt and managed to draw his Beretta even as the noise of the firing threatened to overwhelm him. He got to his feet just as the trunk of the drifting Ford passed by him, leaving him exposed in the street.

He fired a shot into the van – it hit one of the women in the stomach and she collapsed, groaning. The other three shooters still had about a half dozen rounds in their mags and they proceeded to dump them into the staggering detective. He shuddered and fell back into the gutter. The unharmed woman aimed carefully and shot off the top of his head as he lay there. Then she dropped her magazine and pulled out a fresh one.

"What are you waiting for?" she shouted to the van driver. "Go!"

One of the men pulled the sliding door shut as the van took off west on 9th.

One of the PSF officers grabbed the elderly woman at the front of the Starbucks order line and pushed her away.

"What the hell!" the woman shouted. There were a half dozen civilians inside the store, and they all looked over – all except for one man in the corner with his face buried in the *New York Times*.

"You best shut the fuck up," screamed the officer. Kessler ignored the unpleasantness and stepped up to the barista.

"My usual," she said. The barista turned to his buddy.

"The usual," he said. The buddy nodded. Extra loogie it is.

At 7:15, Kelly Turnbull opened the door of the bathroom and stepped out with his black Remington 870 pump action. One of the PSF men was about ten feet away. Turnbull lifted it by its pistol grip, planted the stock in his shoulder and fired a shell full of double aught buckshot straight at the blue's face.

His face was erased, with most of it splattering one of his buddies, some of it catching the old woman, who shrieked and ran. Turnbull jacked out the empty shell and pumped a fresh one into the chamber.

The other security man raised his AK, but Turnbull was quicker, firing straight into his chest. The Kevlar plate in his body armor took the brunt of it, but he still flew backwards and crashed into the pastry case, scattering shards of glass among the indifferent scones and rock-hard muffins that Starbucks now sold.

The splattered officer was raising his rifle next to Kessler when there was a roar and his face blew out forward, and he went down what-was-left-of-his-face first. Behind him, Larry Langer stood unsmiling with smoke curling from the barrel of his .357 magnum Colt Python. Around him, the civilians were diving for cover under the tables.

Turnbull stepped forward and pumped the shotgun, then fired again into the PSF officer entangled in the pastry case. The officer stopped moving. Turnbull pumped the 870 again.

"Nope," said Langer, putting the .357 to Kessler's temple as she struggled to take out her Beretta. She froze, quivering.

"You're Kessler, right?" he said.

"Uh no," Kessler said.

"Then why you wearing her uniform?" Langer asked. Kessler looked down and realized her name was on the breast of her black uniform.

"Don't hurt me," she said.

"You killed my family," Langer said, the anger underlying his words becoming more obvious.

"No, not me," she said. "It wasn't me."

Langer pulled back the hammer.

"We need to move," Turnbull said, covering the door with his weapon. The civilians had recovered their senses and were scrambling to escape. The baristas were gone.

"You can't just shoot a woman in cold blood," Kessler said, desperate.

"Yeah," said Langer. "But I can if I – what do they call that? – misgender you."

"I –" Kessler began, but Langer pulled the trigger.

The cruisers' windshields in the parking lot of the PSF station were shattering one after another. Bullets ripped into the sheet metal, singly or stitching across panels. The shotgun pellets would punch out gaping, jagged holes in the steel, especially as the insurgents moved in closer.

The noise from over four dozen weapons all firing was overpowering.

There were maybe a half-dozen officers lying around their vehicles, with only one or two still stirring. Another five or six were pinned down behind their cars, intermittently returning fire – less aim and squeeze than spray and pray.

The PSF station was a squat, one story brick structure with only a few windows, and those were high on the front face of the building near the roof line. What glass there was the insurgents rapidly blew out.

Every few moments, a PSF officer would appear in the front doorway to fire a random AK burst out toward the attackers. The insurgents caught onto the pattern pretty quickly, and two with scoped hunting rifles patiently awaited his next appearance like they were waiting for an eight-point buck. The next time the shooter swung out to blaze away, he caught one .270 and one .308 round and was dead before he hit the floor behind him. The PSF officers inside stopped trying to shoot at the guerrillas out the front door.

The insurgents had been waiting for the quick reaction force to come rushing outside. The 911 calls reporting the assassinations were supposed to begin coming in at about 7:15 or so that morning. But they didn't. The guerrillas had moved into position in, on, and around the nearby buildings, waiting for the PSF officers to spill out to their vehicles and hurry to the various shooting sites, but five minutes later there was still nothing.

Banks was in overall command at the station. He was positioned with his team next to a hardware store with a good view of the front of the PSF station, and his folks were deployed around the perimeter of the building.

There had been no sentries outside when they first arrived, which boggled his military mind. That made it simple for dozens of the insurgents to slowly move into position, surrounding the station, and to stand waiting for the exodus of the quick reaction force. But the force simply did not appear when expected

"Why aren't they coming out? Do you think they see us?" Banks said to a brown-haired woman with an AR15. Her name was Mary. She had moved into his house a few days before; they had known each other since high school but really connected lying on the ground waiting to pump bullets into passing blues.

"Maybe no one called 911," Mary suggested, not taking her aim from the front door.

"I heard the shots from the Starbucks," Banks said. The coffee shop was a few blocks west. He held his M14, barrel down, waiting. Nothing.

"I don't think anyone called it in," Mary replied firmly.

"I suppose that's good. The people won't help them. Means we have their hearts and minds, I guess," Banks said. On the hardware store's wall next to them were three Carl Hyatt posters that had evaded being torn down the way many of the others had been.

"Well, what do we do?" Mary asked. "They need to come outside or the plan won't work."

"Hold on." Bank leaned his rifle against the wall and pulled out a cheap Motorola cell phone he had taken off one of the dead PVs just in case he needed a burner. The battery was out of it, of course – no sense in walking around with something that would broadcast his location – so he had to reinsert the white power cell into the back of the device to turn it on.

"Still nothing," Mary marveled as they watched. The other insurgents were getting restless. Banks punched 9-1-1 into the phone and put it to his ear.

He waited. And waited. His troops looked at him, puzzled.

"You're kidding," Mary said.

"Hold on," Banks said, gesturing and letting it ring.

Several moments later, he spoke.

"Yeah, hi, hey, some PSF guys just got shot at the Jasper Starbucks on Main," he said, then paused, listening.

"Okay, one was female." Another pause.

"Look, I don't know how she identified. Some PSF officers got shot and I think one is a woman." Pause.

"I don't know what their gender identity is. They're bleeding out because they got shot and they're at the Starbucks and someone better come!" He paused again.

"Me? I identify as anonymous." Banks hung up.

"Are they coming?" asked Mary.

"I don't even know," Banks said, taking up his rifle again.

It was a full three minutes before the quick reaction force of PSF officers began pouring out the front door of the building and heading to the parking lot, most still adjusting their body armor. Banks did not give the signal immediately – actually, there was no signal since the ambush was to be initiated by his rifle fire.

When about a dozen PSF officers were outside and the flow slackened, Banks took aim at one male who was fiddling with his helmet and put a round into his upper torso above his vest – not that the vest itself (as opposed to the trauma plate in front that covered most of his chest) was going to stop a .308 round. The officer was violently thrown onto the hood of a cruiser, and then slid off onto the parking lot asphalt. By the time he hit the ground, Banks was shooting another blue, and all the fifty or so insurgents around the station had opened fire.

The guerillas' bullets bounced off the outer brick walls, the gutters, and cracked the panes of the high row of windows. The PSF inside tried to defend themselves, but it was difficult. The police station was not a fort, and it was not designed to provide the sheriff's deputies inside with the mutually supporting fields of fire necessary to defend the position.

Engaging from the front door was a non-starter – no one had removed the body of the PSF officer killed there and no one rushed to take his place. A couple officers tried to rush out the back door. There were no windows at all at the back, so the insurgents had moved up close. The pair of blues had been cut down by a team of insurgents with three Mossberg 12 gauge shotguns and a silver Henry .45-70 lever action repeater that sent its target flying.

There were not a lot of other options. To fire out the windows running just under the roof, the PSF had to push desks against the outer walls, and then stand with head and shoulders exposed to provide aimed fire outside at the attackers. A couple of them tried it. They each drew a swarm of carefully aimed return fire and fell back on the squad room floor, dead before they landed. That was the last of the attempts to fight from the windows.

Banks waved his force around the flank of the parking lot. The few PSF survivors fighting from behind vehicles realized they were in a crossfire. Within a few moments, most of them were dead or wounded. A couple of them tossed away their AKs and shouted that they were giving up. Insurgents rushed into the parking lot, and spirited them away as other guerrillas took up positions closer to the building.

A bulldozer, its blade low, fired up down the street when Banks signaled it. As it passed, Banks, Mary and a couple others took cover behind the blade and awkwardly moved forward toward the front of the station behind the steel's protection. About 30' from the front door, they stopped. From inside, there were some shots and sparks flew off the outer side of the dozer blade. Everyone returned fire into or around the front entrance, and the PSF's return fire was not repeated.

"Hey, you in there! Come out and talk!" shouted Banks. Nothing. No movement, no response.

Turnbull and Langer rushed over to them, low and fast. Turnbull carried his Remington and had slipped on his shades and a tan ball cap. Langer had not picked up a long weapon yet.

"What's the situation?" Turnbull asked.

"Got probably a dozen already. There's some inside but they aren't really engaging."

"Any contact?"

"Not since they shot at us a minute ago."

Turnbull nodded, and yelled.

"Hey you in there, tell your commander to come out and talk!"

Nothing.

"Hey assholes, I'm not waiting all day. Tell your CO to get out here."

Nothing.

"Dumb shits," Turnbull said, shaking his head.

"I got an idea," Langer said.

"Go for it," said Turnbull. Langer grinned.

"Okay boys," he yelled. "Bring up the gas cans. Get it splashed on there good."

The insurgents shrugged, confused. Banks gestured them to stay put. Turnbull smiled, then yelled again.

"You sure you don't want to talk?"

Then a voice came from inside,

"We, we have prisoners!"

"I know," Turnbull replied.

"You burn us, you burn them," said the voice.

"Yeah, well you ought to be thinking hardest about the 'burn us' part. That should be your priority."

"We should discuss a deal," said the voice.

"I'm sick of yelling," Turnbull said over the top of the blade. "You and me on the front steps."

"How do I know you won't shoot me?"

"If I was going to shoot you I'd have already started barbequing you. The stairs, now!"

"All right," replied the voice after a moment.

Turnbull turned to Langer and Banks.

"If those dicks shoot me, go find some gasoline and burn them out." Langer grinned and nodded. Turnbull stood up behind the blade, came around, and walked up the front steps.

He was greeted by a thin man in civilian clothes.

The man extended his hand. "I am Inspector Kunstler."

Turnbull regarded the outstretched paw as if it were herpetic.

"So you're the head motherfucker in charge?" Turnbull asked.

Kunstler seemed taken aback, but rallied. "I'm in charge."

"You must be PBI. Sorry about all your pals."

"What do mean?" asked Kunstler.

"You're lucky you headed into work early. Your Junior Gestapo guys – we hit them all. Oh, and your PSF chief Kessler too. Her coffee came with extra lead."

"That's no loss," Kunstler said. "So, you have a proposal?"

"No. Here's how this happens," Turnbull said. "You all come out without weapons and we don't kill you all."

"I'd like –"

"Oh, did I give you the false impression that this is a negotiation? Tell your punk pals to leave their weapons and come on out and we won't do you."

"We do have some of your friends inside, and that could be problematic for you if we have to keep fighting."

"I have plenty of friends. I won't miss a few."

Kunstler looked him over. "No, I don't believe you would. You aren't from here, are you?"

"Are we sharing now? You should really be focused on convincing us not to shoot you."

"You're in better shape than the locals, and you carry yourself differently. Military. You're an infiltrator, aren't you? You're the one behind all this terrorism."

"Hey Sherlock, the only terrorism in Jasper is you shitheads."

"One man's terrorist is –"

"Don't say it. I hate that cliché. Now, you talk an awful lot, Inspector, and I think you're about ten words away from me shooting you right here and now, truce or not. Are you surrendering, or do I need to get all Kingsford on your asses?"

Kunstler seemed confused.

"Kingsford. It's a kind of charcoal briquette. You know, for barbequing? Oh, right, you banned grilling because of global warming. I ought to shoot you just because of that."

"It's global cooling. Science tells us we're facing another ice age."

"Enough. Are you coming out or not?"

"How will we be treated?" Kunstler asked.

"I promise not to shoot you all. That's the deal. In or out."

"All right. We'll come out."

The prisoners were zip-tied in the parking lot, about 30 of them including a couple wounded PSF officers. The insurgents searched each one, relieving them of wallets, phones, weapons, armor – everything but the clothes on their backs. They looked miserable.

Kunstler sat and glared; Turnbull ensured his restraints were good and tight. Sergeant Greely sat nearby; they found him cowering in the broom closet. Now Turnbull was focused on giving instructions to the insurgents salvaging the captured spoils. A repurposed municipal bus idled by the street, waiting.

A couple medics wheeled out a stretcher with Ted Cannon. He looked like he had gone ten rounds with the San Antonio 49ers' offensive line.

"Wait," Cannon said as they pushed him past where Kunstler sat zip-tied on the pavement. Kunstler looked up, contemptuous. Turnbull, giving directions not far away, noticed the death stare.

"Hey," Cannon said. "I didn't tell you shit. But I knew shit." He smiled and laughed, painfully.

"Next time," said Kunstler. Turnbull walked over and kicked him in the kidney, and Kunstler glared.

"Next time we cross paths," Cannon said, "I'm killing you." The medics wheeled him away.

"You are lucky I gave my word, Inspector," Turnbull said.

"Someday you will be gone back to your racist red homeland, and I'll be back here cleaning out this right wing filth," Kunstler said, smiling.

"Make that *very* lucky I gave my word," Turnbull said. He picked up the PBI agent roughly by his zip-tie binding, ensuring he stretched the arms at as unpleasant an angle as he could without hearing a snap, and lifted the man to his feet. Kunstler glared even more intensely.

"You pray, right red stater?" Kunstler said through clenched teeth. "You all believe in your magical sky king and pray, don't you? Well, you better pray our positions are never reversed because –"

The Beretta was out of Turnbull's thigh holster and pressed up against Kunstler's forehead.

"If you flap your talk hole just one more time, you're finding out if there's life after death," Turnbull said. Behind Kunstler, two insurgents stepped out of the potential splatter cone.

"Nothing to say? No more penetrating theological insights?" Turnbull asked.

The gun didn't move, not a quiver or a shake, as it pushed on the detective's forehead. Kunstler stood, still and silent, growing pale.

"I didn't think so," Turnbull said, a bit disappointed. "Now get your sorry ass on the bus. You're going home."

12.

Colonel Deloitte's finger ran across the map in his main command post outside Bloomington. His battle captain, the officer who was the central collection point for the information coming into the command post (being old school, Deloitte still habitually referred to it as a "TOC," or "tactical operations center," though the nomenclature had changed), stood behind him watching. His S3, the lieutenant colonel operations officer with a high and tight haircut, stood there as well, cradling a notepad.

Behind them, the map NCO observed the officer huddle. It was *his* map. The staff sergeant made the changes and adjustments to it; no one else touched it. Even the commander did not touch the map to change it. So the sergeant kept his wary eye on the officers to make sure they didn't mess with his work. Deloitte was experienced enough that it never occurred to him to do so, but every once in a while some lieutenant with a marker would start heading towards the map and need to be driven away. The staff sergeant was all over that.

"Have you figured out what the order means yet?" Deloitte said to the S3. "Because I'm still baffled."

XX Corps, the higher headquarters for Midwestern combat units had sent down the order to Deloitte's 172nd Brigade an hour ago and they were trying to make sense of it. Back in the old US

Army, something so unclear and confused would have never gotten out the door, and there would have been a face-to-face orders briefing by the division commander for the subordinate units to make sure everyone was synched.

But the divisions were gone now – cutting out that traditional layer of command and control was a cost-cutting move to free up money to be spent on people who oppression kept from supporting themselves somehow – and the corps commander up in Chicago did not seem to want to engage in actual commanding. She had been selected with great fanfare to take charge of the massive XX Corps and "smash the camouflage ceiling." After an undistinguished career in logistics, and after her first order brief a year ago had been a humiliating fiasco – for one thing, she did not understand her corps order of battle and was surprised to learn the corps had some tanks – she stopped engaging in any activity where she might have to display any tactical knowledge. After that, she just hunkered down in the Windy City, attending parties in her medal-bedecked Class A uniform and sending out long missives about the need to combat the real enemy, patriarchy.

"It looks like there's a declaration of martial law in the south Indiana region, and we're supposed to be prepared to move our forces in to establish order," said the operations officer. "It doesn't say when. Until then, it seems to say we have to keep our ground forces north of Route 150, which runs east-west north of Jasper at

Loogootee. But then we are also supposed to fight insurgents south of there, somehow. I don't get it either, sir."

"Corps doesn't want us sending the ground battalions south yet because the reds will see the movement and they might react," Deloitte said. "But it still wants us to make the problem go away. What's the order say about air assets?"

The operations officer reviewed the three pages of the printed order again. "Nothing about air," he said, annoyed. A comprehensive order would have mentioned air operations in detail.

"If there's nothing saying we *can't* use air, then we *can* use it. And I'm going to push the envelope and say we can insert recon teams," directed the colonel. He stared at the map. It was all red except for a strip a few miles in along the border, which was the Ohio River in this sector. There were several military outposts there, mostly observation positions and radar sites monitoring the red forces. But between there and Bloomington, it was scarlet.

"The interstates," Deloitte said, tapping the map. "That's how they influence the fight now that they've taken Jasper. That's how they stop us from deploying quickly. And that's how they make it known everywhere that we are losing even with the media blackout."

"The PSF already cut off the food, fuel and other deliveries into the red areas," said the ops officer. "Whatever is on the interstates is passing through the area, not stopping."

"Most of it is agricultural products moving to the east coast cities from the farm states," Deloitte said. "Food. They can detour north, but that disrupts everything. If the food stops coming, the cities explode."

"And there's no hiding what's happening," said the operations officer.

"What else?" asked Deloitte.

The operations officer reviewed some notes, then looked up. "There's also a lot here, about two of the three pages, about stomping out phallocentrism in the military command structure."

"Tell Major Little I need a detailed memo on how we can most gender-inclusively execute our anti-phallocentrism mission. That should keep the little shit out of my hair for a while. In the meantime, start planning for combat ops. I want to initiate air ops ASAP.

"I-69 north-south and I-64 east-west are the two main arteries through this region," Turnbull said, the AAA map laid out over a desk in the bank branch they were using as a headquarters. The original idea was to use the PSF station as the headquarters, but Turnbull nixed it.

"That's the first place I'd hit with an airstrike," he said. "Clean it out and leave it empty."

The bank was solid, one of the few reinforced buildings in town. It also had a huge pile of PR currency in the vault, which the workers had forgotten to close when they left. That would make for useful kindling.

Larry Langer and Dale Chalmers stood around the desk where the manager used to sit. He was gone now, having fled north with most of the rest of the Tories. They had clogged the roads out of town earlier. Turnbull had directed that they be let go – no need to have a whiny, fussy Fifth Column among them, agitating about imagined racism and homophobia.

The bank was a hive of activity. Lee Rogers stood a few feet away talking to some people about food stocks. Power was already cut; how long the generators could make up for it was anyone's guess. Food and fuel were going to be problems. Nothing was flowing into the area anymore – but with the freeways still open, stuff was flowing *across*.

"You want to cut the freeways?" Langer said.

"That's right. Cutting off 64 and 69 will prevent them from moving military forces quickly. It'll keep them on smaller roads, where they'll be slower and more vulnerable. But it also has a strategic component. It effectively blocks out the agricultural products from Southern Indiana and Illinois completely, and forces goods from further west around on a long detour north. When the country split, the blue folks forgot who feeds them. They need every inch of farmland they can get."

Langer cocked an eyebrow. "So, how does that help us?" he asked.

"What do you mean?" said Turnbull.

"So they gotta tighten their belt in New York City because they aren't getting all the beans and corn they used to. How does that help *us*?"

"It makes them pay attention to us."

"It might just make them pay *too much* attention to us, if you get my meaning," At Turnbull's direction, Langer had organized a number of teams to head north to Bloomington to scout out the People's Republic Army's forces and their locations and report back. The PRA was sitting there for now, but who knew when it might move south to put an end to their little revolt?

"What are you saying?" Turnbull asked.

"I'm just wondering if this was meant to get them off our backs, or if you've got bigger plans."

"Spit it out, Larry," Turnbull said.

"Well, are you doing this for us, or for the US? Because I don't quite see the end game here. Oh, don't get me wrong – I like to fight. I got nothing to lose. Those blue sons of bitches already killed all my family. I'll shoot them until they shoot me. But how does this end for all these nice people like Dale and Lee here?"

Lee had joined them and was looking at Turnbull. So was Dale.

"What's the endgame here, boss?" Lee asked.

Turnbull paused. "There's a good chance this half of the state is going over to the red," he said. "I don't know how or when, or even if. It's a possibility. They're talking about it, the reds and the blues. Secret negotiations"

"Holy shit," Lee said.

"Are the reds going to invade?" Dale said.

"I don't know. There are negotiations. My mission is to make it easier to lose this place than keep it. And your mission is to keep the PR from treating you like dirt, and you're accomplishing it."

"I feel like we're pieces in a bigger game," Dale said. "Do we matter at all?"

"Do you matter to yourselves? I didn't make you fight. I offered to help you if you did. You wanted to live free. Our interests correspond. So now, what's next?"

"We could just stay put, let this settle down," Ted Cannon said. He had gotten out of the hospital and made his way over to the headquarters. His face still looked like a stretch of Chechnyan ruins, but he was on his feet. He had battle gear on and an AK was over his shoulder.

"You think it will simmer down? You worked with them," Turnbull said. "You know them better than any of us. Do you think they can tolerate people living free in the heartland of the People's Republic?"

"They won't think about anything else until we're back under their thumb," Ted said. "You're right, I know them. They can't stand defiance, and they'll do whatever they have to do not only to get us back under control but to make sure we can never stand up to them again."

"If we don't cut those roads, they can swing in and around us fast with their heavy army units before we can stop them. That's our tactical reason to do it. And there's the strategic reason – hitting them in the stomach," Turnbull said.

"I don't care much about how much they have to eat in New York City," Langer said. "But if those freeways are open they can move on us before we know they're coming. So, that's gotta get done."

"I have some ideas," Turnbull said.

"Me too," replied Langer.

"What else?" Turnbull asked.

Dale spoke up. "I'll get working on the coordination with other areas," he said. While the PSF had not been completely driven out of the regions to the east and west – except for the Hoosier National Forest, which no PSF unit would dare enter – much of the map across south Indiana and Illinois and even Ohio was red. There were enough friends and relatives across the area that hooking up contact between resistance units was relatively easy.

"Good," Turnbull said. "And get the Mayor working to organize the noncombatants. We'll need the hospital up and running even though most of the doctors ditched. Plus, we need the stuff we talked about built."

Lee Rogers nodded. Her logistics portfolio included construction and manufacturing.

"What do you want me to do?" Ted Cannon said.

"You are ex-military, right?" Turnbull asked.

"MP," Cannon replied.

Turnbull motioned him over and bent over the map on the desk. "Okay, while I'm out dealing with the interstates, I need you organizing the defense in depth north of town. Divide into sectors; Dale knows the plan. We need to be able to defeat the main force advance, but we also need to fight the counter-recon battle. If I know their commander, he's going to flood the zone with recon, surveillance, and target acquisition elements. You gotta stop them."

Ted nodded. During a conventional fight, military police abandoned their usual role of pulling over drunk privates driving back from the club and undertook rear area security, meaning locating and eliminating spies and infiltrators.

The huddle broke apart, and they went off in their various directions, all except Turnbull. He surveyed the activity. The locals had slid into their new roles quickly and with remarkably few bumps. Many had military experience, which helped. But mostly these people had been organizing their own businesses, their churches, and their community activities from Little League to parades all their lives. Maybe it was different elsewhere, but here they didn't look to anyone else to do for them. When the PR government left, the Mayor simply created a new one. These people always assumed they would do for themselves, so when someone needed to step up someone always did. Turnbull was providing them some tactical expertise and some guidance, but this war was decentralized, not dictated. They had to fight it if they wanted to be free.

Turnbull watched them proceed with satisfaction. This was becoming a real insurgency. Now all they had to do was not get killed.

Closing the freeway was a two part-operation. Turnbull oversaw Part One.

Six sets of four vehicles entered at various points on I-69 and I-64. There was not a lot of traffic, but there was some – mostly long haul trucks. And they were the target.

Turnbull's team waited by the side of the road west of the Route 161 junction with I-64. Within five minutes a pair of dull gray tractor-trailer rigs passed them. The four vehicles pulled out into the freeway.

"Trail, anything, over?" Turnbull called into the mic from the first vehicle, a Chevy Blazer.

"Negative, over," reported the last vehicle. No PSF in sight.

"Engaging, out," said Turnbull. He put down the mic and picked up the Remington 870. It was full of deer slugs.

He didn't bother cocking it. There was always one in his chamber.

The rigs were doing 60, with the second drafting the first. Turnbull nodded to his driver and the Chevy swung out into the left lane and punched it. The green terrain began flying by at 70, then 80, until the SUV caught up parallel to the first rig and hung there, next to its quarry.

The driver did not look over at him.

"Honk," Turnbull said. The Chevy's horn honked, but the truck driver ignored them.

"Okay," Turnbull said. "So we're playing horsey."

He hung the 12-guage out the window, pointed to the outside tire of the rear double tire and fired.

That the driver reacted to, trying to keep control of the monster truck, which swung across the road and almost side-swiped the Chevy.

Now the driver finally looked over at Turnbull, and Turnbull took the opportunity to pump his shotgun. He pointed his finger at the driver, and then at the shoulder. The driver slowed – the Chevy matched it – and rolled his truck to a stop with the shredded rear tire flapping. The second truck, whose driver had watched the whole thing, did the same with another insurgent vehicle to its left.

"Get out," Turnbull said, having gotten out and pointing the Remington at the cab. The driver complied, terrified.

"What are you carrying?" Turnbull asked.

"Dry goods," The driver said. "Like blankets and towels."

Too bad. Food would have been nice.

"Keys in it?" asked Turnbull. The driver nodded and Turnbull motioned to one of the guerrillas who knew how to drive a big rig. The guerrilla hopped up and into the cab. The driver was baffled.

"We're liberating this truck," Turnbull said.

"I just drive them," replied the driver.

"Well, we're not liberating *you*. You can go where you want. You do need to forget what we look like, though."

"Forget who?"

"That's the spirit. Walk east. I'm sure someone will give you a lift to the next truck stop. And when you get there, you tell them what happened. You tell them the interstates are closed."

The trucker nodded vigorously.

A pair of guerrillas marched the second driver up. He looked inconsolable. They placed him by his friend, and Turnbull gestured east with the barrel of his scattergun. They started walking.

"Beef," said one of the guerrillas proudly.

"Looks like we're grilling tonight," Turnbull said. "Get it to town and turn it over to Lee Rogers."

Turnbull gestured to the guerrilla inside the cab to fire up the rig, which he did. Then Turnbull nodded and the driver pulled the truck across the two lanes, stopped and shut it off. He got out and met Turnbull in the middle of the freeway.

"Perfect," said Turnbull. He motioned for the Chevy Blazer and a Ford F-150 to roll up. Both had winches on their front bumpers.

Part Two of the plan was led by Larry Langer. He and three cars of guerrillas pulled off I-64 at Route 65 a dozen miles west of where I-64 and I-69 crossed. The old Moto Mart sign was faded and forgotten. The new sign read "PEOPLE'S TRUCK STOP." Perhaps 15 trucks and their trailers sat in the lot.

There was no PSF in sight. There had been some guerrilla activity around here so the blues were keeping off the roads. Their cruisers seemed to attract bullets. Langer issued a quick series of orders to his men and took four with him toward the restaurant and store.

The store portion was largely deserted. The old racks that used to hold CDs of long forgotten country western singers and paperbacks by obscure authors were largely empty. The candy bar rack had a paltry selection, and the coolers were only half-filled with sodas and the like. The register girl, who looked like she used to be hefty but had involuntarily dropped a few dozen pounds thanks to the richness of socialism, simply stared blankly when the five men with guns walked in.

"Don't worry, honey," Langer said. "We ain't here for you."

The girl, who made the minimum wage of $19 People's Dollars an hour, felt herself far too underpaid to intervene in whatever was happening. When the five men proceeded on toward the restaurant, she took the opportunity to slip out the back door.

Langer walked into the diner and immediately unloaded half a magazine of AK rounds into the ceiling. A cascade of white tile dust and debris dropped down as the entire place stared, amazed.

"Hi there!" he said. "We are the forces of Free Indiana. If you've heard them calling this 'Indian Country,' well, I guess that makes us the Indians!"

He looked over at a picture of the doddering President Elizabeth Warren on the wall and nodded. "No offense, ma'am."

He walked to the front while his guerrillas spread around the perimeter of the room.

"Now, I want to make an announcement and I want you to carry it far and wide for me," he said. "Relax. I ain't going to hurt you, unless you decide to pick up your cell phone or some other such foolishness. I need you to spread this message for me. Spread the word to all your brother and sister truckers."

"I don't identify as either," one of the diners said, indignant. Langer stared for a moment. One of the other guerrillas walked over and stood by xim; xe got the message and was quiet.

"I ain't here to discuss your plumbing, sir, ma'am, whatever. I'm here to tell you to don't come back. Don't drive your trucks through here. Not during the day, not at night, because this is your gimme. This is your free pass. But the next time it ain't going to go so good."

There was a storm of gunfire outside the diner in the parking lot. The truckers all looked, but the guerrillas didn't flinch. Outside, the other guerrillas were spraying the trailers with rifle fire, punching holes in them, making sure that anyone who saw them understood what a drive through Indian Country meant.

Four PSF cruisers and an orange big rig wrecker marked "Clyde's Towing and Recovery, Bloomington, IA" headed southbound on I-69 toward the two toppled tractor trailers blocking the north-south interstate near where it crossed under Route 125. This was the northernmost of the blocks – there were reported to be others but no PSF had gone past the first one to explore.

These two trucks, one blocking each pair of lanes, had been tipped over next to the overpass and then dragged in close. There was no on or off ramp at 125, so there was no easy way to bypass the block. I-69 was sealed tight.

The convoy pulled up to the toppled trailers, and the PSF officers got out of their cruisers warily. After all, this was Indian Country, even if they never used that term around the brass.

There were some buildings to the west, and tree lines in the distance all around. They formed a rough 360 degree perimeter, AKs pointing outward. Nothing. The leader motioned for the wrecker operator to come forward, which he did – reluctantly. He had not been asked along. He had been taken.

"Well, get going," said the PSF leader. "Clear it."

Clyde the wrecker operator regarded the mess with awe.

"I'm not even sure how I can clear this yet," he said. "I need to think it through first. Look, they dragged them back under the bridge. First, I gotta drag them out. Then I gotta get them upright."

"Just move them to the side of the road," said the PSF leader. "I need this freeway open!"

The wrecker driver was about to respond when the PSF officer's face vanished in a puff of pink goo and his body twirled like a top before spinning out onto the asphalt of the empty freeway. A moment later the *crack* of the .30-06 shot that killed the blue echoed over the open fields.

Then there was a swarm of rounds buzzing over Clyde's head and all around him. Another PSF officer was hit in the leg as he was standing there; the bullet slammed into him from the side at the knee and his lower leg twisted at an impossible angle and he fell screaming. Another bullet in the neck shut him up for good.

Most of the PSF officers were now firing back, on full automatic, off toward the trees and the buildings and everywhere as they scrambled for their cruisers. A few others were hunkered down under their cars or in the ditches that lined the freeway, hoping to wait out the storm forgotten by the invisible insurgent enemy.

But they were not invisible to the men above them on the Route 125 overpass. There were several of them, in tan or camo clothes with battle rigs, firing their AR15s down from the overpass into the PSF officers below.

Clyde, believing discretion was the better part of sanity, ran.

He sprinted as full out as his 55-year old body could sprint toward his orange baby, but the windshield blew out and a tire went and bullets stitched the hood.

The hell with that orange bullet magnet, he thought.

Clyde passed the wrecker and kept on running north up I-69 as the one-sided firefight behind him raged.

The black and white monitor showed freeway, endless, empty freeway, as the Predator drone high above flew parallel to it. They were in a small, but well-air conditioned building watching the feed. Outside, a helicopter was spinning up.

"There it is," said the operations officer, pointing. Deloitte squinted. Another overturned big rig blocking I-64.

"That's nine different overturned trucks blocking the freeways in this sector. We're not using those freeways."

"You can bet every one of them is under direct observation and fire," the colonel said. That was basic Combat Engineer 101. An obstacle that you don't cover is no obstacle at all since the enemy will just reduce it if there's not one stopping him. Some PSF morons out of Bloomington tried to reduce an obstacle on I-69 earlier in the day. That cost four carloads of them.

He remembered back to what Admiral Yamamoto had said: "You cannot invade the mainland United States. There would be a rifle behind every blade of grass." Perhaps the quote was apocryphal

– anti-gun rights fanatics had always insisted it was – but the fact was that there had been over 325 million guns in the United States in the hands of the American people after the gun selling frenzy that greeted the long postponed election of Hillary Clinton in 2020. The People's Republic had gathered up a few million in its confiscation campaigns, but Deloitte had understood the kind of American he was now facing from his time in the Army even if his leaders on the coast dismissed them with contempt. Now here they were, armed and ferociously dangerous.

"Vehicles," the operations officer said, pointing to the screen. Four vehicles moving on a side road, two of them pick-ups. The people in back were definitely armed – he'd looked at enough live drone feeds in the Middle East to see that."

"Follow them," said Deloitte to the drone operator, who sat seated in front of the two senior officers. "What are the rules of engagement?"

"The order says 'Eliminate the racist oppressors using any means necessary.' The Corps JAGs say it means what it says," said the operations officer.

"Then I guess we have a green light. We've got four hostile vehicles. Target the second in line, the pick-up."

"Roger, sir," said the drone operator. The targeting graphics appeared on the screen and locked-on to the second vehicle, some sort of pick-up truck.

"Ready," said the operator.

"Take it out," Deloitte said.

The operator pushed a button and the feed jiggled almost imperceptibly.

Dust, heat, and a roar like he had never heard before engulfed Turnbull as he sat on the front passenger seat of the Chevy Blazer. Something lifted the rear of the SUV up and pushed it along on its front wheels, but it was out of control and the driver had no say as the Chevy flew off the pavement and across a culvert and into a ditch. The grill slammed into the dirt hard.

The airbags deployed as the front end of the SUV dug into the side of the ditch, smacking Turnbull hard in the face and chest behind his battle rig. The Chevy's cab filled with broken glass and a weird, chemical smoke – an airbag is actually just a sack filled with the exhaust gas products of a controlled explosion that vents after it expands the bag.

Ears ringing, Turnbull shook his head and beat down his air bag. There was a moan from behind him. They turned and one of the guerrillas in the back seat had a long, bloody cut on his forehead. Another's neck was at an awful angle and he wasn't moving.

The driver was slowly beating down his air bag.

"What the hell?" the driver said, his eyes half-closed.

"Get out," said Turnbull, shaking away the fog.

"What happ-?"

"Get out now!" Turnbull yelled, pulling his Ka-Bar blade. He sliced off his lap and shoulder belts and pushed on the passenger door.

Stuck.

"Get out of this vehicle. Now!" he shouted at the driver, who slowly complied. *His* door opened easily.

Turnbull maneuvered a leg up and kicked the inside of his door with all his strength. It budged, barely. He did it again, and it reluctantly swung open. Turnbull sprawled out into the muck at the bottom of the ditch. He forced himself to his feet and reached in for his shotgun and radio. He glanced back on the road – it was a Dante-esque tableau of twisted metal, smoke and flames.

Turnbull opened the rear passenger door, flicked the belt release, and pulled out the moaning guerrilla.

"I don't know what happened," said the driver, who had come around the crashed SUV. There was smoke in the air, and not all from the air bags.

"Get over here and help me pull him!" shouted Turnbull. "Move!"

The driver lent a hand and they dragged the injured man toward the culvert that ran under and across the road. It was about three feet wide. Turnbull pulled his cargo inside and the driver followed.

"I still don't –" began the driver, but another thunderclap hit them, and an explosion threw them against the side of the culvert and gut-punched the air out of their lungs. Big and small pieces of debris began raining down outside both ends of the tube.

"Hellfires," Turnbull said.

"What?" asked the driver, confused.

"Hellfire missiles. From a drone. We got droned."

"Drones? They can't use drones on us!" sputtered the driver.

"Why not?" Turnbull said. "I would."

The sun was down, and Ted Cannon was on top of the water tower north of town with a pair of binoculars. He had a map and a red light – for light discipline. And he had the best view in the area.

His teams were out there to the north. He had already divided the map up into grids and assigned teams to defend each one. There would not be a lot of coordination, but then communications were always iffy. The blues had cut cell service to the whole of Southern Indiana, but cells still would have been risky to use since the blues always listened in. As for the radios, they had started to experience strange interference. The blues might be jamming. The guerrillas had to hop frequencies, and that was a pain in the ass to coordinate.

Decentralized execution of the plan was going to be the name of the game simply because there was no way to effectively centrally organize the plan's execution.

Whoomp-whoomp, in the distance. Ted went silent, holding his breath. There was a slight breeze, but that was it. The crickets and the critters below were too far away to hear up there in the air.

Whoomp-whoomp.

Helicopter.

Ted stared hard into the darkness. The helicopter was out there all right, and there was a little moonlight, but he could not see anything. He squinted harder. The sound was out there, northeast, yes, it was coming from the northeast.

The pitch of the sound changed. It slowed – descending? It was somewhere northwest, a mile or two from town. Ted had a mental picture but consulted his map to be sure. He took his radio mic. No interference at the moment. He keyed it.

"Calico, this is Boxcar, you have a helicopter in your area of operations maybe dropping a recon team, over."

"Boxcar, this is Calico," came a woman's voice. "We hear it and we're on it."

The helicopter was back to its normal sound and moving west. Then the sound changed again.

"Budweiser, this is Boxcar, over," Cannon called.

"Boxcar, Budweiser, go ahead, over," came the answer.

"Helicopter descending in your AO, over."

"Roger, checking. Out."

Probably fake drops – a helicopter would mask a real insertion with a half-dozen fake ones. But maybe not. Each of those areas had a team insurgents assigned and each team was comprised of locals who knew the terrain because they had grown-up playing army there. The PRA recon units were at a disadvantage.

Cannon called in three more potential insertion sites when he saw the flashes and the occasional tracer from Budweiser's area. The sound of the shooting took a moment to reach him – and there was plenty. Then nothing.

"Boxcar, this is Budweiser, over," came the call.

"Budweiser, this is boxcar, go ahead, over," Ted replied.

"Boxcar, we got three enemy KIA, over," said the voice. The enemy recon team was dead. "We have one KIA and one WIA of our own, over."

They had lost one of their own people and another was wounded. Ted knew everyone on Team Budweiser. Someone he knew, probably for all his life, had just died. Who? He could ask, but then he thought better of it.

He put it aside and acknowledged. Then he called in medical evacuation.

An hour or more – or perhaps less – passed. Ted Cannon stared out into the darkness to the north. He had listened in to another firefight on the radio, somewhere much farther north. They had gotten the recon team, but lost another guerrilla. Someone's dad or mom, sister or brother, a friend or neighbor.

He could not believe it had come to this.

How the hell had it come to this?

But it had.

Helicopter sounds, different, and more. At least two. Inbound from the north, fast. They weren't like the others, which were almost certainly Blackhawks. No, this was some different kind of helicopter, more powerful, more…angry.

"Ah, shit," he said, as the pair of malignant, insect-like choppers roared past the water tower at high speed. He keyed the mic on the command frequency, which thankfully was not jammed.

"Control, this is Boxcar! You have Apache gunships inbound!"

The gunships followed a course roughly along Route 231 right into the center of Jasper, but the GPS location of their initial target was already fed into the weapons system. Power was intermittent below – it seemed it was coming from generators, since the electricity had been cut off to the whole region. Much of the town was dark, but the aircraft had forward-looking infrared viewers that gave the pilots a look at what was happening below.

What was happening was panic.

The roar of the helicopters sent people running for cover, and their speed over the town made it hard to react before they had disappeared over the neighboring rooftops.

The Apaches banked right, their weapon systems feeding the pilots the targeting data and they fired. A Hellfire missile came off of each helicopter's rails, shooting over the rooftops and slamming into the abandoned PSF station.

The two missiles punched through the walls, detonating inside. The blast ripped through the walls and lifted the roof up, then set it down, collapsing it.

"Sierra-one one, main target destroyed, over," the lead plot radioed.

"Roger, continue mission, out."

The Apaches swung over the town, seeking targets of opportunity. The problem is there were so many. People were scattering and running, and at least a dozen vehicles were moving.

Plonk!

The lead pilot knew that sound from flying gunships in Afghanistan before the Split. These people were shooting at him.

"We are taking small arms fire, over," he called.

Plonk plonk!

A round struck the lead pilot's canopy and cracked it a bit. The aviator was not worried – the cockpit was set inside a titanium tub designed to protect the crew from bullets and the glass was thick and strong. Much of the rest of the craft's critically vulnerable parts were likewise armored. The Apache was not invulnerable to small arms fire, but it was a damn hard nut to crack.

"Looking for targets…armed targets firing in open. Engaging!"

A band of four guerrillas had taken cover behind some cars along North Newton, firing with various types of AR15 knock-offs. The lead pilot swept the sight over them and engaged the M230 30 millimeter cannon mounted under the pilots. The gun slaved to where the pilot's eyes fell and the ship shook as a burst of ten rounds tore downward, followed by another ten.

The cars were ripped to shreds, and the effect on the four guerrillas was worse. There was not a lot left, but the Apache dumped another burst into the area just to make sure.

There was still a great deal of firing from individual shooters. The Apaches swept across the town, engaging and firing at anything that looked hostile. One of their targets was the high school – they put a Hellfire missile into the administration building, which at least gave some of the local kids something to be happy about.

But the fire kept coming from the ground, and some of the rounds hit. One of the Hellfires took a bullet in its canister and would not launch. Both canopies were peppered with cracks.

The lead Apache unleashed two bursts at the fire house – several firemen were firing on it – and destroyed the ladder truck. It swung starboard when the call came in from its wingman.

"Hey, I'm losing hydraulic pressure, over."

"What is it, over?"

"Uh, I don't know. Maybe a bullet cut a line. I gotta return to base, over."

"Roger, expend your ordnance on the way out, over."

"Roger."

The helicopters broke off their attack and began flying north. On the way out they saw several suspicious vehicles, and wiped them out.

Ted Cannon saw them fly by again, this time heading north. He had watched their attack on Jasper from his vantage point, and as they passed he unloaded a clip at them from his AK.

They didn't notice.

Turnbull hopped out of the pick-up in the Courthouse Square. There were fires around town, and several people under sheets in the square.

"Apache gunships," Davey Wohl said, his face tight with anger. "They just came in here and lit us up. And there was nothing we could do."

Dale Chalmers approached. The bank headquarters had not been hit – which told Turnbull that the enemy had no eyes in town. Not yet at least.

"How many?" Turnbull asked.

"At least 20 dead," Dale said. He seemed calm for someone whose friends had probably just been torn apart by the helicopters. "They hit the PSF station, like you said. And the fire house."

"Shit," Turnbull said.

"Yeah, the whole fire crew is gone. And Ted reported that they dropped in recon elements. We think we got them all. But they killed a couple more of us."

"We're holding the interstates, but on the way back we got droned," Turnbull said.

"Droned?" Dale said. "They're using drones on us now?"

"Yeah, drones. We need to assume we're always under surveillance."

"Kelly," Davey Wohl said. "I'll fight anytime anywhere, you know that."

"I know it," Turnbull said.

"But drones? Apache gunships? We don't have anything to stop them. All we have are these hunting rifles and AR15s."

"That's going to be enough," Turnbull said.

"What? We shot the hell out of the Apaches and they kept flying. We can't even see those damn drones. How can we fight them with rifles, Kelly? How?" asked Wohl.

"How?" asked Turnbull. "We shoot the guys behind the controls."

13.

The sun was just coming up. It was quite a beautiful Indiana day.

On a quiet back road, Larry Langer let the wind blow through the tips of his long, stringy hair as he steered the motorcycle north. It had been a while since he had ridden one, but it came back to him quickly. He kept his speed up, just in case someone above was watching. Part of the idea behind the Kawasaki was that one man on a motorcycle was less likely to attract attention from the eyes in the sky. Worst case, he might be harder to hit if they decided he was a bad guy.

His .357 was tucked in his pants and under his zipped up denim jacket. He wore a helmet, which was against his principles, only because it made him less likely to have some random PSF cruiser try to pull him over.

This was a sacrifice. Larry Langer considered helmet laws an unconscionable intrusion upon a man's natural rights.

He pressed on. His target was about 50 miles north of Jasper, just outside of Bloomington.

Langer had been pleased with how his mission to the truck stop had gone – he had repeated it at another further up I-69 later that day. Sure enough, no one had even tried to use the interstates since.

But he had returned to a Jasper in crisis as the townspeople tried to deal with the aftermath of the helicopter raid. Between the Apache and drone strikes, there were about two dozen dead townsfolk and as many wounded, some badly. The real costs of the fight was only now registering on the people.

It was a cost Larry Langer already knew.

He rode on, passing the old, abandoned Navy surface testing facility at Greenwood Lake. The People's Republic was not much interested in building ships – it was a waste of money that could go to subsidizing various constituencies instead. After the Split, the sailors had left and no one ever came back.

He passed under I-69 on a narrow country road where the interstate veered northeast toward Bloomington. The freeway was empty in both directions, and it lent the land an eerie quiet. The motorcycle was about the only sound – the farms were still, and there were no farmers about that he could see. Maybe they had left. Maybe they were in the woods with rifles making sure no one tried to use the interstate.

The insurgent-controlled area extended only a few miles north of I-69, and he soon crossed into the area under the People's Republic's nominal control. Up here, no one was completely in charge. But apparently the local PSF units were exercising discretion – he did not see any PR security forces on the roads.

After another ten minutes of riding, he came to the mile marker that had been agreed upon as the rally point, pulled off the road, and waited.

After ten minutes, a large orange van appeared. Painted in black on both sides were the words "SPECIALLY ABLED PERSONS SPECIAL TRANSPORTATION." In smaller letters was the warning: "Notice: It Is Unlawful To Disrespect Or Shame The Occupants Of This Bus." The van pulled up and the door opened. Three people with hunting rifles looked him over.

"You're picking me up in the short bus?" Langer asked.

"Who are you?" a woman with a Winchester asked. The rifle wasn't quite pointed at him, but it wasn't quite pointed away either.

"A friend from Jasper," Langer said.

"Get in."

"The battle damage assessment is pretty good," said the operations officer. "The Predator took out two rebel vehicles, with multiple casualties. The Apache raid –"

"That's offensive!" shouted Major Little. "They are called Woodrow Wilsons!"

"Where's my anti-phallocentrism plan, Major?" asked Deloitte.

"Don't you think I don't see what's going on here, Colonel," the Command Diversity Officer said.

"What's going on, Major?"

"You're trying to sideline me so you can run this unit in your own racist, sexist, patriarchal image. Well, I won't let it happen," Little said.

"Do I need to have you escorted out of my command post?" Deloitte said.

"There's going to be an accounting," Little said.

"Stand there and be quiet, Major. The soldiers are talking. Go on, Colonel."

The operations officer continued. "The gunship raid eliminated the abandoned PSF station. It does not appear they were using it as their headquarters as we expected. There was heavy resistance, but all small arms. Both Apaches" – Little seethed at that – "suffered significant damage. One is deadlined."

"How long?"

"Maintenance says at least a week. A big round, probably from a deer rifle, hit a hydraulics coupling and, bottom line, they can't get the part from depot. It's back ordered."

"So some guy with his Remington and a two dollar bullet took out a $35 million dollar aircraft that's 25% of my air combat power because the logistic system can't get me a part?"

The operations officer nodded. "And there's another aircraft down. Software issue that will take a specialist coming from depot. They're both sitting on the flight line at Monroe Municipal Airfield, waiting."

"And waiting and waiting, because this army can't do simple things like get helicopters fixed."

"It's inappropriate to disrespect the logistical system," Little piped in.

Deloitte ignored him. "We'll need the two operational aircraft up this afternoon ready to be called in on targets of opportunity. The Predator can do it, or the scouts. How many recon teams are in place?"

"Only one, sir."

"Of three?"

"Yes, the insurgents were very effective in detecting the insertions. We think they are operating a zone defense. The one team in place is the furthest from town, and we don't have anything useful from it yet because it can't see much where it is. I'd recommend shifting them to an alternate position where they can observe better, but the woods are crawling with insurgents and they know the ground like the back of their hands. If our guys move, they probably die."

"But we have Predators up?"

"One's up now doing high loops over the town. We're holding off engaging targets for now, which is good because there are so many targets."

"What do you mean?"

"Sir, Jasper's like an ant colony. They aren't hiding. They're out in the open moving around."

"They're doing it on purpose, giving us too many targets. Hiding the wheat in among the chaff."

The operations officer nodded. Little looked confused; his brain was processing the word "chaff" for possible offensiveness.

"And we have fifteen Hellfires total left."

"Fifteen? I'm surprised it's that many. Don't count on resupply. The whole PRA missile inventory is probably stripped out. No Hellfire engagement without my authorization from now on. We need to save them for the tanks if the US forces come north. We can't waste them on guerrillas unless the target is too good to pass up."

The operations officer nodded. "I'll pass the guidance to the controllers at Monroe. Now, we're still in the planning process for moving south on order. The decision briefing is tonight. I'll have you three courses of action."

"Fine. Anything else?"

"Communications instructions," said the operations officer. "We're changing tactical call signs in case the insurgents compromised the signals instructions the destroyed recon teams carried. Sir, you are Red Eagle. I'm Yellow Hawk." The operations officer turned to the Command Diversity Officer, grinning. "And you are Blue Falcon."

It was 3:00 p.m. when Langer pulled his motorcycle up to the bank and went inside. The court house square was a hub of activity, but it did not appear that there had been any strikes in town since morning. Turnbull was poring over maps by the manager's desk, and that's where Langer headed.

Turnbull saw him coming. "Well?"

"I got a great tour from our pals," Langer said. "Got right up close."

"Good. I have the force waiting. What do we have?"

"Maybe a platoon for security, but no more than a squad on duty at any one time," Langer said. He pulled a folded paper out of his denim jacket and flattened it out on the desk over the map. "Cyclone fence around the perimeter, with barbed wire around the top. There's a tower and I guess it's got a M240. A couple hummers with .50 cals over here. Some 5-ton and HEMMT trucks. Fueler here on the tarmac with JP-8. Now these buildings hold the crews – pilots over here, everyone who doesn't think he's God's gift over here. And in those trailers, the drone jockeys."

"Checkpoints?"

"No, it's outside the PSF perimeter around Bloomington. Anyway, the blue are more concerned with keeping people from heading south than from us coming up north."

"Okay," Turnbull said. "Let's get saddled up and moving."

The force moved out in individual vehicles with four guerrillas each and a map. Each took a different route north, all heading to converge at the rally point near a small hamlet named Hendriksville a few miles west of Bloomington. The rendezvous time was 2000 hours, with the sun falling in the sky.

Turnbull rode in the backseat of a Toyota Camry with Langer, who brought some Pabst. But it wasn't good Pabst. It was the same mass produced swill everyone outside the cities drank, but wearing Pabst livery. Brands were, of course, wasteful. But in the cities, there were microbreweries catering to the urban elite. Somehow, catering to their tastes was never, ever wasteful.

"Beer privilege," Langer snorted, but he still sucked it down.

"How many of those are you going to drink?" Turnbull asked when Langer opened up his second.

"I dunno. How many beers away is it?'

The driver was a young man who had been kicked out of college and returned home after being accused of "gaze rape" by a 260 pound womyn with a nose ring. He had been eager to get involved in the fight, and now he was pointing out the windshield.

"Helicopters!"

Across the open field to the east, at about 300 feet, were a pair of Apaches headed south. The car entered a thicket of trees on both sides of the road.

"Stop!" Turnbull said, and the kid skidded to a halt, then pulled to the side of the road.

"Out and scatter!" Turnbull said, bailing out of the vehicle and sprinting toward the woods. The others followed his example, and they went in four different directions.

After 50 yards, Turnbull stopped, knelt and keyed the mic on his Motorola. "This is Broadsword, Hillary in five mikes! I say again! Hillary in five mikes!" That was the code word anyone on the mission was to give for Apaches approaching. Hopefully Jasper would be ready when they arrived in what he estimated would be five minutes.

Assuming the gunships weren't going to pause to search and destroy the occupants of the Camry they had passed coming north.

After a few minutes, it became clear the Apaches were not going to detour from their route to hunt down one random car – he had been counting on that when designing the decentralized movement plan – and the four loaded back into the Toyota and restarted their interrupted journey.

"Made me spill my beer," Langer complained. "I guess I really ought to thank them."

Turnbull and Langer crawled on their bellies like reptiles, from the soft shoulder under the trees and to the perimeter cyclone fence. Both carried AKs looted from the PSF station, which pleased neither. Turnbull carried wire cutters. Langer had a bolt cutter.

Behind them, in the trees, waited a dozen guerrillas. Another team was cutting its way in down the fence line to the north.

Langer covered Turnbull while he cut. The tower was peeking just over the top of the long general aviation sheds that blocked their view of the flight line, so they kept low. Turnbull snipped one segment, then another, then another. After two minutes and a dozen snips, a man-sized segment of fence fell over. Turnbull pushed it away.

He nodded at Langer and went through. Langer signaled the rest of the team to move up and wait, and then he slithered through the hole as well.

The fence was up on an embankment and they rolled down the little grass hill to the pavement, got to their feet and dashed to the sheds. Carefully, they worked their way down to the south end.

A noise.

Langer raised his rifle, but Turnbull waved him off and placed his own against the shed wall. He drew the Ka-Bar knife from the scabbard on his battle rig. The blade was dark steel, and only the razor-sharp edge he had put on it gleamed in the moonlight.

Footsteps.

Turnbull held out one finger and Langer nodded.

The steps came closer and a man rounded the corner.

It was a soldier in PRA camouflage battle dress, with body armor and a Kevlar helmet left over from the US Army days. His M4 was over his shoulder, and he stopped, trying to compute the two men standing directly in front of him.

They did not compute. He went for his weapon, and Turnbull leapt forward.

The soldier stumbled back, but Turnbull was faster. His left hand shot up and grabbed the lid of the helmet and pulled it down and forward while bringing the knife upward. It entered under his jaw, the thrust coming up met by the weight of him falling forward. The soldier went limp instantly – the blade had gone through and severed his spinal cord.

"Damn," Langer said. "That is messed up."

"Help me," Turnbull said. They pulled the body together and dragged it behind the building, laying him out.

"Overwatch," Turnbull said, and Langer went to the corner, AK up, while Turnbull undid the man's M4A1. It had a selector switch that said "AUTO" instead of "BURST," so it would fire full automatic. Turnbull checked the chamber; there was a round in it. He dumped his AK mags and loaded up with six thirty-round M4 magazines.

"Let's go," said Turnbull, gesturing to the rest of the team.

"You leaving your Ka-Bar?" asked Langer.

Turnbull growled, knelt down and started working the blade out of the corpse's neck as the other team members sprinted over to the shed. They stared at him and the body and then him again.

"What?" asked Turnbull.

No one answered.

Langer peered around the corner and then waved them forward. The team moved swiftly between the buildings, trying to stay out of sight from the guards on the control tower.

They made it to the final shed. Beyond it was the flight line and living area for the aviation unit.

Gunfire and a stream of tracers erupted from the tower, but not directed at them. The second group was drawing fire somewhere to the north.

"Shit," hissed Turnbull. "Larry, the truck. The truck!"

Langer nodded and tore off.

"Follow me!" Turnbull said to the team, rushing around the corner.

The tower was right ahead of them, and the M240 machine gunner was spraying down a target on the other side of the complex. He was certainly not looking at the dozen guerrillas approaching from his flank.

Turnbull switched the M4 to AUTO and aimed as he ran. His weapon erupted in a long burst that sent sparks off the tower walls, but missed the gunner.

That was okay – the intent was to suppress him and get him to let up on his own fire. It worked.

The rest of the teams fired too as they ran. Sparks were ricocheting off the tower and the catwalk. There were at least three shapes up there now. One got off a burst from his rifle before someone's bullet hit him and he went down. The other two soldiers were taking cover.

As the team charged, Turnbull waved three of them off toward the foot of the tower and the stairwell. The rest followed Turnbull's lead. There was more shooting now. Apparently the other team had come out of cover and started suppressing the control tower. But that meant they were not going to be able to do their other mission.

Turnbull darted past the tower and headed toward the trailers and admin buildings at a full run.

Langer flung open the door of a big, green Heavy Expanded Mobility Tactical Truck, or HEMTT, as the troops called them. The cab of the low-slung, vaguely insect-like truck was empty. The steering wheel was chained to a ring welded into the floor – a not-unreasonable precaution since the vehicle had no keys. Langer leaned his AK against the wheel and unlimbered the bolt cutters, set them on a link and squeezed. It snapped through. He cut the other side of the link, pulled the chain remnant out of the steering wheel, and climbed up to the metal landing outside the cab.

"Hey!" Someone was behind him.

Langer swung around. It was a guard with a M4 aimed at him. There was a burst of fire from the tower and the man's eyes flicked to the light of the tracers for just a second as Langer drew the .357 from his belt.

The man's eyes returned to Langer in time to see the barrel of the silver pistol, and they both fired at the same time. The .357 round caught the soldier in the face and he spun backwards and fell in a heap.

Larry pulled himself painfully into the cab and sat. Exhaling, he turned the power switches and hit the button to start the engine. It turned over. With it grumbling roughly, he only then reached down to check the hole in his gut just below his rib cage.

"Damn," he said and looked around. There was a rag on the passenger seat, not exactly clean, but the best he could do on short notice. He took it and jammed it into the wound. That still left the hole out his back, which he could feel leaking. He pushed back in his seat to put pressure on it. It could wait.

He had work to do.

Turnbull led the remainder of his team at a run toward the two large OD green trailers parked next to the tarmac. Wires and cables ran from them and their roofs had dishes and antennae. Turnbull was almost to the foot of the closest one when the door at the top of the metal stairs opened. It was a hatless sergeant in a People's Air Force uniform standing there with a Beretta.

Turnbull put a burst into him.

With the other team rushing the second trailer, Turnbull pumped up the stairs and opened the door. There were two more Air Force techs, standing in front of a bank of TV monitors showing Predator footage.

Turnbull emptied his mag then jumped back down to the ground. There was more firing in the trailer next door.

"Crash the drone and then burn the trailer," he said to one of his troops. The guerrilla pulled a pair of two-liter bottles filled with gasoline from his pack and went up.

Turnbull slammed a fresh magazine home.

"Let's go," he said, charging toward the housing units.

The HEMMT picked up speed as it rolled toward the flight line. Various soldiers were running around, most without weapons, confused and disorganized. Most of them dodged the speeding truck, but not all. The heavy truck did not even notice them.

The crew of the fuel truck saw it coming and sprinted away. Langer laughed behind the wheel, slamming the rear end of the fueler with the side of the HEMMT, tearing off a swath of steel. Raw JP-8 fuel poured onto the tarmac.

Langer groaned – the jolt hurt like hell. But then he smiled.

Up ahead was the row of Blackhawks.

Behind him on the tower, the team Turnbull sent up was shooting it out at close quarters with the surviving guards. The second team was now moving to its two targets, the Predator drone hangers and the maintenance crew housing unit.

Turnbull headed to where the pilots slept, firing a burst through the door as he ran. When he got to it, he kicked it open.

No pilots.

The back door was open and he ran across the sleeping quarters to it. Out the door, in the moonlight, he could see shapes sprinting across the field, many shapes – it looked like the maintenance crews had cleared out too. Some of the guerrillas were shooting at them from the other building. Several fell.

Turnbull didn't bother.

The HEMMT smashed through the tail section of the first Blackhawk, spinning it around so it slammed into the side of the speeding truck as it passed. Glass and steel fragments flew and the truck shook, sending jolts of agony through his gut.

But Langer didn't care.

He smashed through the second, and the third, and then the fourth. The Blackhawks behind him lay as twisted ruins, but ahead lay four Apaches.

Langer smiled even wider, and hit the gas.

The fueler at the far end of the field was on fire. Turnbull watched as the HEMMT slammed through four Blackhawks and then four Apaches in succession. The Apaches crumpled, one after another, like tinfoil, when the armored truck slammed into them, flying off at wild angles, their tails cracking and their rotors snapping. In the end, eight fearsome aircraft were replaced by eight piles of bent, broken sheet metal.

Turnbull grinned. That was a couple hundred million old US dollars down the commode.

He looked at his watch. Time to load up the spoils and go. He trotted back toward the complex where the others were hard at work.

There was one Predator in the hanger, and it too was a smoldering ruin. Someone had liberated one of the hummers with a .50 caliber machine gun turret and brought it over, then riddled the drone with rounds. The big guns on the HUMVEEs would come in handy; they were coming with them back home. Other guerrillas were gathering the ordnance and ammo that they would be liberating.

"Get those 5-ton trucks over here and load this up," Turnbull ordered. With no air threat to worry about, he could safely drive back in the enemy's vehicles. But one that would not be joining them was Langer's HEMMT. It looked like hell as it wheezed and groaned on its way over to join him.

"Nice job, Larry," Turnbull said, smiling, when the door opened.

"Yeah, I clipped their wings," Langer said, rising up and then spilling out of the cab. Turnbull caught him before he hit the pavement. His hand was soaked in something warm that Turnbull knew all too well.

"Shit," he hissed. "Medic! Medic!"

"You think I look bad," Langer said. "You should see the other sumbitch."

The medics gave Langer a couple units of plasma on the ride back and they stuck in a unit of O+ before he even left the ER for surgery at what had been known as Chuck Schumer People's Health Center. It was known as Reagan Hospital now. People were renaming lots of things after Reagan these days.

Dale met Turnbull in the ER as the gurney with Langer disappeared down the hall.

"How did it go?" Dale asked.

"Good," said Turnbull. "Not for Larry, but we did it. The aircraft are gone. The crew we didn't shoot are in the wind. Two other of ours are wounded, and we have a broken ankle from a pothole. Larry's the worst off."

"Will he live?"

"Probably, but only because of sheer stubbornness. What's the situation?"

Dale paused, thinking. "Good," he said. "I mean, as good as it can be. The Apaches swept through and ripped up some buildings north of town. They didn't seem to want to waste too much ammo. Otherwise, we're constructing the obstacles. We're assigning sectors. We're getting it done."

"Do we have enough ammo?"

"Yeah, plenty. These gun nuts laid in enough for World War III and IV, and they've dug it all up. Everyone who wants a gun has one, and usually two."

"We need to make sure they understand how this is going to work." Turnbull said. "They're going to want to fight the first enemy they see, and that's going to get them killed. They have to be smart."

"They'll listen to you, Kelly."

"Then I better get talking to them. But I don't know how long we have until the bad guys come for us."

"They'll call you a traitor, sir," said the operations officer, pleading. But he knew that once the Colonel had decided on a course of action he was hard to sway.

"They can call me whatever they want," said Colonel Deloitte. "But if someone doesn't stop this it's going to spin completely out of control. And a lot more people are going to die."

"You can't talk to the enemy, sir."

Deloitte surveyed the airfield. His personal security detachment was spread out around him in case any of the insurgents were still lurking nearby.

"Enemy," he said bitterly. "I'm not so sure about that."

"I don't understand, sir."

"All this – it's no surprise. Not the tactics, not the strategy. I trained most of their senior SOF. I know the guy who did this. I just don't know who it is yet."

"They'll arrest you if you talk to him."

"They're probably going to arrest me eventually anyway. Racism, sexism, some -ism, some -phobia. It doesn't matter. I don't matter. Someone's got to try and stop this."

"Can you?" asked the lieutenant colonel.

"I don't know," said Colonel Deloitte. "But I can't stop it if I don't try, and after this someone has to."

The runway was strewn with wreckage. The helicopters were smoldering hulks. The drone was a pile of twisted metal and carbon fiber. And the dead still lay where they fell.

"Get those bodies collected," Deloitte ordered. "I'm going to the commo detachment. If they can listen into cell calls, I'm guessing they can get me a number to call and arrange a meet."

14.

"Convoy inbound. Three Humvees, five minutes out, over."

Turnbull gripped the handset as he listened intently, and then paused. It was all proceeding exactly as agreed. But then, he had expected it to. If Deloitte said it, it was happening. His word was good. At least that was true of the old Deloitte he had known a half decade ago in Iraq.

Turnbull keyed his radio mic. "Roger. I'm proceeding. Out."

"You still think this is a good idea?" Wohl asked. Turnbull handed him the radio.

"We'll know in a couple minutes," said Turnbull.

The meet had been set at a remote farm house about five miles west of Route 231, and north of Dogwood Lake. It was as close to neutral ground as there could be, a largely empty space on the map between the two forces.

Deloitte would come in a three hummer convoy, with no air cover and no drones up – not that there was anything left of the 172nd's attached air assets. If Turnbull was going to betray him, there was not much the colonel would be able to do.

But likewise, Turnbull and his small team, out in the middle of nowhere, had nowhere to hide if a Predator or some Woodrow

Wilsons *née* Apaches, or a whole M1 tank battalion, showed up to party. To the extent their safety did not rely upon each other's word that their counterpart would have safe passage, it relied upon mutually assured destruction.

"I'm going up to the site alone," Turnbull told Wohl. They were about 400 meters from the white farmhouse, with it and the whole area under their observation from their position. A half-dozen armed guerrillas were positioned around them in the small knot of hickory trees. Another team was north of the house, covering that approach. Then there were the observers watching the convoy as it came in from the east on the road. Some other spotters watched the main routes from the west in case someone decided to come at them from I-69.

There were not many civilian vehicles of any type on the road anymore. They were alone.

"Yeah, you going by your lonesome is probably better," said Wohl. "If your army buddy is going to sell you out, then it would just be you we lose."

"Well, that's good, I guess," said Turnbull. He picked up his M4 and moved out across the overgrown field. It should have been planted and its crops growing by now. But these days there were lots of things that should have been but weren't.

Deloitte rode in the passenger seat of the center armored Humvee, his ass on the flat olive drab seat cushion and his battle gear secured under the seat belt. He watched the green terrain pass by out the thick glass of the side window. Lots of places to shoot from out there, he noted. If this fight happened, it was going to be a mess.

The vehicles were angular with their bolt-on armor plates. They were also conspicuous in their tan desert livery. The PR claimed it didn't have money to paint them woodland camo after it inherited them in the Split. That was untrue; the PR just preferred to redistribute its money to favored constituencies rather than fund its military. That spending priority decision was causing considerable consternation in the capital right about now. The regime was realizing that it was wrong in assuming that hordes of barely trained welfare cheats armed with hand-me-down weapons would be enough to keep it in power.

None of the three vehicles' rooftop .50 caliber machine gun turrets were manned. That was part of the deal. The gunners sat scrunched up below their roof hatches inside the hummers' cabs, ready to leap up and load their M2s if things went south.

"Stop on the road about 300 meters out," the colonel shouted over the torrent of decibels the engine was tossing off. His driver, Kevlar helmeted with protective eyewear, nodded.

They kept going west for another minute or so, and then the driver halted. They could see the farmhouse down the road and up a driveway.

The other vehicles, seeing what the command vehicle was doing, herringboned. The front vehicle angled north, the trail vehicle south, ready to cover 360 degrees. The convoy had stopped in the middle of an open field with several hundred meters of fields to the nearest tree. The grass was low, and any guerrillas would have a difficult time approaching unseen.

"Stay inside," Deloitte ordered. It would be easier to defend if they could exit, but if his personal security detachment was outside, there was more chance the PSD might take a shot at something and set off a firefight. They might as well wait inside their rides and out of the sun.

"If I'm not back in 20 minutes, get out of Dodge," Deloitte said to his driver. The young specialist nodded. He had gotten the job when the colonel watched him respond to the Command Diversity Officer's inquiry about his preferred pronouns with, "I have a dick, so it's 'he,' xir."

Deloitte got out of the hummer and took his helmet off, threw it on his seat and put on his soft cap. Leaving his rifle leaning against the radio console, he shut the door with a soft "thud" and started walking down the black asphalt road toward the rendezvous site.

Turnbull looked out and saw Deloitte from inside the empty house when he was about 100 yards away and coming up the driveway. Turnbull's men had scouted it out a few nights ago as a possible safe house, and he had decided to use it when the idea of the meeting came up. The owner's family had farmed the spread for over 100 years. A couple months ago, they simply abandoned it. They sold their livestock on the black market and took off for the red – victims of meddling agricultural regulators who insisted they pay for an "animal psychologist" to ascertain the feelings of their milk cows, and of the latest round of bankrupting reparations taxes meant to compensate strangers for the oppressive acts of others that happened somewhere else a century before any of the payers or payees were even born.

Turnbull left his M4 laying on the living room table. He had his canteen in hand and took a drink, looking out through the window as Deloitte walked up the path to the open front door. He had his battle gear on, and his Beretta was in a thigh holster. He watched, sipping water. It was warm, but he didn't care.

The brigade commander hit the creaking steps, his battle gear so tight that it didn't jiggle as he strode up them. Turnbull stepped into the doorway.

"Colonel Deloitte," Turnbull said.

"Kelly Turnbull. Shit, how long has it been?"

"Five years. Since that night in Baghdad."

"I figured the spooks had swooped you up when I got orders transferring you to civilian control. What was your cover? Agriculture attaché or something?"

"Not sure. I've had a lot of covers."

"No doubt."

"It's good to see you, sir."

"I wish it were under different circumstances."

Turnbull waved him off the porch and inside. "Come on in. They left a couch."

Deloitte came into the house and took off his soft cap, then sat down in the fake leather chair that faced where the TV had been. The big screen was one of the few possessions the occupants took.

Turnbull walked around the coffee table and plopped into the sofa. A small mushroom cloud of dust erupted. Turnbull fanned it out of his face.

"Since you're all rustic now Kelly, you got some lemonade for me?"

"I don't think they have lemonade in the PR anymore, sir. I hear it's racist against limes."

"I live that shit every day, so that's a lot less funny than you think from where I sit, Captain. So, what's with the M9? I thought you liked 1911s."

"I do. I can't find any replacement ammo. You got any .45 rounds?"

"What, are you nuts? Those are like gold," Deloitte laughed. Even before the Split, most of the gun and ammo makers had moved into the free red states where the Second Amendment wasn't the red-headed stepchild of the Constitution. That meant the PR had to buy its ammunition overseas, and it did not import that caliber because there was no civilian ammo market anymore, and because it did not issue the .45 round to its forces. The PR preferred smaller, less powerful calibers that were easier to handle by smaller operators. Plus the .45 round was just too all-American, and it was considered offensive to Native Americans due to its association with cowboys.

"Couldn't hurt to ask."

Deloitte's eyes went to the M4 on the coffee table. Turnbull has tricked it out with a new sight, a fore grip and a green beam designator. "Is that one of my weapons under all those mods?"

"Yeah. Pretty clean when I got it."

"I let sergeants do sergeants' business, when I can."

"So how are your troops?" asked Turnbull.

"Good, most of them. A few duds."

"Commanders always spend ninety percent of their time on ten percent of the troops."

"True that. It's different in a lot of ways in the PRA. We usually don't salute."

"Does saluting reinforce patriarchal hegemonies?" asked Turnbull.

"Yeah," said Deloitte, a bit surprised. "How did you know?"

"I just guessed."

"You always were a quick study. You still a captain?"

"Probably."

Deloitte leaned back in the La-Z-Boy. "So, how have you been, Kelly?"

"Just fine. Just doing my thing."

"I've noticed. I should've known it was you from the beginning. You've pretty much gone right by the numbers. You did it just like I trained you, just like I'd have done it in your boots. You've mobilized the masses, and you've provoked overreach by the counterinsurgents."

"Provoked *them*?" said Turnbull. "I don't know about that. They didn't seem to need a lot of provocation to go all stormtrooper on the locals."

"You have to remember, the People's Volunteers are just untrained thugs, and the People's Security Force are not soldiers. They're not really police either."

"Kind of a Gestapo that gives out parking tickets, right?"

Deloitte looked him over. "You think I don't know that the Republic isn't perfect?"

"The *People's* Republic," Turnbull sneered. "I think this abortion of a fake country is a hell of a long way from perfect. I think it would have to work its way up to just being shitty."

"Kelly, that's my country you're talking about."

"Is it? Really? Why?"

"Because it's the one I swore an oath to."

"You swore an oath to the United States first."

"That was a different United States. I don't remember its capital being Dallas."

"You had a choice. You chose them."

"I never saw it as 'them and us,' Kelly. I saw it as a separation, not a divorce. I'm still hoping mom and dad make up and get back together again someday."

"I don't see that in the cards, sir."

"Be that as it may, here we are."

"Here we are," repeated Turnbull, sadly.

"I'm a soldier and I follow orders," Colonel Deloitte said, shrugging.

"My country right or wrong?"

"Always. Just like you."

"Sir, I gotta tell you, I kind of like being in the country that's right."

"Like I said, it ain't perfect, but it's mine. And it ain't yours. Why are you even here? Shouldn't you be back in Arizona or wherever you came from?"

"Texas. I guess I'm here for the same reason you are. I took an oath, and this is where they told me to go."

"This is isn't your fight, Kelly."

"Oh, I don't know about that. I've gotten to know these people pretty good. They're still Americans, even if they ended up on the wrong side of some line on a map. They're real Americans, a little thinner than most Americans, thanks to the bounty of socialism, but still Americans. And they need to come home."

Deloitte leaned forward. "They're Americans who kill other Americans."

"Finish the sentence," said Turnbull. "They're Americans who kill other Americans who tried to take away the rights God gave them. The right to say what they think, to pray how they want, to keep a rifle to protect those rights."

"Yeah, that Second Amendment has been a real pain in our asses," smiled Deloitte. "You know, I tried to explain it to those civilians. They just didn't get it. You remember back in the teens when those two untrained Muslim pussies in Boston shut down the whole city with just a couple of handguns? I tried to warn the powers that be what a few thousand NRA members with dug-up deer rifles out here in the sticks could do, but they wouldn't listen. Now it's my problem."

"That's the thing about our progressive betters, Colonel. They never listen. Especially when it's something they don't want to hear."

Deloitte pulled out his own canteen from his battle rig and took a swig, then leaned back again on the leather La-Z-Boy recliner. It was comfortable, especially after that kidney-walloping hummer ride. He thought about getting one, but these chairs were recently banned in the PR for constituting "comfort privilege."

"You know, it works the other way too, Kelly," Deloitte said. "You have the power to stop this war too. How about I bring my men in, I run things with a soft touch, and your people get left alone? Life as usual."

"Except for the tanks on the street corners."

"I'm offering peace, and no one in body bags."

"Fake peace," Turnbull said.

"What's not fake is that nobody gets killed."

"Sure. They get to live. All they have to do is submit. All they have to do is give up their freedom, and they get to keep on breathing."

"For now. Until things get settled in the PR and we get back on track."

"You think there's hope of getting the PR back on track?"

"Like the guy who just replaced Lincoln in the old Lincoln memorial, I believe in hope and change."

"Here's our proposal. We live as free men and women however we choose."

"I don't think that's in the cards in the short-term," Deloitte said sadly. "Sorry."

"Well, I will bring your proposal to my people as a courtesy to you, because I respect you, but I think I can safely say that they're going to reject your deal."

"A lot of people are going to die," said Deloitte. "Do you want that on your conscience, Kelly?"

"Assuming I had a conscience, it would be crystal clear. These are adults. These are Americans. And if they weren't committed, willing to live free or die, then those fake cops would still be strutting around Jasper like they owned it."

"Let this go, Kelly. Before it's too late."

"Not happening. You know, when the country split, our Special Forces kept the old motto. *De oppresso liber*. To free the oppressed."

"My brigade's motto translates to 'Down with phallocentric role paradigms.' Though it does sound slightly better in Latin."

"These people are being oppressed, and now you're part of it."

"They're disobeying a lawful elected government," Deloitte said, ignoring Turnbull's snort of derision at the idea. "And they're doing it in conjunction with a foreign power. That means I'm their enemy, Kelly. If it didn't, my oath means nothing."

"They're going to tell you to move your brigade down here, aren't they? Because if the US forces come north and you want a chance of holding them back, you need to hold Jasper."

"I want to have a nice chat Kelly, maybe try and work this out, but I'm not going to discuss my war plans."

"I can read a map, sir. You helped teach me to. If you want to hold Southern Indiana, you have to hold Jasper. And thanks to my guerrillas, right now you don't."

"I've got an armor battalion and infantry battalion," said Deloitte. "That's a lot more firepower than you have."

"I've got ground forces too. And unless you get sliced some sorties from the F-16s and F-15s the PR inherited, you have no air power. That's a conventional counterinsurgent's big edge. And those squadrons have, what? A ten percent operational readiness rate on a good day?"

"Well, you saw to that. You killed a lot of my men, Kelly."

"It was nothing personal."

"It feels pretty fucking personal."

"Join us," said Kelly. "Those politician bastards don't deserve having you fighting for them, much less dying for them."

"When have any politician bastards ever deserved us fighting and dying for them?"

"We have a place for you in the USA, sir. In our Army."

"Not going to happen, Kelly. I raised my hand. End of story."

"Someday you're going to say or do the wrong thing, Colonel, and these PR sons of bitches are going to shoot you."

"That's entirely possible. I wouldn't be the first soldier stabbed in the back by civilians," Deloitte replied. "And Kelly, are you so sure your civilians aren't going to do the same to you?"

"Maybe," Turnbull said. "But I think the difference is that I might die because I am expendable in the fight for freedom. You might die because because you're not dependable in the fight for oppression."

Deloitte smiled wanly. Turnbull continued.

"I know that in there, you still believe in the real Constitution and not in that crap some professor invented for a gender study course at Harvard and wrote into the PR's fake constitution."

"Then isn't it that much more important that I stay here, Kelly? Because if I go red, who's going to be left to fight for those rights here in the blue?"

"Why aren't you doing it now?"

"I'm trying."

"I'm just worried that they kill you before you can."

"If you and your guerrillas don't kill me first."

"True enough. If you guys come, it's on. The next time I see you down here, I'm lighting you up. No offense."

"None taken. I wouldn't expect or ask for any less. But there's another side of that coin, Kelly. When we roll down here, we will take Jasper, and we will destroy anybody who gets in our way. I like you and respect you, but we're now soldiers on opposite sides, and I will not hesitate, not even for a second, to blow you and your little army of farmers, insurance salesman, and truck drivers to kingdom come if that's what it takes to accomplish my mission."

"So there we are, I guess."

"There we are."

"One thing. You know we haven't taken any PV or PSF prisoners?" Kelly said.

"We've noticed."

"That's because fuck them. But I'm betting you have a different standard with your soldiers, and that your soldiers are something like soldiers."

"Most of them. There are some you can go ahead and shoot."

"Well, we won't. We'll treat them like real EPWs if we capture them or if they're wounded."

"And your prisoners will get the same fair treatment as long as they're in my custody. Of course, that's all I can promise. Once they are out of my hands...."

"All I can ask for."

"So what now, Kelly?"

"I guess you go back and get your staff finishing up your op order for the move south. You are coming south, right? Not going to try and flank me from I-69, are you?"

Deloitte laughed a bitter little chuckle. He wished Turnbull was on his team instead of his OPFOR.

"It's more fun if it's a surprise, Kelly. Anyway, I'm sure you've got eyes on all my units already."

And you've got your cavalry scouts inserted in here. You still call them 19 Deltas in your army?"

"No, they had a lot of problems with military occupational specialty designators. There was a lot of racism and sexism in there that we were apparently unaware of for decades."

"I see," Turnbull said.

"But you *know* I have scouts too, because you killed some of them."

"Again, nothing personal."

"No, nothing personal." Deloitte got up and extended his hand. Kelly stood and shook it.

"So, was I De Niro or Pacino today?" asked Turnbull.

"I don't think Senator De Niro would approve of you appropriating his portrayal," Deloitte replied. Then it occurred to him that in the movie, Pacino was the one who lived. He did not bring that up.

Instead, the colonel silently walked to the door and stepped out on the porch. He fit his soft cap over his short cropped hair.

Turnbull followed, picking up the M4 and hooking the sling to his gear so the weapon hung out of the way, but was still easily accessible.

Deloitte walked down the steps and behind him Turnbull walked out onto the planks of the porch.

"Colonel," Turnbull said.

Deloitte stopped and turned around.

Turnbull saluted.

Deloitte stared for about a second, then came to attention and returned the salute. Then he turned back around and walked down the dusty driveway.

It was early morning when Davey Wohl handed back to Turnbull the cell phone Clay Deeds had provided. Around them in courthouse square, armed locals were assembling. Lots of men, and a few women. All readying for a fight. Others had slipped away north in the night. Some were just scared. The few remaining Tories had been impolitely invited to leave.

"The email's sent, and then I got one back 20 minutes later. It's on there. It's coded," Wohl said. He had driven out up through the Hoosier National Forest to near Bedford to get cell connectivity again, eluding patrols by sticking to back roads. He had sent the email Turnbull had written, with its long list of very specific requests, and had brought back the reply.

"Any trouble?" Turnbull asked, taking the iPhone and pulling up the reply email from his commander back in the United States.

"No, the roads are pretty empty. They aren't patrolling much. Not yet at least."

Turnbull reviewed the email after applying the decryption app.

"Mission approved. 0100 Local tomorrow. 38°17'39.6"N 86°41'14.6"W. Eliminate radar system vic Branchville Correctional Facility NLT 0030."

"Great," Turnbull grumbled. It was going to happen, if and only if his guys pulled off another raid. That was an unwelcome distraction, but a necessary one.

He quickly found the landing zone on his GPS map app – it was an empty field near the intersection of County Road 570 South and Country Road 85, about a mile south of a little hamlet called Birdseye, remote and hidden from hills but near two egress routes for the vehicles.

It was the radar site that was the sticking point. The area south of I-64 was still contested, and there were more military and civilian security forces the closer you got to the border. The prison looked like it was only a few miles away. But Turnbull understood. Obviously, no one in the red wanted being caught infiltrating the People's Republic – that could spark the conventional war the negotiations were trying to avoid. So the radar station had to be down before the mission could happen.

Turnbull sent Wohl off to find Banks – it would be the Bretzville team that drew this mission. Then he set to studying the satellite map on his iPhone. After about ten minutes, he looked up and said to Lee Rogers, his supply guru, "I need a big truck, a lot of fertilizer and a buttload of propane canisters."

Once south of I-64, they were in enemy territory again, or at least contested territory. Turnbull's people didn't generally operate that far south, and they had no real connection to the local guerrillas who did. They were on their own.

At 2330 hours, a panel truck driven by one of the Bretzville cell members came rumbling down Route 37, followed by an old pickup truck with a steel plate welded behind the cab and blocking the rear window. The old prison was a few miles south of St. Croix, where 37 crossed under I-64. The scouts had confirmed there was no check point. They proceeded south the six or so miles to the old Branchville Correctional Facility.

There had been eyes on the site since early afternoon – as soon as Banks got the mission he had reconnoitered the site from the dense woods to the east. There were about a dozen administrative buildings outside the 12' high razor wire fence which surrounded the barracks that used to house the minimum security prisoners. A large parking lot, with several military trucks, fronted the fence where it bordered the open grassy field where the inmates used to take their recreation. The forest green radar trailers were set up there, about 15 meters from the fence, dishes spinning and their thick black cables snaking to the control rooms in the old guard house.

The PR's prisoners were largely released by the pardons that followed the Split – since convicts were presumptively incarcerated as a result of some sort of oppression – and the ones from

Branchville who had not been released outright had been transferred elsewhere. The site had been taken over by the PR military to provide radar surveillance of that section of the southern Indiana border, which lay a few miles to the immediate southeast along the route of the Ohio River.

Banks counted maybe 30 troops, with only a half dozen enlisted troops on what passed for guard duty at any given moment – they were often out of uniform. There was no evidence that NCOs were checking them – clearly, the command had not inspected it lately. There were no guard towers – the threat of getting sent to a real prison had usually been enough to keep the low-risk offenders from walking off – but there was a water tower on the southeast corner of the facility. The guards did not go up there, Banks noted it as he made his plans.

At night, there was pretty minimal activity. The radar dishes rotated, but there was not much else happening except the occasional guard walking about aimlessly. The barracks lights were still on, but that was it.

At 2343, the Bretzville team that Banks had deployed in the woods on the east side of the facility saw the truck's lights as it and the pick-up turned off Route 37 and into the parking lot. There was no checkpoint outside the wire – there was one guard at the gate in the wire fence located on the southwest corner of the compound by the warehouse. Banks shook his head. What a cluster.

The truck cut its lights and pulled up along the fence parallel to the radar systems on the other side. The driver turned off the engine, got out of the cab, and hopped into the waiting pick-up. A guard walking patrol about 100 meters away inside the fence stared, puzzled. The pick-up turned around and sped out of the lot, the rear armor plate unnecessary since none of the guards had thought to open fire.

Banks glanced at his watch, which had been synched with the rest of the team. 2344 hours.

The intrigued guard started walking toward the truck parked just outside the fence line.

"Cover your ears," Banks told his team.

At 2345, the truck was replaced by an orange fireball that engulfed the truck, the adjacent section of razor wire fence and the curious sentry. Banks and his troops were far enough away that it took a moment for the sound and blast wave to roar through their positon. It was about the loudest thing he had ever heard.

When Banks looked back up, the whole other side of the facility was a combination of dust and fire, with the cloud rising up above it all. Banks took out his radio.

"What do you see, over?"

Nothing.

"What do you see, over?" he shouted.

"I think I'm deaf," came the response.

"Go around and tell me what you see, over!" cried Banks.

Up on the water tower, Banks's observer stood up and slowly came around on the walkway until he was on the north side – he had wisely stayed on the south side so he couldn't be seen while waiting and to shield him from the blast. On the north face, there were now several jagged holes in the tank spraying out water thanks to shrapnel from the vaporized truck. He looked down below at the target.

"It's all fire and smoke," he said into the radio. Then he remembered proper radio procedure. "Over."

"The radars – gimme the BDA, over," Banks demanded, using the acronym for Battle Damage Assessment.

"Can't see – gotta let the smoke clear, over."

"Observe and report, out," Banks said, putting down the radio. He had been afraid of this – he had hoped he could confirm the radars were out of action and scoot, but now he had to stick around until he got confirmation that the units were destroyed.

"Fire," he told his team.

The half-dozen guerrillas near him began to fire their deer rifles, concentrating their shots on the windows of the barracks and the control room. Banks joined in with his M14. The idea was suppression – it looked like the massive explosion had stunned the garrison and the rifle fire would encourage them to keep down as the observer waited for the smoke to clear so he could confirm that they had accomplished their mission and get out of there.

After about 60 seconds, the door of one of the barracks opened and two figures stumbled out. Both were armed. One fired an automatic burst in the general direction of the east. Immediately all the shooters zeroed in on these live targets. After a few more rounds, the non-shooter staggered and fell. A moment later, the shooter dropped straight down – Banks figured somebody's .30-06 bullet had severed his spine at his neck. The team returned to firing at the buildings' windows; no one else came outside or attempted to return fire.

Up on the tower, the observer watched the buildings surrounding the parking lot outside the wire as they burned. But he could now sort of see the field through the smoke and ash and dust. There had been three radar dish trailers. In the flickering light of the fires, he could see that two were knocked over, their dishes bent. One of them was itself on fire. The third trailer was still upright, but its dish was gone – blown completely off.

The observer keyed his mic. "The targets are non-op. I say again, they are non-operational, over," he said.

"Roger. Get back here, out," said Banks.

The observer climbed down the ladder, than dropped the last ten feet to the ground and took off running to the woods, just as he had rehearsed. Not more than ten steps inside the tree line he met up with Banks and the team, and together they followed their planned egress route out to their waiting rides back home.

Two vans headed north on 145 past I-64. Where they crossed the glorified creek that is the Anderson River near a small farm, they flashed their headlights twice and continued north. A quarter mile north, at the edge of the field, Turnbull saw the signal.

"We're a go," he said to his dozen troops. Signal intelligence would detect that the Branchville Correctional Facility radars were out and the mission would commence.

It was 0020 hours. The guerrillas were moving to their assigned positions with their metal buckets. At 0025, Turnbull gave the signal, and each guerrilla lit the lighter fluid-soaked wood in his bucket.

The blacked-out MH-47G had been circling over largely unoccupied territory south of the big bend in the Ohio River a few miles west of Brandenburg for about twenty minutes when the radio call from mission control came in. The crew already expected it – the advanced electronic countermeasures onboard the special ops Chinook had already seen the radar site at Branchville go black.

"Conspiracy 17, Reagan, Reagan," the controller called, using the code word to proceed on the mission. The helicopter, call sign Conspiracy 17 (pronounced "one seven") did not respond – it was on radio silence. Instead, the pilot, a US Army Chief Warrant Officer 4 out of the 160th Special Operations Regiment at Ft. Campbell, vectored northwest through the big, wide gap that just appeared in the People's Republic's radar coverage of its southern border.

The helicopter was a dark hole in the sky, its running and interior lights off and the special engine muffler engaged. That cost them a little bit of power, but they still had plenty of speed, especially since it was a short hop and the ship wasn't wearing its extra fuel tanks.

The pitch black, except for the occasional lighted building below, was no problem. The pilot engaged his forward-looking infrared and followed the pre-programed flight plan.

They crossed over the border south of Derby on the Ohio River and were officially in enemy territory. They flew fast and low on a course that took them just south of Branchville, where the staff sergeant manning the starboard side M134 7.62mm electric Gatling gun got a good view of the fire at the prison and the rescue vehicles that were showing up some 40 minutes after the incident.

The aircraft turned north about 1000 feet east of 145 and headed north parallel to the road. The long black ribbon running east-west that was I-64 appeared ahead of them. There was very little traffic and what there was always came in packs of four or five vehicles – obviously patrols. None of the patrols were close enough to see or hear them – and even if the enemy was using thermal imaging (unlikely, since that investment would take money away from the PR's prioritized welfare spending) the helicopter featured an infrared damper for its exhaust ports to reduce its heat signature in the sky.

About a minute later, the pilot saw an upside down "T" formation of four light sources on the objective up ahead. He slowed as he came in and descended, and he put the wheels down just below the base of the marker, with the long refueling pole jutting forward between the flame buckets. The ground supported the heavy aircraft, as expected, and there was remarkably little dust kicked up by the rotor wash. The analyst who had selected the site had done his job well.

While his men doused the signal fires, the bare-headed Turnbull approached the rear of the aircraft as the ramp lowered. The crew chief stood on the deck, ear protection and goggles on. He signaled and Turnbull and several men moved onboard to push out the three wheeled pallets. Once they were all on the ground, Turnbull turned back to the crew chief, who gave him a thumbs up. Turnbull returned the gesture.

The Chinook powered up as the ramp closed, and Turnbull and his men covered their faces as the rotor wash flowed over them. Conspiracy 17 lifted up into the night sky, almost disappearing in the dark, and then it veered east and left them, heading home on a different course.

Turnbull fitted his cap back on his head as the dust settled, then turned to his troops.

"Let's get this shit loaded up," he ordered. Then men began breaking down the pallets. Turnbull walked around and observed as the guerrillas moved with a purpose. It looked like everything was there. A dozen Javelin missiles. Some AT 4 launchers. The C4 and det cord. The special purpose shaped demolitions. Mines. Medical supplies, including anti-coagulant bandages. But where was his special request?

The men had pulled their 4x4s onto the field and were loading up the truck beds. Lee Rogers, the logistics expert from Walmart who was Turnbull's supply officer, was supervising. Turnbull finished radio checks with the security elements watching the roads for patrols when Rogers approached with an olive drab steel ammo can that was dangling a manila tag attached to the handle by a white piece of string.

"This one's for you – I think," she said.

Turnbull took it, and Rogers began directing the work.

The tag said, "For Michael N."

Turnbull flicked open the latch. There was a piece of paper and ten extended .45 1911A1 mags with hollow points. He unfolded the paper. It read, "They're coming. 48 hours. Don't be their Steppin' Stone."

"We're packed up," Rogers said.

"Load 'em up and move 'em out," replied Turnbull, shoving the paper back into the ammo can and re-latching it. "We have two days to get ready."

15.

The 172nd Brigade's command post was full of soldiers making their final plans for the invasion of Southern Indiana. Deloitte had just returned from the field, inspecting his forces, ensuring they were ready for what was coming. He had been out at the artillery battalion for that last two hours. The unit was supposed to have two M119 105 millimeter towed howitzer batteries and one M777A2 155mm towed howitzer battery, all of six guns each – a fair amount of fire power. The 172nd, thanks to budget cuts, had one battery of four 105 guns, of which three were operational. On top of that was minimal ammunition – less than 200 M1 high explosive shells plus some illumination rounds. Still, the King of Battle would be a powerful asset even in its diminished form. And the battery commander, selected because he scored highest on his oppression ratings, was fairly capable.

That was good, because they were going to war.

The corps order came down the previous night. They were to move south and "defeat the racist terrorists inhabiting the Jasper region and then be prepared to repel the racist red forces."

But because the military always came last in the People's Republic's priorities, his brigade was at far less than full strength, with about only 80% of the allocated personing. He had a tank battalion that was allocated 58 tanks. Only 31 were operational; some had been reassigned to other brigades and the rest were awaiting – endlessly – parts. His infantry battalion was light, not heavy mechanized, so there were no Bradley fighting vehicles or Strykers for the infantry to ride in that could keep up with the armor. That was bad, but the 172nd was still a powerful force. He would have to sacrifice some of the speed of the armor to keep the infantry around it – they would have to ride in 5-ton cargo trucks – but in the end there was nothing the guerrillas had that could hold its own in a stand-up fight against a M1 Abrams.

Well, not "Abrams" any more – in the PRA, it was now formally known as a "Chavez," after Caesar Chavez. General Creighton Abrams had been the Army chief of staff and commander of US forces in Vietnam, so he was declared "a symbol of racist oppression and contrary to the values of inclusiveness and diversity that are our People's Republic Army's true strength."

The colonel would have happily traded all his diversity and inclusiveness right then and there for some more howitzer tubes and tanks.

Deloitte had mixed feelings about his force's fighting ability. Training had been limited and constantly interrupted with stand-downs to address the crisis *du jour*. Some trooper looked at another cross-eyed and then the whole unit was sitting in auditoriums for two days hearing lectures on white privilege instead of being out working on the iron. He had done his best to preserve a firm chain of command, but the PRA's "anti-patriarchal and imbalanced power relationship paradigm" efforts had undercut the authority of his front line leaders. Many were solid, but sergeants and junior officers too often just shrugged their shoulders when soldiers pushed back on orders that were insufficiently fun or fulfilling to them. It did not help that they were constantly being undercut by the new policies that allowed malcontents to go around their chain of command and complain directly to the Command Diversity Officer.

Where was Major Little anyway? Deloitte was relieved that the pest wasn't disrupting his command post, so he did not give him another thought. He went on with the planning and coordination, focusing particularly on the logistics. Tanks and the other vehicles were notoriously thirsty, and they were hungry for ammo. Feeding and fueling was as important as the fighting.

And so were rules of engagement.

"We are seeking to defeat armed insurgents. You can shoot them, but not civilians. We are professionals, not monsters," he had told his assembled officers when briefing them on his plan earlier in the day. "These are fellow citizens. If they shoot at you, engage. If they give up, take prisoners." Little had attended that briefing, and he was visibly displeased.

Deloitte did not give a damn.

Deloitte was busy working when he felt a tap on his shoulder.

"Sir," said the operations officer, his tired face creased with concern. "You need to see this."

They walked outside the tent, past the MPs guarding it, to the large mall parking lot that was their assembly area. The lot was big, and had been empty – the PR closed it the year before as "a symbol of consumerist waste and climate criminality." The tanks, trucks, and troops had only filled half when Deloitte had entered the command post tent an hour before. Now there were dozens of buses, many PSF cruisers, and a variety of civilian vehicles with "PV" spray-painted on them pouring in.

"What the hell?" Deloitte asked.

A group of a dozen men in black tactical gear, with tricked out M4s, was coming their way from a row of black government SUVs. He recognized Inspector Kunstler, wearing tactical gear himself, and Major Little was with him, grinning.

They stopped in front of the colonel.

"What is this?" Deloitte asked.

"Let's go inside *our* headquarters, Colonel," Kunstler said. They all went back into the tent, including the tactical team. The guards did not try to check their identification.

Inside, Kunstler took off his black helmet and put it on a rickety wooden desk cluttered with papers and coffee cups.

"This is the supplementary paramilitary force," Kunstler replied. "My Peoples Bureau of Investigation tactical unit, plus 300 PSF and 300 people's volunteers."

"Why? They'll just get in my way," Deloitte replied.

"Their mission is dealing with the local populace while you defeat the insurgents and prepare to repel a racist invasion by the reds," Kunstler said.

"What do you mean 'dealing with'?" Deloitte asked.

"That is not your concern. Our force will follow behind yours and secure or otherwise address any rebel prisoners. We'll deal with their property as appropriate. Our intention is to eliminate the resistance in this region for good."

"You're going to murder them," Deloitte said. "You'll turn your fake cops and thugs on the people down there, pillage through their homes, burn their towns, and murder them."

"Careful, Colonel," said Kunstler. "You've read the revised martial law proclamation, haven't you? No? Let me share the highlights."

Kunstler pulled a paper from his gear and unfolded it, then read. "The racist homophobic patriarchal and sexist terrorist rebellion will be crushed without mercy. Insurrection and disobedience to the laws of the People's Republic is treason and shall be punishable by death."

Kunstler looked up at the horrified Deloitte. "What are your questions, Colonel?"

"I'm calling my commander."

"You can, but she signed off on the order. See?" Kunstler turned the paper to face the colonel, and his commander's signature block and familiar squiggle were at the bottom.

"So you're just going to sweep in behind us and kill everyone you find?"

"Not everyone. There may be some children who can be reeducated. Naturally, oppressed peoples will not be harmed, since they are obviously victims themselves," Kunstler said. "I've studied this area, Colonel. These people are reactionaries, terrorists. They insist on living on their own terms, as if they still controlled things like they did under the old government. They voted for Trump in 2016, and against President Clinton in 2020. Their attitudes and foolish religious beliefs were themselves an act of violence to progressive peoples everywhere. This is self-defense. We will no longer tolerate their intolerance. They defied us and they must pay. They must be made an example."

"I'm not doing it," Deloitte said.

"You're what?" asked Kunstler, not surprised.

"I'm not having any part of your scorched earth killing spree. My troops are soldiers, not murderers."

"Frankly, I expected this," Kunstler said. "I hoped you might see the error of your ways, but it's clear you won't."

"There's no error. I won't do it."

"Principle, or preference, Colonel?" Said Kunstler. "I think the latter. You see, Major Little informed me that you actually met with the terrorist leader last night. You've colluded with them, Colonel. In a way, you're complicit in this rebellion. Fortunately, the order also places all military forces under my overall command. So I am relieving you of command. Major Little will take command of the PRA force during the operation."

Little grinned widely.

"And you, Colonel, you're under arrest. For insurrection and disobedience to the laws of the People's Republic," the Inspector said.

"Treason," Major Little said, still grinning.

Three members of the tactical team took a hold of Deloitte; one relieved him of his Beretta. The ops officer and some of the troops reached for theirs and the other tactical team members took aim with their M4s. The tent was dead silent.

"No," Deloitte said. "Put your weapons down. Do your duty."

His troops relaxed slightly. The tactical team kept its weapons up; a fight would be a bloodbath. Deloitte would not do that to them.

"I'll be all right," he said to his operations officer.

"No, you won't," said Major Little as the PBI tactical team hustled Colonel Deloitte out of the tent.

"The East Fork of the White River," Turnbull said, standing with his assembled field commanders in the bank headquarters. It was the last briefing before they returned to their units.

"Between I-69 and the Hoosier National Forest," he continued, "there are three crossings, three bridges. Route 231, Route 257 and North Portersville Road. So those are the choke points for forces coming straight south. They could get around our flank through Hoosier, but that's a seam with their unit to the east and the woods are a death trap besides. On the west, we blocked I-69 pretty good. So I think they'll come straight down on those three axes."

"Our teams have not seen any bridging equipment," Dale said. He had sent Liz and the kids south of town with his mother-in-law, and now he was receiving and collating reports from the recon teams the insurgents had deployed around Bloomington to monitor the 172nd Brigade's forces. "We could blow them. We have explosives now."

Turnbull tapped the map. "Not now. If we do it now, we risk trapping our own people north. Plus the US forces might need them going north – assuming they come. Wire them, though."

Dale nodded. They had identified a couple ex-combat engineer veterans among the insurgents. They were immediately designated the explosives experts. Turnbull hoped they still remembered how to work magic with det cord and C4.

"They'll lead with tanks, but they won't go into the urban areas without infantry if they can help it. Their infantry is light – no Bradley or Stryker vehicles, so it's going to be a problem keeping up. They might try to thunder run it, just tear through and shoot stuff, but they can't hold ground with tanks alone. They need boots on the ground. Logistics is going to be a challenge for them, especially with these chokepoints. Since we're operating in zones, we've been laying up our resupply in caches inside our areas so we won't have to resupply over distance as often."

Banks was there watching, having been promoted to lead two elements north of the river. "Why no anti-tank weapons for us?" he asked. "They'll be tearing through our zone and we could get some shots off."

"We'll let the armor get over the river and engage it there and starve it. They'll get into Jasper one way or the other, so we let them. Jasper's where we can get close and neutralize some of their advantages. Target the maintenance, logistics guys, and the fuelers north of the river. Find command posts and attack them. Locate their artillery. That's got to be taken out. Remember, lay low, let forces that can beat you pass by, and then spring up and attack ones that can't. They don't have the numbers to occupy and guard everything.

They'll have to prioritize, which means roads, and long, vulnerable supply lines. You hit them where they are weak."

"I have lots of reports of paramilitaries, PSF and Volunteers," Dale said.

"I'm guessing they aren't front line combat forces," Turnbull said. "You can stand toe-to-toe with those bastards if you have the numbers. Those will probably be the follow on force for local security. They're probably going to focus on civilians. You can probably figure out what that means."

"We've evacuated most of the noncombatants from north of town," Dale noted. "We've got them camped out south of Jasper."

"So we better win," Turnbull said. "It's your land. It's your families. That's what you're fighting for. Good luck."

Ted Cannon moved across the open field and dropped into a stream bed to get closer to his objective. With him were three other insurgents carrying the typical variety of AR15-style guns and civilian hunting rifles. He pulled up the binoculars and looked north toward the outskirts of the small town of Loogootee, about 20 miles north of Jasper where the north-south axis of Route 231 and the east-west Route 150 intersected. The path of Route 150 across the sector was labeled "Phase Line Orange" on the insurgents' maps, and represented what Turnbull expected would be the line of departure for the PRA forces.

There was an assembly area for tanks and a lot of trucks outside to the west near the high school. It was humming – they were getting ready, and he could hear the rumble of tank turbines from a half mile away.

What was going on in the town was more troubling. There were PSF and PV units in the town itself, mostly mounted in civilian vehicles, cruisers and what appeared to be some requisitioned civilian pick-up trucks with their new owners' initials spray-painted on in black. They were going through the town, which the insurgents had never actually held, and seemed to be torching the buildings. The old Dairy Queen and the closed down Wendy's on the south side were in flames. And there was the crackle of gunfire. But there were no armed insurgents deployed in the Loogootee.

"They're shooting civilians," the female guerrilla next to him said.

"Yeah," replied Cannon, not surprised. "I better call it in."

Inspector Kunstler was wearing his black paramilitary tactical gear and had been conferring with the leader of the People's Volunteers element in Loogootee. The PBI agent was happy to hear that the town was completely cleansed of reactionary elements. Now the People's Volunteers were to sweep west and then south behind the main army force. There was to be nothing left standing, or breathing.

"We're ready," Major Little, the new brigade commander, reported.

"Then attack," said Kunstler. "Take Jasper."

"Movement south all over Phase Line Orange," Dale reported to Turnbull. "They are moving on 231, and all the county roads south."

"It's on," said Turnbull. He picked up his M4 from the table. No sense in being in the command post – this was not going to be a synchronized battle with a general moving pieces around a board, at least, not for the insurgents. This was going to be a decentralized fight, a series of separate battles between the enemy and independent guerrilla groups. There was nothing much that he could do to influence their outcomes now. At this point, Kelly Turnbull had more to offer pulling triggers than listening to reports. He headed out the door.

C Company had been nicknamed "Crusader" when it was a US unit. That, of course, was a no-go now. Nor could the tank unit be known as Charlie Company anymore either – that phonetic designation was sexist, as were those of its sister units, Alpha and Bravo Companies. Alpha was patriarchal, and Bravo was too much like "Braves," which might offend Indigenous/First Peoples. Also, they were not referred to as "sister" units anymore; they were "sibling units," since "sister" imposed a narrow gender identity on the units of the armor battalion.

Colonel Deloitte had tolerated the Crusader and other traditional nicknames, but a tirade about those regressive, oppressive nicknames had taken up half of Major Little's final orders briefing to his subordinate leaders. They would use the official nicknames, he proclaimed. So, it came to pass that Caring Company's commander, Captain Jack Cardillo, stood up in the roof hatch next to the mounted .50 caliber machine gun mount, second in the line of vehicles rolling down Route 231, watching for enemies across the flat, open fields.

There were ten tanks in his company, less than the 14 at full strength. His company was followed by a dozen 5-ton trucks packed with infantry, plus a logistics train including a fueler. They had a rougher ride – the tracks of the nearly 70-ton tanks were tearing up the road pretty well.

They were five miles past the line of departure/line of contact and nothing. No people at all, and no opposition. He checked his watch – on schedule, which was good. Route 231 was the key MSR – main supply route – into Jasper, and they could not let it get backed up.

The little hamlet of Whitfield – no more than some houses, barns, and buildings sitting at an intersection with another county road – lay ahead. The woods were getting closer to the road, which made him nervous. He'd prefer to stop, dismount infantry and clear them, but the commander was unequivocal about his commander's intent – don't slow down on the way to Jasper. And also, don't engage in cis-het normative stereotyping.

The second point seemed most important to Major Little.

Cardillo didn't hear the shots behind him over the roar of the 1500-horsepower Honeywell AGT1500C turbine engine and the *clack* of the tracks beneath him. The call came over his radio headphones on the company command net.

"Crusader Six, Crusader One-One, contact left! Engaging!"

The first tank of first platoon was under fire – and replying.

Captain Cardillo turned around to see several M1s stopped and firing their .50 cals into the woods on the east side of the road. One of the turrets rotated its 120 millimeter smoothbore gun left.

"Oh, shit," Cardillo hissed.

Crusader One-One's main gun fired into the trees, and the captain could hear the roar even through his hearing protection. The shell detonated inside the woods – a M830 high explosive anti-tank (HEAT) round meant for enemy armor. The People's Republic had not bothered investing in the canister rounds that essentially turned the massive cannon into a giant shotgun.

Using a HEAT round on guerrillas was like using a sledgehammer for a gnat. And they didn't have enough shells to spare.

"Crusader elements, this is Six! Cease fire main guns, I say again, cease fire main guns! Suppress and move, over!"

He took his own M2 machine gun turned it toward the woods. No targets. The other tanks were moving again now, accelerating to catch up with the rest. But behind them, the infantry trucks were stopping and troops were dismounting. Behind them, the column was halted.

His radio came to life again, this time on the brigade command net. "Caring Six, this is Blue Falcon, you will use the proper call signs! Acknowledge!"

"Shit," Cardillo said, watching the movement descend into chaos behind him and the casualty reports began coming in over the company command freq.

When the tank round hit the tree and detonated, Banks was sprayed with some pieces of wood but luckily he was far enough away that he wasn't sliced by splinters. No one had been hurt by the fusillade of return fire the convoy had laid down after their initial assault on the column. Banks rose up and gestured to his guerrillas to fall back to their alternate positions, just as they had rehearsed. Through the trees, he could see trucks stopped and infantry dismounting. All was going as planned.

The insurgents would be long gone before the infantry organized themselves to sweep through the woods.

The guerrillas had initiated the ambush after letting half the tanks pass by unmolested. The initial volley was some rifle fire, both from the lighter AR15s and various hunting rifles, aimed at the crews riding exposed out of the turret hatches. Four of the tanks actually took fire. One of the crewmen got hit in the arm, and then the trail tanks stopped the convoy to engage the guerrillas while the infantry dismounted to clear the woods adjacent to the road.

But the guerrillas cleared themselves out of the woods. They couldn't win that fight, so they weren't going to fight it.

Farther back to the north, the logistics portion of the convoy was held up too. It sat there, waiting for the road ahead to clear. That was when the second group of guerrillas attacked.

This time the insurgent force was heavier, and reinforced with the two HUMVEEs liberated at the airfield. Their .50 caliber machine guns began sweeping the trucks, wreckers, and fuelers that formed the combat trains of Crusader Company and its attached infantry company. At the same time, riflemen engaged from 500 meters or further. The support soldiers attempted to return fire with M4s, but this was pushing the maximum effective range of their carbines. Outgunned, the support soldiers took cover as their trucks were riddled. The fuelers especially drew fire, one eventually bursting into flames.

After a few minutes, the guerrillas withdrew. By the time reinforcements arrived, the enemy had vanished. The PRA forces collected up the dead and wounded, then pushed the wrecked vehicles off into the ditches at the side of the road and began moving forward again. Now they were behind schedule.

Bravo Company's tanks and infantry rolled through Alfordsville, which sat astride the county road that was one of the three major north-south arteries in the sector. The town was a collection of rustic homes and a church, with a population of about 100 before the evacuation. About two dozen people had stayed behind, the others having gone south or into the woods to fight. Once the army units moved out southward, the PSF and the PVs moved in, about 50 of them. They went house to house, the PSF mostly focused on dragging the civilians to the center of town. A pair of citizens did decide to run; the Volunteers caught them and shot them dead.

Kunstler and his tactical team, in a convoy of four black SUVs, pulled into town and stopped. Kunstler got out and the senior PSF officer approached.

"We have about 20 prisoners," he said. "Old men and women."

"So the young ones are out in the woods," Kunstler growled. There were several bullet holes in his armored Blazer.

"They deny it. They say no one from here's a terrorist. They say all the younger people went south when they were warned what was happening."

"Of course they did," Kunstler said. "Shoot them all."

He went back to his vehicle as all around the PVs carried loot out of the houses that they had not yet torched.

Turnbull watched through the binos as Caring Company's tanks took up defensive positions in an open field on the northwest side of Route 231's bridge over the muddy White River. A quarter mile south were the northernmost reaches of Jasper, with the narrow road lined with cement companies, stores, and abandoned gas stations. It was hilly, with the sight lines broken up by trees.

No wonder the tanks were reluctant to come.

The PRA infantry and the logistics elements were arriving, but for the moment no one was making an effort to advance over the bridge.

Davey Wohl lay beside Turnbull with his Winchester 700 rifle, peering through the Nikon Buckmaster scope. Another three dozen guerrillas were deployed within a quarter mile of them.

"If they come, we can't stop them," Turnbull said, counting the armor. "And I don't want to." The enemy was concentrating in that field, with infantry and the surviving logistics elements moving in. "I sure wish I could call in an air strike right now. They're all clustered up. Just sitting there."

"I can drop one from here," Wohl suggested.

"Look for an officer. He'll be the one moving around a lot and not accomplishing much."

"I got one," Wohl said. He exhaled and fired. Through the binoculars, Turnbull saw one of the tankers stagger and fall. The whole field turned into chaos as troops ran for cover and one by one the PRA machine guns started firing back in their general direction.

"That should set them back an hour or so," Turnbull said, watching with satisfaction. One man with a deer rifle had held up an army.

Ted Cannon placed the butt of his AK on the ground and knelt. The old woman was still breathing, but how he didn't know. With four bullet holes in her, she would soon join her fellow townspeople in the afterlife. He held her hand until the bewildered medic joined them.

"Do what you can," Cannon told her as she opened her aid bag. "But don't use any plasma or anti-coagulant bandages." The medic nodded. Those would be needed for the people who had a chance.

None of his team were from Alfordsville – the town's unit was further south in the area north of the Portersville Road Bridge over the White River – but the massacre still hit them hard. They had moved into town silently from the north after seeing first the black SUVs and then the majority of the paramilitaries leave. They took advantage of the smoke and maneuvered quickly and quietly, catching unawares eight PVs who had found a case of beer and lagged behind the rest.

The Volunteers died in a hail of rifle fire. No quarter went both ways.

The team finished the sweep of the town. No more paramilitaries and no more survivors. He rubbed at his face – he still looked like hell and his jaw ached. But that didn't matter. The policeman in him was arising again. Someone had to account for this. Someone had to pay.

It wasn't about revenge. It was about justice.

"We're hunting PV and PSF," Cannon said. The other guerrillas nodded solemnly. The medic rejoined them, her work finished, her patient passed.

"Let's move out," Cannon said, heading back out of town and into the wild.

Route 257 was the third major axis of advance south, and the farthest west. Alpha Company, now known as Accountability Company under the new nickname regime, approached the bridge over the White River at high speed. It had not taken any fire at all on its movement south, and its commander hoped she could race across the 200 meter bridge that loomed 20 meters above the dark green water before anyone could stop her.

She had sent scouts ahead in hummers, who reported a huge open field to the south past the wall of trees that lined the bank. There were no guerrillas in sight.

As she approached down Route 257 from the wooded north down a low hill that sloped to the bridge, she ordered her tanks to accelerate to 40 kilometers an hour. It was a large, reinforced concrete bridge, and the engineers had assured her it would support their weight.

The first platoon, short with just three tanks, entered the bridge, kicking up chunks of asphalt. The commander's tank was next, followed by second platoon.

There were six tanks on the bridge, with the lead tank was just yards from the opposite shore, when the guerrillas blew it.

The explosives went off simultaneously across the underside of the bridge – the saboteurs had cut the detonator cord into precise lengths to ensure that happened. The special purpose shaped demolitions had been carefully placed by the former combat engineers to scythe through the concrete supports and to shift the bridge off balance. The supported road bed immediately sagged on the right side, and the 420 tons of armored weight on top of it slid in that direction.

There was no stopping it after that. The roadbed cracked and collapsed. Six M1 tanks tumbled over the side, falling ten to twenty meters, landing upside down. Some were not entirely submerged;

others disappeared completely into the muddy water. The seventh tank, seeing the road to its front disappear, along with the armor on it, braked hard, but it was following too closely too fast. It skidded forward on its locked tracks and flew forward off the embankment into empty space, its 120 mm main gun stabbing into the mud and bending on the bedrock beneath.

The woods erupted with fire as several independent bands of guerrillas converged on the backed-up convoy north of the bridge. With its leadership gone and the vehicles trapped, the guerrillas could hit at targets at will along the half-mile long traffic jam.

"Sort of like picking off the legions at the Battle of the Teutoburg Forest," Turnbull had told them when outlining his plan. "They're the Romans, you're the barbarians," he added helpfully.

The vicious struggle went on all night as the survivors desperately fought a losing fight to keep the invisible guerrillas at bay.

The PRA combat engineers waded into the muddy White River water and splashed under the Route 231 bridge to remove the guerrillas' explosives under the watchful gaze of three tanks that had pulled up to the embankment to cover them by fire. Aimed rifle shots every few minutes from guerrillas in concealed positions took one or two soldiers down, but mostly they drew a thunderous volley of machine gun fire in return in the general direction of the shot. That was the idea. Slow them down, burn their ammo.

Turnbull did not blow it. That would have disrupted his plan. Instead, he let them discover the explosives and remove them so they would risk crossing. Turnbull then left Wohl in command south of the bridge and moved back into Jasper proper to make sure the preparations were underway for when the tanks finally got into town.

The tactical command post for the 172nd Brigade was actually three HUMVEEs plus two elderly M577 armored command vehicles. They looked like green boxes on tracks, and they provided a mobile forward command post for the brigade commander. The main command post, remained back in Bloomington; it was not planning to jump south until Jasper was secured.

Inside, bouncing around on the hard bench seats as they moved south on the torn-up asphalt of Route 231, Major Little was receiving updates on the status of his brigade's battle. The rear area was a mess, his S3 explained. Support units were under attack throughout the backfield.

"I'm worried about our logistics, sir," the operations officer said.

"We won't need any if we just take the town!"

The ops officer paused; that was not how this worked.

"You need to understand, sir. Except for the tanks, we're road bound. The insurgents can go anywhere. They choose when to fight and from where. They have the initiative. They engage us with their damn deer rifles at long range and our M4s and AKs can't effectively return fire. They're hitting us in our weak spots, the supporters and logistics units. They aren't taking on our tanks in the open head-to-head."

"They're farmers and racist insurance salespersons!"

"No sir, they're guerrillas fighting on their own ground, to protect their families," snapped the ops officer, trying to keep it respectful. "Just like the dead white men who wrote the old Constitution envisioned when they wrote the Second Amendment. And we're outsiders, here in Indian Country only because some woman in the capital told us to be here."

"Watch yourself, Colonel," Little hissed.

"Loyalty means telling the truth."

"No," said Little. "Loyalty means obedience."

The TAC-CP rolled into the field north of the White River Bridge on Route 231. Major Little stepped out of the rear hatch in a fury. His operations officer followed.

"Why are they all sitting here? Why aren't they moving?" the commander fumed, staring southward.

"Sir, we should step behind the 577," the operation officer said. They were exposed to sniper fire from the opposite bank and the command vehicles were going to be bullet magnets. Sure enough, there was a loud *ding* off the far side of the vehicle and Little practically leapt behind it.

Captain Cardillo had been given a heads up that Blue Falcon was in the area and came back to meet him, zigging and zagging and remaining low. He was well-aware of the sniper threat – he had lost several soldiers so far.

"Sir," Cardillo said, saluting as he reported. Little had hated the patriarchal idea of saluting right up until the moment he took command. The ops officer smiled as Little proudly returned the sniper check.

"Why are we stuck here, Captain? I said move fast and take the damn town!"

"We had to clear the bridge. It was wired to blow," Cardillo replied. "And we had to do it under fire." As if on cue, another rifle round echoed and then the three overwatch tanks all opened up with their heavy machine guns.

Little frowned. He had just learned that Bravo Company had arrived to find the bridge over the Porterville Road blown. And he had heard the reports from the survivors of A Company. Repeating that disaster on the Route 257 Bridge would not do.

"Is it clear now?" the brigade commander asked.

"Yes, the engineers confirmed it. And they think it will hold the tanks."

"What?"

"The tanks are 70 tons combat loaded, Sir. You have to make sure the bridge can support the weight."

"And it will?"

"We think so."

"Then attack, now."

"Roger. I'll alert the infantry company."

"Just get your tanks into Jasper. The infantry can follow."

"Sir," the operations officer said to the commander he outranked. "Sending tanks into an urban area without infantry is risky as hell. The M1s aren't even equipped with the urban combat package. No remote controlled machine guns, no reactive armor. I strongly suggest –"

"They have old hunting rifles and some AR15s. I'm not going to wait. Captain, move out! Use your big guns and take Jasper!"

Cardillo knew better than to argue. He just hoped the infantry would follow quickly. But the ops officer spoke up.

"Sir, we need at least a company with them. We just do."

Little grunted. "Fine." He stomped off, and Cardillo turned to the operations officer.

"Sir, I can't reach my battalion commander. He was supposed to be here."

The ops officer sighed. "A sniper put a slug through his head out on the road."

"Geez." First the brigade commander, and now his battalion commander. At least his battalion commander had been able to go out like a soldier.

"Yeah. Be careful in town. That could turn into a royal clusterfuck real fast. We haven't seen any anti-tank systems yet, but you know there's lots of ways to mess with tanks in an urban area. Hit them hard, but remember who you are. Be careful of civilians. Try and get them to run – those PSF and PV bastards are killing everyone they catch."

"Oh no, you're kidding me."

"I wish I was. We're professionals. We're *soldiers*, not murderers. You remember that. Do it for the boss."

"Yeah," said Cardillo, nodding.

"Look, we're staging the arty now. You'll have priority of fires. The range fan covers all of Jasper."

Cardillo nodded. At least he could call for support from the brigade's three remaining howitzers, and his requests would go to the head of the line. That was something. He moved off to prepare his force to move.

16.

The ten tanks of Caring Company roared over the Route 231 Bridge followed by six truckloads of infantry – the rest would follow – and the TAC-CP. Captain Cardillo's tank was second in sequence and he kept one hand on the radio switch and one on the machine gun mount.

From his position on a hill, Davey Wohl keyed his radio mic.

"Gandalf, this is Hobbit. They're coming. Out."

He turned to his own troops and smiled. "Let's go. It's on." They got up, and began moving toward the road, weapons ready.

"Gandalf, this is Orc, over," Banks said, calling headquarters using the ridiculous name his element had been assigned. He hated those stupid elf operas. Give him a John Wayne movie any day, especially *Sands of Iwo Jima*.

"Orc, this is Gandalf, over."

"No contact yet. Continuing mission. Orc out." Banks waved for his troops to follow him south. The sun was setting, but it might actually be easier to find the artillery in the dark. There were only a few places it could be. And it sure as hell would be impossible to hide once it started shooting.

The PV sedan, a red 2013 Chevy Impala, slammed into the fallen tree just after it made the corner, bringing the vehicle from 40 miles an hour to a dead stop in the space of two feet. The driver and front passenger must not have been wearing seatbelts because they both flew through the windshield and bounced down the road, ending up in two unnatural piles of former people.

The next PV vehicle was a pick-up, and it crashed into the rear, spilling the four Volunteers in the back. Then a couple more PSF cruisers plowed into the crazy daisy chain of demolition.

A fifth sedan managed to skid to a halt without colliding. A farmer named Eli stepped out of his position with a Mossberg 12-guage 590A Tactical shotgun and pumped a load of Remington Express double-aught into the driver's head through the window. He racked in another shell, pivoted and put three blasts in rapid succession into the occupants of the back seat. The one PSF officer in the passenger seat rolled out of the car and immediately raised his hands.

"Don't move, boy," Eli said, taking aim at the prisoner's face.

There were a flurry of shots as the guerrillas finished off the injured in the other cars.

Eli brought the PSF officer to Cannon, having relieved him of his pistol and body armor, and pushed him to the ground. Cannon looked him over. He seemed like an alien, not a fellow law enforcement officer.

"What's your mission here?"

"Nothing. We're just patrolling."

"Tell me the truth. We saw what you people do to civilians."

The PSF officer looked panicked. "I didn't do any of it. I haven't hurt anyone."

"So what's your mission?"

"We're supposed to follow the soldiers and deal with terrorists," the PSF prisoner said, and then realized that perhaps his choice of words was suboptimal. "With the locals."

"Deal with?"

"Look, they shot some, but not me! I didn't shoot anyone! The PBI guy made us. He ordered us to."

"PBI?"

"Yes, he's in charge. He has a tactical team. They have these black SUVs. They told us to shoot everyone. But I didn't! I hid! I didn't do *anything*!"

"What do you want me to do with him?" Eli asked. It was pretty clear Eli would do whatever he asked.

Cannon delayed. "Just stand him up."

Eli took the officer by the arm and hauled him to his feet. A small sack fell out of the breast pocket of the black PSF uniform. Cannon reached down and picked it up.

"That's not mine!" said the prisoner. How many dopers had told Cannon the same thing when he caught them holding back before all this began?

The bag contained wedding rings and watches. Cannon looked up at Eli, who nodded.

"Got it," said Eli, who pushed the prisoner forward and shot him in the chest.

Cannon felt nothing, and it sickened him that he felt nothing. But there was no time for that now.

"Let's move out." They now knew their quarry.

Turnbull watched as the tanks tore down Route 231 into Jasper. The insurgents had set up battle positions in and around both sides of the street at the north end of town. His was in the Walmart – the guerrillas had spent the day knocking out the front windows so it was open to the road.

The tanks were moving fast, about 20 miles per hour, and covering the four miles from the bridge south quickly. No one had engaged them; Wohl's force let them pass right through.

The west side of the road was all houses; on the east, a closed Home Depot, an abandoned McDonald's, and the recently requisitioned Walmart store. The tanks were moving fast. Turnbull hoped that he had trained the other gunner well.

Turnbull engaged the sight on his FGM-148 Javelin missile. With the sun setting, he used thermal. He selected the third tank in line and locked on it. He pushed the trigger and he was surrounded by exhaust gasses as the missile leapt out of the launcher, followed a fraction of a second later by the second from the other missile team.

The missile erupted from the tube and the fins popped into place – not that he could see it. He did see the burning light of the engine jiggle and twist in the air as it made for the speeding Abrams. The missile flew upwards and down in a lazy arc – its target was not the tank itself but the air directly above it. About one meter over the turret, the HEAT round detonated, its shaped explosive forming a stream of superheated plasma that went straight down into the relatively thin armor at the top of the tank.

It was an immediate crew kill, and the second Javelin exploded over the next tank's gas turbine engine and turned it to scrap. The halon fire suppression system inside the crew compartment kept that crew from roasting. Unfortunately, when they scrambled out of the crew compartment, the other guerrillas opened fire, cutting them down before they hit the ground.

"Displace!" Turnbull yelled, abandoning the Javelin launchers. They didn't have any more missiles anyway. Turnbull and the others sprinted to the back of the warehouse as two M1s fired their main guns. The first was the wrong round for the job; in the excitement, the loader had filled the breech with a M829 Armor-Piercing, Fin-Stabilized, Discarding Sabot anti-tank round – basically a titanium dart fired off at several times the speed of sound whose sheer energy would send it punching through tank armor and turn the crew inside the target to a pinkish mist. The sabot shot into the warehouse through the open frontage, flew through a dozen rows of shelves, punched out the back of the building with a barely perceptible loss of speed and finally buried itself 40 feet into the earth.

The second shot was more effective. It was a HEAT round, and it exploded against the back wall, spraying the four guerrillas with fragments.

Turnbull was knocked to the ground, disoriented for a moment by the heat and the noise and the spray of pieces of building. He shook his head and stood, as did two of the others, the ringing in their ears loud and sustained. The fourth guerrilla, whose name he did not even know, lay there unmoving with a shard of rebar sticking out of his eye.

Turnbull ran, but a red curtain seemed to descend over one eye. He wiped it, and as he suspected, it was blood from a cut on his head. He kept running through the "EMPLOYEES ONLY" door into the back area and then was thrown off his feet again. Out in the store area, two more HEAT rounds blew the interior apart. He shook it off again, and they ran through the loading dock and toward the woods.

The appearance of the anti-tank missiles in the hands of the guerrillas had changed everything for Captain Cardillo. He realized his eight remaining tanks were in a kill zone and he did exactly what he was trained to do – punched it in order to get the hell out of there.

The turbines of the eight surviving tanks roared as the drivers demanded their full 1,500 horsepower. They tore off south down 231 into the middle of town.

But that left the trucks full of infantry behind in the kill zone. The infantry company dismounted under a ferocious storm of bullets. The guerrillas with AR15-style weapons and other modern combat rifles focused on achieving fire superiority – that is, they attempted to put such heavy fire on the enemy that the blues would be unable to maneuver or counter attack. The snipers, the veteran deer hunters with the scoped Remingtons and Winchesters, focused on aimed shots at officers, NCOs, and anyone else who looked like he was taking initiative.

As the tanks headed into town and Turnbull was running out to Mill Street, which ran parallel to 231 behind the Walmart. The pick-up truck he had requisitioned was sitting there, keys in the ignition. He put his M4 on the seat and punched it, heading toward the heart of Jasper.

Both sides of 231 were lined with businesses and other buildings close to the road, which to Cardillo was a mixed blessing. The wall of structures made it hard for the guerrillas to engage them with Javelins, but it would also let them get really close. He held the M2 machine gun's dual grips tight, thumbs hovering over the thumb trigger.

Nothing.

And then something, an explosion on the treads of the rear M1 tank. The metal treads flew off and flapped on the road as the vehicle came to a halt.

All hell broke loose and fire started coming from every direction. Cardillo saw flashes, swiveled his turret and fired at them with the heavy machine gun.

The PRA infantry company commander took a 5.56 millimeter round through the throat and fell dead at the feet of a lieutenant, who instantly took charge and rallied his force. The machine guns began kicking and his men and women began returning fire. There was a lot of fire coming from the houses on the west of the road, so he pointed it out to his fire support officer, who checked grid coordinates and got on the radio.

"Quebec One-Seven, this is Crusader Nine! Fire mission! Fire mission! Over!"

As the FSO called in artillery, the infantry lieutenant ordered a casualty collection point in the McDonald's and put one of the medics in charge of the dozen wounded. More people flooded into the restaurant, and he realized they were senior officers. The TAC-CP had pulled up outside and was co-locating in the old fast food joint.

The building shook, and he looked across the street to see 105 millimeter artillery shells exploding among the houses where the enemy was hiding. The fire from the insurgents slackened, and he began to move his company south.

Langer's eyes opened. He was still in the hospital bed. Somehow he had hoped he would wake up elsewhere. There were no beeping monitors because the power was off, but he was hooked to an IV. That came right out. He slid around on his bed in his gown and sat on the bed.

Damn, his stomach hurt.

There were a lot of people running around the hospital floor. Yelling and shouting, but he could hear the shooting and the explosions outside over the noise.

He wasn't staying here. Not while a fight was going on.

He slid off the bed and found he could walk with much less pain than expected. It was probably the drugs, but it didn't matter. He was not sitting this one out.

Langer stepped over to the pile of his clothes, which someone had been nice enough to wash and fold, and started getting dressed.

"You're not leaving," said a nurse from the doorway, shocked that he was upright. "You'll open your incision and bleed out."

"Ma'am," Larry Langer replied. "Where's my gun?"

Banks and his team heard the thunder of the artillery battery from nearly two miles away. It was coming from what appeared to be an open field along County Road 20 about two miles west of 231. An excellent place to set up – everything they needed to shell was within the eight-mile range fan.

"Let's go!" he said, as the artillery let go another volley. Every minute that passed brought more steel death down on Jasper. They moved out fast on a beeline for the firebase.

Cannon had set up his team on both sides of Route 231. The intact PSF cruiser sedan they had captured was parked on the shoulder, and a uniformed PSF officer sat on the hood. There was a fair amount of military traffic, which would ignore the slacker PSF officer. Kunstler wouldn't. This was the MSR, the main supply route. The PBI Inspector had to pass through here some time.

To the south, as he waited, Cannon could hear echoes of the battle for Jasper.

Davey Wohl's mission was to slam the door shut behind the attack force, and that's what his guerrillas did. They moved down out of the hills and woods to converge on the south side of the bridge over the White River on Route 231. That was the door.

The second infantry company tried to cross and was turned back by the volume of fire. The enemy dismounted and the forces shot at each other across the river. The PRA soldiers were not particularly motivated to cross 100 meters of open bridge roadway under the guns of dozens of shooters with scoped rifles.

Davey Wohl moved from position to position, ensuring his people were properly using cover and concealment. He didn't count on the PRA employing snipers too.

The 7.62 millimeter round caught him in the back of the neck crossing Route 231 to get to some of his troops. Two of his men were wounded trying to drag him back in. But no PRA soldier crossed the bridge that night.

The roadblock was at 231 and 8th Street, not far from the courthouse square. The block was a set of logs fitted together and wrapped in razor wire. The tanks could smash the logs, but the wire would tangle in the gears of their tracks. Cardillo saw it and immediately ordered his force to turn off eastward at 9th Street.

While the Crusader Company tanks were fighting through the ambushes on the way to the center of town, Turnbull had driven over and gotten ahead of them. Now he was waiting there for the armor to come, praying his plan would work.

The AT-4 light rocket launchers had made three mobility kills on the M1s along 231 – the guerrillas fired them close, right at the treads, since the rockets would bounce off the depleted uranium composite armor of the sides and the turret. If you got a mobility kill, the tank was still a mighty dangerous pillbox – but it was just that, a pillbox. The guys in it had to come out eventually to eat.

Turnbull paced across the rooftop with several other insurgents, who were preparing their weapons. It was dark, and that gave the armor something of an advantage with its night vision gear. The tanks made the turn and roared under them.

Turnbull waited.

"Come on," he whispered.

An explosion, a big one. He could hear the gears and track grinding below. Turnbull peered over the edge.

One M1 directly below him was up on the sidewalk, smoking. The one behind it, with the commander in the cupola blazing away with his .50 cal, was pulling around it.

"Now!" Turnbull shouted. Lights came up from the high schools portable floodlights hooked to a generator. The entire road below was illuminated like daylight, and that disoriented the tankers for a moment.

The street was covered by dark objects. The lead tank dodged them, but the next didn't. The mine exploded under its body, lifting the tank and blowing out its treads. It stopped. When the commander tried to get out of the hatch, someone shot him.

Turnbull leaned over with his M4 and began spraying the gunners standing in the turrets. Then the rest of the guerrillas arose, with their Molotov cocktails lit, and threw them down on the tanks below.

Flames erupted on the tanks, on their engines, their turrets, their tracks, and on the street itself. One of the fire bombs went into an open hatch and detonated inside. That tank veered left into the abandoned hardware store across the street, stopping about 20 feet inside it.

Cardillo watched his lead tank get taken out and immediately knew it was an anti-tank mine. He screamed it into his intercom, and his driver dodged the two mines lying in the street to his front. He went for his machine gun again, but flaming objects were raining down on him, and he knew what they were too. Just before he ducked into the hatch and pulled it closed, he saw the tank behind him detonate a mine.

Inside his tank he could hear the faint sound of bullets hitting the exterior armor. The guerrillas were on the roofs of the buildings surrounding them. The tactical response was obvious.

Eliminate the buildings.

"Target, right, HEAT!" he shouted and the loader slammed a 120 millimeter shell into the breech. The turret spun.

"Fire!"

The building buckled and collapsed under Turnbull's feet, or at least it felt like it did. The roof split and Turnbull fell ten feet to the second floor in a cascade of dust and debris, along with some other fighters Unfortunately, so did some of the unlit Molotovs, which rolled inside and fell, spreading gasoline throughout the second floor.

"Oh, hell no," Turnbull said. "Get out!" he yelled, and ran to the shattered side window facing the alley. It was another ten feet down. He jumped.

The building shook apart from a second HEAT round as he leapt, and the wall fell inwards behind him. He hit the ground hard, but instinctively executed a passable parachute landing fall. The meat of his buttocks and thigh took the brunt of the fall, and felt like it. But he didn't break his ankles and he could still move.

Cardillo, from inside his tank, ordered the second round into the building where the guerrillas were. That took it down. No more Molotovs.

He keyed the mic.

"Quebec One-Seven, this is Crusader Six! Fire mission! Fire mission! Over!"

"Crusader Six, this is Quebec One-Seven, go!"

"My position! Troops in the open!" He read out his grid coordinates. The cannon cockers acknowledged.

Three M1s were either burning mobility kills or parked inside a building along 8th Street. There was one tank that had gone ahead and another still on Route 231. That one was shooting anything that moved not only with its coaxial and turret machine guns but with its main gun.

The ground shook as the tank fired, and Turnbull could hear the groan of collapsing buildings. Guerrillas were running all around and firing, but with no organization or purpose.

Turnbull pivoted and there was a ghost standing before him. A ghost with a .357.

"Larry? What the hell?"

Langer smiled, but the front of his shirt was drenched with blood. His incision had ripped open.

"I ain't never walked away from a fight before," he said. "Ain't starting now."

"You're bleeding out," Turnbull shouted. "Go back to the damn hospital!"

Langer shook his head. The ground shook as the main gun fired again. A guerrilla position in an empty coffee shop exploded.

"Shit," Turnbull said as he saw he had little choice, and sprinted toward the tank,

The senior sergeant on the firing line of M119s understood what the fire mission meant. The tanks must be in the midst of being overrun or they would not call for artillery on their own position. What the hell was going on down there? The gunners had been firing missions in support of the infantry nonstop since sundown.

The Jasper fight had priority – they were rejecting missions left and right from the units near the bridge. Three guns could only do so much. But they could do something.

He shouted out the next mission and felt like he was punched in the gut. He staggered back and felt another punch. Except it was a .308 round from Banks's M14.

The gun bunnies scrambled, trying to grab their weapons, but the guerrillas were past the sentries and to the gun line too quickly.

With most of the artillerymen dead or running, Banks took out his radio and made the call.

"Gandalf, this is Orc," he said. It still annoyed him, but he persisted. "Mission accomplished. I say again, mission accomplished. They are black on arty."

Bullets zipped around him, pinging off the pavement and the armor of the tank ahead of him. Its gunner was blazing away to the west, and Turnbull was coming from the east. If the guy at the machine gun turned around, Turnbull would be shot in half.

Turnbull was at a full run and dropped his M4, then leapt on the tracks of the Abrams and pulled himself up onto the deck of the tank.

The machine gunner was still firing at targets to the west as Turnbull stood up and drew his .45 from his thigh holster.

He aimed it and fired at the man's head. The gunner dropped into the tank and Turnbull reached the pistol inside the hatch and fired again and again, stopping only when it clicked empty. He pulled it out and inserted another mag, and peered inside.

Thanks to the floodlights, he could see nothing was moving in there.

Turnbull breathed hard and looked up at the 120 millimeter barrel pointed directly at him. The other tank had gone to the end of the block but had come back. They saw him with his gun on the tank containing their dead friends.

I'd do me too, thought Turnbull, and he waited for the HEAT round.

Langer stumbled forward from the alley with something round and black in his hands, right toward the other tank. The tank was buttoned up, so he was in their blind spot until he crossed in front of the coaxial 7.62 millimeter machinegun that was mounted parallel to the main gun.

But by then it was too late. Larry Langer, who had watched Turnbull eliminate the tank that was demolishing his town, had summoned every last bit of strength to pick up one of the anti-tank mines and slam it, contact detonator first, onto the side of the cannon's barrel.

Larry was gone; there was only smoke and flame, and Turnbull took that opportunity to leap down to the street. The smoke cleared and the smoothbore gun was no longer smooth in any sense of the word. It was a curled, charred twisted abomination. The tank itself was still. The guys inside were almost certainly still alive – the Abrams was unparalleled in terms of crew survivability – but they no doubt got their bell rung.

Turnbull caught his breath, supporting himself with his weapon. He shook his head. Only Larry Langer would take on a tank hand-to-hand and win.

Guerrillas were moving past him now. This part of the battle was done. But there was still most of an infantry company in the north of town.

Turnbull let out a sigh, picked up his M4, and began trotting north.

Kunstler slammed the black Blazer's door behind him, but the PSF slacker sitting on the cruiser's hood did not even react. There was work to be done – this area was nowhere near pacified, and this man was just sitting there, on the side of the road.

"You!" Kunstler shouted, approaching the cruiser from behind. The officer just kept looking off into the distance. He probably just did not have the stomach to do what needed to be done to ensure a truly human and caring future. Fine. If he could not serve as an active participant, he could serve as a cautionary example.

"What the hell are you doing here?" Kunstler walked past the car toward the hood where the man was sitting.

"Waiting," the man said without turning.

"For what?"

"For you." Now Ted Cannon turned around. Kunstler saw him and gasped. He drew his Beretta and aimed.

Cannon sat, quietly. Kunstler looked him over, the gun still aimed at Cannon's chest.

"Funny that you'll die in a PSF uniform when you hate them so much," Kunstler said.

"It's a little funny."

"I always hated cops. Fascists. Oppressors. Me? I serve the people, culling out vermin like you."

"I have to say, you sound pretty fascist."

"Get off the car," Kunstler said, and Cannon slipped off and onto his feet.

"You know how I know you're not a cop?" asked Cannon.

"I suppose you'll tell me," Kunstler said. He decided this would be Cannon's last sentence. He was getting bored, and there was work to be done.

"A real cop would have checked the back seat."

Kunstler pivoted as Eli sat up inside the cruiser holding his Mossberg, smiling as he unleashed the swarm of double aught.

The two dozen prisoners from the command post were zip-tied in the courthouse square, having been brought back by truck.

The courthouse itself still smoldered from the artillery hits. A 105 shell had taken out the Ruth Bader Ginsberg statue from the waist up.

The guards were mostly teenagers and old folks. A woman who had to be in her seventies stood guard with a single barrel break action 12-guage; the rest had either deer rifles or M4s.

There were a lot of M4s to be had.

Turnbull checked into the command post in a storefront on the edge of the square. The adrenaline was still running through his blood and he knew it was only a matter of time before he crashed.

"Motrin," he said to the medic. He was handed two 200 milligram tablets.

"Don't toy with me." The medic handed over two more and Turnbull swallowed the 800 milligrams dry.

"Situation?" he said. Dale showed him the maps, old AAA paper jobs with yellow Post-Its representing insurgent units and red ones representing People's Republic Army and other forces.

Several townsfolk were talking into radios and taking notes, then stepping forward to tell Dale's battle captain, Becky the waitress, the information. Then she would have her ops sergeant, a high school friend of Carl Hyatt's, move the Post-Its. No one touched the maps but the ops sergeant.

Dale walked Turnbull through the current status of the Battle of Jasper. The red Post-Its were in disarray and were scattering north with no perceptible rhyme or reason.

"They're running," Turnbull said aloud. Dale looked at the map as if to confirm that it was really true, then went back to his work.

"Becky," one of the radio operators shouted, excited. "There are more tanks coming, lots of them, dozens, on I-69 and 231!"

The command post froze. Everyone understood what that meant. They had barely survived the first time.

Turnbull's mind raced. Dozens? How long could he try and hold out as a rearguard while the rest of the townspeople ran for the border?

Not long. It was over. The silence itself was almost audible.

He and most of these people had held off a brigade, and now they were all going to die.

The radio operator saw the confusion he had caused, and he clarified.

"No, you don't understand. They're coming *north*," he shouted.

Becky came over. "North?"

"It's the US Army. They're coming. They're pouring over the border! They told our people they're heading to I-70!"

I-70 ran east-west across the state through Indianapolis. Half of Indiana was turning red.

The command post broke out in cheers. Townspeople hugged and laughed.

Turnbull was quiet. Dead to alive again in a heartbeat.

Back to the fight.

"Dale, cut some teams south to set up rendezvous with the US forces. We want the passage of lines through our guys coordinated so there's no fratricide. Dale nodded. Turnbull headed to the door.

He still had unfinished business.

Two insurgents lifted the zip-tied lieutenant colonel roughly to his feet. His hair was high and tight, and there was a blood-stained bandage around his right thigh.

Turnbull looked him over, and he stared back hard.

"I'm guessing you were Colonel Deloitte's three?" Turnbull said, abbreviating the term "S3," or operations officer. The TAC-CP was overrun and the staff was captured. The prisoners had not been treated pleasantly, but they hadn't been shot either.

The PRA officer said nothing.

"Some of the troopers told us already, so it's not a secret," Turnbull said. "I've got some questions."

"I'm not telling you shit," said the lieutenant colonel. He seemed resigned to his fate, but determined to go out with his pride.

"If you worked for Deloitte, if he *let* you work for him, I wouldn't expect anything less. I worked for him too."

"So you're the infiltrator?"

"Not anymore. In a couple hours half the US Army will be coming through here and taking everything south of Indianapolis. This isn't Indian Country anymore. It's red. So now I'm not infiltrating anything anymore. I'm a citizen."

The officer said nothing, taking it in. Pretty soon the insurgents would turn him over to the US Army. He'd probably get a choice, go home or go red. If Deloitte relied on him, he was probably squared away. Hopefully, he'd go red.

"I don't need to know any operational stuff. I wouldn't disrespect you by asking," Turnbull said.

"So what do you want to know?"

"I want to know what happened to Colonel Deloitte."

The lieutenant colonel's eyes narrowed, now displaying a different and deeper anger.

"They came in and arrested him," he said. "Then the PBIs took him outside. He looked them in the eyes the whole time. The Colonel said 'God bless America,' then told that bastard to go to hell."

Turnbull was silent for a moment, his fist clenching and unclenching.

"So they shot him?" he said evenly. "Did they say why?"

"Treason, I guess. He said the colonel was guilty of a lot of things, but I guess it boiled down to that."

"Treason," Turnbull said bitterly. That was the last thing Colonel Deloitte could ever be guilty of.

"That's what he said," replied the ops officer. "I think he just resented how the Colonel thought he was a piece of shit."

"*He?*" Turnbull said. "Who is *he?*"

"Our new *commander*," the S3 sneered – never before had Turnbull heard the word "commander" been uttered with so much contempt. "As our Command Diversity Officer, he was next in the chain of command."

"Even though he was incompetent? Should have left the Colonel in charge. Karma's a bitch."

"Yeah," said the lieutenant colonel.

"And where is this new commander?"

The officer gestured with his head. "Him."

There was a major zip-tied nearby, his eyes wide and fearful.

"Pick him up," Turnbull instructed the guards. They dragged Major Little over to Turnbull.

"So you murdered Jeff Deloitte. You aren't fit to lick his boots."

"I'm a prisoner of war," Little said.

"No, I don't see any JAGs around to lawyersplain me the Geneva Convention, and you're no soldier anyway."

"You can't hurt me!" Little babbled. "I'm a prisoner!"

Turnbull drew the .45 from his thigh holster. Little's eyes grew wide with panic.

"Colonel Deloitte was my friend, but he was also my commander," Turnbull said. "So when he said he wanted you to go to hell, I take that as an order."

"But I –"

After 24 hours of fighting, the townspeople didn't even flinch at the sound of the 1911A1.

17.

A platoon of four US M1A3s, with the lead tank flying the stars and stripes from its whip antennae, rolled up Main Street toward battle positions to the north. The bumper numbers identified them as a brigade of the First Cavalry Division out of Fort Hood.

The tanks clanged and clanked past him, just another scruffy civilian with an M4 for all they knew. The combat engineers had cleared the wreckage, or rather, bulldozed it out of the street off to one side to make a path. The Walmart smoldered in the distance, the smoke adding to the unworldly haze.

It looked to Kelly Turnbull like one of the Third World hellholes he had spent much of his twenties fighting in, and not only because of his sleep deprived state.

Locals were moving around examining the damage, most armed. Some were wounded, but walking. Lee Rogers walked by with a handful of guerrillas, some bandaged, seeming dazed. But no one was panicking, no one was faltering.

"Hey!" Turnbull shouted at to a pair of young locals who were dragging a dead PRA soldier in a tanker's jumpsuit toward the field mortuary. "Pick him up."

They stared at Turnbull, confused. Turnbull's eyes were fixated on the dead man's right shoulder patch. It was from the Big Red One. Probably Afghanistan. Probably from when they were on the same side."

"Pick him up and carry him," Turnbull said. "Show some respect. He was a soldier."

The young men hesitated and Turnbull stepped forward, angry. Message received. They carefully picked the PRA soldier's body up off the street and carried it, this time gently.

Turnbull lay down his M4 and sat on a bench out in front of a barber shop. The .45 in its thigh holster rode up, but he was too tired to adjust it. Bullets had pulverized the barber's pole. The shop itself had served as an aid station during the fighting and while the wounded had been evacuated, the floor was still littered with bandages and gore.

Turnbull shut his eyes. His ears were still ringing, but he could make out helicopters. A trickle of blood rolled off his scalp and ran down his cheek like a scarlet tear.

He opened his eyes again, but it took effort. The US infantry was spreading through the town, ready for contact that wasn't going to come. The enemy was gone. Turnbull watched the soldiers advance, too tired to move. A clump of troops approached him, just some ragged, unshaven civilian in battle gear chillin' on a bench in the middle of chaos.

He exhaled.

"Who's in charge here?" asked a nervous US Army lieutenant, geared up and cradling his carbine. On his left shoulder, as with all of them, was the oversized First Cav patch – a triangular shield-shaped symbol with a black diagonal stripe from left to lower right, and a black horse head silhouetted in the upper right corner. His platoon sergeant and radio operator stood behind him, weapons ready. Turnbull just stared at them for a moment.

"Not me," he replied. "Not anymore." With the rumble of the armored cavalry coming up from the south, Turnbull had gone back to the command post and found Dale.

"It's all yours," Turnbull said. "You're in command." And then he left. Dale was too busy to follow him.

The young officer in front of him persisted.

"The locals said you're their commander," said the lieutenant.

"Not me, LT," replied Turnbull. "You're looking for an insurance salesman named Dale, right up the street in the command post. Can't miss it."

That ended that exchange. The platoon leader turned to his RTO, grabbed the handset and began speaking rapidly into it.

"Your guys put up a real fight," said the sergeant first class as he waited for his young lieutenant to do his radio thing. Turnbull noted that the NCO had a Big Red One combat patch on the right shoulder of his uniform peeking out from under his body armor. They had probably walked the same dirt together somewhere along the line.

"Yeah," Turnbull said. "They did."

He'd spent the last few hours organizing the remaining defenders of the town in case there was a counter-attack, making sure there were guides to lead in the US forces, and to setting up teams to evac the wounded and pick up the dead. Plus carrying out his former commander's last order.

None of the townspeople objected. Major Little's own troops basically shrugged. A couple guards had started moving Little's body to the field mortuary where the PRA bodies were being collected, but Turnbull stopped them.

"Not there. He doesn't get to lie with soldiers." They dragged Little off in the opposite direction to who knows where.

"Want a cigarette?" the sergeant asked as the lieutenant continued speaking into his mic.

"No," said Turnbull. "Some ruby slippers maybe, Sergeant. There's no place like home, you know? Assuming you have one."

"Roger, sir," replied the NCO, somehow sensing this was an officer even though he resembled a heavily armed hobo. The sergeant looked around at the wreckage of Jasper. "I'm guessing this is going to be my home for a while."

"Probably a long while. Be careful. Listen to the locals – they know the terrain. They know how to defend it.

"The Joes are already calling it 'Indian Country.'"

"So did the bad guys. Except I guess now the Indians are on your side, despite you being cavalry."

"I hope they don't hold grudges," said the sergeant. The lieutenant signed off.

"Let's move," he told his men.

"Watch yourself," Turnbull said. "Take care of your troops."

"Always, sir."

The trio of soldiers walked off. Turnbull shut his eyes again.

Turnbull collapsed back onto the bench. His eyes forced themselves shut despite his efforts.

Grrrrrrrrr.

Turnbull shook his head, but the growl didn't go away.

Grrrrrrrrr.

He felt a weight on his lap.

He forced open his eyes.

That stupid dog was on his lap, growling at him, the dead frog hanging out of its mouth.

Grrrrrrrr.

"You lived," Turnbull said, a little surprised. "How about that?"

The dog dropped the flattened frog on the bench and came forward and licked his face.

"Oh, no," Said Turnbull, pushing the puppy away. "That's disgusting. You have dead toad breath." But he didn't make the dog get off his lap.

"You're alive," said a lieutenant colonel who had approached from the south. The nametape on his uniform read "FLYNN."

"I don't feel that way right now, Clay," replied Turnbull, petting the puppy and not at all surprised to see him. "Hey, you changed your fake name again."

"What?" Deeds looked down at his nametape. "Oh, right. So, you have a friend. I didn't peg you for a dog person."

"I'm not." The dog growled at Deeds. "But I think maybe I could be."

"Helluva fight," Deeds said.

"Yeah," Turnbull replied. "I'm too tired for my debrief now. But yeah, a helluva fight."

"There'll be plenty of time for debriefing, Kelly."

"You know that they killed Deloitte," Turnbull said. "Apparently he preferred to die like a soldier than live as a butcher."

"We heard that through a radio intercept. I'm sorry."

"There was a time I'd have taken a bullet for him. We were on the same side then. And then we were fighting each other here. I don't mind fighting, Clay, but I'd rather fight people I hate. And I didn't hate him."

"Civil wars are the most vicious wars," Deeds said, sitting. "You take everything bad about a routine war and add betrayal to the mix."

"How the hell did it ever come to this?"

"I don't know, Kelly. It wasn't hard to see where things were headed. It's like we were steering the *Titanic* by committee and no one would turn us away from the iceberg right ahead."

"So what now?" Turnbull petted the dog, which continued to regard Clay warily.

"So, we gave up a little bit of Virginia, and now we have a little bit of Indiana. The bad guys tried to create facts on the ground, and the locals stopped them for long enough for us to move. And when the PR saw they couldn't stop us, they caved at the negotiating table. You were a big part of it."

"So it's all about lines on a map?"

"You don't really believe that, Kelly."

Turnbull looked out across the town, and thought of Langer, Wohl, Bellman, that kid Kyle – all dead. The bodies of those killed fighting had been carried off, but there were still wrecked vehicles pushed to the side waiting to be dragged away. The façade of Main Street was pocked with bullet holes. The Walmart had burned down to the foundations. There was a blood splatter in the middle of the street in front of him. He couldn't tell whether it was from a local or one of the PRA troops.

"What's it matter what I believe?" Turnbull asked.

"It matters to you. I'm just not sure you'll admit it. It matters to these folks. In the end, this place was their home. They fought for it. Without the guys like you to help them, they would have lost it, and probably their lives too. If you hadn't made it ungovernable…"

"I just showed them some tricks. They did the fighting. And the dying. Most of them were amateurs, just regular people."

"That's what the British probably said around 1775."

"Except these were our own people we were rebelling against, at least they had been."

"That's another thing the British probably said around 1775."

"Wait, doesn't that mean you're kind of comparing me to the French?"

"I'd never do that when you're packing heat, Kelly."

"So what now?" asked Turnbull, not truly caring. He'd never been so tired.

"Now we occupy it and defend it. It's ours again. I expect they'll try to instigate instability, make it hard for us to govern."

"Like we did to them?"

"Exactly."

"Not quite. There's one key difference."

"And that is?"

"They're the bad guys," said Turnbull.

"I always enjoyed your rejection of moral equivalence, Kelly."

"I've seen them in action, Clay. PVs, PSF, PBI. And I'm telling you – I'm not going to play nice anymore."

"Did you ever?"

"I tried it out for a little while. I got burned. People died. You don't put your hand on a hot stove twice."

"Good, because we need you again. And your unique perspective on not playing nice."

"I'm not sure I'm finished here yet."

"Sure you are. They can clean up the mess on their own. In fact, they should. It's their home, not yours. You've done your part. Time for you to go home."

"Where is home, anyway?"

"Good point. Maybe you should take some time and find yourself one. After all, you fought for your homeland. You should actually have an actual home in your land, not just a string of FOBs, safe houses, and BOQs."

"I guess he needs a home too," Turnbull said, ruffling the dog's fur. "But I'm too tired right now to think about it."

"You can sleep on the Blackhawk. Get your stuff."

"You're looking at it." Turnbull stood and stared at his M4 for a minute. He left it on the bench. Somebody else would put it to good use here. And he still had his .45.

They walked through town toward the high school, with the little dog trotting along at his heels. The helicopter had landed on the football field and waited with its blades rotating. In the parking lot, a platoon of US troops were mounting up into their vehicles again, ready to head north. Locals wandered by, men and women, young and old, most armed, looking grim, assessing the damage. Turnbull recognized some, but not all of the faces.

One thing he noted – they weren't the faces of civilians anymore.

"Like I mentioned, there's another problem we're having," Clay said. "I think you could help us with it."

"You sure have a lot of problems. How screwed are you that I'm the solution?"

"Very. We can talk on the flight home."

"I don't think so. I'm going to sleep. And I'm not sure when or even if I'm ever waking up."

Turnbull took off his cap, scooped up the dog, and trotted along behind Deeds in a low crouch toward the Blackhawk, the blades whirling above them. They were going to be the helicopter's only passengers.

The crew chief helped Deeds in first. Deeds slid over on fabric seats and began buckling himself in.

Then the crew chief reached his hand out to help, but suddenly withdrew it.

"You can't have an animal on the aircraft," he yelled over the engine's whine.

Turnbull ignored him and climbed into the passenger compartment without assistance, still clutching the puppy. He sat on the canvas seat with the dog next to him. It proceeded to growl at the crew chief.

"I said no dogs on the aircraft!" shouted the sergeant. It was bad enough to have to chauffeur some light colonel and his filthy civilian pal around like they were a couple of general officers, but this mutt was too much.

Turnbull stared, noting the chief's body armor and that thinking between the eyes would be best. His Wilson .45 still had a full mag left.

Deeds leaned in, shouting above the engine roar.

"Son, let it go."

"But Colonel, the regs say —"

"Let it go," Deeds repeated in that voice he used when he was giving a direction, not a suggestion.

The crew chief grimaced, then waved his hand to the pilot. The engine revved up, the blades spun faster, and the aircraft lifted off as Turnbull himself buckled up and put on the headphones. He clutched the puppy tightly, leaned back, and shut his eyes.

"This is bullshit," the crew chief sputtered into his mic, unable to let it go.

Turnbull didn't even open his eyes as he keyed his mic and spoke just one more time before falling into a deep sleep.

"Stop talking."

Author's Note

Note that while there really is a Jasper, Indiana, the one depicted here is not it. While the places somewhat correspond to how the town is laid out on a map, my Jasper is fictitious. None of the characters here are based on real people, except for Indiana radio legend Tony Katz. He's all too real.

Also, you'll note that some of the details involving explosives are vague. That is purposeful. While field expedient explosives are real and can be deadly, this is not an instruction manual for making bombs and improvised explosive devices. You'll have to trust me that the capabilities described here are real. Do not try it at home.

The big idea is that citizens armed with individual weapons can provide a powerful opposition to even a conventional military that is in the service of an oppressive government. The Founding Fathers knew exactly what they were doing when they enshrined the Second Amendment within the Bill of Rights. Let's hope we never have to put their wisdom to the test.

KAS

18 May 2017

Kelly Turnbull will return in

WILDFIRE

About The Author

Kurt Schlichter is a senior columnist for *Townhall.com*, where his work appears twice a week. He is also a Los Angeles trial lawyer admitted in both California and Washington, D.C., and a retired Army Infantry colonel.

A Twitter activist (@KurtSchlichter) with over 100,000 followers, Kurt was personally recruited by Andrew Breitbart, and his writings on political and cultural issues have been regularly published in *IJ Review*, *The Federalist*, the *New York Post*, the *Washington Examiner*, the *Los Angeles Times*, the *Boston Globe*, the *Washington Times*, *Army Times*, the *San Francisco Examiner*, and elsewhere.

Kurt serves as a news source, an on-screen commentator, and a guest on nationally syndicated radio programs regarding political, military, and legal issues, at Fox News, Fox Business News, CNN, NewsMax, One America Network, The Blaze, and on *The Hugh Hewitt Show*, *The Dr. Drew Show*, *The Larry Elder Show*, *The Tony Katz Show*, *The John Cardillo Show*, *The Dana Loesch Show*, *The Larry O'Connor Show*, and *The Derek Hunter Show*, among others. Kurt appears weekly on *Cam and Company* with Cam Edwards, and averages four to five other media appearances a week.

He was a stand-up comic for several years, which led him to write three e-books that each reached number one on the Amazon

Kindle "Political Humor" bestseller list: *I Am a Conservative: Uncensored, Undiluted, and Absolutely Un-PC*, *I Am a Liberal: A Conservative's Guide to Dealing with Nature's Most Irritating Mistake*, and *Fetch My Latte: Sharing Feelings with Stupid People*.

In 2014, his book *Conservative Insurgency: The Struggle to Take America Back 2013-2041* was published by Post Tree Press.

His 2016 novel *People's Republic* hit number one on the Amazon Kindle "Political Thriller" bestseller list.

Kurt is a successful trial lawyer and name partner in a Los Angeles law firm representing Fortune 500 companies and individuals in matters ranging from routine business cases to confidential Hollywood disputes and political controversies. A member of the Million Dollar Advocates Forum, which recognizes attorneys who have won trial verdicts in excess of $1 million, his litigation strategy and legal analysis articles have been published in legal publications such as the *Los Angeles Daily Journal* and *California Lawyer*.

He is frequently engaged by noted conservatives in need of legal representation, and he was counsel for political commentator and author Ben Shapiro in the widely publicized "Clock Boy" defamation lawsuit, which resulted in the case being dismissed and Shapiro being awarded his attorney's fees.

Kurt is a 1994 graduate of Loyola Law School, where he was a law review editor. He majored in communications and political science as an undergraduate at the University of California, San Diego, co-editing the conservative student paper *California Review* while also writing a regular column in the student humor paper *The Koala*.

Kurt served as a US Army infantry officer on active duty and in the California Army National Guard, retiring at the rank of full colonel. He wears the silver "jump wings" of a paratrooper and commanded the 1st Squadron, 18th Cavalry Regiment (Reconnaissance-Surveillance-Target Acquisition). A veteran of both the Persian Gulf War and Operation Enduring Freedom (Kosovo), he is a graduate of the Army's Combined Arms and Services Staff School, the Command and General Staff College, and the United States Army War College, where he received a Master degree in Strategic Studies.

He lives with his wife Irina in the Los Angeles area, and he enjoys sarcasm and red meat. His favorite caliber is .45.